METAMORPHOSIS:

BOOK TWO OF THE *LALASSU*

METAMORPHOSIS:

BOOK TWO OF THE LALASSU

Jennifer Carole Lewis

Praise for Revelations: Book One of the *Lalassu*

"*Revelations* is a quick paced novel that changes the common perceptions of the 'hero', with journeys of self-discovery, acceptance and finding romance in unlikely places and people." – Nada, *Nadaness in Motion* (nadanessinmotion.blogspot.ca)

"This is one of the best love stories I have read in a long time!.... The pacing of this story is written so well that you feel like you're a heartbeat away from more action and emotion than you can handle. The characters are so well developed that they have the feel of real people." – Ella, *Writer in Progress* (writerip.blogspot.ca)

"The imagery and descriptions in this book are phenomenal, and I was on the edge of my seat with 'Oh my gosh, WHAT HAPPENS NEXT?!' almost constantly coming out of my mouth…. If a movie ever gets made based on this book, because one should, I would be first in line at the ticket booth." – Lauren, *Romance Novel Giveaways* (romancenovelgiveaways.blogspot.ca)

"This is a seriously cool book…. I loved the plot and twists and mysteries surrounding the gifted …. I want more!" – Maghon, *Happy Tails and Tales Blog* (happytailsandtales.blogspot.ca)

"Absolutely Magical!.... After reading *Revelations*, I haven't been this excited to pick up the next book in a series in a very long time. Jennifer has a true talent & knack for reeling people in. So proceed with caution if you plan on picking up this book, you'll be hooked!" – Jessica, *Taking It One Book At A Time* (takingitonebookatatime.blogspot.ca)

"What a wonderfully imaginative adventure…. There was just something magical and memorizing about this completely original and vivid world of Lewis's imagination." – Beth, *Tome Tender* (tometender.blogspot.ca)

To all the warriors who have protected us
at the cost of their own minds and bodies.

Thank you.

Ekurru, (Hittite noun) definition: mountain house, a sanctuary

Lalassu, (Sumerian noun) definition: ghost, hidden or secret

The Five Stages of Healing

Hemostasis: stopping the bleeding
Autolyzing: breaking down the dead tissue
Angiogenesis: reconnecting blood vessels
Epithelialization: rebuilding new tissue
Maturation: wound is healed

Part One
HEMOSTASIS

CHAPTER ONE

Snow's ethereal silvery beauty was best appreciated by someone who wasn't having to slog through it, Ron McBride decided as he pushed past clinging white drifts. Halloween might be a few weeks away, but this far north, winter already had a solid grip. Dizzy and nauseous, he shook his head against the illusion of the dark trees merging with the sky to form a cage around him. He'd hated cages even before being held captive.

Without the strength of his enhanced muscles, the cross-country detour would have made him drop hours ago. As it was, he began to wonder if he'd made a fatal mistake. Hell of a thing if his paranoia ended up killing him. *I only wanted to do what was right.*

Four months of running. Four months of carrying the burden that weighed down his jacket pocket as he tried to fulfill a promise with little more than a name. The rules were simple. Never stay in one place for more than a few days. Keep moving north and west. Avoid getting drunk. Don't be memorable. He'd failed them all repeatedly. He'd get caught up in someone else's trouble or find himself lifting more or moving faster than human reflexes allowed. People would notice, and then he'd need to run before his hunters showed up on his trail. Sometimes a bottle offered the only hope of quieting his jangled and exhausted nerves enough to let him sleep.

Yesterday, he'd hitched a ride with a trucker who'd offered to take him as far as one of the remote supply towns in northern Canada, near the Alaska border. Ron couldn't even remember the town's name through the swirling fatigue fog clogging his brain. He did remember the man at the rest stop along the way, though. Dressed in plaid and jeans with a baseball cap pulled low over his features, the man poked at the collection of sunglasses, candy, and toiletries under the harsh fluorescent lights, like all the other truckers. But a jarring addition marred his traditional trucker uniform: expensive leather boots.

He didn't know who the man was or what he was doing there, but he wasn't about to take the chance that it had nothing to do with him. Ducking out the door, he began to walk.

Nearly twenty hours later, his choice didn't seem very strategic anymore. There was a lot of wilderness up here. He could wander for weeks and never come across another human being. The picturesque puffs of snow floating down from the sky might make a lovely postcard, but they clung to his hat, hair, and clothes, melting and refreezing into dense chunks of ice, weighing him down. His fingers shook with cold despite being pressed into his armpits as he walked.

The light faded rapidly into grey-blue twilight. He needed to stop and build a shelter, but his body seemed to have acquired a terrible inertia. It kept plodding forward, his mind and legs equally numb. He forced his arm up to grab at a nearby tree, but his frozen fingers missed, and he smashed into the trunk, rattling his chattering teeth. Dragging himself up, he forced himself to stop and actually look at his surroundings.

Black silhouettes of pine trees jutted into the sky all around him. The steadily falling snow piled into waist-high drifts. He needed some bare ground and a fire. Numbly, he remembered a lesson from his army survival training: birch bark burned, even when wet. Staggering through the snow, he peered into the forest, searching for telltale white trunks.

His frozen fingers bled as he pried strips of bark from a birch and broke branches from a nearby pine. A small gap in the snow offered salvation. Scraping out its sparse accumulation of snow with a branch nearly did him in, but he managed the task and laid out his fire supplies with shaking hands. It took him three tries to get a match to light and another three before he got a piece of birch bark to spark and flame. Luckily, the branches were relatively dry and pitchy, catching easily and flaming brightly.

The warmth hit him like a truck, sparking an irrational temptation to crawl directly into the tiny fire to thaw his body. He clenched his jaw against the pain of blood returning to numb extremities. He'd give himself a little time to warm up, and then he'd go collect more wood and see about a shelter. *Just a little time.*

His weariness seduced him into dangerous unconsciousness. Ron thought he'd only closed his eyes for a moment when a snuffling sound popped them back open. Charred black twigs blended into the ground without a hint of flame, and the cold ground had leached the remaining warmth from his legs. It was dark, far too dark.

His body wanted to collapse back into sleep. A tiny piece of his mind shrieked a warning that if he did, he would never wake again. He needed to stand up and get moving again.

As he rocked back, preparing to rise, the darkness in front of him moved.

Adrenaline cleared away the twin clinging cobwebs of exhaustion and cold. The image in front of him suddenly resolved into perfect terrifying clarity. A bear stood less than five feet away from him.

Ron's hands trembled as he watched the monstrous animal, whose shaggy head was easily the size of a man's torso. Even on all fours, the animal's shoulders would reach Ron's waist, and the massive hump over them would be halfway up his chest. Standing on its hind legs, he guessed the bear would measure ten feet. Dark-brown, shaggy fur blended into the darkness except for a short slash of golden brown over its shoulder, shaped like a crescent moon.

The bear huffed at him, clacking its jaws together. Controlling his fear, Ron carefully moved up, using the tree trunks for balance. If he could go slowly enough, maybe he could get out of range before it took an interest in him. His legs were numb and sore, ensuring he would have no chance of outrunning the creature.

Except it didn't seem aggressive.

It kept looking at him as if trying to figure out what he was. Perhaps it hadn't seen a human before. If ignorance kept it from trying to eat him, Ron wasn't going to push for enlightenment. He thought bears were supposed to hibernate in winter, though. He vaguely remembered reading that if a bear was awake in winter, it was considered especially dangerous.

"Good bear. Nice bear," he croaked.

The bear's ears went flat against its skull, exactly like an annoyed cat. It snorted and shook its head.

"You don't want to eat me, Mr. Bear. Go on and find a pik-i-nik basket somewhere." Ron stopped as the creature let out a low growl.

Okay, so much for the human-voice-calms-wild-animals theory. The bear reached out with an enormous paw and raked through the remains of his fire. A few glowing coals shone amid the ashy flakes. Then it poked at the remaining crisped fragments of birch bark, growling again.

When it turned and began to amble away across the clearing, Ron saw his chance. He eased himself around the trees and started walking slowly in the opposite direction. It was a good plan and might have worked if his legs had cooperated.

His stiff limbs collapsed under him, dropping him to the ground with a massive thud. The bear's attention immediately swung back to him, and Ron's primitive instincts took over. It didn't matter how many times he'd been told to never run from a wild animal—his feet were pumping before his brain could consciously give instruction.

Running wildly through the woods, he heard the bear crashing behind him. *This is it. I'm going to die now.* He tried to summon his enhanced strength for a leap into a tree, but his abused muscles refused. He slammed into the trunk and then rolled down the hill on the far side of it, his backpack flying off and scattering his belongings across the snow.

A tree graciously halted his downward tumble, abruptly catching his head and shoulders with a tooth-rattling stop. Stunned, he could only stare at the top of the ridge as the bear looked down on him.

The life of Ron McBride ended by Canadian wildlife. Embarrassing, but at least no one would ever know. He braced himself for the inevitable crunch of jaws.

The bear, outlined against the inky sky, stared at him. Then it turned and walked away.

It left me. I'm not even good enough to eat. Instead of being a bear's before-bedtime snack, he was going to get to die of a combination of exposure and a concussion. He patted his jacket, feeling for the hard lump. Still intact. He tried to force himself to his feet, but he was too weak. Wearily, he stared at the green and blue lights floating in the sky above. Maybe this was for the best. All the things he'd done and seen… maybe they should go to his grave with him.

Resignation pulled him down into the darkness.

Death felt surprisingly warm and soft. Ron decided it wasn't so bad. He didn't remember his body freezing, which was probably a good thing. He remembered a man's voice telling him it was going to be okay. Maybe his grandfather? Pops had died when Ron was little. His father was still alive, so it couldn't be him. It wasn't how he'd pictured death, but he might finally be safe and home.

He took a deep breath and coughed in surprise. Why did Heaven smell like bacon? His eyes opened, but it took time for his brain to process the images. Blinking helped resolve the warm brown blur into carved wooden panels. Only a few feet from his nose, he could see the individual chisel marks. He looked down, and bright colors flared across his vision. A quilt. Several quilts in eye-popping primary colors. He patted the topmost layer with his hand, surprised at the soft, close-woven fabric.

"Good morning!" a woman's voice cheerfully called out. He caught movement to his right, and a head appeared—one with a bright, merry smile and dancing black eyes framed by long black hair that spilled around her face like a fall of silk fringe.

He jerked back without thinking and cracked his head on the carved wood paneling beside him.

"Oops. Sorry." She reached out to probe the tender spot on his skull. Belatedly, it occurred to him that he might not be dead.

"Where am I?" he demanded, trying to convince his adrenaline centers to relax. He wasn't captured and being held. Not like last time.

"Bear Claw Station, part of Kluane National Park in the Yukon. I'm Lily. Let me see your fingers." She didn't wait for permission, manipulating his hand with strong, supple fingers. He took advantage of the opportunity to study her beyond basic threat assessment.

She was pretty, with creamy skin the color of fresh-baked bread. A pale, fine-knit sweater clung to her full breasts and slender waist. Her touch was gentle as she flexed and examined his hands. To his chagrin, Ron found himself growing hard under the blankets, and he snatched his fingers back. He couldn't remember the last time he'd had the energy to be attracted to a woman. That was something old Ron did, not the new hunted Ron.

She didn't take offence. "I don't think there's permanent damage from the frostbite, but they're going to be sensitive for a while. Are you hungry?"

"Where am I?" he asked as she moved out of sight.

"I told you. Bear Claw Station. Are you sure your head is okay?" Lily popped back into view, her smile twisting into a concerned frown.

"My head is fine. And people don't live in national parks." He shoved the covers away, irritated and suspecting she was laughing at him, playing him for a fool. Suddenly, he realized he only wore an unfamiliar grey cable-knit sweater and threadbare dark sweatpants. "Where are my things?"

"Doc gathered up what he could, but we had to get you back here quickly to keep you from freezing to death. Everything is over there." She pointed to a small pile of folded clothes perched precariously on a stack of bright-yellow plastic bins. Relief sagged in his chest as he spotted the sleeve of his worn jacket poking out.

Lily continued. "This is Doc's cabin. The ranger resupply station is about a half a kilometer away. Are you hungry?"

"I don't need a doctor." He'd had enough of the entire medical profession. He swung his legs over the edge of the bed, jumped out, and promptly tumbled to his knees since the floor was still a good two feet below his heels.

She knelt beside him to help him up. "I should have warned you about the bed platform. Doc likes sleeping up high. Says its warmer."

Yes, she should have warned him. He managed to regain his feet without looking like any more of an idiot in front of her. She studied him with her arms crossed and full lips pursed—neither of which helped to subdue his somewhat embarrassing erection since the pose emphasized her generous breasts and the softness of her mouth. Now that he was out of bed, he could also appreciate her long and shapely legs, outlined in black leggings. *That's not helping. Remember the rules.*

"I'm not sure you should be out of bed yet." She hesitated. "Maybe I should get—"

"You mentioned food?" He wasn't ready to deal with anyone else. He needed to figure out where he was and get moving again.

"Sure. The table is kind of full..."

Full would have been an understatement. Small mountains of paper must have been breeding for generations to create so much accumulation. The cheap card table looked as if its skinny metal legs might collapse at any moment.

"Doc usually eats in his chair. I'm sure he wouldn't mind." She gestured toward a worn-out armchair perched beside the stove.

Ron ignored the chair, reaching for the pile of clothes instead. The familiar hard lump still bulged inside the inner jacket pocket. He hadn't lost it. Releasing the imprisoned air in his lungs, he exhaled as quietly as he could. He might not have much of his old self left to cling to, but he still kept his promises.

"We're isolated. Not thieves," Lily said quietly behind him.

He winced. "I didn't think you'd taken it—"

"What do you have in there anyway?" she interrupted, staring at the jacket in his hands.

He pulled out the sealed grey plastic container. "The ashes of a woman I knew. I promised I'd take them back to her family." It was the least he could do, given how he'd failed to save her.

"Sounds like she was important."

The memory of Nada's final moments flashed in his mind, the pop of the gun firing as blood sprayed across his face. His body wouldn't obey his instructions, moving too slowly to stop it. Ron's heart pounded in his chest, and his fingers curled into fists. He'd failed her. As he'd failed so many others.

Lily's hand on his chest pulled him out of the awful memory. "I won't push. I know what it's like to lose someone close to you. Supper's ready."

As she began to scrape his meal out of the iron skillet, Ron sat down, struggling to find something to say to bridge the awkward silence. He guessed this was a cabin or cottage from the paneled walls. There was only one room, equally dominated by the heavy iron stove blasting out heat and the paperwork cluttering every horizontal surface. His gaze hit the bed he'd fallen out of: a twin mattress resting in a narrow alcove. The only bed in the tiny cabin. "Do you live here?"

"Me? No. My family has a cabin to the east."

He shouldn't have been relieved that Lily wasn't involved with Doc. *You have to keep moving,* he reminded himself. As much as exploring this budding attraction tempted him, he needed to stay focused. Lust intoxicated as easily as liquor.

Lily continued to explain. "I help Doc out. Make sure he's got a hot meal waiting when he gets back at the end of the day. He asked me to do cleaning, too, except then he couldn't find anything after I moved it." She shrugged, handing him a tin plate full of crispy bacon and soft white fish. "What's your name?"

He hesitated. After six months of aliases, the questions should have been easy. But he felt strangely reluctant to lie to this woman.

"You don't have to tell me if you don't want." A sad, sympathetic smile appeared briefly. "Running away from the past is our favorite community pastime."

"Who said I was running?" Ron countered, taking a hearty bite of the fish. Fried in bacon grease, it tasted delicious.

Don't take me for an idiot. Her pointed look couldn't have been clearer with subtitles. "Either that, or you have a suicidal appreciation of Northern wilderness. No one goes out in a blizzard without the right gear or supplies unless they don't have a choice. So, if you don't want to tell us your name, don't worry about it. We'll make one up for you."

"How about Too Stupid To Come Out of Snow?" He hoped it would make her smile.

It worked. Her grin lit up the entire cabin. "Maybe Man Who Hugs Trees. Or we could always go with something less Indian cliché. Like Blue Eyes."

"How is that less cliché?" He chuckled, scraping his plate to get the last of the fish.

"It's a mobster cliché instead of an Indian one. You want some more, Blue Eyes? I have some dried berries and mushrooms here."

He handed his empty plate back. He couldn't remember the last time he'd eaten fresh-cooked food from someone other than a short-order cook. For that matter, he couldn't remember the last time he'd talked to someone more than absolutely necessary.

The realization turned the succulent grilled fish into a flaky stone in his mouth. He couldn't afford to forget what he was running from. And what he'd promised to do. It was the only hope he had.

"Don't go there, Blue Eyes," Lily warned him, perching on a stool.

He swallowed with difficulty. "Go where?"

"Whatever alone place made your eyes go all sad."

"You don't know what I've dealt with," he said gruffly, putting aside the plate and standing up.

"You're right. I don't. And you don't know us." She watched him as he picked up his pile of belongings. "Grandfather will have us all tracking you down if you leave before Andrew says you're healed. If we let you go now, with what you have, it would be murder."

Just walk away. Ron shook out his jeans, fully intending to listen to logic for once. Except she was right. If he tried to go out with his jeans, a worn black sweater, and leather jacket, he'd freeze before he could reach any place with supplies. He was going to be stuck here. "Who's Andrew?"

"My brother. Grandfather and Dad taught him traditional healing, and he did an EMT course down in Vancouver. He takes care of most medical stuff around here, stitches and stuff. He said we should be careful not to let your hands get cold again or you'd lose your fingers." Lily seemed equally comfortable whether he was snarling or smiling. Ron had the uncomfortable impression he'd lost control of the situation.

"What about the doctor?" he asked, feeling like an idiot.

"What about him?" Lily asked, her head tipping slightly to one side.

"Why doesn't he fix people up?"

"Oh, Doc's not that kind of doctor. He's a scientist. He studies bears. Population, behavior, food. All the fun stuff." Lily waved her hand at the piles of paperwork.

"Bears." Her explanation didn't help him to feel any less like an idiot.

"He wants to work out ways for bears and humans to coexist peacefully. A lot of bear habitat is being ripped up with logging, mining, and new subdivisions." Lily pulled another slab of fish out of a glass container and put it in the frying pan. "He thinks bears have a bad rap for being vicious attackers."

The animal he'd encountered hadn't been interested in attacking him. It had seemed curious, not hostile. He thought it might actually have been trying to be nonthreatening, but maybe the concussion was messing with his memories. "What do you think?"

"I think humans and animals aren't as different as they like to pretend." Lily's words were punctuated by a quick jab of the spatula. "They both lash out without thinking, but a bear doesn't even have to be angry to do big damage, just irritated."

A repetitive crunching sound outside of the hut sent Ron's senses into high alert. Footsteps. Coming closer. He glanced over at Lily. She didn't seem concerned with anything other than the skillet. There was only one exit, the door to the cabin. He'd have to fight through whoever was coming.

"You're disappearing again," Lily said quietly, not looking at him. "You can trust us, you know."

Maybe he could trust them, but they shouldn't trust him. Lily and the others had saved his life, and he refused to put them in jeopardy. He owed them the truth. "I have some nasty people looking for me. I don't want you to get hurt, and if they think I've been here…" He couldn't finish. Memories of the dead clutched his voice with cold, stiff fingers.

Lily snorted in amusement. "Who's going to find you? We're past the Arctic Circle, surrounded by primordial forest. It's a three-hour hike along a narrow trail to reach the nearest road. And then another day to drive to the nearest town, home to about two hundred people and a small airport for bringing in freight. Once you leave this settlement, you won't see another human being for days. There are less than a dozen people who live here, and we know every single one of them on sight." She paused. "You should give yourself time to rest and heal. There are worse places."

Ron couldn't quite process her words. A dozen people? Days of travel before reaching other humans? It didn't seem possible. Intellectually, he was aware of the North's isolation, but his mind had trouble grasping the reality. Besides, didn't people come here to get away from other people? Shouldn't they be rushing him out instead of helping him? He tensed, suspecting a trap. People didn't help strangers, particularly the potentially dangerous ones. Not if they were smart.

The footsteps stopped outside the cabin, and Ron tensed at the hollow knocks against the wall before the door opened to reveal a tall, wiry man with a long, snow-dotted grey beard. His glasses steamed up in the heat, hiding his eyes, as he pulled off a snow-laden toque and jacket and shook them outside the door.

"Those tracks to the east are definitely Big Bart's. He's headed out to find a more suitable hibernation spot than the ones around here." The man wiped his glasses and only then seemed to notice Ron standing in the middle of the floor. "Oh good, he's awake. Close call there, boy. Should feel lucky."

"You must be Doc." Ron had been prepared for a fight, but the old man standing in front of him completely failed to register on Ron's paranoia-enhanced internal threat meter. He looked like a doting grandfather, the kind who carved wooden toys for a horde of grandkids.

"Sure you don't want to tack an 'I presume' onto the end of that? Don't get too many chances for that line." Doc grinned as he continued peeling off layers of protective clothing. "Osmund Svensson. Doc is fine. I assume Lily's told you I'm not actually the useful kind of doctor."

"She mentioned you study bears." Ron started to wonder if everyone here suffered from some kind of shared delusion. Maybe their isolation made them eager for new faces. *Or maybe they're genuinely nice people who don't deserve to get caught up in my mess.*

"Then there's no need to go over it again and bore you to tears. Andrew said you should stay put for a while until your hands and head are fixed up. Plenty of room in here. And Lily is a fantastic cook." Doc winked at the girl.

"Only compared to you." She smiled sweetly back at him, her laughter barely concealed.

"True. True. I burn everything." He chuckled indulgently. Ron half expected him to pull out a pipe and settle in front of the fire like some kind of lean Santa Claus. For a moment, Ron let himself feel the envy roiling in his gut. He wished he could go back to the innocent days when he didn't know what lurked behind the curtain of normalcy. He wanted to laugh with his parents and repeat jokes they'd told each other a thousand times. He wanted to not worry about strangers and questions and secrets.

"Gerry asked me not to keep you late tonight." Doc passed on the message to Lily with a good-natured, conspiratorial grin.

Lily's cheeriness froze, but she quickly put on a polite smile. "Supper's on the stove."

Ron wondered what she was hiding. An abusive family? A surge of protective violence tightened his shoulders and knotted his fists.

"We'll see you in the morning, then." Doc glanced over at Ron.

Lily gathered up mittens, hat, and a thick parka. As she bundled herself up, she paused to meet Ron's eyes. "Don't disappear on me. Give Bear Claw a chance."

She slipped out into the twilight, leaving the two men alone in the cabin. Ron forced his hands to relax. He couldn't walk away if she needed help.

"Great Ghost of Ursus, you weren't thinking of heading back out there?" Doc asked, his bushy eyebrows poking above his glasses in surprise.

"It's not good for me to stay in one place too long," Ron answered honestly. "For me or the people who live there. Only I don't think I'll be ready to go anytime soon. Not if I want to survive the trip."

Like Lily, Doc seemed to be completely deficient in survival awareness. He didn't blink at the news of possible danger, focusing only on the practicalities. "True. I'm sure we can find some gear for you somewhere. I don't know what you're running from, but this is a good place to catch your breath. It's got to be pretty bad for us to find you slumped over a burned-out fire in the middle of the forest. Especially without mitts or a parka." Doc's shrewdness peeked past his jovial exterior. "We're not about to let you head out to freeze, so you might as well relax and indulge an old man with some company. Have you tried the fish?"

Lily hurried through the woods to the steeply sloped log cabin she shared with her brothers and grandfather. She wasn't looking forward to the conversation she knew was coming. With luck, Lou would still be in the bush. Grandfather and Andrew she could deal with. Lou would be another story. She missed her twin, Mark. He could always be counted on to find the less serious side of life.

That faint hope died when she heard dogs barking. If the team was home, then Lou was back. Sure enough, a dozen dogs were frisking around their elevated squat boxes. She lingered among them, letting them sniff and jump around her in a frenzy of reacquaintance.

"Hey there, Pepper, Ginger, Molasses," she called out softly, rubbing their wide heads with her mittened hands.

"Lily." Her grandfather's gentle voice cut through the dogs.

Without another word, she left the animals and went into the house. She'd been dreading this moment since Doc had first brought the man back to Bear Claw. She hung up her outer clothes with meticulous care, her stomach heavy with trepidation.

Out of the corner of her eye, she watched her brothers in the common area. Lou hunched over the table, his thick fingers twisting wire into traps. He glared at her, a roughly made leather cap jammed over his long black hair. He only wore clothes he made himself out of the animals he trapped out in the forest and tundra. Andrew was his twin's opposite, reclining in his chair by the fire as if he hadn't a care in the world, but his sharp eyes missed nothing. He kept his hair neatly trimmed and ordered all his clothes from catalogues.

Grandfather cleared his throat, signaling an end to her delaying tactics. He sat quietly, unaffected by the tension. As a shaman, he always seemed to be prepared for disaster.

"Is he awake?" Andrew asked. No need to clarify who.

"He is." Lily lifted her chin defiantly.

"And?" Lou prompted gruffly.

She took a deep breath before answering. "I don't think we'll have to kill him."

Chapter Two

"He's a threat," Lou growled, his heavily muscled frame straining against his handmade leather garments. Lily had tried for years to convince him to try Georgette's hand-knit and handwoven garments, but he always refused, saying they were too flimsy for proper use.

"He's hurt and lost." Lily kept her voice level. Pointing out Lou's paranoia wouldn't help the situation. He had some justification, having tracked too many hunters and poachers. She understood the need to protect Bear Claw but couldn't agree with his ruthlessness.

"He has to go," Lou snapped back.

"I did not put effort into treating him only to have him banished. He needs to stay." Andrew sounded amused, speaking in the same tone he used when training the puppies for sled duty. Dressed in plaid flannel with soft, wool-lined slippers, he refused to play to the stereotype of a medicine man despite Grandfather's training. He'd returned to Bear Claw because of the family's obligations, not out of any distaste or discomfort for twenty-first-century society.

"He is running from himself, from his memories," their grandfather interrupted.

None of the Charging Bull siblings bothered to ask how he knew. Their grandfather had long ago mastered the knack of maintaining an otherworldly mystique in all circumstances. Lily personally believed he made up at least half of it as he went along and took credit for things he hadn't considered or intended. But then, she'd never been terribly spiritual. She preferred to concentrate on practical matters.

She'd never admit her doubts to his face. Although Grandfather was shorter than all of them, his commanding presence could not be denied. His age would be impossible for an outsider to guess. His hair was still dark, with only a thin scattering of white and grey. Pulled back neatly in a tail and tied with a leather thong, it framed his face in a smooth oval. Multiple layers of wrinkles folded into each other, a mixture of age and weathering. He looked as he had always looked for as long as Lily could remember. He might be older than anyone else in their settlement, but he wasn't so old or weak that the siblings could dismiss one of his irritable cuffs across the backs of their squabbling heads. Grandfather poked another log into their antique enameled stove before turning to Lily. "What else did he say?"

"He doesn't want to talk much about himself. Every time I got close, he pulled back." Lily took a deep breath. Her obligations were clear, but when she thought of the pain she'd seen in Blue Eyes's face and heart, she couldn't turn away. She might not be a shaman, but the drive to help still ran deep. "He needs us, *Uzumati*."

His formal medicine title caused Grandfather to raise an eyebrow. "Your brother is correct in his concerns. The trouble chasing this man may find him here. We already have too much attention on us with the geological survey's discoveries last year."

Lily winced, remembering the flurry of excitement when the surveyors had discovered a large deposit of rare minerals beneath Kluane. Mining companies immediately began sniffing around, trying to revoke their national park status and offering bribes and considerations to the local tribes and settlements.

"I know, *Uzumati*. But this is one man, someone who will die if we don't help him." She needed to turn her family's focus away from all the other dangers they faced. If Grandfather could just see Blue Eyes as a man, there was a chance.

"He's not a lost puppy, Lily." Andrew failed to hide the hints of amusement tugging at his mouth.

"He's dangerous to us," Lou snapped.

"He's lost and alone, and we're talking about whether or not to kill him. I'd say we're more dangerous to him." Lily knelt by Grandfather's worn, padded chair. "Are our hearts as frozen as the river? He deserves our compassion."

Grandfather nodded slowly, considering her point. "You argue from the heart. Is there a strong motivation behind your words?"

Because I couldn't possibly want to help someone without the impetus of destined fate driving me. Lily kept her gaze fixed on Grandfather's face to keep from rolling her eyes. Blue Eyes might be cute, but she could want to help someone without it being part of true love or biological drives. She had enough to occupy her.

"You can't mean—" Lou jumped to his feet. "Not with an outsider!"

"Calm down. This isn't anything more than human decency. Shouldn't that be enough?" She turned back to her Grandfather.

He glared at Lou. Grandfather never had much patience for sibling battles. "Very well. This man needs time to recover. For now, we will refrain from judgment. It will be best if he is allowed to leave without realizing we are more than a collection of social misfits. Andrew will continue to treat him. Lily, you pleaded for his life. You will be responsible for him."

"Yes, *Uzumati.*" She lowered her eyes respectfully. Her grandfather clasped her shoulder for a moment. In any other family, it would have been a hug. They both understood what he meant.

"I don't like this," Lou growled.

"Perhaps you can check the southern trap lines again if his presence so disturbs you." Grandfather's voice was mild, but Lou flinched under the rebuke. "I have made my decision. You will all abide by it."

"The others will have to stay out of sight while he's here." Andrew stretched in his chair. His twin's belligerence never seemed to get under his skin.

"An unfortunate result of having temporary strangers here. But a necessary one." Grandfather got to his feet, preparing to end the discussion.

"We don't need to operate blindly." Andrew pulled his cell phone out of his pocket and held it up. Lily frowned. The lack of cell service was part of why they'd chosen this particular pocket to settle in. "I took his picture and gave it to Bob. He's on his way to Juneau for a pickup. He'll send the picture to his contact and find out who our mystery man is." A freight pilot and a member of their community, Bob checked out the rangers posted to Bear Claw and the occasional tourist for them. Still, Lily couldn't help feeling she'd made a mistake in telling anyone about Blue Eyes.

"It could bring his troubles right to our doorstep," she protested.

"Bob understands what's at stake. I trust his contact. He's found information for me before. It doesn't have to be all drum circles and visions." Andrew glanced at Grandfather, making it clear whom his last sentence was intended for. They must still be arguing about his commitment to the shamanic path.

"You know how I feel about modern technology. It spreads lies and weakens the spirit." Grandfather thumped his fist on the table.

"Ignorance isn't protection," Lou said reluctantly. "We need to know everything we can."

Lily straightened. She wouldn't have expected her traditional brother to ever support Andrew's course of action. She'd dismissed his gruff outbursts as just his typical personality, but if he was truly worried, she'd have to be even more careful.

Grandfather saw it, too. He nodded, accepting the decision even if he didn't like it. Which left Lily with no choice except to do the same. She served up the evening meal, trying to distract herself from the ominous feeling souring her belly. Grandfather and Andrew settled by the stove with a game of chess. Lou continued to work on his traps. After years of living in close quarters, they all knew when to walk away. Small grievances quickly turned into major fights if allowed to develop, and none of them had the option of leaving Bear Claw permanently, so they needed to maintain at least a veneer of civility at all times.

"You will not eat with us, Lily?" Grandfather asked.

"I ate at Doc's. I think I'll go to bed." It was a polite way of saying she needed to retreat. She walked away from her brother, disappearing into the tiny curtained alcove she called her own—a small handmade bed with built-in drawers for her clothes, overhung with a shelf for her books and trinkets. Making sure the curtain had closed completely, she opened the top drawer to pull out a pamphlet and package of letters. The pamphlet had once been glossy, but she'd gone through it so many times that the pages were soft and worn. She could still see the Northstar Communications logo clearly, though.

Her family would have a fit if they knew she had it. Lou and Grandfather would, at least. Andrew and Mark might have some sympathy, given their own leanings toward modern society. Bear Claw couldn't possibly afford the kind of exposure a mining operation would bring, but this company was different. They wanted the minerals, but they also were offering to use the various settlements in Kluane National Park to launch a prototype for a communication network that could link isolated communities and give them easy, cheap, and reliable Internet. It could open up the whole world.

Edyta, the Russian expatriate who ran Ptarmigan Shipping, had given her the pamphlet, and the two of them had been exchanging letters for the better part of a year. Lily's family didn't trust Edyta, especially since the businesswoman frequently used her influence to pressure the local communities. As the only source of shipping, she held a lot of power. But Lily liked the tiny, blunt businesswoman. Edyta and Evonne, Lily's best friend, were the only two who knew how much she dreamed of connecting to other people and places. She would never abandon Bear Claw, but if there was a way to reach out without endangering them all… her train of thought was as familiar and worn as the pamphlet.

Maybe that's why I feel such a connection with Blue Eyes. He wasn't one of the dozen people she'd grown up with. He'd been to places and seen things she'd only dreamed of. That made sense, much more sense than Lou's fears and Grandfather's hopes. She didn't have room in her life for setups with a cosmic dating service, and only a fool would believe in the fantasy of instant connection and lifelong partnership. Lily prided herself on being practical. Evonne was the dreamer and had been since they were little girls. She'd married Bob after only knowing him a few months, though they were still together after five years, so there must have been something there.

"She shouldn't go back there," Lou growled from the common area. Lily kept quiet. Her brothers never remembered how good her hearing actually was. A little sister needed to use whatever tools she had.

"She'll be fine. You worry too much," Andrew replied. Grandfather must have been out or in bed for them to be talking so freely.

"You've seen him. Should I be worried?"

"I can't speak for Lily, but he's not really my type." Andrew would be smirking. "You can't have expected her to never be interested in a man."

"He's not one of us," Lou said. "She should stick to her own kind. For all our sakes."

"She may not have a choice." Lily heard the chairs scrape across the floor as Andrew continued. "We need more wood for the fire."

The door closed, and Lily decided she'd hidden long enough. The events of the day left her muscles twitching in restless agitation. She needed to go out, burn off some energy.

She crept outside, avoiding her brothers, who were still talking loudly by the woodshed, arguing about her. She made the familiar dash to the woods, headed for her own private sanctuary, a small cave near the cabin. Usually she went there to read or have a little privacy. Tonight, she stripped off her clothes and stuffed them into a thermal-lined bag to keep them from freezing.

There wasn't much time before her exposed skin would crystallize and freeze. Lily closed her eyes, letting her consciousness sink into the sounds of the forest: the echoing creak of ice-gripped wood shifting in the lowering temperature, the endless hiss of wind scraping across the frozen ground, the almost inaudible plop of tree-caught snow losing its battle with gravity to fall to the ground. It was the familiar melody of her life, one that had soothed her since birth.

The icy wind would have ripped the life from her naked body if she had been human, but Lily's ancestors had long ago claimed this arctic land as their own. Even as the cold beaded her skin in intricate patterns, a thick coat of fur began to sprout from her tan flesh. Evonne had told her that the change was disturbing to watch, describing it as painful, but Lily never felt that way. It wasn't any more uncomfortable than stretching muscles after a period of being hunched in a single position. Everything stretched outward, finding new equilibrium and balance.

She dropped to her forepaws, the bulk of her alternate form settling around her, lending weight and strength to every step. The power of her grizzly form both reassured and intoxicated her. In this shape, she need not fear any natural creature. Only unnatural hunters such as humans could threaten her, and they would not find her easy prey.

Things were simpler in the fur. Moral ambiguities had a tendency to disappear, leaving her mind clearer and more focused. She found it both alluring and terrifying. Her great-grandmother had retreated deep into her animal form, abandoning her family to live in the forest. Lily always worried about succumbing to the same fate.

Pointing her snout toward Doc's cabin, she breathed deeply. It was time to patrol and hopefully find more answers about her mystery man.

After struggling out of a nightmare-filled sleep, Ron poked about Doc's tiny cabin. With no clock, and having broken his watch during the fall, he had no way to gauge how much time had passed. He only knew it was the next day because Doc told him so before leaving to do his morning rounds, as he called them. He'd promised to return to the cabin soon, but Ron was already stir-crazy. There was no TV, nothing except masses of notebooks and sample containers. He'd hoped Lily might come back, but instead, the hours dragged on endlessly, broken only by a few scientific books about bear behavior and anatomy and a battered Tom Clancy novel with the last three pages missing.

He was torn. On the one hand, this looked like the perfect place to take the recharging time he desperately needed. He could figure out a plan, maybe even figure out a way to safely go home. The idea sent a surge of longing through him. The last time his family had seen him, he'd been headed straight for an ugly death and an anonymous grave. If only he could talk to them, tell them he was trying to get better and stay sober. But if he did, he'd lead his pursuers right to them, and he couldn't risk that. Not without a plan.

His head shrilled with too many competing alarms. The man from the truck stop—if he was connected with Ron's captors, he could conceivably find this little community. In fact, from what Lily had said, there weren't many other options. If he kept moving, he'd stay ahead of them. Every time he'd let himself be seduced into staying still, they'd found him. There were already too many deaths on his conscience. He pushed the heels of his hands into his temples, trying to silence the pounding headache in order to think rationally.

Lily might have something he could take to ease the pain. Ron sagged in the chair, realizing that no matter how he tried, his mind kept circling back to her brilliant smile, her gentle touch, her delightfully curvy body. He groaned, feeling like a randy teenage boy trying to catch a glimpse of a girl between classes. But he wasn't a teenage boy. He was a man, one who knew better than to let his selfish desires put someone else at risk.

A knock at the door caused him to jump up, banging into the tiny table and sending the piles of paper tumbling to the floor.

"Who is it?" he called out, squatting to pick up the papers.

The door opened, revealing an older man with weather-tanned skin, dressed in a fur hat with flaps covering his ears and a brown parka. "I'm Bill Miller, the senior ranger for Bear Claw. Doc mentioned you were up and feeling better."

Why would Lily and Doc have betrayed him like this? Ron forced himself to keep still despite his mind screaming at him to lash out before he could be recaptured and made helpless again. The mental noise drowned out what Bill was asking.

"—out there?"

A crackling told him that he'd crushed the papers in his hand. Ron sat down, putting the crumpled pieces carefully on the table and rubbed at his head. *Stay calm.* "Sorry, could you repeat that? My head is still killing me."

Bill's tired eyes narrowed slightly, but he nodded pleasantly enough as he took the other chair. "I asked what you were doing out there."

I can do this. Keep it simple. "I got lost."

"Have to be pretty lost to end up in Bear Claw." Bill started stripping off his gear, revealing a worn blue-denim shirt and jeans, ending Ron's hopes of a quick interview.

Ron decided to go with a variant of the truth. "I've been traveling a while, trying to keep a promise I made." He pulled the hard plastic box out of his jacket. "I said I'd bring her home to her family, and I've been searching to find the place ever since."

"That's one heck of a promise." Bill didn't reach for the urn, although his long fingers twitched toward it.

"I was told it's on the border near the Yukon, Alaska and British Columbia. It doesn't show up on any maps. I hoped once I got closer, I'd find someone who knew about it." He felt more confident now. The ranger was distracted from wondering how Ron had ended up alone in the woods. With luck, that part of the story wouldn't come up again until Ron was well on his way.

"We've got pretty extensive maps of the area at the ranger station. Show a lot of the individual cabins and smaller settlements. What's the name of this place?" Bill asked.

"Ekurru." Ron pronounced the word awkwardly. Walter Harris had refused to write it down for him.

Bill's eyes widened, and his lips pressed together. The mood shifted from curiosity to hostility, raising Ron's already tense nerves to painful alertness.

"Who are you?" Bill demanded.

Ron bolted to his feet, his adrenaline firing and ready to fight. He would not be caged again. Bill leaned back in his chair. His hands were spread with rigid fingers, prepared to defend himself, but the casual pose seemed designed to defuse the situation rather than antagonize it.

Ron took a deep breath, trying to regain his composure. His hands were shaking, and his headache swelled with each thumping heartbeat.

"Didn't mean to upset you. Easy now." Bill kept his voice level, giving Ron time to calm down.

"What do you want?" Ron retreated from the table, putting his back to the wall.

"When I came here, I planned to file a report about you being found. Let your family know you were all right and call off any search-and-rescue efforts." Bill relaxed slightly, but his right hand still hovered near his belt. Ron suspected the man had a weapon there. "From your reaction, I suspect it wouldn't be a good thing."

"I don't have any family, and no one is looking to rescue me."

"I can see this is difficult. Sit down, son, and I'll put my cards on the table if you'll do the same." Bill held up his hand before Ron could object. "I'm not asking for your secrets, but it might be best if you stopped asking about Ekurru."

Ron slowly sank into the chair, his body still thrumming on high alert. There was no way Bill would still believe he was an innocent lost hiker. Rationally, he should cooperate. Emotionally, his legs twitched, ready to smash and run—anything to escape the older man and his accurate suspicions. Rational thinking scraped out a victory by a very thin margin.

"I take it there's trouble following you. Trouble you're looking to avoid."

Ron nodded.

"Is it likely to follow you here?"

"I don't know. I was hitchhiking, and then I saw someone I thought was following me. I took off into the woods to get away. I got lost and tried to build a fire, but I fell asleep and then there was this bear—"

"What kind of bear?" Bill's attention sharpened even more.

"A big one, brown. Had a little golden crescent on one shoulder." Ron described the animal, the muscles bunching even tighter around his spine. Why did the ranger care about the bear?

"That's Litonya. One of Doc's." Bill frowned. "What happened next?"

"I woke up here."

"And no one on your trip told you anything about this Ekurru place?"

"That's right."

Bill relaxed, raising Ron's suspicions even more. He wondered if Walter had given him a fake name, something to flag him as he traveled. Maybe that was how people were tracking him. His brain shied away from the memories of his captivity.

"I don't want the people around here getting hurt. I won't put you in any official report, but I want you out of here as quickly as possible." Bill stood up and started pulling on his gear. "Understood?"

Ron nodded. His mind and body still raced in high gear, refusing to give him the space to think and act. He barely noticed Bill leaving—he was too overwhelmed and exhausted from the constant struggle to control himself. His palms crushed against his eyes as if he could physically force his brain to close down. He couldn't quite seem to breathe. The air kept getting sucked back out of his lungs faster than he could pull it in.

A drink. I need a drink. If he didn't get some relief from his hyper-awareness, he was going to be sick. He remembered Doc telling him how he kept food and other supplies in a storage bin beside the front door. *No need for a fridge,* the old man had chortled. *Not when it's thirty below out there!*

Ron's body bolted for the door before he could consciously finish the thought. He struggled with the locking mechanism for the bin before managing to open the lid. He scanned the contents, praying Doc would have a little something to warm up with on a cold night.

The bottle of vodka was nearly full, and Ron breathed a sigh of thanks. His bare fingers stuck to the chilled glass, reminding him that he had dashed outside in socks, jeans, and a sweatshirt. The cold woke his brain to the implications of his actions. *Remember the rules.* One drink would inevitably become more, and he'd suck down the entire bottle in pursuit of temporary oblivion. His fingers refused to let go of the smooth, chilled glass. As he retreated back to the house, his mind raced so quickly that he could barely grasp his own thoughts.

The bottle called to him, promising to blunt the raw nerves locking his body and mind in hyper awareness. His nails scraped along his cheek, and the pain gave him room to think. He wasn't safe. *Just one. I can do just one this time.*

He fumbled the screw cap off and managed to pour a generous amount into a mug. Tipping it down his throat, he welcomed the icy burn of the alcohol. It stole along his nerves, muting the alarm like a hand pressed against resonating guitar strings. *Just one more. Then I can stop.*

"Lily, we weren't expecting you! Bob took your letter with him when he left last night." Evonne greeted her warmly from her place by the squat little stove. Her black hair was pulled into a loose braid over one shoulder, and her grey-tinted fingers were busy knitting an intricate pattern.

"I was hoping to talk." Lily's socks could barely grip the satiny-smooth wooden floor. The matching walls gleamed in the lamplight, broken only by the brightly painted doors. When they were little, she'd envied Evonne for having a solid frame to keep her space private instead of a simple curtain. Several new woven blankets hung on the walls, done in soft blue-green geometric patterns. "I see Georgie's been bored again."

"She's testing out some new designs on her loom." Evonne shrugged, unimpressed by her sister's talent even though the rugs and blankets Georgie made were the family's major source of income. "Tea?"

"Please." Lily chose a mug from the shelf and filled it from the kettle warming on the stove. The heat seeped pleasantly into her fingers.

"So, are you going to tell me, or do I have to drag it out of you?" Evonne put aside the knitting, careful to only use her elbow to open the bag where she kept her works in progress.

"There's been a new development," Lily said carefully. She'd spent the night staring sleeplessly into the darkness.

"Is it because of the new guy hanging out at Doc's?" Evonne asked breathlessly.

"You heard about him." Lily had hoped to break the news herself. Her fingers tightened around her mug. She hoped Evonne wouldn't see her interest in Blue Eyes as a potential betrayal of the community. Lily couldn't bear another lecture.

"Bill stopped by and warned us to keep away from him. He was pretty upset, went to talk with Doc up at the Colony." Evonne turned around, her big eyes wide. "Did they find out about Northstar?"

Lily shook her head and took a swallow of tea to warm and loosen her voice. "Not yet. But things are happening faster than I expected."

"You haven't done anything wrong. It's talk—nothing to be ashamed of." Evonne might make a good show of determination, but she and Lily both knew what was at stake. Evonne's grey fingertips were actually covered in nearly invisible sensitive hairs, giving her incredible tactile sensitivity and condemning her to a life of isolation. Ekurru was the home of the Marked, the *lalassu* whose physical characteristics made it difficult or impossible to blend with typical human communities.

"That kind of thinking is what got us into trouble in the first place." Lily grinned, sipping her tea.

"What we want isn't wrong, Lily. No one should have to live in a cage. It might be made of ancient trees and traditions instead of cold iron and concrete, but it's still a cage." Evonne hesitated, biting her lip. "I've been thinking, and I want you to bring the new guy here."

Lily had no idea what to say in reply. *Are we planning to offer him smoked salmon with a side of freak-out?* She carefully put her mug down on top of the stove. "Are you serious? Does Bob know?"

Evonne looked at the wedding photo on the wall. Bob beamed at the camera, his round, pale face almost split in half by his grin. In the picture, Evonne looked nervous, her hands covered by delicate lace gloves to disguise their color. Bob's head only came up to Evonne's chin. He often joked that his small size made him the perfect freight pilot since he didn't take up much extra weight. He never let his stature slow him down or backed away from a fight. Evonne had told her that when they first met, she'd loved that about her husband. His protectiveness made her feel safe. Yet Lily knew that somewhere along the way, safe became a prison.

"He doesn't know. He'd freak out. He wants me to stay in this cabin all the time. We had a fight last night. He told me to go up to the retreat while he was away. Georgie's already there."

The hot tea turned cold in Lily's stomach. The retreat was a bunker dug into the tundra, a final place of retreat if Ekurru was ever discovered. The dank, cold, and claustrophobic tunnels would be torture for Evonne and Georgie. Their tactile sensitivity easily overloaded them with information. *If Georgie went down there, she must be terrified about Blue Eyes and whoever is after him.*

Evonne continued. "You remember how I stopped going on the sales trips? It was because Bob worried I'd expose myself and get lynched. I'm tired of it, Lily. He gets more scared each year, and I'm starting to feel strangled. That's why I want to meet this man."

A surge of jealousy surprised Lily. Evonne was married. She shouldn't have been looking for someone else. Lily might not be sure she wanted to act on her attraction to Blue Eyes, but she certainly didn't want to compete with her best friend. *Don't get caught up in fantasies. Keep your feet on the ground.* Something of her thoughts must have leaked through, because Evonne hastened to explain.

"Bob thinks any normal person who meets me would be freaked out. If we can show him that this man knows who I am and what I can do and isn't hurrying to find pitchforks and torches, then it should help him to relax."

"What if he does freak out?" Lily needed her friend to look at the possibility. "What then?"

"We can control the meeting. He won't have any proof, and if he runs away, blabbing about strange people in the North, he's only one more crazy person. But I don't think it will happen. I don't think people are as afraid as Bob believes they are."

Lily considered the plan. "It feels like we're taking advantage of Blue Eyes being lost and alone. It doesn't feel right. Last night, my family was deciding whether or not to kill him, and it was close, Evonne. This would put him in even more danger."

"It's not like we have a lot of lost hikers to choose from," Evonne insisted. "We don't have to let your family know."

Keeping a secret in such a small community was impossible. On the other hand, Blue Eyes obviously had practice keeping his mouth shut if he was running from something. *No, I can't.* Lily shook her head.

"You like him." Evonne's eyes lit up.

Of course, her best friend figured it out faster than she had. "Yeah. I do. I think. I don't know—he's also one of the only men I've ever seen who wasn't related to me. Whatever I'm feeling, it doesn't mean we're mates."

"I never said anything about the m word. Besides, you don't like Steve, and he's not related to you." Evonne leaned back in triumph.

Lily's lip curled automatically at the mention the latest temporary ranger assigned to help Bill. Steve kept flirting even when she made it clear she wasn't interested. He refused to back down, and she'd been tempted to solve the problem with a few well-placed rifle shots. "Dr. Damali is welcome to him."

"I wish they'd both leave," Evonne grumbled. Every stranger meant additional danger for the *lalassu*. Between Steve and Dr. Damali, a fellow biologist who drove Doc up the wall, tensions had been running high.

"Forget Steve. Back to this Blue Eyes. If you like him, you should go for it," Evonne suggested eagerly. She'd always been the more romantically inclined of the two of them, devouring the romance novels that Edyta sent them every other month. They'd spent many evenings together with Lily reading the books since Evonne couldn't handle the texture of the pages. Lily liked the stories, but they were just that: stories.

Not the basis for real life.

"Give me details." Evonne kept her fingers tightly together as she slid her hand through her long but narrow mug handle, picking it up with her palm to avoid touching it with her fingertips. It fit snugly in her hand.

"Blue eyes. It's the first thing I noticed. Like glacial pools, deep blue with little green flecks in them. He's tall, but thin, like he hasn't been eating well for a long time. Light-brown hair, cut short and curling a little bit under his ears. Nice shoulders. He says he came here to bring a woman's ashes back to her family." Picturing Blue Eyes relaxed Lily. It had been such fun to try and coax smiles from his serious face.

"An old girlfriend? A wife?" Evonne sipped her tea, keeping the mug balanced with her lips and palm.

Why had that particular jealousy-inducing possibility not occurred to her? Lily's contentment fled. "I don't know. He didn't say."

"Either way, she's dead. Not exactly competition." Evonne waved away the possibility.

A knock at the door interrupted them. Lily frantically reviewed the last few minutes of conversation. She'd been so preoccupied she hadn't heard footsteps approaching.

Evonne called out, "Come in."

Andrew poked his head inside. "Good morning, Evonne. Lily, we need to talk in private."

Lily bit back a sarcastic reply and got to her feet. "Sure. I'll be back later, Evonne."

"Don't rush. And think about what I said." Evonne waved them off cheerily, and Lily found herself wading through the fresh, loose snow behind her brother in the Arctic early-afternoon twilight.

"Your rescuing impulses have landed us in some serious trouble." Andrew slogged ahead, his voice grim. "Your new friend asked about Ekurru."

The wind's chill bit deep into Lily's cheeks as they drained of blood. "How?"

"He told Bill that he promised to bring someone's body home. He claimed it was the name of the town and that it was near the three borders."

"He did show me a plastic container which he said held a woman's ashes." This latest upheaval was too much for Lily to begin to process. At worst, she'd suspected Blue Eyes might be a refugee or fleeing some criminal situation. Given a thousand years, she would never have guessed that he would spill out one of Bear Claw's guarded secrets. She couldn't even begin to think what this meant for Evonne's plan. "What else did he say?"

"He gave no hint of Ekurru's true purpose, but Bill is not a skilled interrogator. Your Blue Eyes would have quickly realized something was wrong. Doc and Bill are waiting for us." Andrew's long strides cut easily through the snow.

"What did Grandfather say?" Had the death sentence been put back into place? Lily's ribs clung together, refusing to part long enough for her to draw breath.

"He wants to know more—who this man truly is and what he knows of us. We can guess who he carries." Andrew never glanced back as Lily fell farther behind."Nada." The old woman usually came in spring and fall to visit her nieces, Evonne and Georgette. This year, she hadn't arrived. Lily's mind couldn't quite accept the idea that she might be gone. Nada had always seemed like an unstoppable force of nature.

"We've heard nothing of her death. And we should have been informed." Andrew's voice was grim and strained. Their communication network with their fellow *lalassu* relied on dead drops and passed messages. The links could all too easily be broken. They'd heard very little over the last few months. But it couldn't be anyone else. No one was missing from their little community.

The ground had been steadily rising beneath them as they walked, but now it dropped away in a steep cliff. A series of pathways were carved across the irregular cliff face, linking the various caves. Lily glanced into them as they passed. Most held furry lumps curled into the back, and the smell made guessing unnecessary: the caves were all occupied by bears.

Any student of bear behavior would immediately recognize this place as unusual. Bears did not den close together. They didn't tolerate fellow members of their own species except during mating and raising cubs. Yet these caves held a dozen bears happily hibernating together.

One bear slowly uncurled as Andrew and Lily approached. She ambled to the entrance of her cave, each dinner-plate-sized paw stepping as delicately as a lady picking her way across a puddle.

"Hi, Setsuné." Lily offered her hand, unafraid of the giant animal. She'd known this bear since she was a child. Setsuné had always taken an interest in Lily's comings and goings. Her name meant "grandmother" in their language.

Setsuné clacked her jaws in greeting, allowing Lily to bury her mittened hand in her thick ruff of winter fur.

"How's your friend?" Lily smiled at the enormous bruin.

"What friend?" Andrew asked.

Setsuné's fur bristled and rumbled with her growl. Lily hastened to reassure her. "It's all right. Andrew won't cause any trouble." She turned her attention back to her brother. "I've seen signs that she's sharing her cave with another bear. A smaller one. I'm not sure who, and she doesn't like me poking around."

"We have more to deal with than Grandmother's roommates. Doc and Bill are waiting for us." Andrew gestured for her to hurry.

"Sorry, Setsuné. I'll be back soon," Lily promised. Setsuné yawned and ambled slowly back into her cave to nap again.

The siblings picked their way down the switchback to where the ranger and biologist were waiting by the circular firepit. Surrounded by four-foot-tall walls made from massive river stones, the bed of embers sent up a wave of heat. Bill tossed a fresh chunk of dry wood into the firepit, and it quickly began to flame.

"I assume Andrew brought you up to date?" Doc asked.

Lily nodded.

"Bear Claw is getting too crowded. First, Dr. Damali poking around." Bill ignored the automatic grumbles from Doc at the mention of the other biologist. "Then, the visitor that I'm still not asking questions about. Now, this man who's claiming to be a lost hiker returning a body. It can't all be coincidence."

"We've always drawn our share of hunters for the size and abundance of our game. Not to mention the occasional Sasquatch enthusiast," Andrew reminded the others. "We're too small a community to tear ourselves apart looking for traitors who may not exist."

"He might not know about Ekurru," Lily interrupted, a new possibility crystallizing in her mind.

"He asked for it by name," Bill interjected, his lined face full of worry.

"Nada knew about Ekurru. She told me that she wanted to be buried up here, away from the electronic noise of the city." Nada's gifts made her painfully aware of any electronic field, no matter how faint. Lily's voice caught as she realized it might be time to honor her final wish. "If she died, she would have wanted to be brought up here."

"She could have asked any number of *lalassu* to bring her here. Why take the risk with someone unknown?" Doc asked the question as if it were part of a scientific inquiry. He wasn't condemning her theory, merely exploring the hypothesis for holes.

"We don't know the circumstances of how she died. She may not have had a choice," Lily argued. "Blue Eyes can't know what Ekurru really is. Otherwise, he never would have mentioned it to Bill. He's asking as if it's a town like any other."

"He is running from something. It could be whatever killed Nada." Andrew nodded thoughtfully as he spoke. "If he is risking himself to fulfill a promise, it speaks well of his character."

"We still need to gather more information." Doc threw another chunk on the fire.

"If he doesn't know of Ekurru's special nature, perhaps we can stage something suitable," Andrew suggested.

"I think we'd be better off taking him down to Kluane and handing him over to the authorities." Bill wearily wiped at the soot-smudged walls of the firepit. "There are too many moving parts to keep track of."

Lily opened her mouth to protest, but Andrew beat her to it. "We have to keep him where we can watch him. Between the four of us, we can surely manage to prevent him from causing any trouble."

"He's been left alone all day. I suppose I shouldn't have done that." Doc's beard and moustache folded together in consternation. "Only… Elxeli's been hurt, and I've been trying to get him to let me see what's wrong. I didn't want to leave him."

"You go ahead. I'll take a look at Elxeli. He and I get along well." It would give her time to try and untangle the knotted skeins of her reactions. The situation was more delicate than she'd ever imagined, and she couldn't risk making it worse. She made her way to Elxeli's cave. The massive bruin growled softly as she stepped into the cave. She chided him. "Don't be silly. I won't hurt you."

A loud huff expressed his skepticism more than adequately.

Lily knelt down beside Elxeli, trying to make out details in the dimness. "I need a flashlight."

When the bear didn't react, she clicked on the tiny penlight she carried in her pocket. Leaning closer, she saw Elxeli cradling his front paw closely, refusing to put it on the ground. She held out her hand. "Show me."

The bear rumbled softly.

"Don't be a baby. Show me," Lily insisted.

He extended his paw, gingerly resting it in her outstretched hand. Lily turned it and immediately spotted the problem: a deep puncture in the second toe. It wasn't hard to guess what had happened. Elxeli had earned his Dene-inspired name as a cub, using his paws to drum on trees, rocks, cabins, or whatever he could reach. Even as an adult, he couldn't resist a hollow tree. He must have crashed through and jabbed himself on the splinters.

Lily shone the light into the puncture, checking for remaining fragments. She couldn't see any inside. A tap on her shoulder told her Andrew had slipped into the cave. He held out a tin of her grandfather's healing ointment. It would prevent infection and numb the pain until the wound healed.

"All right. I'm going to put some of this on. Try not to lick it off." Lily stripped off her mittens and spread a generous fingerful on the wound. Elxeli shivered and tensed but didn't growl or snap. "It should be better in a few days."

The bear's dark eyes slowly slid closed, and he laid his head down on the cave floor to sleep. Lily and Andrew crept out of the cave.

"You have a natural gift," Andrew praised her before flipping back to criticism. "You should concentrate on developing it."

"Thanks, O Wise Elder." His comment gave her an idea. Blue Eyes might be skittish about sharing his secrets with humans. But they weren't the only willing ears around here.

Chapter Three

This is impossible. Karan studied the computer screen, searching for an explanation. According to the information, the people he was searching for did not exist. Had never existed. Danielle Harris and her brothers, Eric and Vincent, were figments of his imagination. They had humiliated him and his boss, snatching valuable assets out of their hands and forcing them to retreat to their stronghold in Eastern Europe. Overlooking the Black Sea, their Ukrainian chateau was an ancient citadel of polished stone and stained glass. It was pleasant enough, but Karan loathed being forced into any action. Still, if he had to be exiled from his comfortable set of identical apartments, then this was an acceptable substitute while he repaired the situation.

McBride's records were still intact, although he seemed to have once more disappeared below their radar. Karan's agents had not been able to confirm a sighting for weeks. McBride was not being protected by whoever had altered the Harris-sibling records. Without witnesses nearby, Karan allowed himself to indulge in a frown. He had found his targets before through their high school records, but since then, someone of considerable patience and skill had subtly changed the photos and contact information. An uncomfortable possibility began to occur to him.

"*Pan* Samil?" The elderly housekeeper tapped on the open door. Her cringing pricked Karan's lingering irritation raw. He had been forced to be overly strict with her initially. She saw him as a fellow servant and had attempted to engage him in camaraderie. It had taken several extended conversations before she understood the nature of their relationship. *A*

"What is it?" He did not look at her. That made it easier to ignore her perpetual wringing hands and darting glances.

"*Pan* Samil, this was delivered for you." She held out a narrow cardboard cylinder in her trembling hand.

"Put it on the table."

She obeyed quickly and vanished back into the depths of the house. Karan paused to evaluate the situation. A little fear was acceptable—it bred respect and reduced chances of betrayal. But too much reduced effectiveness and increased the chance of rebellion. He and Dalhard were relying on the staff's discretion to conceal their presence here. If the woman could not regain her composure, she would be useless—or worse, reveal them through fearful babble. The requirements of laying low would make finding a replacement difficult.

He would need to find out if she had anyone in her life likely to cause trouble if she abruptly disappeared. With luck, his preparations would be unnecessary, but he did not rely on luck to make his way in the world.

The cardboard tube rattled when he picked it up. Opening it, he discovered a data drive inside along with a note of verification from one of Dalhard's North American agents. The drive held a lengthy report along with a few blurry surveillance photos of a man in heavy winter clothing, his face turned away from the camera. The report claimed the photos were taken in northern British Columbia near the border with Alaska.

The man could well be their asset. Yet another point of frustration: Karan had allowed the former soldier to escape when the effort to retrieve him might have negatively impacted their own flight from the authorities. There had been a number of suitable subjects waiting to undergo the transformative protocols, and he had deemed it unnecessary to indulge in further risk. Unfortunately the subjects had not survived the treatments, leaving him with no choice but to retrieve the Harris siblings or the soldier. Karan approved the agent's request for bribe money and wired funds from an untraceable Swiss account.

Dalhard wanted all assets retrieved for his own purposes. Perhaps he still hoped to breed his own supernatural army instead of genetically modifying one. Karan would have scrapped the venture as too costly for the potential reward, but it was not his decision. His employer kept himself locked in his suite, communicating with a wide network of legitimate contacts to chase down even hints of rumors, looking for new potential sources of supernatural test subjects. Lately, the focus had been on a project near the Alaska border, based on stories of unusually intelligent bears.

His boss's obsession and isolation left Karan free to do the work needed to rebuild Dalhard Industries, including the mining project to cover the Alaskan interests. A significant portion of their North American businesses had come under scrutiny during the investigation, forcing him to pull back and present a veneer of legitimacy. Scrubbing the records of any hint of impropriety from such a distance had not been easy or cheap, but their people had accomplished what was necessary. Only in the last few weeks had he been able to turn his attention to potential new sources of income.

Not everyone could think logically about long-term risks and goals. Karan accepted the limitations of others and used those limitations to achieve what he wanted. With Dalhard, he'd achieved power and influence without any personal risk. Should any of their illegal activities come to light, Karan Samil could easily vanish, leaving André Dalhard as the responsible party. He had nearly done so, but he was glad he had waited. The situation was still salvageable.

His opponent might have hidden some of the pieces, but the game continued. Eventually, the missing pieces would have to be brought back, or the game would be forfeited. And once they were back on the playing board, it was only a matter of time. Karan never lost, no matter how long it took to achieve his victory.

Lily caught up with Doc before they reached the cabin. Despite living up here for over three decades, he'd never quite mastered the fine art of breaking a trail through loose snow.

"Do you think we can trust him?" she asked, knowing Doc would be brooding about it as much as she was.

"Can we trust him? That's one question. The better one is whether or not we should trust him. He's dropped into our circle out of nowhere. We'd be idiots not to be suspicious." Doc's breath puffed ahead of him in shifting clouds.

"He was scared and alone. He couldn't even build a fire to keep himself warm." Lily knew her anger with Bill and Andrew was unreasonable. She understood the stakes as much as anyone, but she couldn't seem to keep herself from snarling whenever someone doubted Blue Eyes.

"I didn't say I didn't believe him. But he's not telling us everything. Even if he's harmless, what's chasing him might not be." Doc stopped, his bushy brows dipping below the rims of his glasses. "Something's wrong."

A scuffling, scraping sound echoed through the trees, and Lily's hackles began to rise. She held up her hand, silently telling Doc to wait while she checked it out. Reaching into her pocket, she pulled out a pistol loaded with flash-bang rounds. If this was local wildlife, the miniature firecrackers would send them running. If the threat was more than just an animal, she would shift to the fur.

She came to the last few trees on the edge of the clearing. She could see the back of Doc's cabin clearly. A strange crashing and crunching barked through the air. Lily eased forward slowly, making a wide circle around the cabin.

Rounding the corner, she saw a black bear trying to bite into a frozen mass of caribou meat. Its teeth scraped noisily along the ice-locked flesh, managing to cut slushy grooves but not break off a mouthful. Picking up the chunk, it flung the meatsicle against the trees to shatter it, revealing the source of the crashing. She recognized the animal by the white patch at its throat.

"Big Bart." She shook her head.

The animal looked up at her, blinking comically like a brat caught sneaking cookies before supper. Lily might have sympathized—after all, the little bear was only a year or two old. He needed to learn to stay away from humans, or else his odds of survival would be slim.

"Go on!" she shouted, raising the pistol and firing. A red whirligig burst out of the muzzle, and Bart hightailed it in the opposite direction.

Doc came out of the woods and joined Lily a few minutes later while she inspected the damage. Bart had ripped into most of the contents of Doc's cold-storage box, looking for food. Except the locking mechanism wasn't damaged. It looked as if it had been left open, but Doc was too experienced to be so careless.

"Oh dear." Doc picked up the mangled caribou. "This isn't going to look good on a report."

"Not much is left. He even tried crushing the tin cans before he found the meat."

"And you know Dr. Damali will use it against me. The woman won't be satisfied until we're all packed up south." Doc continued his rant. "Do you know the woman dared to ask to use my plane to bring in some stupid equipment? As if I'd risk the *Angel* in this weather."

"I'll have Lou haul the remains somewhere safe," Lily said as he paused to draw breath. "And we have enough to worry about without bringing Dr. Damali into it."

"The woman insists on being in it," Doc huffed.

"The door is still intact. He didn't get inside." Worry for Blue Eyes made Lily's fingers clumsy. He would have been terrified hearing Big Bart ransack the storage bin outside the door. It surprised her that he hadn't called out to them when he'd heard them talking.

She opened the door and stopped in her tracks.

Blue Eyes hadn't called out because he lay passed out in the chair by the stove. An empty bottle of vodka rocked on the floor beside him, and some of Doc's research notes were singeing on the stovetop. Lily rushed in, pulling them off the hot surface before they could burst into flames. The baked-leather backing cracked in her hands.

Obviously, Blue Eyes had taken the vodka from the storage bin and neglected to lock it afterward. Lily's teeth locked together in fist-clenching fury. His carelessness could have gotten him killed. As it was, Doc's winter supplies were destroyed, and a careful season of encouraging Bart to forage instead of scavenge had been undone. They couldn't just run down to the local grocery store and get more food. They would have to order it at exorbitant prices and have Bob fly down to pick it up from the closest supply point. A baby would have more sense!

She snatched at the vodka bottle. Only a few drips remained in it. Her curiosity broke through the clouds of fury. *Why? What happened to make him rush for the bottle?* He hadn't been drunk in the woods when he'd been found. His face and hands didn't show the signs of prolonged alcohol abuse. And people didn't typically swallow entire bottles of liquor to relax.

"Is there any more?" she asked Doc.

"More what? Oh, there was another bottle in the bin." Doc fiddled with his fogged glasses, peering myopically at Blue Eyes. "It doesn't really seem the time for a drink."

"I think we should move it. Get it out of reach while he's here." Lily folded a blanket over Blue Eyes. He looked worn-out and vulnerable, like a moose brought to bay at the end of a long chase. Dark circles stood out against his pale skin, and even asleep, his face stayed pinched in habitual fear.

Doc coughed, and Lily had the distinct feeling he was suppressing laughter. "I'll take it over to your house and see about getting something to tide me over until we can get more supplies. At least the river hasn't frozen yet. Still plenty of water."

She heard the door close behind him but kept her attention on Blue Eyes. The fire had burned low, and his skin was cool under her fingers. He shifted under her touch, his eyes half opening.

"Blue Eyes?" she whispered, wondering if he was truly waking up.

He smiled sleepily at her. "Lily. Glad you're here. You make it all quiet. Can think and breathe." His eyes started to slide closed again.

"What happened?" she asked. There was no one around to hear if he confessed something horrible. He might be aware and reacting, but his conscious functions had taken a break, which wasn't like any drunk she'd ever seen. One or two junior rangers had spent their time up here completely wasted.

"Got scared. Too much in my head. Don't want them to find me. Bad monsters." Blue Eyes's fists and mouth tightened.

Lily's hopes started to feel more like a burden pulling her down. "What monsters?"

"Chase me all the time. Can't think. Can't sleep. Always waiting for a mistake." His agitation grew, his shoulders starting to twitch and writhe as if preparing for a fight.

Whatever he feared, it went right down to his core. Even in his sleep, it haunted him. She struggled, wanting to soothe him, but she needed answers. She decided to give one more little push. "Mistakes like Nada?"

His face crumpled, raw and naked with regret and guilt. "I tried. I couldn't save you. So sorry."

Lily looked away, giving him back the privacy she'd violated. She couldn't torture him like this. "Shh. It's okay. I'll keep the monsters away."

He relaxed immediately, sinking back into true sleep. Lily sat back on her haunches, even more confused than she'd been a few hours before. She'd had the perfect opportunity to find out more, maybe even plant a suggestion or two. Instead, she'd patted him on the head and wished his nightmares away. She'd dedicated her life to protecting the Marked, and suddenly this man was creeping ahead of them on the priority list. Her stomach twisted as she wondered if she was betraying her people for the sake of a pretty face and hints of a sad story. She'd never felt so vulnerable or uncertain. She didn't want this to be a mating bond, but she couldn't deny the strength of her instincts. They were impossible to fight, which meant Blue Eyes was disrupting all her carefully maintained plans and routines.

"I should send you on your way," she whispered to the sleeping man. "It would be safer for you and for us. So why does the idea strike me as so unthinkable? Like abandoning one of my brothers?" She dared to stroke his cheek with her fingertips, the rough stubble catching on her calluses. "I wish I knew more about you, Blue Eyes."

"Ron," he murmured. "Name's Ron."

She snatched her hand away, embarrassed. Blue Eyes settled into a deeper sleep. His trust unsettled her. Awake, he was wary and suspicious. Drunk, he'd handed her his name. She wasn't worthy of such a prize. "Ron. We'll talk more when you wake up. There's more going on here than either of us realize."

Bob slipped quietly into the Internet café in Juneau, safely anonymous among the crowds of tourists from cruise ships busily checking their email and uploading their vacation photos on the ranks of bulky monitors. He paid for an hour of computer time and sat down among the jabbering throng to wait and sip the overpriced coffee. After years in Ekurru, the press of strangers overwhelmed him. He found it hard to remember his life in Vancouver. It seemed like a fairy tale of constant hurry and demands, not like an experience he'd actually lived.

The day he'd found Evonne had been the best moment of his life. Something about her made him believe in Cupid's arrows. When they first met, he felt as if a bolt from above had struck him, stopping his heart and realigning his entire world around her. Even after all these years, the feeling still hit him hard every time he looked at her. The idea of losing her drove him crazy. He'd do anything to protect Evonne and her family. The little data card in his pocket burned like a beacon. This so-called lost hiker could expose all the Marked if Bob wasn't careful.

The computer chimed, and he uploaded the photo from Andrew's phone and sent it to his friend in Vancouver. Ken was a brilliant investigative reporter with a full-time job at the *Vancouver Sun,* and the two of them had been friends since college. It hadn't been easy keeping the secret of the *lalassu* from him, but Ken had encouraged him to move to the North, threatening to personally kick Bob's ass if he didn't take a chance on the girl of his dreams.

Ken immediately emailed back. *Is this guy dead?*

No. He's hurt, and we're trying to find out who he is. Can you do the face-recognition thing for me again? Bob sent.

Ten minutes later, another email. *Call me.*

Bob pulled out his cell phone. "Ken, what's wrong?"

"I thought it might take a long time to pull up the records, but they popped up right away. There was a big story a few months ago. I think your man is Corporal Ronald McBride from the US, and if he is, it could be bad." Ken's voice was tight, as if the words were squeezing out against his better judgment.

Bob's fist tightened around the phone. He'd never heard Ken so worried, which sent his own heart pumping. If the hiker was McBride, the man was only five miles away from his wife. "What did he do?"

"He's linked with a bunch of suspicious deaths, starting with his own platoon in Afghanistan," Ken said quietly.

"He could be a murderer?" Bob's half-strangled shout attracted all sorts of attention from the tourists around him. He grabbed the memory card and headed out, pulling his hat down tight.

"It says he's a person of interest, and there's a number to call if you've seen him." Ken gave him the information, and Bob struggled to imprint it on his brain.

"Thanks. I owe you. I have to get home as fast as I can."

"Take care of yourself and Evonne. And call me back when you can. You know I'm going to worry until I hear from your sorry self." Their usual banter fell flat.

"Don't tell anyone that he might be there. I'll call you soon." Bob shoved the phone back into his pocket and threaded his way through the crowds, going right for the Juneau airport. The faster he got his wheels up, the better.

Ron's skull thudded painfully to awareness, giving him time to realize his tongue tasted as though a small animal had been using it as a burrow. The blurry nightmares had sapped his strength and left him with stiff muscles.

"Good morning, Sunshine!" Doc's voice rang out cheerfully. And loudly.

Ron winced, his memory of the previous night returning. Shame rivaled the hangover as he remembered draining the vodka bottle in his pursuit of chemical oblivion. Not exactly ideal house-guest behavior.

Doc wasn't above a little revenge, it seemed. Ron refused to believe making breakfast required such a godforsaken level of clatter. Doc banged the metal spatula against the iron fry pan, rattling the tin plates and whistling an off-key, merry tune.

Ron groaned. "Is there any water?"

"Sure thing." Doc handed him a plastic cup. Ron gulped the frigid water gratefully.

"Breakfast is a little thin this morning. We had a visitor last night." Doc put down a plate with fried strips of meat.

"I'm sorry about the vodka. I'll find a way to pay you back for it." Ron's father had taught him to be upfront about his mistakes. The man would be horrified to discover how his son had lived for the last few years. The thought of his dad's disappointment always left him ready to crawl into the ground and disappear.

"It wasn't so much the vodka, though I will miss it through the winter. It was the rest of the supplies." Doc settled into a chair and began wolfing down his own meal.

"But…" Ron trailed off, wondering if he'd been worse off than he'd thought last night. He didn't remember taking anything other than the vodka.

Doc's friendly demeanor vanished. "You didn't lock the bin, and one of the local troublemakers found it. Little black bear named Big Bart. I've been trying to teach him not to scavenge from humans for most of his life. And your carelessness last night gave him a big setback."

It never occurred to Ron to wonder why the supplies were locked. In retrospect, it seemed obvious. Of course animals would scavenge for food. The worst he'd ever dealt with were a few crows picking at his garbage bags. Or maybe a determined raccoon. Not an animal that weighed as much as any man and could inflict serious damage with a casual swipe.

"Bears who scavenge get shot. Folk call them nuisances," Doc continued, frustration making his voice rough and gestures sharp. "Bart's mother died before she could teach him how to forage properly. That little bear's been looking for trouble ever since. He keeps coming back around here no matter how many times I drive him off. I thought I'd finally convinced him humans weren't great to hang around."

"I'm sorry." Ron rubbed his face with the heel of his hand, feeling like an idiot and a public menace.

"I'm headed out to track him down, make sure he keeps going north and doesn't try to head south for easy pickings." Doc put away his dishes.

"Can I help?" Ron straightened, willing to try and fix the mess he'd created. He didn't have the slightest idea how, but walking away without making the effort wasn't an option. He'd sunk low enough. Time to start being the man he was raised to be again.

Doc paused and looked at his guest. Some of the angry tension drained away from his shoulders and face. "I appreciate the offer, and I will take you up on it. But not today. You don't have the gear to go out there without getting hurt. I spoke to Bill about it. He'll see what he can do. He seems convinced we should get you on your way as quickly as possible."

"It's probably safer for you all that way," Ron admitted. He'd only been here a little over a day, and his instincts were already tied in knots. He felt like a pale copy of the person he used to be, before Afghanistan and before his capture.

"Maybe. We're a stubborn bunch who don't like to be told what to do." Doc plopped a thick, shapeless knit hat on his head. "I'll be back in a few hours."

Left alone with his guilt and thoughts, Ron didn't bother trying to go back to sleep. What he'd done yesterday had been more than stupid. Aside from the impact on Bart and Doc, his little drinking binge had left him vulnerable. He could have stumbled out into the snow and frozen to death. Anyone could have found him in the cabin, and he'd have been helpless. Worst of all, the binge reignited compulsive cravings, making him want to do it again and again. His hands and legs twitched, wanting to search for more liquor or drugs, anything that promised a surcease of pain.

No more lying to myself. Thinking he could stop on command was a delusion. He'd had breakdown binges since escaping from his captor, and they always made things worse. And yet he could never stop himself from giving it another try when the opportunity presented itself.

He gritted his teeth against his frustration as he made himself useful, scrubbing dishes and generally tidying things up. He decided to wrap himself up in blankets to try chopping wood for the fire, but the near-zero temperatures drove him back inside quickly, his hands stinging as if they were being attacked by bees.

A knock on the door halted his round of self-recriminations. Hoping it might be Lily, Ron quickly opened it. Instead, he found himself staring at a petite woman whose heart-shaped face peered out at him from a fluffy black-fur wrap. She carried a heavily loaded sack.

"You must be our mystery guest," she said, pushing past him into the cabin.

"Who are you?" Ron closed the door, his adrenaline rising sharply.

"Dr. Damali. Rachel." She smiled and winked at him, and the hairs went up on the back of his neck. Her bared teeth might have been intended as charming, but all he felt was hunted.

"Bill intended to bring this over. Some of Steve's older gear. I offered to do it for him." Dr. Damali indicated the heavy bag she'd dropped by the door. "He said you were close in size, but I think some it might be a little small." She raked an appraising look over his body before turning to examine the cabin. "Oh dear. I knew Doc liked to play the absent-minded professor, but this is too much."

She shrugged out of her outer garments, revealing a snug-fitting white sweater over black leggings. Generous hips and breasts swelled out of a tight, svelte waist. Ron yanked his gaze away but not before Dr. Damali caught him looking at her. And smirked. "See something you like?"

"Doc's not here." Ron backed away from the tiny woman only to find himself hard against the stove.

Dr. Damali burst out laughing. "Well, I didn't think he was hiding under the table. I'm more interested in talking to you anyway. Steve mentioned that you saw an unusually large bear out in the woods?"

"Who's Steve?" Ron demanded.

"Bill's partner. Professional, not romantic. He's the other ranger posted to this park." Dr. Damali picked up a notebook and began to flip through it. "He passes on things of interest to me. Like unusually large bears."

"You study bears, too?" Ron wondered if everyone in Bear Claw was crazy or just determined to take advantage of getting to see a new face.

"I do," Dr. Damali purred, putting down the notebook and running her fingers along a set of hair samples in clear plastic baggies. Her almond-shaped eyes never left Ron, heightening the impression of a cat toying with its prey. "I'm interested in making sure they have enough space to live their lives without human contamination—unlike Dr. Svensson's foolish catering to loggers and miners, with his silly spouting off about humans and bears sharing an environment."

"I don't know anything about it." Everything about this woman hit a false note, and Ron didn't want to find out what was under the constructed façade. He just wanted her gone. Whatever it took to make her walk back out that door, he'd do it.

"I'm sure you don't. This is virgin forest, virtually untouched by human hands." Dr. Damali made a circle with her slim, pale hands. "Even the native tribes didn't spend much time around here despite the richness of the local resources. Because of the unusually large bears. Bears who were supposed to be able to avoid any trap and who towered above the hunters. I've been looking for evidence of those bears. If the animals here are significantly larger than the norm, then it would prove that the specimens we've been studying down south have been dwarfed by their continual interactions with humans. So, why don't you tell me how big the bear was?"

"It was big, but I don't know if it was bigger than usual. I haven't met many bears." Playing the rodent in this verbal game of cat and mouse wasn't getting him anywhere. *Give her what she wants, and get her out.*

"Taller than you?" Dr. Damali widened her eyes, cupping her cheek with her hand.

"I was sitting down. Its head was higher than mine." If he gave her what she wanted, she'd go. He gritted his teeth against the ache in his heart and pride.

"Fascinating. And it was a light brown?"

"With a little golden crescent on one shoulder."

"Easily identifiable. Could you take me there?" Damali stepped closer, naked greed shining from her eyes.

"No. I have no idea where I was. That's what lost means. I was unconscious when Doc brought me back." Ron stepped behind the chair, clenching the wooden back with whitened knuckles.

"Too bad." She clucked her tongue like a teacher telling the student he needed to stay in for recess. "I heard what happened with Doc's supplies. You'll need work to pay to replace them. Now, I have some grant money set aside for an assistant. I could make sure it went to you, if you were willing to help me."

"Doing what?" A few weeks ago, he would have said yes. But old instincts stopped him. Shoving aside the constant sirens of alarm sounding in his head, he studied the biologist carefully. She wasn't actually attracted to him, he guessed. Her behavior felt like an act, a manipulation tactic. If he could convince her to drop it, he'd have a chance to find out what she was really after.

"You act as if you're afraid I'll eat you alive." Dr. Damali's delighted grin held more than a trace of predatory glee.

"I prefer to be honest, ma'am." Ron straightened his shoulders and forced himself to let go of the chair. He'd done enough running for one day. "I might be the only new man you've seen in a while here, but I don't think you're so hard up or desperate that you'd push where you aren't wanted. Why don't you drop the flirting-belle routine and tell me what it is you're looking for?"

"You'd be surprised how many men respond to a little flirting." Dr. Damali still smiled, but her posture firmed up, becoming more businesslike.

"I'm not one of them." Now that she wasn't actively hunting him, Ron relaxed. But he still kept the chair between the two of them.

Dr. Damali gracefully took a seat and began to tap her fingers on the table to emphasize her points. "Very well. I was hired by AD Mining Industries to do an ecostudy. They're particularly interested in the local wildlife and the stories of large, unusually clever bears. They're negotiating with the government for the mineral rights to this area."

"You're working for a mining company, and you slam Doc for catering to miners and loggers?" Her hypocrisy annoyed Ron.

"Not at all. AD Mining made it very clear that they would not dig a single hole if I could prove there was unusual wildlife here that might be harmed by mining efforts. Given how Bear Claw has been resisting any development, I thought they would be eager to help my efforts, but instead, they've done everything except tie me to a sled and haul me out of town." She pouted.

"Sounds like you're not so good at figuring out when you've worn out your welcome." Ron crossed his arms over his chest, ready to end the conversation.

"I don't intend to let a bunch of xenophobic yokels with delusions of living as one with the local wildlife stand in my way," Dr. Damali snapped. "There's something unique here, and it needs to be properly documented by someone with actual academic credentials. Doc has decades of data lying around this cabin. I need it." She bent to pick up a notebook.

"I think you should leave, ma'am." Ron plucked it out of her hands. He wasn't about to let her rummage through Doc's things while the man wasn't present.

"Think about my offer." Dr. Damali shrugged into her parka. "I've been playing by the rules until now. A few words from me, and Doc could find himself yanked back south, and Bear Claw could lose its protected status. They'd all have to leave. Is that what you want?"

"Threatening me isn't a good idea." Ron had no respect for bullies of any stripe, and he refused to run from one again.

"It's not a threat. It's a message, one you should pass on to your housemate. Doc may want to believe I'm the bad guy, but he's making choices that impact a lot of people." She pulled her furry hat back down on her head. "If you change your mind, I have a bunk at the ranger station."

Ron watched her leave, hiding his conflicting emotions behind his best poker face. He wanted to go searching for another drink but held himself back. He didn't dare let himself fall again. How did a community with fewer than a dozen people in it have so many political landmines to tiptoe around? He didn't know anything about mineral rights or ecostudies, not even enough to guess at what wasn't being said. He'd seen a bear, and suddenly everyone was focused on that fact. Dr. Damali's concerns seemed sincere, but so had the last pitch he'd listened to. The man had offered him a chance to be a hero, to be stronger and faster than other people and go where they couldn't. If Ron could have done that before Afghanistan, Adam and Brian would still be alive.

The sense memory of dust and sand clogging his nose and coating his mouth made him choke. He heard the popping sound of the sniper's rifle again, and his body froze. For a moment, the walls of the cabin swam hazily, looking more like tan adobe walls baked in desert heat. Ron closed his eyes, despite his training shrilling at him to take cover and return fire. He needed to focus on the moment, or else he'd be caught up in the past. Without drugs or alcohol to numb his fear, it hit him full force.

I'm in the North. Near the Arctic Circle. Not Afghanistan. Afghanistan was five years ago. He kept repeating the words to himself over and over. *There is no sniper. No IED. No wounded.*

Eventually, the phantom sounds and smells vanished. Ron tentatively opened his eyes, relieved to see the little cabin instead of heat shimmers and sand. The effort of keeping himself anchored in time left his body drenched in sweat and his hands shaking. Everything hurt, his muscles clenched beyond stretching.

His body might not have moved past the dangers of the Middle East, but his mind had picked up on the real and potent dangers waiting to strike here. He couldn't afford to forget how he had participated in a kidnapping and witnessed a murder. His captor had presented himself as a businessman interested in helping others, only showing his true colors when facing resistance. Ron rubbed at his face, his palm scraping over rough stubble. He'd let a monster experiment on him, and when it came time to stand up and protect the innocent, he'd found himself quietly taking a stance beside the man. They'd tried to tell him that it was because the man had some kind of psychic powers, but others had managed to fight back. Ron could barely bring himself to remember the man's face, let alone his name. The truth was clear: he'd failed because of the same flaw that had left his friends to die under the desert sun.

Make him faster. Make him stronger. Make him sober. It didn't matter what he tried to do. Deep inside, he was still the same man who'd hesitated when seconds counted. That was why he hadn't been able to stop the shootings. He couldn't be relied on, and his weaknesses were fatal to anyone who trusted him. Heat shimmers began to dazzle his vision again. *Not Afghanistan. Afghanistan was five years ago.*

Chapter Four

Lily heard Ron muttering to himself as she arrived at the cabin. Something about Afghanistan and a sniper. She opened the door and saw him crouched by the chair, his fists tight against his temples and his eyes buried between his cheeks and eyebrows. His powerful shoulders contorted painfully inward as if shielding himself from blows. Tears glimmered in the folds as he rocked back and forth.

Her hands twitched forward, wanting to take him in her arms and hold him until the terror went away, but she didn't want to make his panic worse by touching him without warning. She knelt beside him and whispered his name. "Ron?"

His eyes opened, and he jumped backward, or tried to. He ended up knocking into the table and falling onto the floor. He stared at her as if he couldn't quite place who she was, his gaze clinging to her as if she were his only lifeline to sanity.

"It's all right," she said softly, taking his hands in hers. His fingers were shaking so badly that they rattled against hers until she held them tight.

He shook his head, his shoulders slumping in despair.

"It's all right," she repeated, tugging his hands gently to pull him toward her. He collapsed against her shoulder, shaking. Guessing anything like a restraint would only make things worse, she kept her grip light, resting one hand on top of his while the other gently stroked his back.

She had no idea how long she held him. Time vanished as she focused on soothing his obvious terror. Frost whitened the cabin walls, feathering out from the open door. They were close enough to the stove to keep from freezing to death, and luckily, she didn't have to make the choice of abandoning him to restoke the fire.

She could tell the instant he regained awareness of his surroundings. He stiffened and pulled away from her, apologizing.

"It's all right." She slid her hand along his pale skin, which was dry and flaking from the cold. Her own skin looked dark next to his, like a spring hare against a birch tree. "Come and sit next to the fire."

He took a chair while she brought in supplies for supper and put fresh logs in the stove. She pulled the other chair closer and sat across from him, watching as he tried to pull himself together. He froze in place suddenly. "You called me by name."

Lily kept her voice low and her movements slow. She suspected it wouldn't take much to send him into shock again. "Do you remember yesterday? You were half-asleep when you told me your name."

"It's not something I want to get around."

"I'm fine with sticking to Blue Eyes if you want." She shrugged, studying him. He wasn't relaxing. His fingers and feet were moving as if getting ready to run. "You said something about monsters."

A definite reaction: his leg started to vibrate, the knee bouncing in place.

"Sometimes monsters aren't so scary when you get to know them." She tried to keep her voice casual, but inside, she wanted to beg him not to crush her dreams of acceptance. "Want to tell me about them?"

"Not really. Just some old bad memories." Ron wouldn't look at her.

The lines of pain on his proud face cut deeply into her protective shell. All of her rational explanations crumbled. Bad memories, regrets— they could torture as much as any physical blade. In that moment, something shifted in her mind, and she no longer cared about long-term consequences. In the moment, she couldn't hold herself back. Leaning forward, she kissed him.

It was a soft, schoolgirlish kiss—a split-second of pressing her lips against his, tasting the salt of tears on his lips. His mouth remained hard with surprise, and Lily withdrew, feeling very awkward about her presumption. She tried to make light of it. "Now we can both be embarrassed."

"You kissed me to even some humiliation scale?" Ron tilted his head to one side, rubbing his palm across his cheek.

"I kissed you because I wanted to." Lily shrugged, offering him a smile of appeasement. "It seemed like the thing to do in the moment."

"And now?"

"Now I'm worried I may have overstepped." She laughed, hoping it would disperse the awkwardness. "I don't usually maul strange men on impulse."

Ron smiled at her, and she was relieved to see the haunted look in his eyes fading away. "I wouldn't call it a mauling."

So much for the wisdom of romance novels. I should have stuck with practical and professional. At least her dark skin hid the effects of her embarrassment. She tried another joke as she stood up to find the frying pan. "Are you planning to report me to the rangers for taking advantage of you?"

Instead of turning away, he stood up and kissed her. This time, there wasn't anything hesitant or innocent about it. His wide hands cupped her back and buttocks, pulling her close against him. His lips played against hers, tasting and exploring. She ran her hands over his broad back, her belly burning with sensual heat. His masculine strength excited her more than she'd ever imagined it could. It didn't feel like glowing coals that could heat a room through the night. Instead, it struck like lightning, searing through her, forever altering her in an instant.

All with a kiss. Ron broke away, leaving her breathless and ready for more. *Okay, points to the romance novels.*

"I don't think we need to call the rangers." He still cradled her in his arms, his hands keeping their bodies in full contact.

"Is that why you kissed me, Blue Eyes?" she asked breathlessly.

"Ron."

Lily blinked at him, not quite sure how to make the single syllable into an answer.

"I want you to call me Ron," he said quietly. "Although I do like Blue Eyes. And I kissed you because I wanted to and it seemed like the thing to do in the moment."

"And now?"

"Now it sounds like the best idea I've had all day." He traced her cheekbones with his fingertips as if learning the shape of her face. The gentle caress sent shivers of electricity sparking along her nerves. She leaned into the caress, catching the rough callus of his thumb with her lips. She wasn't completely ignorant in these matters despite her overprotective brothers. Only it never seemed worth the fuss. Now, she finally understood what the books were talking about as Ron ignited a chemical reaction in her blood. She didn't care about the differences between them or the fact that they couldn't possibly have a future. Kissing him was too addictive and intoxicating to give up after only a brief taste.

His breath panted against her forehead, rough and ragged. "I shouldn't be doing this."

"That makes two of us." Lily nibbled tiny kisses along his throat.

He moaned, his arms tightening around her. "I can't stay."

"Ron, listen to me." She pulled back, meeting his tortured gaze. "I won't pretend to know what you're going through. There's something bigger going on than you want to say, and I can accept that. I'm an adult, and despite what my brothers would like to believe, I'm neither naïve nor a virgin. Right now, it's only a kiss." The words were for herself, too, a reminder that this could never be more than an interlude, a memory to cherish.

His hands tightened around her waist. "I don't want to hurt you."

She wondered if he would feel the same once he knew the truth. Their secrets yawned between them like a deep canyon, threatening to pull them both in. Was it horribly selfish of her to want to kiss him before telling him who and what she was? To take what she wanted before he could reject her? She was a skinwalker, protector of her tribe's secrets. She had more responsibility than any outsider could comprehend and was more alien than Ron could hope to grasp even if she shifted to the fur in front of him.

"Believe me when I say I wish I could stay and make this more than a kiss. Every woman deserves more than that." His heartbeat drummed steadily against her cheek. "I wish we had the time."

She stopped him with a finger across his lips. "Take it a day at a time. If you decide you have to go, then you have to go. For now, you leaving doesn't sound like a good reason not to kiss you." She didn't mention her own rapidly accumulating mental list. Every kiss would make it harder to be impartial, compromising her role as guardian. Right now she didn't care about it, but the entire list hovered in her subconscious, waiting to slam back down on her later.

"I'm not really a girl-in-every-town kind of guy." Ron looked up at the ceiling. "My father would be horrified if I were. He raised me better than that."

Her grandfather had raised her to put everything else second to the welfare of her people. To protect the Marked at all costs.

"Lily?" Ron asked.

"Sorry. Lost in thought. So, how many of these town girls do you have stashed away?" She kept her voice light and teasing.

He smiled down at her. "You'd be the first, I promise."

"I can live with that." She lifted up on her toes to kiss him again, but crunching footsteps outside interrupted.

Ron frowned, stepping away from her. His fingers curled as if searching for a weapon as he moved to the exact spot on the floor where he'd have a clear line of sight to the door without any blocking furniture. The frost on the walls had melted, leaving gleaming trails of wetness on the wood.

The visitor knocked at the cabin door. "Lily, you in there?"

She recognized the ranger's voice. "Steve?"

He opened the door as soon as she answered. Tall and broad shouldered, he styled himself as a modern cowboy. He even wore a Stetson over his toque and belted his parka with a massive metal horseshoe. "Is Doc here?"

Lily shook her head, glancing briefly at Ron. Steve glared at him as if he were a poacher.

"Doc left this morning. He said he was going after Big Bart," Ron told the ranger.

"Yeah." Steve's drawled answer left no doubt he'd heard about the open supply bin. "He was supposed to meet up with Bill this afternoon, only he never came in."

Alarm overrode any of Lily's lingering embarrassment or awkwardness. "When was Doc supposed to be there?"

"About two hours ago. Bill is out with your grandfather and Lou, looking for him. He sent me to see if Doc was over here." Steve's suspicious glare never left Ron. "You sure he left okay this morning?"

"Right after breakfast." Ron straightened, but his arms and back stayed relaxed.

"Can anyone verify that?" Steve snapped at Ron like an irritable dog.

"What are you saying?" Lily broke in, annoyed at Steve's blindness. They should be focused on finding Doc, but there was no way Steve would put aside his accusations. Better to get them over with.

"I find it suspicious when someone finds a lost hiker in Bear Claw with no hiking supplies or winter gear. I find it more suspicious when that person doesn't want to be reported and ends up destroying Doc's winter stores. And now Doc has vanished." Steve adjusted the leather rifle harness slung across his back, drawing attention to it. "Stay here in case Doc comes home."

He left without saying good-bye, shutting the door with too much precision to qualify as a slam.

If she'd had any intention of listening to Steve, she would have been even more annoyed at his dismissal. Instead, Lily began collecting her gear. "We should go look for him."

"Agreed." Ron began pulling outer clothing out of a large bag. Lily recognized it as some of Steve's old gear. "Is he always like that?"

"He wanted to be a police officer, but something happened to prevent him. He joined the Forest Service instead, and I think he imagined himself arresting poachers and trespassers. It's pretty quiet up here, though." Lily shrugged, not particularly interested in any further discussion of Steve. "I know where Bart hangs out and where Doc was likely to go. I have the best chance of finding him."

"I owe him. I'm not going to sit tight if he needs help." Ron glanced around. "What if he does come back?"

"If I'm right, we'll only be a few hours. If he's not there, we'll come back and coordinate with everyone. Meanwhile, we'll make sure the stove is stoked so the cabin will be warm if he makes it back here."

The preparations only took a few minutes, and then they were outside. Ron walked behind her, trusting her to find the landmarks to guide their path. If he hadn't been there, she might have considered shifting to the fur, but she gratefully accepted the excuse to avoid it for now. She could do this search in the skin. Carrying the prepared survival pack, Lily led him through the darkened forest easily. She'd been roaming these woods since she was a child and knew them as another woman might know the furniture in her living room.

Using lanterns to light their way and provide some warmth, they found signs of Doc's trail along with Big Bart's. Lily knelt to pick up an expended flash-bang round. The snow around it had melted and refrozen, making a frilly ice collar around the blackened firecracker.

"Did Bart attack him?" Ron asked.

Lily shook her head. "No. He would have used this to drive Bart off. Then he'd have followed for a few kilometers to make sure Bart kept going."

They only walked another ten minutes or so before they heard a hoarse shout. "Hey! Over here!"

Lily rushed through the trees, expecting to leave Ron behind. Instead, he easily kept pace, crashing through the clinging snow as if it were paper instead of ice. Suspicions nibbled at her awareness, but worry for Doc shoved them aside.

They found the biologist tucked under a massive pine, using fallen branches to insulate himself against the snow.

"Doc! What happened?" Lily knelt, searching for signs of injury.

"Slipped on some ice, chasing Bart. I think my holler scared him more than the flash-bangs. He lit out of here like I'd set his tail on fire. I thought I was okay until I tried to stand." Doc winced as she touched his leg. It was hot and swollen even through the insulating layers of clothing and the chill temperatures. Lily glanced up at Ron, who held the lantern steady to provide light.

"It's broken, I think." Doc's face twisted in pain as he tried to move. "I nearly blacked out when I put the heat packet in my boot."

Lily noticed the matchbox-sized bulge of additional heat packets in Doc's mittens and breathed a sigh of relief. With those, the chance of frostbite damage was considerably reduced. Only idiots went out without them around here.

Idiots or the unaware. She glanced over at Ron, the gaps in his story suddenly opening wider like a maw that might swallow them all. He'd lied, and while she assumed it was to protect herself and the community, liking him was no guarantee that everything would work out. She'd been busy kissing him while Doc lay alone out in the snow. "We need something to brace the leg with."

Ron quickly found two relatively straight branches and began snapping off the extra pieces. His efficiency impressed Lily as she pulled the rope from Doc's survival pack. Together they strapped the branches on either side of Doc's broken leg, working like two halves of a machine. The partnership was effortless and natural, making it hard for Lily to remember that she'd only met him a few days before.

They knelt on either side of Doc and hoisted him between them, letting him sit on their interlocked arms with an arm around each of their shoulders. His broken leg jutted out stiffly, and he'd gone white, but he nodded to them to continue. Ron didn't seem to find Doc's weight a burden and was unsurprised by how easily she carried her share. The fears welled up in her mind as they walked, rising out of subconscious fog to snap at her comfort with sharpened teeth. Doc's injury, Evonne's crazy plan to show Ron the Marked, Steve and Bill's suspicions, Ron's breakdown, and the kiss all jockeyed for position inside her skull.

No matter how much she thought she should, she couldn't bring herself to regret the kiss. She'd had no idea it could feel that way. When she'd let Robbie Fisher take her to his house, kissing him had ended up being disappointingly technical—a mashing of lips and tongues.

Ron's kiss hadn't been any different in technique, yet the mechanics had been lost in a swell of emotional reaction. Even now, her womb clenched at the thought of it, sending a rush of electrical elation flooding through her veins. She wondered if the unknowns made the difference. She and Robbie had known each other from childhood, when they'd attended the school at Kluane. She'd known almost everything about him, whereas she knew almost nothing about Ron. Maybe the element of danger and mystery turned her on more than the man. That happened sometimes in the romance novels she and Evonne read, in which couples hated each other but couldn't resist the attraction of peril until they finally fell in love.

Those were stories. It couldn't be that way in real life, could it? Confusion stole away her confidence. She wished she had a mother to go to. Setsuné might be a good listener, but she was short on useful advice even when she wasn't preoccupied.

Doc's cabin emerged from the darkness as the yellow circle of lantern light crept over it. Ron braced Doc on the bin while Lily got the door open. Together they got him inside and into his chair with his bound leg resting on a stack of notebooks. Suddenly, the tiny cabin felt as if it were shutting down on her, closing like sprung trap. Her fur side roared, desperate for an escape. Lily couldn't fight it and bolted backward out the door. She barely found the presence of mind to offer an excuse for her abrupt departure. "I'll go get Andrew and let Bill know we found Doc."

Ron didn't even have time to agree before the door closed, the sturdy wood sealing Lily away from him. Doc's bushy grey eyebrows poked up above his fogged glasses. "What happened between the two of you?"

What indeed? A kiss, a lie. He'd been given what should be any guy's dream: an offer of no-strings attached and no hurt feelings. With Dr. Damali's aggressive flirtation, he hadn't hesitated in saying no. But with Lily, the possibilities tantalized him, making him forget everything else. He didn't know what he felt, and he wanted to figure it out. What answer could he possibly give Doc? Instead, Ron took refuge in practical matters. "I should get you something warm to drink."

"Coffee's up on the shelf. But I could use help getting out of this jacket first."

Ron put a kettle of water on the stove to boil then helped Doc to extract himself from his damp layers. He pulled the quilts from the bed and bundled them around Doc. His head whirled. Too much had happened since he'd woken up hungover and humiliated. Time to start reducing the unknowns.

"Doc, have you heard of a place called Ekurru?" Ron asked, watching the biologist carefully. If he reacted as strongly as Bill, Ron would have to leave quickly. Even if it meant leaving Lily.

The pause might not have been noticeable if Ron hadn't been watching for it, but Doc definitely hesitated before giving his overly casual answer. "Only in old stories."

Relief eased the tension in Ron's shoulders and gut. "What kind of old stories?"

"I suppose they'd count as legends. It's a place of sanctuary. Such and such a hero is wounded and spends time in Ekurru to heal. Or he needs magic help and finds it in Ekurru." Doc shrugged as Ron handed over a mug of instant coffee.

Ron was fairly certain Doc wasn't lying, but he wasn't telling the whole truth either. He decided to be subtle as he pressed for more information. "So, it's local to this area?"

"The name isn't Dene or any other native language I know of. So I couldn't really say where it was from. Bill mentioned you'd asked about it."

"Why would Bill mention I asked if it didn't exist?" Ron extended his conversational trap carefully, hoping he wouldn't spook Doc into shutting up.

"We get a few people looking for it sometimes. I suppose it's Bear Claw's equivalent of El Dorado or Shangri-La. There was a fellow from one of the mining companies who got real interested in the old stories. Sent a lady from the university to record them all for posterity. It's how that Dr. Damali heard about my bears and decided to come running to see them for herself." Heat flared in Doc's eyes at the mention of his rival, but he shook it off. "Why are you so interested in it?"

"I made a promise to take someone there." Ron didn't let his eyes flick toward his worn jacket with the urn still wrapped inside. Instead, he kept his focus steady on Doc and caught the brief whitening of the other man's knuckles. Doc might not be freaking out the way Bill had, but he didn't like that Ron was asking about Ekurru. This was more than academic rivalry or small-town xenophobia. They were protecting something, and Ron needed to tread very carefully to keep his promise.

"How's the leg?" Ron asked, changing the subject to let Doc relax. He didn't need to push further right this minute.

"Hurts like heck now that the shock and cold are wearing off," Doc answered honestly. "Andrew can't get here quickly enough for me. Be nice if there was some vodka to take the edge off." Doc's grin took the bite out of his words.

Ron took a deep breath. He needed to accept that the bottle was never a solution and make it stick this time. "I think I've done enough drinking for now." He smiled back, but it didn't go more than lip deep. He needed to keep on his toes. "Guess we'll have to find another way to distract you from the pain."

Doc studied his guest. The light reflecting from his glasses turned his gaze into a blank enigma. "This leg is going to slow me down a lot."

Ron nodded, suspecting Doc was laying his own conversational trap. "Did Steve bring that gear by for you?"

"No. It was Dr. Damali, actually." Hiding the truth served nothing. It would come out eventually, and Ron didn't need any more lies to keep track of.

To his surprise, Doc laughed. "I should have guessed she'd take advantage of the opportunity. Let me guess: she asked you to spy on me."

"She wants information on the bears. She hinted she'd pay for it." Ron suspected he wasn't the first one to get the offer.

"Well, then I can see an easy way to repay your debt. You'll work for me." Doc gave a delighted grin.

Ron was less enthusiastic. He didn't have the time to get caught up in some wilderness field-study feud.

"Hear me out," Doc said. "I'm going to need someone to help me hobble around out there. Even with crutches, I won't be able to carry my pack with my notebooks and such. You come with me and take notes for Dr. Damali—a few empty den sites where she can't cause trouble."

"It sounds dishonest." Ron could practically taste a bitter pong of irony in his objection. Lies had kept him alive for months. But he just couldn't promise something he had no intention of delivering. It scraped against the grain of the last remnants of who he'd been raised to be and hoped to be again. Even on the run, he'd been careful not to make false promises.

Doc shrugged. "The information she wants isn't for sale, and she wouldn't believe it even if you offered it to her. She's chasing myths, trying to make a name for herself."

"I won't do it." Ron needed to draw a line in the sand even if it was arbitrary and ended up delaying him. No more convenient choices. "I'll help you and pay you back for what I've cost you, but I won't pretend to sell something I won't deliver."

Doc nodded, accepting the terms. "It means staying here until my leg heals. You okay with that?"

"I'll stay unless I have evidence I'm placing you in danger. Lily told me how isolated this place is. She said anyone would have trouble finding me here." Ron's gut clenched tight, refusing to play the odds. Staying in one place was a calculated risk, but maybe he would end up getting to leave Bear Claw with his pride intact for once.

"She's right. It's as safe as can be for a man in your position. Let me offer you a little free advice. Don't rely on silence to keep your secrets. People accept explanations much easier than stonewalling." Doc stretched. "Now, tell me what happened between you and Lily."

"Nothing happened," Ron insisted.

"What did I say about stonewalling? I've known that girl since she was a little cub. Something happened. Do I need to worry?"

Exhausted with the weight of silence, Ron went with the truth. "We kissed."

Doc nodded slowly, his beard and moustache bristling as his lips pursed in thought. "And does the kiss have anything to do with why you accepted my offer?"

"Yes. No. I'm not sure." Ron rubbed his palms along the length of his thighs, scrubbing at his anxious thoughts. "I've spent a long time doing things I'm not proud of. I offered because I don't want to be that guy anymore. But I don't really know if it's safe for me to stay, and I don't want to hurt Lily… or anyone else."

"Well, some more free advice: I'd figure it out quickly if I were you. Definitely before you kiss her again." Doc leaned back, closing his eyes. "Lily's brothers are overprotective."

Overprotective. Ron wondered again if that was code for abuse. Lily seemed unusually upset whenever the idea of her family came up. There was more than overprotectiveness here. *Is that why she insisted on no strings?* "I told you, I don't make promises I can't keep. I can't even guarantee tomorrow. She deserves better than that," Ron said softly as if volume might betray feelings he'd barely begun to acknowledge.

"That she does. But she also deserves a chance to be happy, even if it's only for a little while." The biologist looked at him shrewdly. "Think you can give her that?"

The man he'd been raised to be could make her happy. The man he'd become would only disappoint her, the way he'd disappointed and failed everyone else. Ron closed his eyes, letting the warmth from his mug ease his stiff fingers. At the VA hospital, the therapists had told them not to long for their old bodies but to accept their scars and push past them. Realistically, he knew he couldn't go back. But maybe he could find a way to work past the scars in his soul.

Chapter Five

"Doc's been hurt. It might be a broken leg," Lily announced as soon as she stepped down into the family cabin. Lou sat at the long trestle table, warming up with a bowl of soup. Andrew stood up quickly, abandoning his chess game with Grandfather.

"Where'd you find him?" Lou demanded.

Lily described the area as Andrew came back into the room with his medical kit and began to dress to go outside. She saw her opportunity to escape once again. "I should go and tell Bill that Doc's been found."

"No, Lily, you stay. We need to speak. Lou, go to the ranger station and tell them Doc's been found." Grandfather's piercing dark eyes never left Lily's face.

Lou nodded, slipping out behind Andrew. The door thudded into place like the closing of a tomb. Lily took her time hanging up her clothes and putting her mittens, scarf and toque in the birch-bark basket beside the door, hoping Grandfather would say something. A reprimand for dawdling would have been a welcome distraction. Instead, his silent presence and judgment loomed behind her. Finally, she couldn't delay any longer. She turned, feeling like a seven-year-old being prepared for a scolding.

"Change comes in many ways," Grandfather began, settling into Shaman Storyteller mode. She could practically see the face paint and feathers instead of his plaid-flannel button-down shirt. At least the buckskin pants Lou had made matched Grandfather's Wise Elder tone as he droned on. Long years of futile argument had conditioned her not to press him to skip to the point. "Sometimes it comes slowly, like the seasons, giving all time to adjust and find their place. And sometimes it comes quickly, like a lightning strike, leaving everyone to scurry in panic. Your Blue Eyes is a lightning strike, and I fear you are not prepared to guide the flames. A wildfire could leave us all exposed."

"I have no idea what to say to that." With the constant snap and play of her own conflicting emotions, Lily couldn't summon the energy to play respectful student. "I'm well aware that none of you are happy with having him here."

"Blue Eyes is the least of our problems. We've received a message from Edyta asking for a meeting. She is not pleased with how we've been delaying matters." Grandfather pulled a sheaf of letters from beside the chair.

Lily recognized the packet of Edyta's letters and the battered Northstar pamphlet. Her first instinct was a child's one: to deny everything and hope not to get in too much trouble. Reminding herself that she was an adult took a moment.

"I want you to go speak with her." Grandfather laid the letters on the table beside the chessboard. "Lou leaves for Kluane in the morning to meet with Bob."

Whatever information Bob had found about Ron could tip the still-uncertain death verdict. If she was there, she could have a chance to find out first. Her animal side snarled and growled inside, not happy at the idea of leaving familiar territory. Or was it because of Ron? *I need to figure this out.* She couldn't hope to plot the proper course with her bearings all twisted and scattered. She needed some distance. "What do you want me to say to Edyta?"

"I've been following your conversations since your first meeting. You've handled her well so far." Grandfather's stoic mask slipped briefly, giving her a glimpse of his discomfort before settling back into place. Even secondhand, the stories of his encounters with Edyta were explosive. "Convince the squawking she-gull to give us more time."

He'd known the entire time. Her mind seized on the morsel of knowledge and prepared to worry it into pieces like a dog with a bone, but instinct warned her that there was more at stake than a need to delay negotiations with the mining companies. They didn't dare directly oppose the bidding. It would only encourage the companies to start poking around in Bear Claw, which could send their secrets flying away like summer birds.

"This is about Blue Eyes." Lily didn't speak his true name. Until he chose to reveal it, they would not hear it from her.

"Do you deny your responsibilities?" She couldn't point to any portion of Grandfather's face that changed, but it hardened, the mask firming to stone instead of wood. "You chose your path, Lily."

His implied accusation ignited a snarling wave of internal fury. She champed down on it, keeping her voice and gaze level. "If Blue Eyes chooses to leave, you will let him go."

"You would let him disappear with our secrets?" Grandfather stood up, looming over her.

Ron had said it himself—he couldn't stay. The world reframed itself into dull greyness, thudding back into position. She would go, giving him the space to do the same. Their kiss would be a memory, nothing more and nothing less. She would do her duty to Ekurru and the Marked. "Bear Claw can't stay isolated forever. We have to look ahead."

Grandfather's lips twitched downward for a split second, as much of a frown as he would ever allow himself. "You still deny a mating connection between yourself and this Blue Eyes? A bond would take priority."

"He is not my mate, but that doesn't mean I want to leave him here, helpless, with people who are ready to kill him any minute. Especially when he's not any danger to us." She wouldn't take an easy lie even if Grandfather would allow her to get away with an untruth. She should be walking away, not pushing the confrontation. This was the sort of dispute that could lead to feuds. None of them could afford that.

"You know what is at stake. Something has changed—a second lightning strike that followed the first of his arrival. Tell me."

"I kissed him," Lily admitted defiantly. "It doesn't change anything. I can like him without being biologically bound to him."

"What will happen when he realizes you are not human? You are as much animal as human, Lily, no matter how you try to hide your other half. Both are your true form." Grandfather thumped forward, his footsteps echoing and creaking against the floor. "It is even more necessary for you to leave now. You cannot afford the distraction of this man."

She might have decided that for herself, but hearing Grandfather say it set her teeth grinding and her blood boiling. Closing the gap between them, she glared into his flinty eyes with all the implicit challenge of prolonged eye contact. "He wouldn't hurt us. He needs help."

"He is a distraction." His grip tightened on her chin.

Lily refused to flinch. "Then promise you'll allow him to leave unharmed."

Grandfather let go, and although his expression didn't shift, Lily sensed he was unsettled. He limped slowly back to his chair, his right leg dragging along the floor. "His physical injuries were minimal, but Andrew felt there was a greater trauma, something that struck Blue Eyes's heart and soul."

Lily hadn't told her brother about finding Ron curled in a ball, trying to pull himself back from overwhelming memories. "Since he arrived, Blue Eyes has remained on guard, looking to protect others despite the cost to himself."

Grandfather sat silently for a long time. When he retreated into his mind like this, he didn't move. His eyes stared straight ahead at a single point instead of flicking around as most people's did while thinking. His fingers didn't twitch, his toes didn't tap, and he didn't shift his weight in his chair. It was as if his mind detached entirely from his body, leaving it empty and waiting while he contemplated. Perhaps the stillness was part of the shaman's training, but Andrew hadn't achieved it yet.

Lily waited. The negotiations were done. If Grandfather agreed, she could leave Bear Claw with a clear conscience, knowing Ron would be safe from her family. He would go, remembering her only as a girl he kissed one time. He'd never know how close he'd come to a predator.

Grandfather spoke, startling her. "You are overwhelmed, pulled in too many directions. What if we could remove some of these concerns?"

"How?" she asked suspiciously. *He'd better not mean* remove *in the Mafia sense of the word.*

"If he is in need of our help, then his presence cannot be a coincidence." Grandfather tapped the arm of his chair. His gaze refocused on her, pinning her in place with its intensity. "We will offer him an opportunity to walk the path to restored health."

"What do you mean?" Lily's lips tightened in an effort to keep from voicing her fears.

"Andrew can help him, offer him a chance to find his own solid ground rather than clinging to you."

It should have been an easy decision, but she selfishly wanted to be the one to help Ron. Lily began to pace, her feet scuffing along the uneven planked floor. "Andrew doesn't trust him. He sees a puzzle, a chore to be completed."

"Andrew struggles more than you know. The path of the shaman is not easy. Be grateful you were not chosen to walk it."

The mild reproof stung deeply. Five steps took her to the wall, and the same number brought her back to the opposite one. Like an animal in a cage, she couldn't stop searching for an escape. Grandfather watched her, his face impassive. Only his silence betrayed his concern. "I will give Blue Eyes a chance for true healing. I swear it, Lily."

Her breathing came a little easier. Grandfather's promise meant something. There might still be the danger from whomever was chasing Ron, but she didn't have to worry about her own family hurting him anymore. *Think of it as repayment for the kiss. I get a memory, and he gets a chance to heal.* "I'll go with Lou in the morning."

"Very well. A final word, Lily."

Of course he has to get the last word. She waited.

"I see danger in these papers. More than the greed of men wanting wealth. Whatever you feel for Blue Eyes, you cannot afford to lose sight of the larger storm bearing down on us. We cannot offer a sanctuary bathed in blood."

Ron looked up hopefully when he heard the footsteps approaching. When Andrew opened the cabin door, Ron couldn't help craning his neck to see if Lily was behind him.

"I'm afraid you will have to settle for the Charging Bull sibling with actual medical knowledge," Andrew said.

Ron's lips tightened in irritation. He didn't like Andrew's ready sarcasm and little jabs. His fist curled, ready to confront the other man, but common sense and the reality of his situation managed to haul back the reins on his more primitive protective instincts. "Doc's in a lot of pain."

Andrew looked at the biologist, lying back on the chair with his leg propped up on a pile of notebooks. Doc's eyes were closed, although the tight lines around his eyes, mouth, and knuckles revealed he wasn't asleep. "I have painkillers. Is there hot water?"

Ron nodded, shifting the kettle from the table to the stove. It immediately started to whistle. Andrew prepared a tea for Doc and warned him, "I'm going to have to examine your leg, and it's going to hurt rather a lot."

"Do your worst, Medicine Man." Grimacing, Doc drank the tea down without opening his eyes. "This tastes like crap."

"Of course it does. Otherwise, how would you know it worked?" Andrew studied Doc. Ron watched anxiously, his irritation at Lily's brother disappearing under concern for the injured man. After a few minutes, the pinched folds in Doc's face began to smooth. His hands spread out over his grey sweater rather than clenching it in his fists.

"Hold him steady while I get a look at the wound." Andrew delivered the instruction as smoothly as any ER doctor, holding a slim blade that gleamed in the lamplight. Fighting an automatic urge to tackle Lily's brother for the weapon, Ron moved to stand behind Doc, his hands on each of the biologist's upper arms to keep him from jerking around. Andrew slit the torn, filthy trouser leg and long underwear with practiced knife strokes.

As Andrew uncovered the joint, Ron was relieved there was no blood breaking past the skin. He might not be a doctor, but he assumed it was a good sign. The leg was badly swollen, though, and a deep-red bruise coated the skin above the ankle. Andrew held the limb as gently as possible, massaging and manipulating it to determine the extent of the injury. Doc paled and clutched the armrests tightly enough to dent them.

"It is not broken, but it is a bad sprain. You'll need to keep off it for at least six weeks." Andrew's eyes flicked to Ron.

"I've already said I'd help him out." Ron straightened, recognizing the unspoken challenge.

"I see. That may not be the…" Andrew hesitated, clearly searching for words that wouldn't reveal any secrets. "Wisest solution."

"I owe him for saving my life, and I need to repay him for the loss of his supplies." Ron squared his shoulders as he faced Andrew. If he wanted to get back to the person he'd been before Afghanistan, he had to accept more risk. His head never shut down anyway—he might as well have a reason for the alarms.

"An admirable goal. But the work is demanding. You are also recovering." Andrew suddenly grabbed Ron's hands in a painfully tight grip. Ron tried to pull back, but the shaman held him easily. Sweat burst on Ron's neck and back. Since his transformation, no one had ever held him when he wanted to break free.

"What is it?" Doc asked, frowning.

"They're healed. As if they'd never been exposed to cold." Andrew's dark eyes narrowed as he studied Ron, releasing his patient's hand.

"I heal quickly." Ron stepped back out of reach. Maybe he should have been paying attention to his internal alarms.

Doc and Andrew exchanged a look. Ron knew it well: the look of two people who shared a secret and were deciding whether or not to tell a third person. Perhaps he should tell them he was aware of the *lalassu*, but if he was wrong about that being the secret, he'd be painting a giant target on them and him. After what he'd been through during the last year, he wasn't going to assume he knew all the possibilities. Maybe he could talk quietly to Lily the next time he saw her. He trusted her more than her brother.

"As you wish. I'm going to collect some birch bark for a cast to allow Doc to move about." Andrew took the knife and small axe, closing the door with a precise, annoyed click.

"I take it he doesn't like me." Ron hoped his voice didn't betray his rapidly pulsing heartbeat.

"Some of it is his charming personality. But yeah, I'm pretty sure he doesn't like you." Sweat shone on Doc's face, darkening his iron-grey hair. "It's times like these that I miss access to the good drugs."

The silence stretched out, made awkward and brittle with secrets and pain. Ron listened hard for any sign of Andrew's return. Doc's features were set in the fixed stare of a man white-knuckling his way through an excruciating test of torture. At his direction, Ron put a large pan of water on the stove, ready to heat and soften the bark. It had only begun to simmer when he heard Andrew's footsteps crunching in the snow.

They boiled the long strips of pale bark. Once pliable, Andrew let them cool before wrapping them around Doc's foot while Ron held Doc steady. Soon, a rigid cast supported Doc's ankle and calf.

"Check him in the night. The bark will shrink more as it cools. Make sure it's not too tight." Andrew gave Doc another cup of tea. "Better to sit in the chair close to the stove. You'll need to stay in bed tomorrow. You can have more tea every six hours."

Doc's eyes started to close. Ron took another quilt from the bed and laid it over him while Andrew packed up his supplies.

"Is Lily coming back tonight?"

As Andrew stood, Ron saw the hostility flare in his eyes. "You are my patient. Lily is my sister. I will make sure you are healed enough to survive out of our care. Beyond that, I don't owe you anything." He disappeared into the night, leaving Ron alone with a bad feeling. Was Lily safe?

Ron dimmed the lantern to let Doc sleep, but his nerves were jangling too much to let him slip into unconsciousness. He'd been placed on guard, and his instincts wouldn't let him relax. Nor would they let him stay inside the windowless cabin. *I need something to take the edge off.* The thought lingered seductively in his mind, but he reminded himself it wasn't an option. His only choice was to suffer through the nerves and try not to let them push him into doing something stupid.

After over an hour of staring blankly at the ceiling, twitching upright every time he thought he heard something outside, he realized sleep wasn't in his future—unless he exhausted himself past the nerves. He put on his outdoor gear and slipped outside, trying not to make noise and wake Doc from his needed sleep. Outside, the moon lit up the snow brightly enough to make a lantern unnecessary. Ron's breath hung in an icy wisp in front of his face, and he decided to make a few circuits around the cabin to familiarize himself with the landscape.

Despite his indulgence last night, he felt better than he had in a long time. Funny how something as simple as letting Lily know his real name had lightened his burden. Or maybe it was the silence of the trees and snow, promising to hold his secrets fast in their frosty, inhuman grasp. Whatever the cause, the despair hanging on him fell away. Reclaiming himself wouldn't be easy, but if—*no, when*—he did it, he'd be able to face his family again. He'd need to find a way to do it safely, without attracting the attention of his captors. One challenge at a time.

The snow crunched loudly under his feet, the almost plastic creaking noise echoing through the quiet forest. "I guess I don't have to worry about anyone sneaking up on me," he muttered. Unlike the snow, the trees' monolithic hush stole away the sound of his human voice. It felt like a rejection, as if nature was snubbing him, reminding him that he didn't belong there.

He tried to shake off the sensation of being an intruder, but it lingered, seeping through the carefully defined perimeter of his mind. His nerves shrilled at him, making it hard to concentrate. Too much information tried to clamor for his attention. Ron reminded himself that he had a task to do. He needed to focus.

As he came around the corner of the cabin, he saw a massive shape outlined against the glowing white snow. His city-raised brain took a moment to process the information and parse it into its proper identification. A bear.

It sniffed at the door, its nose about halfway between the doorknob and the top even though all four paws rested solidly in the snow. Ron guessed the heavy hump over its neck was probably close to his own height of six foot four.

He had no weapon, not even a stick to whack it with. His mind began to whirl with the first stages of panic, flinging him back to being helpless under the desert sun.

The bear turned, and its large brown eyes met his. Ron wondered if he were going insane, because he could swear he saw hints of laughter in their depths. Slowly, the bruin began to amble toward him. Ron glanced up at the roof of the cabin. He could make it up there. Of course, this bear was big enough that it might be able to follow him up there.

A paler crescent of fur on the animal's shoulder caught his attention. "Litonya?"

The bear tossed its head back in an unnerving approximation of a nod. It—no, *she*—halted only a few feet away, close enough to confirm his guess about her size. He'd heard bear paws described as dinner-plate sized, but hers would be more like serving platters. Long, narrow black claws extended from each toe, doing nothing to assuage his panic.

Except she wasn't being aggressive. She held her ground, watching him carefully, and it felt more like a hostess waiting to see if an anxious guest was about to bolt than a predator waiting for a meal.

"Did you come to check on Doc?" Ron asked.

Litonya tossed her head again before extending her muzzle briefly toward Ron.

"Doc… and me?"

Another head toss, this time with a low rumble. It sounded like a giant cat purring. She settled into the shallow snow near the cabin door, delicately tucking her paws underneath.

"You're not what I expected." Ron took a careful step, preparing to circle around her.

Litonya clacked her jaws together, creating a pop of noise. It sounded like a bark of laughter.

"I guess I don't know many bears," he admitted, moving slowly.

Now he was certain that he saw laughter in her eyes as she watched him. Her long, golden-brown fur shivered as if she were suppressing giggles.

Ron smiled back, relaxing, even though the intellectual side of his brain remained completely focused on the proximity of an animal that could kill him with one paw. "I guess you're worried about me. Just like I'm worried about Lily."

Litonya raised her head swiftly at Lily's name. Something about the gesture encouraged Ron to continue talking.

"She took off right after we got Doc back, after we…" He eyed Litonya, wondering if she'd get upset. Then he questioned his sanity. She was a bear. She couldn't possibly understand him, no matter how much it looked like it. "After we kissed. Her family doesn't like me, and every time we start to get close, she gets scared. I'm scared they might be hurting her."

Litonya huffed and shook her head back and forth.

"You don't think they're hurting her?" He wanted to believe it was true.

A sharp crack cut through the night. Litonya sprang to her feet, peering at a point in the distance. Ron froze, ready to leap out of her way if she charged. Instead, she began to steadily walk toward the noise, her paws not making any sound. After a half-dozen steps, she glanced back over her shoulder at him. She jerked her muzzle toward the sound as if expecting him to go with her.

Following a bear didn't sound like the craziest thing after everything else he'd seen over the last year, but it would still rank fairly high on the list. It didn't stop him from walking behind her, trying to keep his footsteps as quiet as possible. Whoever or whatever had made that noise, he needed to know. With the prospect of actual danger, the alarms in his head worked for him.

She led him through the trees but seemed to lose the trail quickly. She swung her head back and forth, snuffling loudly.

"What is it, girl?" Ron asked.

Litonya's ears went back, and she glared at him as if she understood about *Lassie* references.

"Sorry. Did you find something?"

She shook her head, which looked more like rolling her neck on its axis than heaving it side to side but was still a clear negative. She humphed in annoyance.

"Maybe it was another animal. I should get back to the cabin."

Litonya didn't seem eager to leave. She nosed the ground and the nearby trees. He waited, but the growing growl suggested she wasn't discovering anything.

No matter how friendly she seemed, Ron wasn't quite comfortable with the idea of turning his back on her. He exhaled in relief when she began to pad in the direction of the cabin, letting him follow. When they reached the clearing, she stopped and approached him.

Her massive jaws looked capable of biting a car in half, but Ron trusted her. He held still as she stretched out her neck and nudged him with her head. Even though she'd obviously tried to be gentle, the gesture nearly knocked him off his feet.

She waited patiently for him to regain his balance before nudging him again. This time, he stayed upright. She took a few steps to the door and poked it with her muzzle.

"You want me to go in." Ron studied the silent trees. "I should warm up, but I also should stay out here in case someone is skulking around."

Litonya shook her head again as she settled by the door.

"You're saying you'll keep watch tonight?"

She threw her head back in her bearish nod. *Can I really trust a wild animal to protect me?* The fact that his instincts said *yes* made him wonder if he should be checking into a mental institution. Bears didn't understand humans and communicate with them. Except this one did.

For the first time in years, Ron felt at peace. For once, he could trust someone else to take up the burden.

"Wake me if something happens," he told her, kneeling down so that their heads were even. He held out his hand the way his father taught him to do with new dogs so they could get his scent.

Litonya stretched out her neck and took a deep sniff, the cold air rushing past his fingers. He got the sense she did it more out of politeness than need. Ron opened the cabin door and stepped inside, pausing to look back at the silhouette of his guard bear. "Goodnight, Litonya."

She clacked her jaw at him, and he shut the door on the most surreal evening he'd ever had.

The next morning, the massive depression in the snow outside the cabin told him it hadn't been a bizarrely detailed dream. Ron followed his footprints and Litonya's but couldn't see any other signs of an intruder. He wasn't sure if he should trust his instinct that the noise had been caused by a human. It might only be his paranoia speaking. On the other hand, there really were people out to get him. Disconcerted by his thoughts, Ron decided to retreat back to Doc's.

The biologist seemed better this morning, sleeping quietly. Ron checked the birch-bark cast and prepared another mug with Andrew's medicinal tea and set water on the stove to boil. He decided not to mention the incident in the night. Doc might be open-minded, but it didn't mean he was ready to accept that Ron had followed a bear to look for someone who might or might not have been spying on them and might or might not exist.

He woke Doc and made him drink Andrew's tea. The biologist immediately sank back into sleep without complaint, which worried Ron. He tested the other man's cheek. It was warm, but Ron wasn't sure if it was warm enough for a fever. He worried the biologist might become seriously ill and he'd fail to recognize the signs. He couldn't even go to Andrew's house since he had no idea which direction it was.

A tap on the door interrupted his worry. Lily poked her head in. "Is he awake?"

"You're okay." Ron exhaled, taking her hand and tugging her into his arms. He held her tightly, letting himself relax in the awareness that she was unharmed.

He felt Lily smile against his chest. "I'm fine. But I'm afraid I have to go."

"What?" Ron pulled back, his hands tightening on her arms.

"Some companies have approached Bear Claw about developing different resources. I've been talking with one of their representatives, and that makes me responsible for handling some of the negotiations." Lily shrugged, rolling her arms as if his grip was too confining.

Ron let her go immediately. He suspected this trip had something to do with him. Andrew had made his disapproval clear. "Is it a good idea to leave the park right now?"

"If I don't, they might come here looking for us, and that would be worse." Lily's face tilted down, but she peered up at him through her long eyelashes. "Are you upset that I'm going?"

He hesitated, unsure how to answer. What could he say to make her stay? The strength of his desire left him no mental room to open his mouth.

She deflated. "Sorry. Too blunt. I don't have a lot of experience talking to men after kissing them."

"No, it's okay." He hurried to reassure her, hating that he'd inadvertently hurt her in her confidence. "I'm out of practice, too. To answer your question, I'm going to miss you, and although I'd like you to stay, I don't feel I have the right to ask you."

An overly loud cough interrupted the awkward conversation. Ron finally noticed the thickly built man, draped in leather and fur, standing by a pair of dog sleds. The lapse in awareness set his fingers vibrating with alarm, not helped by the palpable glare coming from underneath the newcomer's low-slung leather cap.

Lily waved. "That's my brother Lou."

Ron frowned. Even from twenty feet away, he could feel the hostility. "Are you going to be okay with him?"

"Lou is my brother. He'd never hurt me. None of my brothers would." Lily didn't look like a battered and terrified woman. But he still sensed an undercurrent of fear he couldn't explain and didn't like. It roused his protective hackles.

Lily took his hands in hers, squeezing them. "I promise, Ron. None of them would ever hurt me. I've been more worried about them hurting you."

"Doc mentioned they can be overprotective." Ron noticed the man by the sled shuffling in place.

"Lily!" the man barked.

"We have to get going, or we won't hit the midway campsite before it gets too dark to travel," she whispered. Her tongue darted out to moisten her lips, and Ron felt a hard jolt of desire swell. "There's just one more thing I want before I go."

"Hurry home." He bent and stole another kiss, not caring about the hostile stranger watching from the sled. All that mattered were Lily's sweet lips moving under his. Breaking away from her was the hardest thing he could imagine doing. He wanted to kiss her again. His body ached with the urge to draw her closer and explore the fantasies playing in his head. He wanted to forget Doc sleeping three feet away and the people after him and just lose himself in the moment of exploring Lily.

From the ragged breaths she sucked between trembling lips, the same thoughts were going through her mind. She ducked her head to press her lips against his palm. As his body shook with an intense surge of pleasure from the brief contact, he almost missed her words.

"It's never been like this for me before." Smoky desire darkened her bright eyes as she watched him.

He managed to dredge up a coherent sentence. "Me either."

"It's comforting to know we're together in our ignorance."

Another loud cough from Lily's brother snapped the mood. Lily's tan skin ruddied with embarrassment. From the heat in his own cheeks, Ron hadn't completely lost the blood above his waist, though it certainly felt as if it had all been diverted to an inconvenient part of his anatomy.

A slight moan from Doc reminded Ron of his other responsibilities. "Is Andrew coming later? I think Doc might be getting worse."

"He'll be here soon." Lily bit her full lower lip, leaving a luscious indentation. "I have to go."

"I know." Ron watched Lily and her brother drive away before he realized he'd completely forgotten to tell her about their intruder in the night.

If someone was searching for him in Bear Claw, he'd already lost his opportunity to keep Lily and her family safe. Panic started to surge through his mind, and he shoved it down, concentrating on his purpose. If his former captors came looking for him, he'd make sure they regretted it.

Part Two
AUTOLYZING

Chapter Six

Sitting at his glass-topped desk in the chateau's antique-filled library, Karan stared at the glowing computer screen as if he could see past the displays and interfaces to track the digital trail back to its source. If what he suspected proved to be true, then the fiasco in Perdition was larger than he'd initially thought.

When the Harris girl had exited the plane, her eyes had glowed red. The significance had escaped him at the time—he'd been too focused on extracting himself and his employer before the authorities arrived. The phenomenon kept returning to his conscious mind, nagging at his thoughts and sending him to the private archive. After combing through a set of journals that predated the Renaissance, he realized their danger might have been even greater than he had realized at the time. The journals' parchment pages had darkened over centuries, making the handwritten Latin even harder to parse, yet the sketch inside one of them was clear enough: a young girl, draped in a classic Greek robe, languidly embracing a nude man. The stain marking the edges of her eyes had faded to a dull brown, but the notes with the sketch indicated they had once been red. Further notes explained the red rings were part of a transitional phase of the Nox Dea's Chosen Priestesses.

The Priestesses were some of the most powerful *lalassu*. Karan did not believe in divine powers, but he knew better than most what secret gifts lay out there. If Danielle Harris was a descendant of the Priestess lineage, then he and Dalhard had inadvertently netted a much more dangerous prey than they'd planned. The Priestesses could neutralize men through sex, like the legendary succubi. The journals were very clear on that point. The lineage was also prone to receiving visions of the future, which they claimed came from their Goddess.

Two things did not match the profile of the Priestesses in the crackling pages of the journal. First, Danielle Harris was much older than the teenage girls mentioned in the book. Second, she was physically powerful, not a psychic. Vincent Harris had claimed his mother was "like the original High Priestess." Could he have been referring to the Nox Dea, the Night Goddess?

A lesser man might have cursed himself for not taking the opportunity to interrogate the Harris brothers while they were in his custody, but Karan was not one to dwell on missed opportunities. If one was patient and persistent, new opportunities inevitably arose, often better than the originals.

If the Harrises were descended from the Priestesses, then their ability to electronically disappear took on a new significance. He would waste no further time and resources chasing digital ghosts. He had waited a long time for this opportunity. Even if he were wrong about the Harrises, the time was right. He had resources of his own now.

He chose the website at random. The frame did not matter. All that mattered were the eight words he typed into a comment.

Caligo, *come out, come out, wherever you are.*

Ron swung his axe hard, sinking it deep into the rough-hewn log balanced on the chopping block. Squinting against the painfully bright sunlight, he hoped the repetitive exertion would allow him to sleep later. His mind kept whirling with the implications of his decision to stay in Bear Claw. The thought of putting Lily or Doc in danger made him sick, but if the noise last night had been someone, then it was already too late. The idea of his captors sending goons in was bad enough, but if he wasn't there to protect Lily and Doc… his fists tightened on the wooden axe handle, twisting his skin painfully inside his gloves.

"After an extended consultation—"

Ron spun around, axe raised to strike, before the speaker had finished his sentence. Recognizing Lily's brother, he locked his arms into place, preventing himself from launching a lethal attack.

"—I believe I have taken entirely the wrong approach to your situation." Andrew seemed unaffected by Ron's reaction, completing his statement as if discussing the weather. He glanced at the upraised axe with an arched eyebrow. "Perhaps I ought to have coughed first."

Panting, Ron forced himself to lower the axe. His arms burned with the painful effects of having restrained his blow. He hadn't heard Andrew approach or sensed his presence. The sudden revelation of how vulnerable he was wreaked havoc on his internal alarm system. Part of his mind crashed into despair while the other part screamed and ran in circles. There simply weren't enough unoccupied cells to allow himself to respond.

Lily's brother watched him, and Ron felt like a science project being measured and evaluated. Finally, Andrew spoke again. "You can't speak to me right now, can you? Every part of you is caught up in your internal battle. Judging from the tension in your arms and shoulders, your instinct was to kill the intruder, and you held back only when you recognized me. At great cost to yourself."

Ron managed a low growl. "What do you want?" His lungs strained to hold onto the oxygen he sucked in with rapid shallow breaths.

"You're recovering faster than I would have thought. You've been struggling with this for some time, haven't you?" Andrew held up his hand. "Don't bother speaking. I already know the answer. Now that I know what to look for."

"What are you talking about?" Ron tried to draw a deep breath, except his jaw refused to unclench his locked teeth.

"Scars on top of scars," Andrew said quietly as if reporting to someone else. "I'd like you to come with me."

"Doc." Ron made the single syllable into refusal and explanation.

"I brought Bill to stay with him." Andrew raised one eyebrow, apparently annoyed at the implication of negligence. "He's been friends with Doc a long time. He'll make sure Doc is fine for the relatively short time we'll be away."

Ron nodded, unable to gain enough breath to speak. It didn't seem to bother Andrew at all. He began to walk away, not waiting for a response.

The axe handle weighed heavily in Ron's hands. An ordinary man could kill with one of these. In his hands, the tool was capable of much more. Andrew hadn't liked him from the beginning. Doc was incapacitated, and Lily had been sent away. This smelled like a trap.

Andrew paused, evidently realizing Ron wasn't going to follow him. "Perhaps I erred, and you enjoy being tormented by flashbacks and constant paranoia?"

"What are you planning to do?" Ron demanded, his fingers gripping the handle with enough force to dent the seasoned wood.

"My grandfather has some experience dealing with trauma. He's offered to help you, and since I've seen the damage, I'm willing to help." Andrew's sardonic poise softened briefly. "I can understand why you don't trust me. But I am a healer, and I don't like leaving someone in pain."

Ron had heard promises from various therapists over the years, all of them claiming they could help him. All of them had been proven wrong. And yet, an unbidden creeping of hope still managed to stir.

"It would greatly assist my domestic comfort if you would give me a try. Lily has been vocal in her protests about us misjudging you. When she returns, I'd like to have a chance to eat a meal in peace without hearing about it anymore."

A simple decision lay in front of Ron. He could accept Andrew's word and begin building a bridge of trust between them. Or he could refuse and ruin any plan for staying in Bear Claw. He might not trust Lily's brother, but what choice did he really have? He put down the axe.

"Thank you." The words sounded genuine, not sarcastic.

Andrew led him around the cabin, where a half dozen dogs were attached to a sled. Unlike every dog Ron knew, these were quietly waiting in the snow instead of leaping around. When they saw him, they got to their feet, eager but patient. Andrew checked their harness, leaving Ron to eye the flimsy-looking sled. A few pieces of wood and some leather stretched across the front. It couldn't possibly be safe, even if it managed to support him. He wondered again if Andrew was leading him into an ambush, someplace his body could be quietly dumped and forgotten.

"If I planned to kill you, I could do it in considerably more comfort and with less effort right here." Andrew never glanced up from the dogs, casually ruffling their fur as he dropped his verbal bomb.

Fresh alarms began to prickle the hairs on the back of Ron's neck. "You know what I'm thinking?"

Andrew shook his head, looking up with disappointment. "I'm a shaman, not a telepath. But I'm also not an idiot, and neither are you. Get on the sled."

He'd already decided to trust Lily's brother. A little more wasn't any greater risk. If there was a chance Lily's family could stop his body and mind from constantly overreacting, he'd let them try. He climbed into the sled, wincing as it creaked under his weight. The wood was stronger than it looked, though.

Andrew snapped out a command to the dogs, and they began to jump and plunge forward along a trampled path. The sled jerked unevenly for a few yards before quickly settling into a smooth pace. Ron grinned as the cold air swirled past his face, stealing his breath. It felt like rushing down a hillside on a sled, only it didn't end after a few seconds. They kept flying over the snow, skimming across the crust.

He could have enjoyed it for hours, but their destination wasn't far. A rounded mound of leather layers rose above a small patch of cleared ground with wispy steam emerging from a central hole. Ron recognized it from the movies: a sweat lodge.

Andrew knelt and uncovered a small pottery vessel near the entrance, pulling out a smoldering bundle of cedar leaves. "Take off your outer clothes. From this point on, be silent and respectful."

Ron complied slowly, still fighting his urge to flee. Andrew began to chant under his breath in what Ron assumed was his native language. Gritting his teeth, Ron held still as Andrew moved around him, waving the cedar bundle to disperse the smoke evenly. His skin crawled at the idea of anyone being able to strike him from behind.

"I will take care of your possessions. Go inside," Andrew ordered.

Ron pulled back the flap covering the entrance, releasing a cloud of steam to condense in the chill air. He bent and awkwardly half crawled into the dim interior, trying to be as quick as possible. The heat wrapped around him tangibly like a blanket, beginning its slow penetration to his frozen core. Ron inhaled the thick air gratefully. He'd almost forgotten what it felt like to be completely warm.

"Not beyond all repair." A low chuckle came from the far end of the lodge. "Come closer, Blue Eyes."

A low fire provided dim light, enough to see the outline of a bare-chested man on the other side. His long, loose black hair held a few threads of grey as well as a string of brown-and-white feathers. Ron wondered if they were eagle feathers or from some other bird. The elder shaman's tan skin showed many pale scars crisscrossing back and forth in an irregular map of historical violence. His nose was flattened against his cheeks, like Lily's, and his piercing gaze was framed by fine wrinkles and weathering. Ron guessed this was Lily's grandfather.

"My name is Gerald Charging Bull. Call me Gerry. I've heard many conflicting stories about you from my grandchildren. You hide your truths under your skin, muddying the waters of friendships. You run like the fleet deer of the forest, hoping your speed will carry you beyond the interest of predators. Love snared you tighter than any claw trap. You must decide whether to gnaw yourself free, leaving a piece of yourself behind and making yourself less than you have been. Or to accept the trap and cease running."

Ron wasn't sure if he should say anything. Andrew had specifically ordered silence, but Gerry's words sounded like the opening of a conversation.

Gerry took a pair of wooden tongs and lifted a smooth rock out of the fire, dropping it into a pile of similar rocks. Fresh steam billowed up as he poured a dipper of water over them and pulled a few rocks out of the pile to add back into the glowing embers. "This is a sacred place, Blue Eyes, but it is not a traditional lodge. We have combined many rituals and cultures to make this place. The Greeks purified themselves with steam, as did many other cultures, like the Babylonians." Gerry's sharp eyes snapped onto Ron. "We have merged the traditions to reflect both sides of the people who shaped us. Much as you will find new balance within the different sides of yourself if you are to heal."

"Easier said than done." The words burst out before Ron could stop them. He tensed, wondering if Gerry would order him out. Gerry had looked at him when mentioning Babylon, perhaps fishing to see if Ron knew about the *lalassu*. Was he fishing as a predator or to see if Ron was a trusted insider? He longed for his life to be simple again instead of tangled in so many layers of secrets.

The corners of Gerry's eyes wrinkled with a suppressed smile. "If it was easy, anyone could do it."

The brief glimpse of humor reassured Ron, but the shaman's stoic mask swiftly reasserted itself. Gerry continued, poking at the blackened rocks on the embers, adjusting them to his satisfaction. "I asked Lily to leave us for a time. It was necessary for your benefit as well as her own and Bear Claw's."

His suspicions confirmed, Ron tensed. Her family had sent her away because of him.

Lily's grandfather raised an eyebrow. "No need to get upset. We all could see that you needed healing. Part of that will be finding your balance before this attraction pulls you askew."

"Isn't love supposed to heal everything?" Certainly, his parents had encouraged him to go out and date instead of spending his time brooding at home. Some of the vets at the meetings claimed focusing on their wives and children helped, although others said the burden of being responsible for their loved ones only made it worse. With Lily, he could relax. She helped him feel more confident, ready for anything.

"Love?" Gerry repeated the word with only the faint inflection of a question.

Ron pushed his palms into his thighs. He hadn't quite meant to say that. He liked Lily, certainly. Was it love? He wasn't quite ready to go there.

"Love inspires, uplifts, and makes us into more than we could ever believe." Gerry stared into the mist, a faint smile suggesting he remembered loves in his own life. "But it does not heal, thank the gods."

Ron had never heard anyone suggest being in love might be bad. "Wouldn't that be a good thing?"

It was obvious where Andrew had learned his withering stare. Gerry's made Ron feel like a particularly stupid pupil. "No, it wouldn't. It would be an unfair and horrible burden to put on the ones we loved. To make them responsible for our entire well-being. How could they seek their own lives, knowing that it came at the cost of our suffering? It would be a wearying burden for any person to carry, bowing their shoulders and spirits. Love can only offer a crutch, one that injures both parties even more in the long term. True healing only comes from within. It cannot be imposed, only encouraged."

Ron flushed and hoped Gerry would think it was because of the steam. He'd never thought about it in that way. A lot of soldiers carried tokens of their families: a picture or other memento. Brian had carried a piece of fabric with flowers on it. It had been wrapped in a little plastic bag and tucked into his helmet. He'd sniffed it every night to give himself sweet dreams. Ron had forgotten all about it until now.

Fresh guilt swelled in his throat, blocking his breath. The arrogant selfishness of having survived, when Brian hadn't, beat at him like monastic flails. *I should have found it to send home. Or put it in his coffin. Something.*

"Let it go, Blue Eyes. The dead do not bear grudges," Gerry said softly.

Ron remembered the little girl from the plane. Bernie. She'd said Nada wasn't upset with him. That she only wanted to go home. He shoved the thought aside. "I could have saved them. If I'd been faster or smarter—"

He remembered the old lady laughing behind the duct tape sealing her mouth. Their captors had told her to restart the plane, but she'd refused. He'd known what was coming and tried to stop them. The gun had been only a few feet away. If he'd been faster, he could have knocked it aside.

Nada was a captive, like him. Yet somehow she'd found the strength to defy them while Ron, a highly trained veteran soldier, had sat like a lump of clay and watched it happen. The memory sank deep into his mind like sharp fangs. Another failure.

Gerry stopped him. "It is what happened. Living in the past does not change it. It only denies and destroys the present."

"I let them all down," Ron whispered. "I kept trying, but I let them down."

"Let it go," Gerry repeated. "Come back to this moment in time. Feel the steam on your skin, the sweat trickling. Feel it slide into your lungs, heavy with moisture. Concentrate on what you feel now, not on what you wish you had done differently."

Ron tried, but he felt as if his mind were splintering. Parts of it refused to let go of the memories, hanging onto the shards tightly enough for them to slice deep wounds. His attention kept flickering between the past and the present like a television rapidly switching between channels.

"Don't fight it. Your struggle for control holds you back. Accept that the world is too large to carry in your hands. You do not have the power of a god—you should not take on the responsibility." Gerry poured water on the stones for a fresh burst of steam.

Ron gulped the scalding air. Sweat sheeted off his body, soaking into his clothes and darkening the leather padding on the floor. He shook his head. "I can't."

"Not today. I would have been surprised if you could. Eventually, you will find the path, and it will be sooner than you might think. We will try again tomorrow. For now, simply breathe, and allow your body to relax even if your mind cannot."

Ron did his best to obey Gerry's instructions but found it hard to relax when he was also struggling to catch every exterior noise. He wasn't sure how long he spent raggedly breathing in the steam. Eventually, Gerry doused the fire and told him to go home with Andrew.

Heavy with disappointment, Ron left without saying a word. The ride back to Doc's cabin seemed to go faster than the ride out to the sweat lodge. Despite his inability to surrender to the moment, Ron did feel lighter—not carefree or cured, but for the first time in months, he had the mental energy to think further than the next moment.

"Thank your grandfather for me, please?" Ron asked Andrew as they stopped in front of the cabin. He didn't want Gerry to think he wasn't grateful for the help.

Bill emerged as they arrived, a rifle in his hand. He nodded at both of them before retreating back into the cabin. Ron's sense of peace faded at the sight of the armed ranger. If Bill felt the need to protect Doc with a rifle, then things were worse than he'd feared.

"There are a lot of large predators around here. Only fools go unarmed." Andrew whistled sharply. Bill came back out of the cabin with his gear. He nodded briefly at Ron before getting in the sled.

As Ron watched the two men leave, he wanted to pace, his body filled with a restless energy. He guessed the whistle was the equivalent of honking a car horn in the driveway. His father always despised people who did that, although Ron found himself wondering if it might be excusable here. It wasn't fair to make the dogs stand for long in the cold.

Unseen eyes watched him from the forest, adding to his restlessness. "Time to get in."

When he went inside, he found Doc awake and eating fried fish and mushrooms. "Ah, Blue Eyes, welcome back. Bill made some dinner. Don't tell Lily, but sometimes I think he's a better cook than she is."

Ron helped himself to a heaping plate, and the two men ate in comfortable silence for a time. "I'm glad to see you feeling better."

"Never underestimate the resiliency of the human spirit, along with a little chemical assistance." Doc winked, holding up his tea mug. "Looks like Lily's family have decided to accept you. At least for now."

"It's all turned around so quickly. Yesterday they couldn't wait for me to go. Today, I get the feeling they'd hunt me down if I tried to leave." The meal and the heat pulled him down into drowsiness. Part of him still suspected a trick, but he was suddenly too tired to wrestle up the necessary energy to care. If it was a trick, he'd deal with it.

He might have fallen asleep then and there if a loud crunching and snuffling outside hadn't cracked the lid containing his adrenaline. Doc frowned, struggling to raise himself up.

Ron waved at him to stay seated, creeping noiselessly to the door. Holding the lantern in one hand and the latch in the other, he bellowed out, "Who's there!"

He flung open the door and held the lantern high. If it was an intruder, his shout should send them scurrying off, but he wanted to get a look first.

Instead, he saw a familiar dark outline. "Litonya?"

The bear stepped forward into the light, and Ron's muscles fear-locked. This animal's fur was considerably darker than Litonya's and did not have a golden crescent on its shoulder. It raised its head level with Ron's. He kept his voice calm, not wanting to provoke it. *Large predators. Armed. Right.* "Doc, we have a problem."

He heard a scuffling sound from behind him but didn't turn, not wanting to take his eyes off the bear. He considered closing the door quietly and hoping it went away but rejected the idea. It looked powerful enough to come right through the wall if it chose to. The axe was still outside, and Bill had taken the rifle away with him. There was no other weapon in the cabin unless he wanted to try defending himself with a frying pan. He was prepared to take the animal on, hand-to-hand, if it attacked.

Movement to his right caught his attention, and he flicked his gaze sideways to see Doc bracing himself on the low shelf by the door, his face white with pain and effort. The biologist looked out the door and then exhaled sharply. "It's all right, Blue Eyes. I recognize her. Her name is Setsuné." He reached out to Ron. "Help me back to the chair."

Turning his back on the bear went against every survival instinct, but Doc needed his help. And after Ron's previous encounters with Litonya, he could take a little on faith. He lifted Doc up and placed him gently back in the chair.

"Careful—don't hurt yourself," Doc gasped.

Ron mentally cursed himself for his lapse and trotted out his usual excuse before trying to change the subject. "Adrenaline, I guess. What should we do about our friend out there?"

"I would guess she's come out to check on us. Close the door so we can keep the heat in." Doc winced as he adjusted his seat and carefully lifted his bark-wrapped foot into a better position.

Ron couldn't resist taking another look out the door. Setsuné ambled slowly out of sight around the cabin's corner. He closed the door, but he could still hear her snuffling and moving nearby through the thin walls. His nerves crawled under his skin at not knowing what was happening.

"Litonya's been coming around?" Doc asked, his voice unbelievably casual.

"I have trouble sleeping, and I ran into her last night. She's different from what I expected." Ron saw Doc's lips tighten and knew he was treading on a sensitive subject. "At first, I thought she might attack me, but she seemed more interested in protecting me."

"I've known her a long time. You don't have to be afraid of her." Doc glanced at the door. "I wish she hadn't, though. She should be more cautious around strangers."

A slow simmer of anger built up in Ron. "There's more going on here than you've told me."

Doc nodded, not denying the charge. "You of all people should know the value of carefully choosing the people to share your secrets with. Get a good night's sleep. Tomorrow, you'll help me check out my bears, and I'll explain what I can."

Traveling with Lou was never going to make anyone's top-ten list of Northern tourist attractions. As he and Lily guided their dogs over the snow-packed trail, he barely said a word except to bark directions. He'd always been a forbidding figure to Lily, and the fact that he was constantly away for days at a time only made it worse. He was more comfortable expressing himself physically than his twin. He hunted for the entire community, tracking down game and bringing it back singlehandedly.

Which was why it surprised her when he started talking to her as soon as they settled down at their fire for the evening.

He grunted. "You're attracted to him, aren't you?"

"That's none of your business." Heat flushed Lily's skin, and she hoped it was too dark for Lou to notice.

"You are my business." He ripped off a piece of jerky with his teeth.

Lily waited for him to explain what he meant by that, but he seemed to think his comment was self-explanatory and continued to tear the jerky to pieces. It was so unlike him to make an effort to communicate that she decided to try patience. "Lou, I know it was hard to take care of things after Mom and Dad died, but I don't need you to watch over me."

"I know." Lou's neck briefly appeared as his head lifted and his shoulders dropped in a display of surprise. "You're an adult."

"Then what's the problem?" Lily tilted her head in confusion.

"How many of us are left?" Lou resumed his hunch, elbows resting on raised knees.

What does that have to do with anything?

"How many skinwalkers are left?" Lou clarified.

Lily blinked. They never talked about their heritage openly. Their entire family could shift between the fur and the skin. Some spent more time on one side of the divide than others. She always assumed Lou spent most of his time as a bear. "I—I don't know."

"Not many. And every generation, there are fewer."

"Ah." The secret responsibility they really never talked about but which weighed heavily on Lily's shoulders. Between isolation, low birth rates, and systematic prejudice, the population of both skinwalkers and their tribe was steadily shrinking. Young women like Lily faced tremendous pressure to have the babies needed to increase the population. Knowing that her personal choices could lead to species extinction sucked. "Still definitely not your business."

"Isn't it? Do I have a mate? A partner? Even a prospect of one?" Lou rumbled, more upset and animated than she'd ever seen him. "There's no one for me, Lily."

The evident despair and frustration made it hard to maintain her position of autonomy. "I'm sorry, Lou. I didn't know you thought about it."

His stern mouth flicked upward briefly in a smile. "I don't like to complain."

"I'm glad we're talking now. I'm not volunteering for enforced breeding or anything, but if that's a goal, shouldn't you be encouraging me?"

"He's not one of us. He's normal, and we're not, so we can't even be sure you're genetically compatible. Assuming he doesn't run screaming the first time you shift." Lou's blunt words slashed through the illusion of pretense she'd been clinging to. "He wouldn't understand, and he could destroy everything here."

Lily's hackles rose at the implied blame. "You mean the people chasing him could destroy everything."

"No. He could. He freaks out and calls in the government, and everything collapses. Wouldn't take much. Pull in the environment-nuts. Start with imposing maximums for taking caribou and other wildlife. Give the mining companies the excuse they've been looking for to take over. We've had enough trouble with Damali and her threats." Lou obviously spent a great deal of time thinking on the topic.

"You don't believe her when she says she's here to help." None of them did, but moving the topic away from Ron seemed like a smart plan.

"She says the mining company will pull out if she can prove the existence of the unique wildlife. I think they'll use it as an excuse to move us off the land. Once we're gone, let the buzz die down, and in a few years, they have unfettered access." Lou poked the fire. "She should have given up and gone home weeks ago. She must have something. Maybe she suspects the Colony."

"She just has the old legends," Lily protested. "Doc, Bill, and I, we've all told her that's all they are. Legends. Like Sasquatch."

"Last thing we need is for anyone to figure out the truth in the legends." Lou got to his feet. "We need more wood."

He disappeared into the woods without another word. Lily suspected he'd used up his quota of conversation for the year. But the fact that he'd made the effort spoke volumes. Over and over, their problems circled back to the twin issues of isolation and secrecy. Maybe Evonne was right. If they didn't have to keep the existence of the Marked secret, then Lou could travel and meet someone. Maybe they could start their own online dating site. *Freaks Seeking Freaks.* The idea made her smile for a moment until she reminded herself that Ron would not have been on such a list.

Grandfather and Andrew would be hoping distance would weaken the attraction as if she were a character in a Jane Austen novel. She'd asked Setsuné to keep an eye on the cabin so Ron could sleep. He needed the rest, but he'd have to drive himself into exhaustion to get it. Looking up, she knew Ron would be outside, restlessly patrolling and looking at the same stars. "Sleep tight, Blue Eyes. May the forest watch over you."

CHAPTER SEVEN

Andrew did not rush to the Colony. Rushing was undignified and suggested a lack of ability to cope. But he didn't waste any time, either, in view of what he'd found outside of Doc's cabin: a length of rope snagged in an upper branch and a fresh scar nearby on the trunk, suggesting the rope had been attached to another branch that had proven insufficient to support the weight of a hidden watcher.

He didn't pause to exchange greetings with any of the bruins enjoying the brief midwinter sun. Instead, he marched to the northern end of the narrow valley, to the tiny clapboard cabin. The metal roof had been dulled with branches and mud. More netting and branches concealed the cabin from casual view. Andrew opened the door without bothering to knock.

The hut's occupant tried to block the light with a pale hand. His eyes were rimmed in bright red, and the hut stank of liquor and his unwashed body. His dark curls clung greasily to his scalp as he laughed bitterly. "I don't remember ordering a wake-up call."

Andrew frowned. "This is not a time for humor, Vincent."

"Then is it a time for complaining? I'm thinking of putting up a scathing review about the food here. You people have really taken serving gods-awful fish meals to an extreme." Vincent hunched closer to the stove.

"We gave you sanctuary," Andrew reminded him. The depth of Vincent's rancor kept surprising him. It was so unlike how Andrew remembered their guest before his capture. Then, Vincent had been the party clown, larger than life, always ready with a joke to lighten the mood and never thinking beyond the shallow needs of the moment. Now every word came out stained with self-disgust and sarcasm. A cutting edge accompanied every joke, pricking and slicing at the listener. One day, Vincent would turn those blades inward if Andrew couldn't find a way to disarm him.

"Yeah. It's been great being locked up here," Vincent snapped before the bitter, careless jester returned. He seemed shrunken, reduced, as he curled up in the darkness. "I know this is an exile. I've been sent to the fucking Arctic like Frankenstein's monster at the end of the book. Maybe I should vanish into the darkness, riding an ice floe. Maybe your new friend should join me."

Andrew knew better than to express interest. Vincent would take vicious pleasure in holding it over his head while refusing to share another word.

"They sent me up here because they were afraid of what's in my head. The Beast could have made me into a fucking Trojan horse," Vincent muttered, taking a long slug of vodka directly from the bottle.

Andrew noted the grimy glint of other discarded bottles. Too many. Doc had given in again and ordered another case of liquor. He believed Vincent shouldn't have to face the memories of his ordeal without chemical blunting. Andrew doubted it helped, and Vincent still refused to give any details from his capture, not even the man's name. Vincent's family told him that the captor had used psychic powers to mentally override Vincent's personality and memories. Without his patient's help, Andrew couldn't begin to break past those barriers, and Vincent still refused to call his captor anything but the Beast. The denial was so complete that Andrew wondered if the emotional state might have been manufactured by the Beast.

"Should be worried about your new friend. Keep me locked up here, and you let him wander free. It's funny since we're both alumni from the same school of bullshit and betrayal." Vincent grinned maliciously.

Only long practice kept Andrew's face impassive as his mind flickered through the implications. "You're saying Blue Eyes was there with you and the Beast?" Could Vincent's memory be trusted in such a case? Between the psychic manipulation and the alcohol, his brain must be a chemical mess right now.

"Ron McBride, a corporal. He was a proper little soldier to the Beast. Did whatever he was told, including delivering a little girl back to the Beast instead of rescuing her. But who am I to judge? I'm the one who told him everything about how to find us." The energy seemed to drain out of Vincent. "Go away. Save someone else. I'm done."

"Vincent, we're here to help you, but we can't do it without your cooperation," Andrew reminded him.

"I don't want your help. If I were you, I'd make sure someone watched your new friend. Wouldn't want something nasty to happen." Vincent yawned.

"Is that what you were doing—watching him?" Andrew pulled out the rope. Vincent thought they didn't know how he went wandering the forest each night. He barely slept unless he drank himself into a stupor. His trails had disappeared a few weeks earlier, and Andrew suspected he'd begun moving from tree to tree, staying off the ground.

Vincent didn't answer but stared sullenly at the glowing red coals in his stove.

"Were you thinking of hurting him?"

No answer.

"Maybe killing him?"

Andrew caught the faint flinch, a brief wrinkling of the flesh beside Vincent's eye. So, Vincent wasn't as indifferent and despondent as he liked to pretend. They'd taken him to a sweat lodge, but Vincent had slashed it open and run back to the Colony, threatening to slit the throat of anyone who tried to make him do it again.

Vincent's pain battered at Andrew's awareness, biting at him like a pack of dogs bringing down prey. It gaped vast and raw, driving Vincent to lash out in desperate attacks, trying to inflict maximum damage to give himself a little breathing space. Without Vincent's participation, Andrew was frustratingly helpless. Healing could not be imposed.

Entirely unsatisfied, he left Vincent to his sulking. For the moment, Andrew had other priorities—such as finding out if there was a grain of truth to Vincent's claims about Blue Eyes.

Lily stood in the dingy community hall, sipping harsh coffee from a paper cup. The linoleum under her boots was scuffed and darkened from decades of meetings, dances, and celebrations. A ring of yellow nicotine stain coated the walls below the ceiling, although no one had been allowed to smoke in here for the last ten years. While Lou picked up supplies and met Bob at the tiny airport, she'd come here to listen to Ptarmigan's latest attempt to drum up local community support for mining operations—a well-detailed but succinct presentation with an emphasis on new jobs for the area. Northstar had sent a short video clip but no representative.

"Lily!" Edyta called. The tiny Russian woman stood on tiptoe to wave, her russet hair making her stand out among the native crowd. Lily made her way between small clutches, catching bits and pieces of conversation. It was mostly about hunting, with some concern about predators going after food supplies.

Edyta's thin fingers snapped around Lily's arm like a trap, pulling her to one side. "What did you think?"

"It's interesting. Some good theories. But theories don't always work out here." Lily glanced at the table full of glossy booklets. "Ptarmigan Industries put a lot of work into this."

"Not just us. We've gotten renewed interest from Mr. Dalhard for both AD Mining and NorthStar. Between you and me, I hadn't heard from him for so long I thought he might have given up and begun looking elsewhere. Then he called yesterday and told me he was determined to find a way to make it work in Kluane. He asked me about Bear Claw in particular." Edyta led them to a pair of unclaimed cheap green plastic chairs with metal legs.

"Did he? We're not so interesting." Very deep primal instincts warned Lily of a predator on her trail. She needed to be careful and cunning, using all the resources from both sides of her nature. "Not like the traditional villages—"

"Mr. Dalhard isn't interested in re-creations for tourists. He wants something more genuine, although he's asked a lot of questions about

106

Dene legends and customs. He sponsored Dr. Damali's work to ensure the local wildlife is preserved. I know we've all heard a lot of promises before, but he seems genuinely committed to doing more than government-mandated minimums." Edyta sounded smug as she leaned back in her chair.

"I know. Yet I keep searching for the hook in all this delicious bait. What do you think is in it for him?" Lily asked. Dalhard's people were all far too persistent. They could find other communities for their prototypes with less effort.

"He's spending a lot of money and time on things that have nothing to do with his comsat network prototypes," Edyta replied in her typical blunt fashion. She had succeeded in running her airfreight business in a hostile environment for over thirty years. She never wasted time or breath on polite lies or dissembling. "Why are you all so reluctant to believe him? And don't give me the abuses-of-the-white-man speech. There's more than that."

Lily took a moment to collect her thoughts, well aware Edyta would mark the hesitation. "We're not a reservation. We don't have any political standing other than national park status."

"Come on. Until Bob married Evonne, you used to send someone to Kluane twice a month to pick up your mail and supplies. Your grandfather refused to set up any kind of airdrop, let alone a landing strip. He doesn't want anyone in there." Edyta shook her head, setting her short red hair swinging. Glints of grey underneath the dye caught the light.

"We have Doc and the ranger station." It was a feeble counterpoint, and Lily was all too aware of it. The irregular walls of the community center started to close in. Her animal side swelled up, causing her muscles to twitch.

Edyta pressed on. "What are you afraid people will find out if they come up there? You can't think they'd want to stay for the weather."

Lily closed her eyes, forcing the fur down and concentrating on the skin. It worked, but the difficulty left her wondering if she would soon find herself living in the forest full-time.

"Are you all right?" Edyta asked, her skinny fingers gripping Lily's arm.

"Fine. Bad coffee." Lily hoped she looked like someone with an upset stomach rather than someone trying to hide a secret.

"Lily, I've known you a long time. I've been sending you books and magazines for years." Edyta let go of Lily's arm. Lily suppressed the urge to rub the area. "I know you're interested in the outside world, and still, whenever I invite you to join me for a little while, you refuse. Why?"

"I have responsibilities at home. They need me there." A reckless urge to reveal the truth snipped at her control, but decades of silence helped her hold her tongue. Edyta had carved a place for herself and fought her way to the top of a male-dominated industry. She would surely have some sympathy for people kept isolated because of their differences. Lily could certainly use an outside perspective to try and pull herself together again. She wondered if Ron would understand if she tried.

"Your brothers could figure out which end of the fry pan to put the fish in for themselves for a few weeks." Edyta snorted. "I don't think you know what you want, Lily. You're torn between your family and your own heart. The sooner you figure it out, the happier you're going to be."

Edyta's words helped to crystallize Lily's thoughts. "It's more than what I want. It's about what's best for all of us. I don't think we can huddle in the forest and pretend the rest of the world doesn't exist anymore. Loggers, miners—they're all coming, and they want in. If we're hiding, then they can sneak up on us. If we're connected, we can sway public opinion and tell our side of things. You've seen the damage these people do, Edyta. Lakes full of poisoned chemicals or drained into lifeless pits. The companies move on, and everyone forgets about those of us who are stuck trying to survive up here."

Edyta put down her cup of coffee. "Quite the speech. There's more than the environment for you, though. Don't try to hide it."

"Of course there is. I like learning about other people, but I also love my culture and my family. Right now, I have to choose. Either I leave them to go somewhere with ready access to the outside world, or I cut myself off and stay in a tiny patch of tundra my entire life. I shouldn't have to make that choice. Grandfather thinks if we bring in the Internet, it will erode our culture, turn us into a mirror of southern society. I think we're eroding it a lot more by forcing people to either abandon us and integrate or remain isolated. Why shouldn't I have a chance to see the world or fall in love—" Lily clamped her lips shut too late to prevent the traitorous words from escaping.

"Fall in love?" Edyta seized them like a bear snapping at the salmon runs.

"Just an example." Lily looked into her own cup to avoid the other woman's eyes.

"Not a random one. Is there someone new in Bear Claw?"

Lily started to feel like a rabbit under the gaze of a fox. If she mentioned anything about Ron, it could get back to the people chasing him.

"I know that look." Edyta chuckled. "There is someone."

"I shouldn't. I have responsibilities." Lily straightened her shoulders, trying to project a confidence she no longer felt. Everything had gotten so tangled.

A wistful expression softened the older woman's hardened features, and she patted Lily's leg. "There are always responsibilities. I'm going to tell you something you need to know, Lily. In the end, those responsibilities don't matter."

"Of course they do." Lily was shocked.

"They're important, but they're not everything. I walked away from two chances at love because I was too busy building my business. I didn't think I had time to do both. And I've regretted that choice for most of my life." Edyta wiped at her eye with a finger.

"You accomplished so much."

"I'm proud of what I've done. Yet, looking back, I could have had both. Maybe it would have taken a little longer to get to where I am now, and maybe neither of them would have worked out, but walking away from what could be love leaves a scar. It never really heals, and it left me feeling empty."

Lily didn't need to ask what she meant. Ron had carved out his own place in her heart, one that couldn't be filled with duties and obligations. Unlike Edyta, she wasn't sure she could have both. *But are you sure you can't?* Ron would be leaving, maybe even before she got back. The attraction might be thrilling, but romantic thinking died a quick death when faced with the realities of Northern life. The Arctic was too unforgiving to dreamers. She needed to stay practical and keep her feelings in perspective.

Edyta shook her head briefly, and the practical, hard-nosed woman replaced the wistful one. "Back to business: you should meet with Mr. Dalhard. I was suspicious, too, before we talked. After a few minutes, I figured out he was the real deal. He wants to help us."

"You trust him." A big endorsement. Edyta didn't trust new people easily. She'd had too many potential business partners try to walk all over her because she was a woman.

"I do. Hell of a thing, but I do. And I think you should, too. Meet with the man. Talk to him like I did."

"Maybe. I'll think about it—about everything you said," Lily promised. "I should get back to the airport. Lou will need my help."

Edyta let her go graciously, and Lily breathed a sigh of relief. She hurried through the muddy streets. Despite semi-regular visits, it still seemed strange to see so many houses so close together. Light and noise from one would invariably spill over onto the others. What would it be like, to always know there were other people nearby? She shivered at the thought. She wanted to retreat into her own cave sanctuary and hibernate until things started to make sense again.

Kluane's airport was mostly a hub for freight to the surrounding communities. A few different freight carriers used it, but mostly Ptarmigan. Bob stored his snowmobile and cargo sled at the hangar. Lily picked her way to the half-moon corrugated-tin building and slipped inside, only to stop in her tracks. Tension filled the air like powdery snow, shoving aside the oxygen and resisting her attempts to breathe.

"Get in, and lock the door," Lou growled. Bob looked up, his face pale and his mouth twisted as if he were about to vomit. The red-and-yellow-striped sweater he wore made him look even sicker.

Lily did what they asked, flipping the sign from Open to Back in 5 Minutes. "What's going on?"

"He's a murderer," Bob snarled, his pate flushing red through thinning brown hair. His thick fingers clenched into even thicker fists.

"Who?" Lily's gaze flicked between the two men.

"Blue Eyes," Bob said. "And you left him with Evonne!"

Lou stood up, glaring at the other man. "His real name is Corporal Ronald McBride, and he's under investigation for the deaths of his squadron in Afghanistan and the murder of Nada Sanchez."

Lily grabbed at a chair as the universe spun around her. She recognized Nada's alias. She'd often pretended to be Latina instead of native. It made things easier down south and meant less chance of being tracked back to Bear Claw or one of the other enclaves. Lily's mind clung to those details in a desperate attempt to avoid facing what Bob had revealed. "Where did you get this information?"

"From Ken," Bob said. "I called the contact number for the RCMP, and they told me to stay away from him. He's dangerous and delusional. We have to get home right away."

"I don't believe it," she whispered.

"I'll get the dogs ready—" Lou began.

"No. I mean I don't believe it," Lily repeated more firmly. This had to be a lie. "We knew someone was after him. What better way to isolate him than to spread false stories?"

"We know Nada is dead," Bob insisted.

Lily fought down the fur. "Why would her murderer bring her ashes back to us?"

"To trap more of us." Bob sputtered as he got angrier. "Maybe he's some kind of Van Helsing, looking to rid the world of monsters."

"He's not—"

Lou interrupted Lily. "We don't know him well enough to say one way or another. We can't afford to be involved in an RCMP investigation."

"He's not a murderer," she insisted, trying to subdue the growl rolling through her back muscles. Whatever had happened to Ron, she could not believe he could kill an innocent person in cold blood. He'd been so worried about her getting hurt, and he was taking care of Doc despite the personal risk.

Lou studied her, his eyes cold and judgmental. "We all could be murderers in the right circumstances."

"We don't have time for this. We have to get back before he hurts someone." Bob opened the door and left without another word.

Lily stopped Lou from following, putting her hand on his chest. "Promise me we'll give him a chance to tell his side of the story."

"And if we get back, and he's hurt Evonne, Doc, or Andrew?" Lou asked, his mouth set in stony determination.

Bob was ready to serve as judge, jury, and executioner. Lou hadn't wanted to give Ron a chance to survive in the first place. *What if I'm wrong? What if he really is a killer?* She tried to make herself consider the possibility but couldn't. She couldn't make herself see Ron as a danger to them. Which made it easy to say the words Lou needed to hear. "Then I'll take care of him myself."

Ron rolled his shoulders to resettle the weight of his heavy backpack full of supplies. Andrew had reluctantly given Doc permission to go out, mainly because the only way to keep him in the cabin would have been to sit on him. The biologist was impatient to check on his bears and make sure "the Damali woman" hadn't been bothering them. Andrew supplied an oversized boot to lace over the cast and told Ron to carry all the gear and break the trail through the snow. Now he and Ron were out in the forest and snow, trudging along to Doc's directions.

Ron felt as if he were being watched. The sensation came and went at all hours. But despite lengthy patrols through the short day and endless night, he had yet to find someone. The sensation grated on him. Too bad he couldn't recruit Litonya as a full-time watcher. A week ago, he couldn't have imagined being comfortable with a wild bear so close to him. When she'd been there, he'd felt oddly safe. Setsuné didn't inspire the same sense of security. They'd come to a mutual understanding in which he ignored her and she ignored him, but she still made him uneasy.

He wished Lily were back. Knowing she was out there—out of reach, beyond his ability to protect—only heightened the paranoia-fueled adrenaline keeping him on edge. The memory of their kiss kept him awake for entirely different reasons. It was more than simply liking her. She'd somehow breezed past all of his carefully erected barriers without him realizing, taking up residence inside his heart and mind. Every time he smelled bacon, he missed her.

Ron shoved aside his depressing thoughts as Doc slowed down. They were approaching an abandoned log cabin, its rounded walls coated with lichen and moss. The roof was missing, probably scavenged long ago, leaving the inside heaped with snow. Doc made his way around to the back, where a low lean-to shed crouched in the shadows. He peered into the dim interior and smiled. "There you are, Buttercup."

Ron's breath caught in his teeth, steaming out in icy wisps. Inside the shed slept a black bear, perhaps a third the size of Litonya, nestled in an insulating bed of leaves and branches. As they came close, she opened her eyes and lifted her head. She watched them cautiously but with none of the intelligence he'd seen with Litonya.

"There's a good bear," Doc said softly, not approaching. "Blue Eyes, I'll need those branches now."

Ron stripped a young spruce tree of its branches, building up a pad near the shed entrance. Once he'd made it thick enough to satisfy Doc, he spread a blue plastic tarp and a soft wool blanket on top. Getting Doc down to the padding took some work, but soon the biologist lay with his elbows outstretched on either side of his head and his chin resting on top of his bright-yellow mittens. His attention was solely on Buttercup. "No need to be afraid. I know he's new, but he won't hurt you, and I need the help."

As he'd been instructed, Ron retreated, finding a relatively clear spot to wait in. Finally back with his bears, Doc had settled in and wasn't in any hurry to leave. Sometimes he would grab his pencil and notebook to scribble an observation. Mostly, he talked with Buttercup.

It wasn't like with Litonya, where she seemed to understand English. Doc made long, low vocalizations, like a mix of yawning, purring, and growling. Buttercup would sigh, huff, and growl back. Ron wasn't an expert on bear body language, but he could see Doc relaxing as the strange conversation continued. The old man's shoulders retracted from their hunch toward his ears, and his sound leg stopped twitching. He looked like a man enjoying a cup of coffee with an old friend, not a scientist studying his subject.

"All right. I'll let you rest now. See you soon, Buttercup." Doc struggled to get to his feet, and Ron hurried to help. He checked Doc's watch and surprised himself when he discovered more than two hours had passed. Two hours, and he hadn't felt trapped or bored or pursued. He savored the rare sensation.

"Thank you, Blue Eyes. I needed this." Doc sighed in contentment. He must have caught Ron's puzzled look because he hastened to clarify. "It's one of the reasons I've stayed here as long as I have. I could have gotten a teaching job or another research position. But whenever I tried, I missed them too much. I lost sight of who I was and got caught up by the clock and other people's expectations. After the last time, I swore I wouldn't go back."

"I've never seen anything like it. It was like watching two people converse in a foreign language. " Ron packed up the blanket and tarp.

"Sometimes I think I was born in the wrong body. I was meant to be a bear and live up here, finding my food and sleeping at my own pace." Doc whispered his secret to the skies. "It's the only place I've ever felt whole. It makes me envy Lily and her family."

"What do you mean?"

Doc shook himself, his arms and legs drawing inward in unmistakable fear. He'd said something he wasn't supposed to. "I-I guess I mean how they… how they… how they've made their home here. They fit with the land."

Ron hid a grin. Doc was not an accomplished liar. "Is this one of things you're going to tell me later?"

"Bear Claw is full of secrets. Just like you," Doc replied.

"Fair point." Mirth from the brief exchange faded quickly. Despite the teasing, Ron was still an outsider. A wave of homesickness pulled down his contentment, though he wasn't sure which he missed more: his family or the army. He'd ruined both with his drug and alcohol use, trying to cope with what had happened to him.

The thought caught him by surprise. He'd always blamed Afghanistan before. Now he understood how his own fear and guilt drove him to seek chemical numbness. *Maybe the sweat lodge wasn't as useless as I thought.*

While he'd been recovering with the Harrises, Virginia had told him stories to distract him. One about ghosts stuck with him—how they walked among the living constantly, unseen and unable to affect anything except in rare circumstances. He'd tried to be a ghost, slipping invisibly through life without having to connect or interact. Now it wasn't good enough for him.

"You know, bears are good listeners." Doc balanced carefully on his carved walking stick. The head of the cane was a good likeness of a grizzly bear.

"Only if you speak their language," Ron teased, trying to lighten his mood as he easily hefted the bulky backpack.

"Even if you don't. You can tell them anything, and they'll never betray it. In some cultures, they are the keepers of wisdom and healing." Doc wiped at the frost on his beard. "Litonya will be back soon."

"You have a radio tracker on her?" He hadn't seen a collar, but maybe there were other methods.

"More like experience. Litonya isn't likely to stay away once she's gotten curious about something." Doc smiled fondly, as if describing a beloved and mischievous granddaughter.

"I feel comfortable with her even though I never thought I'd say that about something with four-inch claws and matching teeth," Ron admitted. "She's not just a bear, is she?"

"She is and she isn't. It's a complicated situation."

"She's the reason you don't want Dr. Damali poking around the bears, isn't she?" Ron was starting to understand some of the strange interactions he'd observed.

"You are perceptive, Blue Eyes." Doc's shoulders crept toward his neck.

"Ron." Enough secrets. It might be reckless and stupid, but it felt right to offer his real name to Doc.

A low growl interrupted Doc's reply. Ron's reflexes snapped into adrenaline mode, letting him hear the faint brush of pine needles scraping against one another. A large black bear snarled in the clearing ahead, intimidating a smaller bear. And neither of them looked the least bit interested in a conversation.

Chapter Eight

Come and find me, Pujari. The answer to Karan's challenge hung innocently in cyberspace. A link glowed below, an invitation to a private chat room.

Karan's thoughts twisted uncomfortably in his skull, and his palms were damp with perspiration, making him second-guess his decision to break the long silence. He could no longer hold all the possibilities in his mind and plan for each one. This contact opened up too many options, potentially pitting him against an opponent who was nearly his equal. *Nearly, but never actually equal,* he reminded himself. The decision had already been made. Too late to back out. He needed to remember how far he had come.

He clicked on the link, perhaps a little more forcefully than he'd initially intended. A small, innocuous box opened up. Text immediately appeared.

Caligo>> It's been a long time.

Karan did not hesitate in his response. **Pujari>> Too long and not long enough.**

Caligo>> You will forgive me if I don't immediately accept your claims. I've visited the grave too many times.

Pujari>> And where did you end up burying me? Karan's breathing eased with each new line. This exchange was going as he had hoped.

Caligo>> I put up a small stele in the Valley of Kings. I thought you'd feel at home there.

116

Pujari>> You will confuse the hell out of the archaeologists. I assume you have a test in mind. We have so many secrets to choose from.

Caligo>> Why did you stay away?

Pujari>> You threatened to kill me. Staying dead seemed prudent. And it gave me the chance to explore new options in my life. The pain from their old arguments had faded somewhat, but Karan still felt the ache of frustration from so many times of trying to explain and meeting only with brick-like stubbornness.

Caligo>> Why come back now?

Pujari>> We already crossed paths. But neither of us knew. And it led us both into disaster.

Caligo>> What do you mean?

Pujari>> You were always the genius. Figure it out.

Karan clicked the dialogue box closed, pleased to see his hands were steady and his plan was progressing. Only a shadow of his former hatred remained, not enough to cloud his mind. His partner never saw things clearly, never understood how the world truly worked. He saw Karan's practicality as a cold-blooded lack of morality. He constantly failed to see how one could help more people from a position of power than from invisibility.

Even their nicknames came from opposite approaches. He had chosen Pujari, which meant "priest" in Hindi. He believed in deliberately guiding the lower masses to appropriate choices. His partner chose Caligo, Latin for shadow or darkness. He always chose names having to do with something intangible such as smoke or fog. Something that could not be caught even when it was right in front of you.

His partner would not be satisfied with their brief exchange. Karan remembered their final encounter as if it were yesterday…

Caligo had caught up to him in London. Out of nowhere, someone grabbed his arm, forcing him to halt and spin. Karan's umbrella fell to the ground, letting the pounding rain drench his hair and shoulders immediately. He glared at Caligo. "This is not a good time."

"Did you think I wouldn't find out?" His partner's hair was plastered against his skull. "You can't do this, Pujari. It's not what we agreed."

Karan wrenched his arm free and hissed back. "I never agreed to anything. I simply stopped arguing with you. I am the one who kept us safe. I did what needed to be done."

"You've killed people!" The accusation echoed in the relatively empty streets. None of the few passersby bothered to look at the two men shouting. They hurried past on their own errands, shoes clicking against the paving stones.

"Like your hands are clean. Would you rather they killed us?" It hurt, a sharp pain in the heart he thought he had silenced long ago. He had earned more trust than this. More faith.

"Go through with it, and I can't turn away. I'll have to end it by any means necessary." Caligo's expression was a jangled mixture of fear, regret, and determination. He meant every word of his threat.

Karan's sharp pain hollowed out into an empty ache like a bubble inside a glacier—frozen and desolate with no chance at anything beyond destruction. He thought he had long since broken the tie with Caligo, but some remnant still clung to cause this kind of pain. Caligo had actually meant to kill him. After everything they'd done together, fought for together, been through together. It had all meant nothing, apparently. "Do what you must."

Karan walked away on that day. Until today, he had never exchanged another word with his former partner. Caligo might have been sentimental, but he had sent a hail of bullets to cut Karan down in the middle of combat. It would have been child's play for him to betray Karan's position to the enemy, achieving his goal without dirtying his hands. A hypocrite to the end.

"Karan!" Dalhard's voice barked through the intercom. Composing his face into an impassive mask, Karan walked the short distance to his employer's suite. Heavy velvet drapes blocked the light from the twelve-foot windows. The air stank of staleness and old sweat.

Dalhard crouched over a paper-strewn desk, his dark hair lank and uncombed. Stubble clung to his cheeks and chin. The man's meticulous grooming regimen suffered in the face of vengeful obsession. Yet, when he looked up, his eyes were saner than they had been in months. "Karan, I finally have the answer."

"You've found the Harrises?" Karan could not contain his surprise.

"No. They'll have to wait. She couldn't see the beauty of my vision."

Dalhard swept his hand over the desk like a knife slicing a throat. "I've found what we really needed. Human soldiers are limited by nature. We need something more powerful."

Another chimera chase. If it kept his boss happy and harmlessly occupied, then Karan would indulge him. "Such as?"

"Bears with the intelligence of humans. Large bears, able to fight with claw and fang. We'll make a fortune!" Vindictive light glinted in Dalhard's eyes. "We'll be able to recover our property as well."

Karan noticed the agent's thumb drive lying on top of maps of Alaska and British Columbia. He had delivered it, although he had not expected his boss to actually read it. "You saw the report on McBride."

"Where is Bear Claw? I can't find it on the maps," Dalhard demanded, irritably shuffling through the stacked papers.

"It is not listed on the maps, but it is approximately here." Karan pointed to an area near the junction of British Columbia, Alaska, and the Yukon. "I received confirmation McBride is there this morning through our false RCMP information line."

"We need to go immediately." Dalhard ran his hand over his chin and scowled. "Fetch me a razor, and make sure we have a full tactical team. Contact Ms. Golov from Ptarmigan—she should be able to get us precise coordinates. She's eager to secure a percentage of the mineral rights."

"I'll draw up the paperwork." Karan nodded. He and Dalhard were still wanted for questioning, but perhaps a quiet excursion could be managed.

"And cages. Large enough for bears."

Ron took a deep breath as he stared at the two snarling black bears in the clearing. He didn't need to worry. Doc was a bear expert. Together, they'd be able to handle this. As his mind calmed from the initial adrenaline surge, he noticed the ragged carcass in the snow between them—a few scraps of meat on unidentifiable bones, perhaps a rabbit from the size.

"Bart!" Doc cried out, holding out his hand as if he were about to dash between the two combatants.

Both bears looked at the biologist in surprise. Ron took a deep breath to stay calm. *Doc is an expert. He knows what he's doing.*

Bart took advantage of the older bear's distraction to snatch the carcass and run into the trees as fast as his furry legs could carry him.

The larger bear roared, but Bart had already vanished. Its gaze swung back to Doc and Ron, no longer seeing them as intruders but as potential prey.

"Oh dear," Doc whispered.

Ron didn't need to hear another word. He grabbed Doc by the waistband as the bear began to charge them. Summoning every ounce of his enhanced strength, he jumped as high as he could, reaching the sturdy pine branches twenty feet over their heads.

Landing was a trickier matter. His feet slipped on the bark, and he let go of Doc with one hand to grab at another branch. The biologist cried out as his sprained ankle banged against the trunk. Ron gritted his teeth to keep going. Ignoring the ripping sensation across his back as his arms struggled to hold his weight and Doc's, he gently lowered the other man onto the broad join of their chosen branch.

Doc scrambled a little but managed to hold on, his legs draped on either side. Ron let him go and concentrated on getting himself into a safe position.

"Great Ghost of Ursus. That was… most unexpected." Doc peered down at the ground below. The bear circled the tree, glaring at them. "Can you do it again?"

"What?" Ron looked at him in surprise. If he was thinking about running freaking scientific tests…

"You've heard the old folk saying about how to tell what type of bear is attacking you? Climb a tree. If it climbs up after you, it's a black bear. If it shakes the tree until you fall out, it's a brown bear. If it knocks the tree down, it's a grizzly. If there are no trees, it's a polar bear." Doc's smile looked a little shaky as he gestured back at the ground. "That's a black bear. He might decide to come up after us."

"Oh." Ron looked around, spotting another tall pine thirty feet away.

"I might be able to make the tree over there."

"Your confidence is not encouraging. Let's see if I can dissuade him." Doc pulled his little pistol out of his pocket and fired a flash-bang at the bear, who was beginning to hunch his way up the trunk. The red flaming pinwheel and loud bangs were too much for the beleaguered predator. The bear dropped down and took off into the woods. "That should work if we give him time to get far away."

"Are you all right?" Ron asked anxiously. Doc looked quite pale, and his mittens were curled into fists.

"Sore but considerably better than the alternative." Doc studied Ron. "Quite the jump, my boy. Explains why you were asking about Ekurru."

"It's part of the reason." To his surprise, Ron wasn't upset about having revealed his secret to Doc. His brain kept trying to lock him down in paranoia, but his muscles stayed relaxed. He could focus on the situation instead of preparing to flee as fast as he could.

"Part of the legends is true. It's a sanctuary for those who are different." Doc's significant glance left no doubt. He wasn't talking about television or food preferences, or anything equally trivial.

"You mean the *lalassu*?" Ron had never heard the word before escaping his captor's custody, but now it fell from his lips easily.

"Not just *lalassu*. The Marked," Doc said as if the two words explained everything.

Maybe he should have stayed for the remedial classes with the Harrises.

"The Marked are *lalassu* whose gifts have physically marked them. They only have a few choices: find sanctuaries like Ekurru, stay mobile and avoid attention, or play up their gifts as sideshow attractions," Doc explained, a hint of anger in his voice.

Ron struggled to understand. "Sideshows? Like from the circus?"

"Not all of them. Even at the height of sideshows, only a small portion were *lalassu*. Most were a mix of theatrical makeup and genetic outliers." Doc leaned back against the trunk, struggling to find a comfortable position. "My grandfather worked for one of those shows. He told me all sorts of stories about when he was a boy, told me there were any number of mysterious and fantastical beings in this world. I never thought I'd meet any until I came up here."

"What happened?" Ron began to wonder if he'd been the only person to not suspect the existence of the *lalassu*.

"I stumbled into Ekurru, quite literally. I'd been chasing two cubs, Litonya and her brother, Lokni. Their mother was killed by another bear, and I tried to take care of them for a time." Doc paused, and Ron suspected the biologist was holding something back. "It took some time to convince them I was harmless. Luckily, Bill came in to speak in my defense."

"Bill knows?" Ron interrupted in his surprise.

"Only a few people up here don't know. You, Steve, and Dr. Damali. This isn't something we tell transients." Doc sighed. "I wish you had told me earlier. We could have saved everyone a lot of worry."

"It's not something I want to advertise. It's already gotten me into enough trouble." Ron hesitated to explain the truth. He wasn't really one of the *lalassu*, just an escaped experiment.

"What about your family?"

Ron looked away. "We don't really talk anymore. I've disappointed them a lot." They would still be wondering what happened to him, a nagging ache throughout the day. His mother used to scan the newspapers, looking for drug-related deaths. She and his father would be dreading hearing from some official, telling them their son never pulled his life back together. Ron hoped to spare Nada's family some of the same wondering. "I didn't know Ekurru was connected to the *lalassu*. I only wanted to bring Nada home."

Doc's spectacles fogged up from the tears in his eyes. "When she didn't arrive, I suspected… though I'd hoped for something else. She was a good lady. When Lily gets back, we can take you to her family."

Ron had carried the box for months, but now he realized he'd have to look into the eyes of Nada's family, knowing that if he'd been faster or smarter, they would still have a mother and grandmother. How could they feel anything but hatred for him? The cowardly voice inside urged him to give the urn to Doc and Lily. They could comfort the family, and he could disappear, finding somewhere to stew in his guilt and remorse.

"Easy there, Ron. Whatever it is, let it go." Doc's tone was the same one he'd used when talking to Buttercup, coaxing and gentle.

Ron forced his emotions back into his overstuffed mental box. Now wasn't the time.

Doc glanced down, and Ron thought the man might be giving him space to recover until he asked, "Did you have a plan for getting out of the tree?"

"It's been more improvising than an actual plan," Ron admitted. "I can carry you as I jump down."

"Before we do, one more question. The people who are after you, is it because you're *lalassu?*"

Was he? Ron didn't know the answer to that. He'd been genetically altered, an experiment gone wrong. He went with a reply that avoided the tricky explanation of nature vs. experimentation. "They want to use me for what I can do."

"Understood. We should get down and go to the ranger station." Doc patted at his pockets, doing inventory.

Ron went perfectly still. "Are you turning me in?"

"What? No." Doc shook his head slightly as if the answer were obvious. "We have to let them know about the bear. He's not one of ours, and this could get bad in a hurry."

"Why?"

"It should be hibernating now. Don't they teach you anything in school these days?" Doc tried to hide his smile under the cover of his beard, but Ron saw his lips twitching.

"I slept through that class," Ron said dryly. "Besides, none of the others are sleeping. Litonya, Big Bart, Buttercup—they're all up."

"They don't exactly sleep when they hibernate. Sometimes yes, but they stay aware of what's going on around them. Bart doesn't have enough fat stored up to hibernate. He has to keep scavenging for food, although I suspect someone is feeding him. It would explain why he keeps returning to this area. Litonya is a special case. The bear down there should be like Buttercup, holed up in a warm den for the winter. If he's not, he's sick or starving. Both of those are bad. Even worse, that bear is not scared of people. He's a bad statistic waiting to happen."

Doc's explanation was plausible, but the idea of going to the local authorities set Ron's internal alarms blaring. He'd trusted his captor, and look how that ended up. The cynical side of him told him to ditch Doc at the base of the tree and start running. Someone would find the biologist before long. Since the escape, Ron had listened to that voice. It had kept him alive more times than he wanted to count.

Now his old internal voice rose over the cynicism and paranoia. He had an obligation to these people, to Doc. If this was a trap, then so be it. He'd deal with it then. But he wasn't going to run anymore. He bent and picked Doc up, balancing him easily. "Let's go find the rangers."

Despite Doc's assurances, Ron still found himself brooding as they walked to the series of squat grey-clapboard huts that made up the ranger station. Some of the buildings were for supplies, some for equipment. Doc mentioned he stored his plane in one of them. They expected to find someone in the main office, one of the first cabins they came across.

Of all the many paranoid possibilities running through his mind, walking in on a make-out session hadn't been one of them. Dr. Damali and Steve were locked in a passionate kiss, leaning against the map table, one of her legs wrapped tight around his waist and his hands busily moving under her sweater.

Doc hadn't bothered knocking, but now he banged his walking stick against the wall, causing the pair to jump and break apart. Steve flushed red with embarrassment, grabbing his Stetson and jamming it onto his head. Dr. Damali kept a Cleopatra-cool composure, her almond eyes flicking from one man to another as if considering whether to issue a complaint or an invitation.

"I suppose it's too much to expect certain standards of decorum during field assignments these days." The bristly hair around Doc's mouth thrust forward as his lips curled in disgust.

"Oh, Doc. You are priceless." Dr. Damali laughed, running her fingers through her short dark hair. "We're consenting, unattached adults. And here I thought you were a child of the free-love movement."

"What's going on, Doc?" Steve eyed Ron suspiciously, puffing out his chest as he tucked his thumbs into his belt. "Is he giving you trouble?"

"Great Ghost of Ursus, no! Where's Bill? I'd rather speak with someone who is thinking above the waist," Doc snapped.

"He's out," Dr. Damali purred. "I'm sure Steve can handle the situation."

Steve's expression twitched between being pleased and proud of her statement and wanting to maintain a certain professional demeanor.

"What brings you in?"

"I spotted a rogue bear. Not one of the local population. He's skinny and desperate and could cause problems," Doc reported. Ron admired how he'd gone ahead with the report, especially in front of Dr. Damali. Acknowledging the rogue would only give her more ammunition in their scientific squabbles.

"I'm surprised you're not suggesting feeding him like that other little rogue you adopted." Dr. Damali's eyes narrowed.

Doc lost no time rising to the bait. "Bart lost his mother. He needed to be fed and protected for another year at least. I gave him a chance to survive."

"And encouraged him to scavenge locally." Dr. Damali shrugged one shoulder. "At least your delusion of personally educating every problem bear appears to be coming to an end. Perhaps if you'd accepted a more scientific approach when I arrived, you could have avoided getting hurt."

As the tension escalated, Ron's fingers twitched to pull out a field weapon, although he hadn't worn one in years. Flooded with panic, his instincts screamed at him to lash out to protect himself. His only option was to lock himself down and try not to vomit as waves of disorienting flashbacks started to hit.

"Your narcissistic delusions of scientific adequacy aside, I fail to see how you harassing my bears would have avoided me slipping on ice." Doc stood right in front of him, but in Ron's mind, he kept flickering interchangeably with a young private in desert camouflage. Ron couldn't remember the man's name and didn't dare try now. He needed to keep himself anchored in the present. *I'm not in Afghanistan. I'm in Bear Claw, in the Arctic. Concentrate on the now, like Gerry said.*

"Now, now. Don't you know it's not popular anymore to assume women are incapable of higher intellectual pursuits?"

"I have no problem with women. This is about you and your—" Doc's voice rose with each word. The shouting mingled with memories of barked orders and cries of terror. Ron shut his eyes. *I am in Bear Claw. Afghanistan is over.*

"You all right?" Steve's words broke through the cascading memories.

Ron grabbed at the mental anchor, opening his eyes. To his relief, the overlapping images and sounds vanished, leaving only the cabin and three other people. Doc and Dr. Damali were both staring at him, although Steve looked suspicious. Ron rubbed his palms along his arms. "Yeah, I'm fine. Still getting used to the cold."

"The cold…" Steve let his voice trail off even as he shrugged his shoulders. Every inch of his posture told Ron that the ranger wasn't buying his story.

"We've given you the information. Go and chase the rogue to your heart's content, with my blessing." Doc thumped his cane on the floor as he turned to leave. He started to wobble, and Ron caught him before he could slip. The near accident didn't derail Doc's irritated exit in the slightest, and Ron hurried to catch up with him.

Doc limped back to his cabin, muttering under his breath the entire time. The sense of being watched returned, and Ron spent his time scanning the trees, hoping to spot his observer. His nerves started to feel as though they'd been splintered into raw fragments and spread out over the landscape.

Bill had left a pot of soup simmering on the low-banked coals on the stove. Ron served it up in silence while Doc finished his one-sided tirade on politically correct idiots who thought they understood nature but were actually scared of it. Ron tuned him out, trying to keep his reaction trembles contained. He thought he finally had them under control when Doc startled him with a question. "Is that what Andrew took you off for yesterday?"

"What do you mean?" The warm soup seemed to dry up on his tongue.

"Whatever happened at the ranger station. You were standing still with your neck and arms tight enough to pick up a five-hundred-pound log. You couldn't hear us anymore." Doc's tirade had vanished, replaced with concern.

"Oh." Ron bought himself some time to think by putting his soup bowl down carefully on the table without disturbing the various notebooks and papers scattered across it. "I guess that was part of it."

"You don't want to tell me." Doc's mouth folded down in sadness.

"I don't like talking about it," Ron answered honestly, the words tumbling out of him in frustration. "Talking doesn't help. Once you tell someone, then they know, and they want to know more. Is it getting better? Is it getting worse? No one ever wants to hear that it's not going to get better."

Doc nodded slowly. "I can understand that, but I think you need to let it out." He spread his fingers briefly to stop Ron's automatic retort. "Don't tell me or Andrew if you don't want to. But tell someone or something. Shout it to the trees if you have to—whatever will let it get outside of your head."

"Is everyone up here some kind of therapist?" Ron asked in exasperation.

"Not really." Doc smiled, but his eyes were still sad as he stared into the fire. "I was in the service a long time ago, and I lost friends. It's one of the reasons I first came up here. I was looking for a place where no one would be waiting for me to fall apart. But it kept coming up in my head, and I found myself telling the bears all about it. I talked until I was hoarse, and then I found myself starting to heal." He shrugged. "There are worse ways to go around it."

"Except the bears here aren't exactly normal," Ron pointed out. He heard the old pain in Doc's voice and instinctively recognized a fellow survivor. But the connection didn't mean Ron could discard his caution. Some secrets were better buried than revealed.

"Some are and some aren't. I think bears like Lokni and Litonya might be the reason for Sasquatch rumors up and down the West Coast. They're smart and don't behave the way people expect bears to behave, and so stories sprang up. But they're just as vulnerable to loss of habitat as any other animal, for all their intelligence." Doc's attention returned to the present with an almost audible click. "Enough changing the topic. You need to get yourself sorted out sooner rather than later."

"Why?" Ron clenched his fist. *As if it's that simple.*

Doc's answer surprised him. "Because of Lily. You like her, don't you?"

Ron's flushed face and abrupt severing of eye contact must have answered Doc's question adequately, because he continued.

"You need to get yourself sorted out before you break her heart. Because that girl has three determinedly protective brothers, all of whom can take out a caribou with a single rifle shot from five hundred meters."

Chapter Nine

"Your twitching is driving me crazy," Lou growled at Bob as they sat around a campfire, giving the dogs a well-deserved rest and a chance to eat and warm up. This was usually one of the best parts of the trip for Lily, when they'd break into the fresh supplies for some treats. Instead, the tension kept thickening.

Lily didn't blame her brother for his frayed temper. Bob had been jittering constantly since they left Kluane. If his knee wasn't popping up and down, then his fingers were tapping, or his head swiveled around like a barn owl, or his shoulders twitched. Some part of him stayed in perpetual motion the entire time, a nonverbal shout to *HURRY UP* before it was too late. It got on her nerves, and Lou had far less patience than she did.

"How much longer?" Bob demanded, bobbing up and down on his seat as if expecting to hear instructions to get back on the trail at any second. All his gear was packed into his multipocketed parka vest.

"The same amount of time it takes us every damn time." Lou got up and walked off into the darkness, the thick fur pelts swaying with the force of his steps. Lily had no doubt he'd left to avoid some drastic and dramatic retaliation.

"He doesn't understand." Bob's head swung around as he tried to find the dogs across the fire in the dusky half-light. "Are they ready to go again?"

Gritting her teeth, Lily tried to be sympathetic and understanding. "We all care about Evonne. None of us wants to see her hurt."

"You should have killed him!" Bob shouted back. "Not welcomed him with open arms. And legs."

His rage lashed out at Lily like a sudden squall swinging in from the ocean—the same disorienting sensation that hit when the skies were sunny one moment and swarming with thick black clouds the next, as if they'd been teleported in. Bob's continuing onslaught kept pounding at her, triggering an instinct to protect herself.

"If he goes to the press, what do you think will happen?" Bob's ugly words ricocheted from the trees, slamming into Lily from all sides. "You think the world will really welcome us with open arms and sing a song of brotherly love? When it goes wrong, who's left in the trap? Certainly not Lily Charging Bull with the option of pretending to be normal! Do you really think he'd want you if he knew you were a skinwalker? Not even human!"

"Enough!" Lily shouted back, the volume and weight of building rage surprising her. She never got involved in conflict. Grandfather had taught them to retreat rather than risk damage to the close-knit community. The dogs began to shift and bark, disturbed by the argument.

Bob hesitated as she rose to her feet. The muscles in her back were crawling with the need to attack back, and he must have seen some warning of it in her painfully rigid face. He swallowed whatever vile poison he'd been about to spew.

In that moment, Lily hoped he choked on it. "You have no idea what you're talking about. You haven't been trapped in the valley for generations, watching the world get smaller and smaller. You've known Evonne less than five years, and you think this somehow makes you an expert? You know nothing about it. You're not one of us. Are you sure this isn't your own disgust?"

Bob's pale face flushed dark purple. "How dare you—"

"How dare you!" Lily flung the accusation back in his face before he could finish. Her jaw ached from years spent biting back what she thought. The dogs' howling rang in her ears, an unearthly chorus of fear and alarm.

"I'm not the one sucking face with a murderer!" Bob jumped to his feet.

"He's not a murderer." The words didn't come easily through the swirling miasma of anger.

"Why? Because you like him? That makes you an expert because you want to fu—"

The expletive vanished in a sharp crack of knuckles on flesh as Lily slugged him. She'd never learned the art of the feminine slap. Instead, she punched him the way her brothers taught her, straight from the shoulder.

He fell backward over the log they'd been using as a seat. Her fingers ached, and a sharp pain radiated from her knuckles, but it didn't stop her from wanting to rake her claws across his face and chest. She raised her arm, feeling it grow longer and heavier.

A thickly muscled grip clamped around her wrist. She snarled and turned, ready to strike whoever might be in range.

"Back it down!" Lou thundered at her. His features blurred and refocused, swimming between her brother and a threat. Lily closed her eyes, mentally clawing to resummon her calm, but the emotional storm continued to batter at her defenses.

"You can do it, little sister. Breathe, in and out." Despite his encouraging words, Lou still held her in an unbreakable grip.

Finally, she returned enough to herself to relax. She opened her eyes and nodded at Lou.

He let her go, and she dropped to the ground, cradling her numb hand to her chest. It was too much effort to try and get back to her feet, so she curled up into a ball, ignoring the chill snow.

"Idiot!" Lou managed to inject the three syllables with scorn, sarcasm, and fury as he turned on Bob.

"I didn't… Lily, I'm sorry. I'm so worried." Bob sounded terrified and contrite. As he should, considering what he'd nearly unleashed.

"Leave her be," Lou snapped. "Go gather wood. Make yourself useful somewhere away from here!"

She heard Bob's footsteps squeaking away. Lou picked her up and held her. "It's okay, little sister. It's okay now."

Tears burst out of the swollen knot in her throat. There was simply too much emotion wracking her to hold the sobs back. A horrible jumble of shame pounded at her: the near disaster with Bob, uncertainty about Ron, guilt for wondering if Bob was right, worrying about Evonne, the heavy burden of a life of responsibility and duty. All of it was too much to bear without some kind of release.

It came and went quickly, leaving her cheeks sore and beginning to freeze from the wind. Lou let her go when she started wiping at her face with her scarf.

"Lily," he began, treading as carefully as he would on late-spring ice. "You feel strongly for this man—"

"I'm not talking about it." It couldn't be a mating. *But what else could it be?* Ron was going to leave. He would walk away, and she would be left with a few memories to stave off devastating isolation. She sprang up to her feet, stalking away from Lou. "Leave me alone."

"What are you and Evonne planning?" Lou called out.

Lily stopped, all too aware that her widened eyes and pale face gave her away too much to risk a lie. Maybe Lou would understand, given how he felt about the lack of mates. "She's feeling trapped and isolated. We both are."

"Go on." Lou gestured, impatient and irritated. He could never tolerate being simply told their conclusions. He was too much of a hunter. She needed to show him the trail and then let him take it on his own.

Picking her words carefully, Lily began. "We stay isolated because we're afraid of how people will react to us. We've assumed we would be hunted, but what if we're wrong?"

Lou got up, fury tightening his face.

Lily stepped in front of him, words tumbling out. "Evonne wants to tell Blue Eyes about the *lalassu* and the Marked."

Lou's breath hissed in through his teeth, his horror paling his face. "The *lalassu* have been a secret for thousands of years!"

"Then isn't it more than time we looked again at our policy?" Lily countered. "People are exposed to many different cultures and ideas now. It's not small, closed societies anymore. Besides, how can we keep the secret when there's so much recorded? If we reveal ourselves, we can at least control how we are portrayed." She took a deep breath. "We weren't planning to jump out and shout 'Here we are!' to everyone. Just one person."

"I'm glad you have that much sense. People might like the idea of special abilities in stories, but they'd turn on us if they thought we really had them."

"You don't know that. None of us do." Her heavy heart made it hard to drum up any real hope.

Lou nodded slowly to himself. "Have you thought about what you will have to do if he reacts badly?"

"Why do you think I've been hesitating?" She sank back down onto the log to stare into the fire.

Lou hunkered down in front of her, blocking her view. "First things first: we get home and see what we're dealing with. I know you like him, Lily. But if he's a threat, we have no choice. We can't let him leave."

Anger flared through depressive inertia. "I won't let you hurt him."

"That's not what you said before we left."

"I said I'd take care of him. I didn't say how." Lily expected another fight, but Lou simply nodded and went to check on the dogs, leaving Lily to wonder if he understood or if she now stood on the wrong side of the family line.

Ron could not sleep after Doc's offhand comment about Lily's brothers' skills with a rifle. The woods were unusually quiet with no sign of Lokni or Litonya. Just silent trees standing sentinel over snowy ground. Still, he felt the sensation of being watched. No matter which way he faced, it crawled along his back like spiders.

That girl has three determinedly protective brothers, all of whom can take out a caribou with a single rifle shot from five hundred meters. The words echoed through Ron's head yet again. His nerves kept his senses in high alert, trying to parse the shadows into the shapes of potential snipers. Out in the open, he might be vulnerable, but it was nowhere near as difficult as trying to cope with the obsessive certainty *something* was sneaking up outside the cabin. The sturdy log walls seemed like paper, sturdy enough to block sight but too fragile to stop whatever hunted him.

Despite the light of stars and moon, the darkness ruled everything except a narrow ten feet of visibility around the clearing. Anyone could be hidden beyond the dark barrier. Seen through a thermal scope, his body would stand out like a beacon against the cold trees. No matter how often he told himself that he was being paranoid, that no one could be out there sneaking up on him, his body refused to relax. Adrenaline sparked through his veins, keeping every nerve jangling in readiness.

He wanted a drink, wanted to dive into the chemically induced numbness and pull it down on top of him. Doc's bin was cleared out, but Steve looked like a man who enjoyed a beer after work. The strength of Ron's craving undermined his good sense, making a trek across unfamiliar terrain and breaking into someone's home seem like a simple matter of logistics, no worse than going to the store to pick up a bottle.

Ron pressed his hands to his temples as if he could squeeze out the siren lure calling to him. He sucked in a deep breath, the icy air freezing in his nose and mouth. All around him, cold, dark trunks reached up to the star-drenched sky. Back in his former life, he never imagined there could be so many stars visible to the naked eye. Now, in the absolute darkness, he had a front-row seat to the oldest light show in existence.

Cautiously putting each foot down to avoid the betraying crunch of snow, he concentrated on his patrol. He couldn't do anything about the clearly visible footprints, but at least they'd keep him from getting lost.

The weight of the trees and sky and snow pressed in on him, making him feel smaller and, at the same time, like a bright-red target in a grey world. The land was ancient, steady, and strong. It had faced everything in all of history and still stood, unchanged. It was harsh and unforgiving, ready to kill the unwary, unprepared, and unlucky with equanimity. But it wasn't cruel—only demanding.

Movement in the forest pulled him out of his thoughts. Something large passed quietly between the silhouetted trunks. Ron held still, letting his eyes resolve the shadows. "Litonya?"

She emerged out of the trees, the golden crescent of fur shimmering in the starlight. She huffed at him, the sharp exhalation sounding like a curious inquiry.

He smiled. "I missed you."

As soon as she stepped forward, the sense of vulnerability vanished—no more watchers crawling along his spine or sense of having a target on his back. She answered him with a rumble, one with a definite sense of agreement. She pointed her muzzle back toward the cabin.

"I couldn't sleep. My mind won't stop replaying memories," he confessed. "It happens a lot."

The bear swiped at the ground with a massive paw. Ron frowned, unsure what she was doing. Digging for food? Except she wasn't digging into the dirt. She kept sweeping until she made a snow-free patch large enough for a man to sit on.

"Is that for me?" Ron asked.

She lightly patted the clear ground again and stepped back.

Doc's idea of talking to someone sounded like a smarter plan than breaking into the home of an armed government employee in search of liquor. Recklessly, Ron decided to give it a shot. The bear couldn't ask questions or tell anyone else what he'd said. "All right, Dr. Bear's Woodland Psychology Service. Let's give it a shot."

Litonya snorted, sounding amused. She settled herself near the patch and waited for him.

Ron pulled a few thick branches off a nearby spruce and laid them over the cold ground for insulation. Then he made either the smartest or stupidest decision of his life. He sat down.

Litonya gave off a low rumble of satisfaction and approval.

"You want me to spill all my secrets?" From where Ron sat, he could see the bear clearly. Her deep-set brown eyes invited confession. "It's not pretty."

Her shoulders shrugged as if she wanted to disagree but was too polite to argue with a guest. Ron chuckled at himself. Ursine therapy. He was about to launch into the most painful details of his life less than a foot away from an animal that could kill him. Even Doc had kept his distance from the bears this afternoon. If he told anyone about this, even Doc, they'd think he was crazy. Maybe he was.

"It started when I got posted overseas. I was excited. I'd wanted to be a soldier since I was a little kid. I'd make my family proud and be one of the heroes in camo gear. I saw myself as a protector, standing up to bullies and keeping families safe." Ron could clearly remember his idealistic feelings, but they no longer felt entirely real. They were more like something he'd read somewhere or seen in a movie. "It wasn't like I thought it would be when I got over there. Sometimes my fellow soldiers were a bigger danger than any of the hostile terrorists we were supposed to be fighting. They'd bully people they saw as weaker, taking whatever they wanted from them. Sometimes the commanders took care of it, and sometimes they let it go, saying it wasn't important. It was more important to keep the sense of camaraderie."

Litonya balanced her forelegs on the ground and rested her head on them. She stood close enough for Ron to feel the heat radiating from her body. He continued. "Mostly, I did convoy duty. Driving stuff and people from point A to point B. It sounds simple, like a delivery guy but with more sand." Ron shook his head at his naïveté. "Except you've got snipers shooting at you and IEDs hiding under roadside trash, and you never know if the kid running toward you is wanting candy or is planning to explode. It screwed with everything I thought I knew, and I got numb. I couldn't tell the bad guys from the good guys anymore. So I focused on doing my job and staying alert. I told myself: *don't think about the possibilities.* I wouldn't let myself think about home or what my family would say if they knew how I was acting."

He smiled, leaning back to stare at the sky. "I had a couple good friends in my squad. Adam and Brian. Those guys were freaking funny. Brian always played these practical jokes on people. Like swapping out nametags on gear when it went to get cleaned. Adam did impressions. He did Obama and Clinton so good you'd swear they were in front of you. He could imitate our CO, and one time Brian convinced him to do it over the radio. They ordered a couple boxes of whiskey from supply. And when it arrives, the two of them look as surprised as everyone else. The CO goes red in the face, shouting at everyone, trying to find out who did it. We never told anyone it was us." The urge to laugh faded, and he took a deep swallow before continuing.

"We were delivering food and ammo to a forward group when we got a call that the compound they were using had been laced with explosives. Some of their guys found them the hard way. Bomb unit would have taken more than a day to get there, and this place was supposed to be majorly strategic, so we were ordered to help with the sweep." They'd had basic training, but none of them were qualified to deal with bombs. He'd thought at the time that maybe they should protest, try and convince command to wait until the experts could get there, but Adam and Brian thought it would be great fun. Ron agreed easily enough, seeing a chance to be a hero again. The weight of that mistake never stopped tugging at the raw wounds in his mind.

"We pulled the trucks up behind some basic shelter, met up with the others. They said there were at least two snipers positioned outside the walls. The snipers had shot two of the guys trying to get away from the explosions. The squad shot back, and there hadn't been any more activity when they collected the wounded and brought them to the back of the compound." Why hadn't he insisted on fresh recon? The guilt swelled in his throat, making it hard to talk.

Litonya offered a low rumble like a mother giantess trying to sing a lullaby. Her eyes looked sad, as if she understood every word. Ron scrubbed at his eyes. Maybe Doc was right about being born in the wrong body. She seemed more human than the lost souls he'd fallen in with after Afghanistan. The compassion in her eyes made it easier to continue. Doc had been right: talking to someone, even a bear, helped. "We were being careful even though we thought the worst was over. Careless gets you dead in a hurry out there. We all knew that lesson. We unloaded the supplies so we could take the wounded back on the truck. Not great, but choppers wouldn't come into the area. It was really quiet out there. Most forward places, you hear gunfire in the distance, or explosions. In the back, you hear ordinary sounds, goats or kids, people talking. Out there, nothing. Even the wind was quiet."

Despite the years, the memory still hit him with a percussive force strong enough to knock him off his feet if he'd been standing. "Suddenly, the back half of the compound went up in bright-yellow fire. The shock wave knocked me back. It felt like the noise of the explosion shoved me down before the fire could get to me. I couldn't move." If only he'd been able to move...

"Adam and Brian were behind some cover. They got up right away to start pulling people out of the fire. Never hesitated, just ran as if they'd done it a thousand times before." He closed his eyes, his face contorted in grief. "Bastards ran right into enemy fire."

Litonya huffed in sympathy and surprise. He couldn't cope with opening his eyes as he heard her weight shifting. He didn't care anymore if she was leaving or coming to eat him—he was trapped deep inside the cursed memory, forced to relive it without any hope of altering the outcome.

He saw the first bullet hit before he heard the blast of gunfire. It plowed into Adam's shoulder, knocking him backward. Adam's helmet fell off as he tumbled onto his back. He always forgot to do up the chin straps. Ron's body ached all over from the pulverizing blast of the explosion, every nerve signal shrilling an alarm of major damage. He needed to help his friend. His future self screamed at his past self to move faster, that time was running out, but the second shot still hit Brian before Ron could manage to pull himself to his knees. Blood sprayed across the dusty sand, the grains drinking it up to leave rusty remnants behind.

He looked to the side and saw the sniper. The bastard wasn't even trying to hide—he was perched up on the wall with his rifle. A third shot ended Adam's life and Ron's grip on sanity and common sense.

Pain got shoved into a mental box, and Ron ran at the sniper. He didn't shout. If he'd made a noise, the man might have had time to pull his head out of the scope and shoot him, too. Instead, Ron leapt up onto the top of the hood of the jeep parked beneath the wall. The other man heard the thud of him landing, but Ron was too close by then. Another few steps, and he grabbed the sniper, yanking him down into the compound. The rifle was poorly assembled and broke into pieces when it hit the ground. Ron pounded the man with his fists as the sniper struggled to break free. The burst of adrenaline had only lasted long enough to knock the son of a bitch out before collapsing beside him, struggling to breathe through cracked ribs.

"I could see Brian only a few feet away from me," Ron heard himself say. "He was still alive. He had a hole in his throat, and he was still alive. He was terrified. I'd never seen him scared before. And then he went away. His face and body went slack. One second I could see the person, and the next, there was just some meat that kind of looked like someone I used to know. Not even a whole second. No transition. Just one thing and then something else."

Thick fur tickled his hands as they rested on his knees. Opening his eyes, he saw Litonya had moved closer and was only inches away. She watched him out of one eye while gently brushing against him with the long, soft fur around her neck. It never occurred to him to be afraid. Instead, he leaned forward, burying his face in her ruff as the tears came.

She smelled of pine and sweet berries. "I should have gone to help him instead of taking out the sniper. There were other guys there, firing at him. They had to hold back when I attacked. Maybe I could have helped—" He squeezed his eyes shut again and thudded back against the tree. So many people had told him again and again that he couldn't have saved Brian even if he'd tried. But they couldn't know. People surprised doctors all the time.

An odd low rumble, like a cat purring, echoed through the air. Ron made himself finish. "The squad drove me and the other injured back. Got me to the medics in time. I spent weeks in the hospital. Turns out between the blast and the attack, I got some pretty major internal injuries. I've never hurt like that before. Like the pain was trying to force me out of my body so it could take over." Litonya felt sturdy under his hands and strong enough to take any pain and draw it out of him. Like a primal Mother Earth.

"They fixed me up, gave me therapy to help me walk again, slapped a medal on my chest, and sent me home. Called me a survivor, but they didn't know. My friends died because I pretended I could still be a hero. It made me feel dead inside, like I died that day, except my body kept moving around. My folks didn't really know what to do with me. I'd wake up screaming in the night, ready to slash at anything near me. The only thing that helped was having a good stiff drink or two before bed. But then it wasn't only one drink. Pretty soon it was a whole bottle. They took me to AA, where I found another vet who told me about other things that could take the screams away. Pot, heroin, Vicodin… I tried them all." He winced, remembering how desperate he'd been for the next fix—whatever would drive the anxiety away.

"My folks tried to make me stop, but they didn't get it. I walked out, started living on the streets so I wouldn't disappoint them anymore. It was easier to get drugs, and since they made the screaming in my head stop, they were all I cared about." Ron found himself rubbing his fingers over his inner elbow. He'd swear he could feel the rough track marks even through the parka. He forced his hand away, hot shame burning away at his resolve to be honest. "I've done so many things I can't live with, Litonya. I wish I had died back there. I wouldn't have disappointed my family, and I wouldn't have spent the last years living a nightmare.

Without the drinks, my head thinks I'm still back there. I'm always checking for snipers and bombs. I can't live like this, always running on screaming fear, trying to stay alert." But he realized that he didn't feel that way now. He trusted Litonya to warn him if anyone came close. He pulled back, stroking the bear's fur.

"I should leave," he said quietly.

Litonya shook her head and made a disgusted sound.

"I should, but I don't want to," Ron continued. "I'm starting to feel like myself again. Like I might not have killed the only good side of myself. It gives me hope that I can go home someday and show my family that they were right not to give up hope for me. I feel like I'm coming back to myself here. I like helping Doc out. This place feels bigger and more intimidating than anywhere I've ever lived. But I like it and… I like Lily."

His quiet confession sparked a reaction in the giant animal beside him. Litonya began to purr again. Ron chuckled. "She's not like anyone I've ever met before. When she's there, everything gets brighter and warmer. And when she smiles… it's like the sun."

With that thought, his mood tumbled again. "She wouldn't want to be with me if she knew what happened. She shouldn't have to deal with stuff like this. And her brothers would use it as an excuse to run me out of here. I don't want to walk away, though. Guess that makes me crazy, huh?"

Litonya shook her head before lifting it suddenly, growling.

Ron got to his feet, his joints numb and stiff. His bare hand stayed buried in Litonya's fur, letting her senses guide him. Her fur was so thick he couldn't reach the skin beneath, only a springy cushion of shaggy hairs. The world stopped being terrifyingly unpredictable, and everything seemed to slot into place. His senses sharpened, collecting information on all levels. The forest might be visually impenetrable, but he could hear sighing wind and creaking branches. Vibrations filtered up through his boots, and he could feel, rather than hear, Litonya's growl rumbling through her fur.

A few crunching steps were his only warning before Andrew emerged out of the forest twilight. He looked down at Ron's hand on Litonya's shoulder, and his eyebrow shot up in judgmental surprise.

Litonya reared up on her hind legs, still growling. She stood between Ron and Andrew, dwarfing the two of them. She didn't seem friendly anymore. Now she looked like the dangerous predator from documentaries and movies.

Andrew reached into his pocket and pulled out a small wide-mouthed pistol. When he aimed it at Litonya, Ron didn't hesitate. He shoved her aside, although it felt more like trying to shove a parked car away. Then he threw himself at the other man to spoil his aim.

He only had time to grab Andrew's arm when the gun went off. The two of them fell against the tree and went sprawling across the snow. *No! Not again!* Ron's brain kept screaming at him, everything falling into a hyperalert state as he prepared for his next attack.

Andrew broke free of Ron's grip and rolled easily to his feet. He raised the gun again, and Ron shouted at Litonya, "Hurry! Run!"

He jumped at Andrew, but the other man sidestepped him and fired. Flashbacks of Nada's death sprayed across his mind—how the bright flash burned across his retina while his mind screamed for his body to do something. *Anything!* Despair ripped away any thought of self-preservation, and everything moved in slow motion as he prepared to take Andrew down. It didn't matter what the other man did. Ron would take whatever damage was dished out as long as he could strike back in return.

A whirling firecracker exploded against the trees, sparking and banging loud enough to wake the dead. Litonya growled again, dropping to all fours.

"Go," Andrew ordered as though scolding an errant younger sibling.

Ron hung in a miasma of uncertainty. A second before, he'd been ready to die to avenge Litonya's death, except Andrew was firing the same sort of flash-bang rounds that Doc used. They were meant to drive away, not to hurt. Litonya met Ron's anguished gaze. She stepped toward him as if to protect him yet again.

"Please, don't let him hurt you," Ron whispered, ignoring the sharp glance Andrew fired his way. He spoke only to the bear. "Please."

She backed into the woods, her wary gaze never leaving Andrew and Ron. Her giant shadow merged seamlessly with the night's shade under the trees.

"Are you quite satisfied?" Andrew asked, completely ignoring the fact that he was covered in snow.

"I thought you were going to shoot her." Ron blinked frost from his eyes. His body and senses were struggling to return to functional normality.

"Shoot a grizzly. With a pistol." Andrew's tone made it perfectly clear what a stupid assumption it was.

Ron slowly got to his feet, feeling foolish. He'd seen Doc use something similar, but in the heat of the moment, a nonlethal option hadn't occurred to him. There was no sign of Litonya anywhere. His body was stiff with cold, and it annoyed him that Andrew had no trouble moving smoothly as he brushed clinging ice crystals off his clothing.

"You were lucky I came along when I did," Andrew continued. "Were you planning on dying of hypothermia or the more traditional route of being eaten?"

"I came outside to think. And she didn't try to hurt me." Defending Litonya was entirely natural.

"Not even Doc takes such foolish chances. Do I have to escort you to the cabin?" Andrew tilted his head back so that he could look down his nose at Ron.

As if he could get lost when it stood less than twenty feet away, the only source of light visible. "I'll be fine." Ron didn't break eye contact. He had no intention of allowing Lily's brother to bully him.

"Then I will leave you here. Enjoy your evening." Andrew began trekking in the opposite direction, back the way he came.

Ron watched him go, unwilling to show anything that might be construed as weakness. It was a foolish tactic. Competing with Andrew on a survivalist level was a nonstarter given that the other man had grown up in the North. But Ron's pride had taken a heavy blow tonight.

Andrew never looked back, and Ron returned to the cabin. The unpleasant encounter hadn't spoiled the sense of relief from telling his story to Litonya. He'd never told anyone else what exactly had happened—not the commanders debriefing him, not the therapists the military had assigned. Not even his family.

Instead, he'd told a grizzly bear. *Not any bear*, he corrected himself. *Litonya.*

He hoped she wasn't hurt from the flash-bang. Even if sparks fell on her, they hopefully hadn't been able to penetrate her heavy coat.

Doc was still sleeping when Ron eased himself back into the cabin and crawled into his cot. For once, his brain felt tired enough to let him surrender to exhaustion. Closing his eyes, Ron let out a deep breath and prepared to slip into sleep.

Until his mind jolted him awake with a very important question: what had Andrew been doing out in the forest in the middle of the night?

CHAPTER TEN

Vincent hated being cold. And ever since his family had shipped him up north, he'd been cold. Even sitting practically on top of the fire only meant part of him got warm. The half of his body away from the flames stayed frigid.

They should have killed me. He'd heard all the excuses. Gerry Charging Bull would be able to heal him. The shaman knew more about the mind and spirit than any *lalassu* living. The injuries the Beast had inflicted were all internal, invisible to science and medicine. The healers in New York hadn't been able to do anything for nonorganic damage. They couldn't tell if the Beast left something behind, perhaps some kind of sleeper command that could have him waking up with his family dead at his feet.

Eric is the one who killed someone. I didn't do anything. Yet he'd ended up getting exiled while his brother stayed home. Typical fucking Harris family logic. Shove the problem somewhere out of sight and then never speak of it again.

The bark of his chosen tree bit roughly through his jeans, and the tips of his fingers were numb. He heard snatches of McBride sharing with the bloody bear. The animal was even larger than the bears in the Colony. Something about war trauma. *You think you've had fucking trauma? Try getting mind-fucked by some asshole and then kicked out by your family.*

He should be curled up in his hovel, not sleeping. He never slept more than a few hours anymore. Instead, he spent the never-ending Arctic nights roaming through the trees, watching Ron Fucking McBride circle blindly around the cottage and play with a bear who could eat him without pausing to chew.

When he'd first heard rumors of a lost hiker, Vincent suspected an agent of the Beast's, sent to kill or capture him. Recognizing McBride came as a complete shock, but Vincent wasn't ruling out the idea that the ex-soldier might be an agent. McBride had been the Beast's planned poster boy, after all.

But Vincent hadn't seen anything other than the same restless nights and taut anxiety that he suffered from himself. They were both broken.

A sudden bang made him jump and curse himself for losing focus. Know-It-All Andrew was struggling with Fucking McBride while the bloody bear looked ready to kill them both.

Vincent leaned forward. This could be the moment he'd been waiting for.

Except the tussle didn't last long. The two men switched to arguing. His hopes sank as he realized it wasn't a real fight. This wasn't the moment when McBride proved himself to be the real traitor. A hateful little voice inside him reminded him that the Beast could have created two traitors as easily as one.

Who am I kidding? This was never going to end in any kind of good way. Each word in his thoughts weighed him down like a massive stone placed on his shoulders. They held him in place, locking him into numb misery.

"Are you quite finished imitating a Popsicle?" Andrew's nearby voice slashed ineffectively through the crushing mental stone.

Ah, sweet sarcasm. The rapier verbal thrust to distract and discourage. Vincent remembered wielding it well. He refused to acknowledge Andrew's presence and continued to stare at the silent forest—at least until something tugged on the rope holding him in the tree, and he went tumbling to the ground at the other man's feet. He glared up at the shaman, who was wrapped in his puffy layers. Andrew should have looked ridiculous, but instead, he looked dignified and disappointed, like a butler discovering his employer's children playing with the antiques.

"Perhaps we'll try advanced knot tying as part of your therapy." Andrew did not offer him a hand up.

Pain shot through Vincent's chemically numbed senses. He'd have giant bruises dotting his shoulder and legs from where he'd landed. At least his feral abilities allowed him to roll enough to prevent serious injury. He glared up at Andrew.

"I will never understand why visitors to our fair park are so determined to freeze to death, but allowing it would reflect badly on our hospitality. It's time to go back."

"What do you fucking care?" Vincent struggled to his feet, his jeans starting to grow cold and wet from melting snow.

"I could go into a lengthy lecture about you being my patient or you spying on my sister or the risk you pose to my community—the same old tunes you've heard before. Tell me why you are so determined to destroy yourself, and I'll consider leaving you to it." Andrew shrugged as if indifferent to the outcome.

"Why isn't McBride locked up?" Vincent blurted, shoving his numb fingers into his jacket pocket.

Andrew quirked a sardonic brow. "We don't have a prison. And if you are implying that you are a prisoner, then we are doing a poor job of containing you."

"I know why I'm here. Everyone's afraid of what the Beast left in my head. What about McBride's?" Vincent seized the opportunity to lash out in order to see someone else hurting worse than he did. A deeper part of him felt ashamed over his pettiness, but it was buried beneath layers of pain and anger. He was tired of being the worst case in sight.

"You refused to work with us to determine the extent of your mental injuries. You threatened to kill us if we even tried, which caused considerable difficulty in treatment." Andrew's mild words left Vincent feeling like a scolded child.

Perversely, it made him want to throw an even more immature tantrum—stomp his feet and scream that it wasn't *fair*! Instead, he mumbled, "He's dangerous."

"We're all dangerous in the right circumstances. The more interesting question is why you are so determined to wallow in a past not of your choosing?"

But I did choose it. Dani had resisted. Eric had resisted. Even McBride had resisted, to a point. Vincent was the only one who swallowed the Beast's influence whole and didn't look back. The man convinced him that murdering a random person as part of a product demonstration was an acceptable way of doing business. Vincent had spent days locked in a concrete box after being shot by a guard while trying to escape. Even after that, he found himself forgiving the Beast.

When he struggled to picture the man who had held him, his memories refused to sharpen, staying as blurry shadows without context or detail. A part of him still saw the Beast as a savior instead of his enemy, someone who would lead him away from the terrifying uncertainty of a life lived on the edge of society. He'd spent too many days scrounging for cash in day-labor jobs. He'd liked the idea of being rich and powerful, a valuable commodity. He'd never be hungry again, and all that Scarlett O'Hara stuff. He'd wanted it so badly he'd been ready to fight for the privilege of a golden collar and chains.

Right up until the moment the Beast left him on the tarmac, he'd have gone with them, done anything for them. And they'd walked away without even considering him. As if he'd never existed. That moment had shattered him into tiny splinters.

Even now, he'd go back to them in a minute if they appeared, like a faithful dog returning to its abusive owners again and again. It sickened him, and as much as people told him to blame the Beast, what had happened was his own fault. The knowledge kept him in his squalid shack, sucking up whatever intoxicants were available—anything to blur the certainty branded in his mind. He'd wanted it. Which meant he deserved whatever happened to him.

"I see," Andrew said quietly. He glanced up at Vincent's perch. "Quite ingenious, really. I assume you traveled a fair distance by tree before setting up here, avoiding leaving tracks."

Vincent glared at him. The bastard wasn't a telepath, so he had no business pretending he knew what went on in Vincent's mind.

"I think we'll try a new approach in the morning. For now, I would like to get some sleep before dawn." Andrew helped Vincent up. Cold, wet, and exhausted, he didn't bother to resist. Glancing back at the darkened cabin, he wished McBride a rotten, nightmare-filled night.

"You want to travel to North America under your own identity." Karan barely managed to keep the word *idiot* out of the sentence. He held out his boss's coat for Dalhard to slip his arms into, playing the role of the helpful assistant.

Freshly shaved and dressed in a designer suit, Dalhard looked like his former self, only a little thinner. His ordeal only showed in the looseness of the jacket across his shoulders and paper-like wrinkling of his skin. Even diminished, the man still struck a powerful chord of intimidation. It was his eyes, Karan decided. They still were not quite sane. People would instinctively pull back, their instincts warning of an unpredictable predator. "We need to put the nail in these inconvenient investigations."

"I sanitized our business records, but we could still be facing possible assault or even murder charges if the Harrises end up testifying." Karan hoped he could convince his employer to take the prudent path for once.

"They won't." Dalhard examined himself in a mirror, studying the nuances of his changed appearance.

Karan would not allow himself to be swept up in his employer's delusions again. "You cannot be certain. They worked with the policeman, Detective Joe Cabrera. McBride might be hiding in Canada, but it does not mean he has not contacted the American authorities. We should travel under false papers until they are all back under our control."

Dalhard smirked. "They won't testify. You should have more faith in me, Karan."

"Do you have assurances you have not shared?" Irrational anger threatened to burst Karan's meticulous control. His ability to succeed depended on predicting all possibilities and planning for them. To discover his boss withheld vital information threatened everything he worked for.

"Watch yourself, Karan. You work for me. Not the other way around." Dalhard frowned.

Not yet. Compose yourself. "My apologies, sir."

Dalhard straightened, trying to adjust the suit to a proper fit. "They won't testify because I won't allow it. It's an old failsafe, one my mother and I perfected. Those who come under my influence are unable to speak against me or act against my interest. They can't even say my name in a negative context."

"I see." Karan laid out an assortment of ties for his employer to choose from. A failsafe against testifying could be useful if it were real. His boss had overestimated his own abilities before.

"My mother read a great deal of science fiction. She claimed it was the best source for truly understanding the possibilities. She became fascinated with a set of programming laws for robots to make them into the perfect servants. It took a great deal of fine-tuning for us to realize how to replicate them and how to plant them deeply enough to ensure they would be effective." Dalhard selected a deep-blue tie with a subtle pattern in the weave. "She disliked killing. It creates too clear a trail even in the best of circumstances."

A prudent observation. Karan began to recalculate the optimal path. He had not trusted his informants when they told him no witnesses had come forward to testify against his employer. He believed they were waiting to see if the business investigation bore fruit before committing themselves. After all, the siblings lived on the fringes of society, and the soldier was a drug addict. None were the sort of "good" witnesses a district attorney preferred before launching an indictment.

Karan had prepared records that would further sully the reputations of witnesses, should any choose to come forward. If his employer's claims were true, then they'd be doubly reluctant, giving Dalhard and himself a significant safety margin.

"Your mind has always been your chief asset, Karan. It gets so tiring to have to explain everything in excruciating detail. You see it all clearly now." Dalhard's smile did nothing to soften the anticipatory thrill in his eyes. "They don't have enough to cause us any real problems."

True enough. The brothers and soldier should still be under conditioning, including the failsafe. Danielle Harris had broken free of her conditioning, but her direct knowledge of events was limited. What she had seen could be explained and minimized. After all, she had been in their custody less than six hours, which made charges of kidnapping and coercion difficult. The building destruction had all the proper permits, albeit inserted into the system after the fact.

His old partner still posed a challenge. Given Caligo's connections to the Priestesses, Karan could guess how Dalhard's financial information had been leaked to the authorities. He might be able to undo their work of sanitizing the records. However, Karan could be certain his old partner would not insert false information in an effort to incriminate. Caligo always held himself to an inconvenient moral code.

He looked up to see his employer watching him through the mirror. Karan flinched, instinct overcoming a lifetime's practice of controlling his emotions. Dalhard's mask of sanity and purpose had fallen aside, leaving naked spite and obsession.

"I want them, Karan. They must be crushed. Destroyed as if they never existed." Dalhard hissed the words.

Karan could understand his boss's need for revenge and would even help him, at least for the time being. After that, he would recalculate the potential ratio of risk and reward. It all came down to the numbers.

Ron watched the darkness of night shift into the greyish twilight of the Arctic morning. He gave up pretending to sleep and went to stoke the stove to warm the cabin. Doc got up a little while later and started some water for oatmeal.

"Rough night?" Doc asked, limping on his birch-bark cast. He gripped the furniture to help him navigate.

"A lot to think about." Ron poured hot water for tea.

"Want to talk about it?"

"Hell, no." Ron shook his head emphatically.

Doc laughed, pouring hot water into his mug for tea. "Even without sleeping, you look better than you did yesterday. I'd guess you took my advice and talked to the trees last night." He raised his hand to stop Ron's protest. "I won't pry. But I'm glad it's out of your head for a while. A man shouldn't have to live with his demons full-time."

"They're never going to go away," Ron said quietly to himself, accepting a steaming bowl of cereal.

"You'd be surprised what goes away in time—lost opportunities, words you regret, mistakes you would take back in a heartbeat. Time grinds them all away like stones on a seashore. It's only when we insist on recarving them day after day that they stay deep and fresh." Doc smoothed his beard into his shirt and started on breakfast.

Ron paused, spoon in hand. "Very deep. You should write it down. Doc's Words of Wisdom from the North."

Doc grinned. "Then there'd be a never-ending stream of people pounding their way to my cabin, eager to do anything for my teachings. I'd never get to see the bears."

Ron surprised himself by barking out a spurt of laughter.

Doc's grin spread even wider. "That's good to see. When you first came here, you looked like a dead man walking. Everything as serious as a death sentence."

"Everything feels lighter now." Even the unseen watchers were gone. "Lily's due back today, isn't she?"

"Is she what it takes to make you smile?" Doc chuckled and sipped at his tea. "I can show you the way after breakfast."

Ron couldn't deny that the idea of seeing Lily again put a smile on his face. When they were together, things were simpler and less overwhelming. She'd woken up his heart and his body. He thought about her all the time, which caused physical complications that hadn't been a problem since the early days of high school.

The idea of a relationship without strings still made him uncomfortable, but his desire to be with Lily overrode that. He reminded himself that both of them understood this was a temporary situation and, eventually, he would have to leave. Hopefully, he'd do it as a better man than the one who'd arrived.

As he and Doc trekked through the woods, Ron noticed the biologist moving easier than he had the previous day. Which meant he hadn't permanently damaged Doc's sprain by jumping them up the tree. Anticipation and the lack of tension left him giddy, and he reminded himself Lily might not be back, and even if she was, she might have changed her mind.

He heard the dogs long before they got to the clearing where Lily's family cabin sat, a steep-sided log structure built to the small scale he was beginning to find normal. A few other structures huddled nearby, and the lack of chimneys or smoke led Ron to guess they were for storage. Squat raised boxes were scattered between the buildings—a veritable forest of doghouses.

"Looks like they're back. I don't see too many empty spots." Doc wiggled his fingers at the sled dogs in greeting.

The door opened as they came close. Ron recognized Andrew and guessed that the other man, dressed entirely in layers of leather and fur, must be Lou. The brothers' eyes widened briefly in surprise.

Andrew opened his mouth to say something, but Lou put his hand on his shoulder and shook his head. "This is more important."

Andrew didn't look pleased with his twin's interference but didn't argue. Instead, he fixed Ron with a sharp look. "I will come for you after lunch. Be ready."

Ron nodded, irritated with the delivery but too eager to proceed to make a protest. If sweating in a tent and talking to bears could accomplish what two years of therapy couldn't, he'd sweat his skin off and talk until his voice was gone. He would do whatever he had to.

Three short steps led down into the cabin, making it larger inside than the outside suggested. *Built below ground level for warmth.* Every time he thought he understood life here, he'd be hit with a new reminder of how harsh and precarious living above the Arctic Circle could be.

He'd expected the inside to be dark and cramped, but the cabin's single room was surprisingly bright, lit by a few small windows high in the south-facing wall. It was also eerily quiet, and Ron realized he didn't hear the underlying hum of a generator like the one at Doc's. A large table and benches took up most of the room, but Ron noticed a curtain, stretched across an alcove near the kitchen, in nature-true shades of brown and green intermingled randomly to evoke leaves and shade. Instinctively, Ron guessed it marked Lily's space.

"So, the stranger comes to visit at last," a dry, gravelly voice pronounced.

Ron managed to avoid jumping in response, though his heart pounded hard enough to make his temples throb. Gerry sat on a battered but comfortable chair, clearly visible. Yet Ron had been completely unaware of his presence until the old man spoke. Even now, his eyes tried to skip over the old man rather than focus on him.

Doc chuckled. "Playing an old Indian trick?"

A ghost of a smile flickered in the depths of Gerry's eyes, the only sign of amusement in his otherwise impassive features. Ron relaxed slightly. He wouldn't have guessed the old man had any trace of practical joker in him. "Let's say my schedule hasn't been entirely my own choosing."

Doc barked out his laughter, plunking himself down on the bench and stretching out his injured leg. "You have to give him a point for that, Gerry."

"I suppose I do." Lily's grandfather turned his piercing stare toward Doc. "Has he come to make his honorable intentions clear?"

Ron hesitated. Was this another joke or some kind of tribal custom? He could still barely accept his decision to stay. His instincts kept shrilling a danger alert at him.

"Of all the idiotic things to say." Lily's voice came through the closed door seconds before it slammed open. She stopped on the stairs down. "Oh."

"Hi." Ron started to wonder if he'd presumed too much. Lily didn't look as though she'd only just arrived from a long journey. Realizing she must have come back the previous night but not visited him brought a swamping wave of disappointment. Maybe a few days apart had brought her the distance her family hoped for.

A slow smile crept across her cheeks. "They didn't tell me you were here."

Gerry interrupted the poignantly awkward reunion. "Lily, remember what we have spoken of."

The blooming smile retreated far more swiftly than it had appeared. Lily looked stricken by her grandfather's words, and Ron found himself easing his weight forward to place himself between them. She visibly wrenched her attention back to Ron. "This house is starting to feel a little crowded. Would you like to join me for a walk?"

He nodded, glancing briefly at Doc, who waved the couple on quite happily. Once they were both outside, he couldn't help exhaling sharply.

"I know, they're a lot sometimes." Lily took his hand. "I missed you."

Her admission sent his doubts into retreat. Whatever was happening between them, he hadn't lost his chance with her. He couldn't stop fondling the slender imprint of her fingers through the soft leather of their mittens. "I missed you, too. I've been thinking about you nonstop."

"Me too," she replied softly, her long lashes caressing her cheeks the way he longed to. "How did the sweat lodge go?"

"I think it might actually be working. I'd forgotten what it felt like to not be crushed under fear, not thinking, only reacting." Ron took a deep breath. "I'm not running anymore. I won't spend my life like that."

"Does that mean you're giving Bear Claw a chance?" Lily smiled.

"More than a chance. You all have given me an incredible gift. I still worry about putting you all in danger, though." He reminded himself not to get too caught up in the high of recovery. It was just as treacherous and artificial as any chemical equivalent.

"We're not entirely defenseless here."

"I know. But I don't think I could live with myself if you got hurt." He bent his head to kiss her.

"Wait." She stepped back. "Not here with my family right around the corner."

"Do you have somewhere else in mind?" Anticipation left him hard and aching.

"I have my own private sanctuary." Lily took his hand and led him toward the woods. Ron resisted the impulse to go in and say a proper good-bye to his host. His grandfather's lessons in politeness and manners warred with the building pressure in his veins.

"Does your family bother you that much?" he asked softly as they walked.

"I've lived my life in their protective shadow. They're all terrified something will happen to me."

"Why you in particular?" he asked. "Is it a protective guy thing?"

"Yes, but not in the way that you think. There aren't many of us left." Lily held aside a branch as she led Ron through a narrow gap between pine trees. "No one wants to contemplate extinction, but for the last dozen generations, our population keeps getting smaller and smaller. Young women are valuable, too valuable to be risked."

"What do you think?" Ron asked. Her clipped and hasty delivery suggested the situation frustrated her, but she also seemed resigned to it. The idea of her family forcing her to hook up with someone for breeding purposes brought a jab of sharp jealousy.

"In an abstract way, I can support and agree with them. But since it's my life they're insisting on padding with pine needles, I can't quite get on board with it." Lily led him past a tall outcropping of dull-grey rock. She glanced back at him, her teeth worrying the corner of her bottom lip. "I've never shown this place to anyone before."

Her doubts about sharing her space couldn't have been clearer if she'd written them on a billboard. Ron wondered if he should offer to go back without intruding. It might cause him to explode with frustration, but he wouldn't push where she wasn't comfortable.

"It's where I come when I need to get away. Things can get tense, and Grandfather always taught us to walk away rather than risk shattering our community bonds. There's nowhere to go if someone's feelings get hurt. Everyone can end up taking sides in a disagreement, and if someone says or does something hurtful, we depend on them for our survival. So, we all have places to retreat to where the rest of us know not to follow. Lou goes out into the forest or up onto the tundra, and Andrew has a private sweat lodge. Mark built a tree house, and Grandfather kicks us all out of the cabin when he needs time." Lily pulled aside a bower of thick spruce branches to reveal a tiny cavelet. "This is mine."

It was too low to stand up comfortably in but deep enough to stretch out at full length without poking one's head or feet outside the protective branches. Lily knelt and picked up a piece of round metal, which looked as if it had been cut from the top of a barrel. A tube poked out of the top, curving off to the side. As she lifted it, Ron caught sight of the blackened interior and a pile of ash underneath. She swept out the debris and piled fresh kindling into a rounded teepee. A quick strike with a match, and soon a cheerful flame blazed. As she settled the barrel end back in place over the flame, he realized the object was a portable stove. The tube was actually a chimney, forcing the smoke out of the little cavelet. A hole in the side allowed her to poke fresh fuel into the interior without lifting it again.

The ingenuity and simplicity of the design impressed him. As she lit a primitive lantern using melted fat for oil, he realized she wasn't meeting his eyes. Her movements were smaller and more hesitant than he was used to seeing. He gently stroked her arm to catch her attention. "This place is amazing."

She glanced briefly at him. "It must seem primitive to you."

"That's not what I was thinking. This place is entirely yours. You're not dependent on anyone else here—not for supplies, not for help, not even passively for heat or electricity. This is all yours." He tugged off his mittens. The stove warmed the small space faster than he could have imagined. "I'm glad you've had this sanctuary."

"Thank you. It took me a while to put it together the way I liked." She suddenly looked up, capturing his eyes with hers. "Did you kill Nada?"

The blunt question shocked him, knocking him out of his romantic anticipation. He closed his eyes, remembering watching helplessly as the man raised the gun. The blast of the shot had deafened him as it echoed inside the plane's fuselage.

"I was there when she died." He forced the words out, each of them scraping hoarsely against his throat. "I couldn't save her."

"I shouldn't have asked like that." Lily looked back down at her hands.

"Why…?" He couldn't make his vocal cords shape another syllable no matter how hard he tried.

"Bob found some articles saying you were a suspect in her death. We figured something must have happened to her when she didn't come for her usual visit. And you said you were carrying a woman's ashes."

"That made you think I was a killer?" The hurt slashed deeper than he could have imagined, a razor carving into the fleshy muscle of his heart. Pressure built in his chest as if it were filling from blood from a physical injury instead of an emotional one.

"No!" Lily rose up on her haunches, taking his hands in his. "No, I never thought you were. I was sure there was a mistake. I wanted to hear your side."

The ferocity of her protest eased the ache somewhat, letting his mind realize what was happening. His captors were setting him up to take the blame for their crimes. "Those bastards!"

"The people who held you, they killed her?" Lily asked, her gaze never wavering from his face.

"Right in front of me. They'd done something to me, to my mind.

When I saw her die, it woke me up. I knew I couldn't go with them and that I needed to stop them. I was so weak and confused I didn't know what to do." The walls of the cavelet pressed in, making him feel as if he were back there, trapped inside an ironically enhanced body that still wasn't enough to make him the protector he should be.

She pulled him into her arms, holding him tight as his body shook with the intensity of the memory. He tried to focus on Gerry's advice from the sweat lodge. *The dead do not bear grudges.* He clung to her, using her as an anchor to keep him from drowning in the past.

"Living in the past doesn't change it. It only destroys the present," she whispered.

"That's what your grandfather said." He remembered Gerry's other advice about how crippling it was to expect someone else to heal you. The thought sparked guilt about taking comfort from Lily's embrace, but he hated the idea of pulling away. "He also said I shouldn't rely on you. It's why he sent you away."

"I know." A glint of steel in her compassionate gaze revealed her strength. "He's a big believer in standing on your own feet. But I don't see any harm in an occasional leaning."

Ron wanted to kiss her. The mixture of light and shadow danced over her full lips, so close to his own. He wanted to throw aside caution and lose himself in her until his memories vanished. But he refused to place such a burden on her. He took a deep breath, bracing for the worst. Except the panic attack had passed. This was the first one in months that hadn't left him mentally incapacitated.

"The news story," he began slowly, not trusting his voice. "It's fake. Designed to force me out of hiding."

"People aren't comfortable protecting a murderer. It would keep you isolated. It's a lot of work, though. The people after you must be eager to get you back."

"I'm a science experiment to them," he said bitterly. "I wanted to help people, and instead, I ended up being driven farther away."

"Or maybe you were being driven to where you needed to be," she suggested.

"I don't believe in fate. If there is a plan, and someone chose this to happen to me, then whoever it is would be a vicious psychopath. I can't believe in a higher power that would kill innocent people to bring me here." Angry and reckless, he could have shouted his irreverent defiance to the heavens.

"Wouldn't it be worse if there was no purpose to all the horrible things that happened to us—if it was all random and meaningless?" Her dark eyes were full of wisdom and mystery.

Did it have to be indifferent coincidence or an all-knowing plan? As much as it would soothe him to believe his suffering had a purpose, he couldn't forget how it had come about. Every cell of his body rebelled at the idea of Brian and Adam as expendable, mere pawns designed to force him onto a particular path. He hadn't known Nada long, but she'd knowingly risked her life to save the little girl. While he'd only sat there. He didn't deserve to be the hero of any story. His earlier giddiness was long gone.

"It's hard to get over not trusting people. It's easier to hide behind duty and responsibilities." Lily sounded more as if she were speaking of herself than about him.

The cavelet warmed significantly while they spoke, making him uncomfortable in his parka. He unzipped it, and the rasping noise seemed to wake Lily from her thoughts.

"We should get more comfortable if we're going to continue with deep discussion." She opened up a large plastic bin and unfolded a quilt in sunset colors of red, orange, and yellow.

"What's that for?"

"The bed." She spread it over a thick pile of bracken that took up half the floor space. It was knee-deep and densely packed. He'd naively assumed it was a woodpile. She pulled out a second blanket, this one in sea colors—greens, blues, and whites. She unzipped her parka and shrugged out of it, tossing it at one end of the bed. "Care to join me?"

The thought of getting into a bed with Lily left Ron's mouth dry and his jeans painfully tight. He reminded himself to take things slowly. She'd invited him to talk, and he didn't want to presume anything else. She lay down with her back to the cave wall, and he carefully stretched out beside her. The bed was more comfortable than he would have imagined. The bracken gave slightly under his weight, supporting him like prickly memory foam. The two quilts kept any sharp branch edges from poking him.

The light from the lantern sent flickering shadows dancing around the cave. His shadow caressed Lily's body, highlighting the beautiful full curves of her face and figure. Ron couldn't resist following them, letting his fingers trace her cheekbones and soft, plump lips.

"You've changed since I've been gone," she said quietly, resting her hand on his chest. "You're quieter inside, not living in the future and the past."

He understood what she meant. When he'd dashed into the wilderness from the truck stop, he'd been reacting, not thinking. He hadn't allowed himself the luxury of thinking in months. "The sweat lodge helped. And I found someone to talk to. It's giving me hope that I can reclaim my life from the mess it's become."

He winced, thinking she might be jealous. Or worse, ask him who it was, and he would have to explain he'd spent the night playing Freud and Friends with a bear.

Instead, her face lit up with the beautiful, compassionate smile he craved. "I'm glad."

"I've got a long way to go, but I'm more myself than I've felt in a long time." He lifted her hand from his chest to press a kiss against the slim fingers. "And I have you to thank for it."

"You did the work, Blue Eyes."

"Because of you. Lily, there's so much about me that you don't know, and maybe you won't want me here anymore when you learn it, but I feel like I'm starting to wake up after years of just existing. I've done things I'm not proud of, things that haunt me to the core of my soul. I'd given up believing it was even possible to be anything else." The words flowed easier than he'd ever imagined. It felt right to be open with her. Guilt and shame weren't pulling him down anymore. Instead, he had hope.

His jubilation cooled slightly as he saw Lily's reserved expression. "You don't know me either, Ron. There are things I haven't told you about me and my family."

"Like Ekurru?"

Lily's body went stiff at Ron's words. Her thoughts were racing.

He must have seen her surprise and fear because he hastened to explain. "Doc told me. How it's a retreat for *lalassu* who are visibly different, the Marked. I understand. I've been hunted because of what I can do. I have special gifts, too."

He was one of the *lalassu*? Why hadn't he said anything? Her brain halted on realizing how disappointed Evonne would be. She couldn't use him as an example of tolerance to convince Bob to lighten up. It was easier to dwell on her friend's potential disappointment than to wonder if his status would make him any more accepting of a skinwalker.

Ron continued, speaking slowly and carefully. "Doc explained that you protect Ekurru, keeping the people there safe. And not only the people. I guess you protect the bears, too. I've met some of them, and I know they're more than ordinary animals. It's funny, but I feel safer with them than I have in a long time."

His words melted her heart. He needed to feel safe. She ignored her nagging conscience. "The bear is a protector. Bears stand guard over those who cannot protect themselves." Lily remembered the legends her grandfather had told them. If Ron could accept her, then maybe she wouldn't need to fight so hard to keep her distance. "They will fight beyond a death wound to keep those they care about safe. Do they bother you?"

"A few years ago, they might have. Now it feels good to have some fellow soldiers around, even if they have four legs and fur." He shrugged. "The world is bigger and stranger than I ever would have guessed, growing up. I'm more interested in getting to know you, though."

His blue eyes were shadowed, and the lamplight turned his fair hair into a glowing corona. *This is the moment. Tell him about skinwalkers before it's too late.* Coherent thought flew out of her head as his thumb caressed her lip, the rough edges of his callus catching at the soft folds. She leaned in to meet his kiss. His lips were cool and sweet against hers, like fresh clear water on a summer day. His tongue brushed against her lips, and she opened them in invitation.

She tugged at his shirt, wanting to feel his skin under her fingertips. His hands, buried in her hair, stroked the line of her skull as the thrust and play of his tongue drove her past any thoughts of discomfort or judgment. It awakened something in herself that she'd only seen glimpses of. She slid her hands inside his shirt, enjoying caressing the smooth muscle and soft skin. She even thrilled at the crisp snag of body hair against her fingertips.

His lips nibbled along the line of her jaw with tiny biting kisses as he leaned over her. Tugging down the edge of her sweater, he revealed the curve of her bra underneath. Lightly gripping the edge of the bra cup, he whispered through swollen lips. "Is this okay?"

She nodded breathlessly and gasped as he pulled down the cup and fastened his mouth on her bared nipple. Her fingers clenched together, scoring his skin with her nails as she tried to pull him closer. The exquisite suction sent her blood racing through her veins to settle heavily in her eager womb. A distant part of her mind reminded her that this far outstripped her previous encounters. Everything was more: more pleasurable, more intense. It was as if her nerves were stripped raw, quivering before his touch. She'd never imagined it could feel like this.

"Lily!" The urgency in Lou's shout overrode her immediate impulse to knock her beloved older brother into the middle of next week.

Ron rolled to his feet just as quickly, crouching low to avoid smashing his head into the ceiling. He yanked his sweater straight as he pushed aside the concealing branches at the cavelet's mouth. He moved cautiously, sizing up the situation and placing himself between her and any possible danger.

She put her own clothing back in order and followed Ron outside. Lou waited a few steps away, a silent silhouette against the trees. "Andrew needs our help."

"What is it?" she demanded, dozens of fears coalescing in her mind and fluttering in the dark shadows of worry.

Lou wouldn't elaborate. "Hurry."

Chapter Eleven

Andrew packed up his equipment with expert efficiency, his mind still brooding about the earlier conversation with Lou. They'd watched Blue Eyes and Lily vanish into the trees behind the family cabin. Andrew had shaken his head. "This can't end well."

"It's worse than you think. They're mated." Lou had dumped the sentences into his brother's mind like a too-heavy load of firewood crashing onto the floor.

"Are you sure about this?" Andrew strove to keep his voice neutral. He hadn't seen any evidence of his twin's suggestion, but Lou didn't deserve a cynical response—even if he wasn't known for his people-observation skills or social insights.

"She acts as if she's mated," Lou repeated, the irritated growl in his voice suggesting he wasn't entirely pleased with the situation either. "She defends him like a sow with her cub. And she came close to ripping out Bob's throat. She began to shift." He leaned against the cabin's log walls.

Andrew began to pace. "But he's not one of us." The mating instinct was powerful among their people, one of the areas where they were more animalistic than human. They didn't get a choice once the biological urge asserted itself. The only option was to try and minimize exposure to unsuitable potentials. The instinct couldn't be denied any more than the need to eat or drink. "There must be a mistake. She said he wasn't her mate."

"She can say the sky is green. Doesn't make it so." Lou's shoulders twitched and rolled, signs he was having trouble maintaining his human form. "If she bonds with him, there's nothing any of us can do. I think it's too late."

The mating bond didn't allow for second chances. Would Blue Eyes even consider staying in Bear Claw? If Lily survived him leaving, she still wouldn't consider a new mate from among their people. If his kind went extinct, who would protect the Marked? Andrew shook his head as if he could dislodge the uncomfortable thoughts. No clear decision presented itself. "We can't make this kind of decision in haste."

"We might not be able to make it at all," Lou pointed out. "She'll fight us if we try and separate them again. I wouldn't want to stand against her. She reminded me of Mom."

Andrew remembered his mother, standing on her hind legs and roaring at the poacher who'd killed his father. She'd ripped most of his skull to pieces with a single blow from her massive claws. Andrew had only been a boy, barely eleven years old, and the image still haunted his nightmares. In the moment of her mate's death, his mother hadn't cared about anything except vengeance. Once the poacher lay dead on the ground, she'd curled up and refused to leave their father's body. He and Lou had crouched, shivering in the cold, unable to shift into bear form. They'd pleaded and screamed for their mother to help them, but she remained deaf to their needs. Eventually, Grandfather came looking for them and brought them home. Their mother stayed away for almost two weeks before staggering home, gaunt and exhausted. If she hadn't been pregnant, Andrew doubted she would have returned at all.

Hefting his bag, Andrew left the cabin. He hoped Lou was wrong. His sister didn't deserve that kind of torture.

Karan had barely opened his laptop before the message appeared. He had hoped to have a few minutes to himself after a long and tiring flight. Dalhard already held court in the main suite with the local senator, a long time supporter of the company and recipient of many campaign grants.

Caligo>> We need to talk.

Amusement broke the impassive line of Karan's mouth. Caligo was ever predictable. **Pujari>> The time for talking ended a long time ago.**

Caligo>> You're working for André Dalhard.

Pujari>> A man must seek employment somewhere. *Come, old friend. Put the pieces together.* **He needed my particular skills.**

Caligo>> He's hunting *lalassu*.

Bravo. He can be taught. **Pujari>> It is a competitive market. Every edge counts. I assume this is about the High Priestess line. That was an error.** True enough. He would never have touched the Harris siblings if he had been aware of their heritage. Expecting to contain them with Dalhard's limited resources would be rather like catching lions bare handed. It could be done, but it was far easier with the right preparations.

Caligo>> You expect me to believe that?

Pujari>> I have not seen any members of their line for over seventy years. We were recruiting bodyguards, not looking to begin a war. He did not doubt a Hunt had been called, and preparations were underway to deal with it. With a little effort, perhaps he could delay Caligo from becoming involved.

The computer remained blank for three steady heartbeats.

Caligo>> That's why you contacted me.

Caligo always put too much faith in sentimentality. The five words on screen practically oozed with hurt. As if Karan would reach out after decades of silence to renew the friendship of a man who had already betrayed him once. **Pujari>> I need you to convey to them that our actions were in error. We did not target them intentionally.**

Caligo>> They aren't the only ones you've taken.

Pujari>> The company recruited people with exceptional skills. Much as you and I used to do. Our actions have been cloaked in secrecy, true. Because I understand how important it is to keep our people secret.

Would Caligo believe him? In the end, it did not truly matter. He had shoved the seed of doubt into the dirt, and even if it failed to grow, it would poison his old partner's actions and slow him down for the critical milliseconds that Karan needed. After centuries of watching Caligo, studying him and his reactions, Karan could predict that the man would want to give him the benefit of the doubt. Caligo was prone to focusing on insurance and prevention rather than understanding the rewards that a little risk could bring. Karan had underestimated him only once.

Caligo>> You should come home.

The fly was ensnared in the web. Now he could devour it at his leisure. **Pujari>> Perhaps one day. For now, my place is here. Will you pass on my message?**

Caligo>> Yes. It will be hard for them to accept. There has been too much damage.

Pujari>> I regret that. As I always have.

Jabbing him about the circumstances surrounding their parting ensured Caligo would be too wrapped up in guilt to effectively counter him. In truth, Karan's only regret lay in not recognizing how his partner's inconvenient conscience would prod him into surprising directness. He turned off the transmitter, making his computer appear to be offline, before printing off the documents he had come for in the first place. Choosing an exit point in any negotiation was vital in achieving a business goal.

He returned to the sitting room of their elegant penthouse suite. Dalhard and another man were sitting by a crystalline fireplace, sipping bloodred cognac.

"Senator Paterson, I have the papers you asked for. My apologies for the delay." Karan bowed respectfully, holding out the package with both hands. The senator believed himself to be progressive but was deeply uncomfortable with non-European cultures. Karan often played up his Indian origins around the senator to keep him off balance. It left the man more vulnerable to Dalhard's psychic influence.

"Thank you, son. Not to worry." The older man waved off the issue, wanting to appear magnanimous. "Gave us more time to talk. Shame how everything got blown so out of proportion."

Appearances mattered to the senator. It was the key to manipulating him. Karan noted the telltale seams of an expensive toupee to hide thinning hair, although the color and texture matched the man's remaining white locks. His healthy tan came from a booth, and colored contacts made his eyes a more vivid blue than nature had given him.

Stylists likely chose his clothing to make him appear approachable but still powerful. To Karan, the effort only served to betray the man's inherent insecurities.

"Indeed, I'm most anxious to have my reputation restored." Dalhard's crocodilian smile never quite reached his eyes. He patted the senator's bare hand, squeezing it slightly.

Paterson's expression glazed under the influence of Dalhard's persuasive gift.

"You will ensure the charges are dropped when you return to your office, won't you?" Dalhard suggested. "After all, they are based on falsified evidence from dubious sources."

"Yes, of course. Of course. Dubious sources. Never should have trusted them." Paterson nodded obediently.

Dalhard's reptilian grin widened. "Wonderful. Now, shall we order room service?"

To Ron's surprise, after telling them to hurry, Lou didn't take them back to the Charging Bulls' cabin. Instead, they headed deeper into the woods. He cast a wistful look over his shoulder at Lily's sanctuary cave. Lou's terse message piqued his curiosity, but the thundering anger and pain radiating from Lily's brother made Ron wonder if he really wanted to know the answer before he needed to.

"Lou, tell us. What happened?" Lily demanded, easily keeping pace with her brother through the unbroken, clinging snow.

"Don't know. Bill came, said Steve and Damali were hurt. A bear attack," Lou grunted.

"How? Where?" Ron asked.

Lou didn't answer, his hunched, fur-covered shoulders as silent as the mountains they resembled.

"Do you think it was the rogue bear?" Ron asked Lily.

"What rogue?" Lily grabbed his arm, her eyes wide.

"Doc and I ran into it a few days ago," Ron explained, filling in the details of the encounter with Big Bart and the rogue, although he left out his superhuman leap. "Doc didn't recognize it, but I could tell he was worried."

"He should be. Rogues are dangerous, especially if they're not afraid of people." Lily rubbed her finger along her nose, thinking.

Ron shivered, imagining a bear as large as Setsuné or Litonya going rogue.

Bright lights ahead silhouetted the trees like bars in a prison cell. Ron followed Lily and Mark into the crime scene. Five lanterns hung on poles, turned up to their brightest illumination to dispel the Arctic twilight gloom. The garish gleam made it impossible to overlook the irregular crimson splotches and pink-tinted puddles. Unlike the dry sand in Afghanistan, this frozen ground rejected the violence done to it, leaving it all on the surface to bear witness.

Lou headed inside and knelt beside one of the depressions, studying it like a man scanning a newspaper for a particular article. Ron held Lily back, a vague recollection of cop shows reminding him not to contaminate or destroy evidence. They made their way around the outside of the clearing to where Andrew and Bill knelt beside Steve. A bright-blue tarp was spread out beside them. It might have been for Andrew's medical supplies except that the tarp bulged and dipped too much to be a good surface. He didn't see Dr. Damali anywhere.

"Looks like they unleashed a full can of bear spray, and Steve fired a couple of shots." Lily pointed out the fresh chips and holes in the trees as well as the bright-orange patch of snow.

It hadn't helped. Blood coated Steve's face despite the large swatch of fabric pressed against his forehead. Ron might not have a lot of respect for either the ranger or the biologist, but no one deserved to lie in the snow, injured and alone.

"I'm telling you it was Big Bart!" Steve shouted, jumping to his feet.

The words spilled out of Lily's mouth as if she couldn't deny it quickly enough. "It couldn't be. He's a scavenger. He's never attacked anyone."

"He killed Rachel," Steve snarled.

Ron stepped between Steve and Lily, his throat drying as he realized what lay beneath the tarp. If he hadn't left Doc's supply bin open, then

Bart would be far away from here. It made him responsible for this.

"She told you he was dangerous." Steve turned to Bill, tears leaving lacy white trails of frost on the edge of the tracks.

"We need to get him inside so I can sew him up," Andrew said quietly.

Steve looked down at the tarp, his mouth twisted into a rictus of pain. Ron felt an identical emotional echo in his own heart. He had refused to leave Adam and Brian's bodies even though he knew they were beyond feeling any pain or disrespect. If it were Lily lying there… the thought struck an emotional earthquake, rattling through him physically.

Bill picked up the tarp-shrouded corpse while Andrew led Steve toward the ranger station. Lou stood up, brushing the slush off his knees and mittens.

"It must be a mistake," Lily insisted. "Big Bart wouldn't do this."

Her staunch defense of the little bear made Ron smile. She wouldn't believe the worst of her loved ones.

"The scene is a wreck. The snow got chewed up to slush. No tracks to read to confirm or reject Steve's story," Lou replied. "I see a variety of prints. Could be one bear, could be two. I've got a few human footprints over here, which is odd. There are several trails leading out of here."

Lily stared into the forest, looking at the first set of tracks. "Those go right toward the Colony."

Lou leapt to his feet, shock and astonishment widening his usual taciturn scowl. His head whipped toward Ron. The muscles in Ron's neck, arms, and back tightened, preparing for a fight.

Lily waved away Lou's unspoken objection. "He's one of us. Doc already told him about Ekurru."

"Doc's chatty these days," Lou growled. "Follow those tracks, and see if they go to the Colony. I'll start with the others."

Ron found himself following Lily into the deepening gloom. After the brightness from the lanterns, the darkness of the forest seemed impenetrable. He caught himself wishing his captors had given him enhanced night vision as well as the enhanced strength, stamina, and senses. Lily seemed to have no trouble navigating the forest path. He waited until they were well away from her brothers before speaking. "What's the Colony? Another name for Ekurru?"

"No," Lily replied, still focused on the ground. "Doc told you about the unusual bears here. You've seen them."

"They're hard to forget."

"The Colony is where they live. They don't think like animals. They can plan and be patient to get what they want," Lily explained.

Ron thought of his encounters with Litonya. "So, they have human intelligence."

Lily didn't answer right away. She seemed to be struggling to find the words, her mouth periodically opening and then closing again as she discarded potential explanations. From the difficulty, he guessed this was something she took for granted and describing it was as baffling as coming up with an explanation for the difference between the ocean and the sky. "No. It's not like a human thinks either. They're still bears, but they're not dependent on instinct. They can reason and figure things out for themselves. They can recognize traps and avoid bait or find ways to trigger the traps without getting caught. My family has helped to protect and take care of them for generations."

Ron frowned. That didn't match what he'd seen. Litonya acted like more than an animal with higher reasoning powers. The more he thought about their encounters, the more he realized the bear had been trying to protect him. She'd checked his fire to see if there were any live coals to rekindle it. He suspected she'd gone to fetch Doc after he'd fallen down the hill. She'd recognized his emotional distress and reacted by trying to soothe him. Wild animals didn't have that kind of empathy. Rather than challenge Lily's assertions, he decided to change the subject. "Are we still following the tracks?"

Lily nodded, the gesture only visible because the paler outline of her face stood out from the shadows. "They're the right size to be Bart's." She sounded defeated. "I'd really hoped they were wrong."

"I can't see anything. I can barely make you out."

Lily's head jerked up in surprise. "You should have said something." She reached into her pocket and cracked a glow stick. It cast an unearthly yellow gleam across the forest. "We're not far now."

Feeling a little like a potential UFO sighting, Ron followed Lily. His instincts all shrilled that she was hiding something from him. He should trust her, but the idea of a secret triggered a powerful fight-or-flight impulse. The last thing he wanted to do was to hurt her with a fear-based gut reaction. The trees thinned out as they walked, and after a few more minutes, the forest was replaced by frost-rimed masses of rock thrusting out of the ground. Lily led him to one side of a chunk of rock the size of a small strip mall, where the trail of compacted snow revealed a gap between outcroppings. Stepping through, he paused to absorb what he saw.

The ground dropped away, plunging deeply to create a steep-sloped valley. A switchback trail went back and forth across the cliff face, dotted by too many murky cave mouths to count. At the base of the trail, red coals gleamed in an enclosed firepit. He thought he could see the outlines of a small hut crouched off to one side of the valley floor, almost buried behind frozen dirt and branches.

There's no snow, Ron realized. Someone had gone to the trouble of removing all the snow from this narrow valley. He couldn't guess how Lily was still tracking the bear, given how the ground was rough-cut stone, but she stopped on the second switchback, at the first cave on the trail.

"Setsuné?" she called out softly.

A low growl answered.

"Please come out." Lily knelt down and placed the glow stick on the ground at the cave mouth. "We need to know if he's in there."

At first, Ron thought he was looking at a large rock taking up most of the room in the cave. When it shifted, the profile broke up into the jagged outline of fur. His first instinct was to grab Lily and put himself between her and the animal. If he hadn't spent time with Litonya, he might have done just that.

The bear was easily the same size as Litonya—double the size of any bear he'd ever seen before. Her teeth were bared, and her ruff stuck out like a lion's. Ron didn't need Doc's expertise to recognize a thoroughly pissed-off bear.

"I'm not going to hurt him, Setsuné. I promise." Lily showed no sign of fear. Instead, she sounded like someone speaking to an irritable older relative—respectful but not afraid.

Setsuné's ruff slowly settled, and she twisted her head back to grunt into her cave. Ron recognized the white markings on Big Bart, although he looked ludicrously tiny and cub-like next to the massive Setsuné. He whimpered as he came close to Lily. He'd inch forward and then scuffle back, clearly unsure what to do.

"How did you know he'd be here?" Ron asked.

"I knew Setsuné was taking care of someone she didn't want us to see, and Bart kept coming back to this area no matter how often we chased him off. I guessed the two might be related." She made no move to touch Bart, which kept Ron's jangled nerves from leaping into overdrive. He could see the intelligence in Setsuné, but Bart was still a wild animal. She glanced back at Ron. "He's been hurt."

A wet mass of fur behind Bart's neck gleamed black in the yellow light. Ron could smell the coppery blood. Setsuné licked at the wound and whined at Lily.

"I know. You've been taking care of him. He needed a mother, or a grandmother. He was lucky to find you." Lily sighed. "I wish you could tell us what happened."

"Can he?" In his old world, the question would be idiotic, but since they were having a rational conversation with a bear, he didn't want to rule out the possibility.

"He can't. But I can," a new voice interrupted. One that haunted Ron's nightmares.

This time, he didn't hesitate. He grabbed Lily and turned, putting her between him and the rock face, the most protected position possible. Then he turned back to face the man approaching from the valley floor.

"Hey, Corporal. Still pretending to be the hero?" Vincent drawled as he rounded the last turn.

"What are you doing here?" Ron spat out the words, scanning the trail for a weapon.

Setsuné swung her massive head and snapped her jaws together, mere inches from Vincent. The other man paled and stepped back, heeding the warning.

"She's right. We don't have time for this nonsense." Lily put her hand on Ron's shoulder. "Vincent came here so Grandfather could help him."

"Came here." Vincent laughed bitterly. "It sounds so mutual that way."

"Enough, Vincent. You said you could tell us what happened. Tell us, or go crawl back into a bottle." Lily's voice came out harsher than Ron had ever heard her speak. Chafing shame burned through him. He'd crawled into bottles, which meant he wasn't any better than the bitter man standing in front of him.

"I was up in the trees when I spotted Ranger Rick and his sidekick. I was bored, so I decided to follow them. I stayed up in the trees so they couldn't see me." Vincent bit off each word as if he resented the breath to say them. "I saw him and the biologist getting groiny, and I was about to leave to vomit in peace when the bear started to charge."

"Bart?" Lily demanded.

Vincent shook his head. "It wasn't this one. I've seen him hanging around. The attacking bear was all black. No white bits. He swiped at the ranger and knocked him off his girl, holding her down. She screamed, and I jumped down out of the tree to try and scare him off, but he bit her head. I heard the skull break."

Ron winced. He knew exactly what sound Vincent meant, and it wasn't one that anyone should ever have to hear.

"I shouted, and he dropped her. He looked crazy, ready to charge at any minute. The girl was dead, and I thought Ranger Rick would be next. I didn't know what I should do until that little fellow showed up. He charged at the crazy bear and knocked him aside. I think the cub here got bit, but between the two of us, we drove the other one away. Then the little guy came back and started licking the girl, like he wanted to wake her up." Vincent's defensive sarcasm had fled, leaving only raw pain. Ron heard the familiar regret that would torture the other man for the rest of his life—the guilt of not being fast enough, of making the wrong choice.

"What happened after?" Lily asked.

"Ranger Rick came to, and he pulled out his shotgun on the little guy. I knocked him back and hustled this guy back here. I'd seen him with Setsuné. I knew she'd take care of him." Vincent shrugged, looking much younger than his usual façade of bravado made him appear. "I could hear Bill shouting. I knew he'd find Ranger Rick before it was too late."

"Funny. Steve didn't mention you being there." Ron kept his voice neutral.

"Don't think he liked knowing someone knocked him down. Or maybe he got confused from being hit in the head. I'd care, but I really don't. I just don't want to see Bart hurt for something he didn't do." *Like I was.* The words hung unspoken between them. Ron wondered how long the other man had spent in captivity before the two of them met. It didn't take long for their captor to break a man beyond repair.

In the end, it didn't matter. He believed Vincent was telling the truth, which meant a dangerous animal was loose. "We need to tell the others and find the rogue before it hurts anyone else."

Setsuné raised her head, clacking her jaws together.

"Don't worry. We'll make sure they know Bart had nothing to do with it," Ron reassured the giant bear.

"Thank you for telling us the truth, Vincent. I know it wasn't easy." Lily stepped out from behind Ron, her hands raised to embrace Vincent.

Selfish pleasure thrilled Ron as Vincent stepped back to avoid Lily. "Doesn't make a difference. I'm still a monster. Like him." The venom in his gaze when he looked at Ron could drop a dozen horses in their tracks.

"He's not a monster!" Lily dropped her hands to her hips, glaring down at Vincent.

Her defense warmed him, but he didn't deserve it. "I am. He knows it better than anyone. I failed when it was most important."

"Do you still hear him in your head? Telling you to keep quiet and come back?" Vincent asked, naked fear and hope battling in his face.

Ron shook his head. "I feel his mind crawling into mine, locking up my muscles to hold me back when I most need to move."

"He never goes away." Vincent's shoulders slumped in defeat. "Only way to win is with a bullet in the brain. And then he still wins because he's alive and we're dead."

Vincent began to walk back down the trail, and Ron hurried after him, completely ignoring Setsuné and Bart. He grabbed Vincent's arm. "I don't think it needs to be this way." "You're some big expert on mind control now? Took a minor in military college?" Vincent's protective sarcasm fired with all barrels.

"No. But they are." Ron nodded back at Lily. "Her brother and grandfather can help us. They helped me get past the panic attacks that were driving me to booze and drugs. I think they can get rid of whatever blocks that bastard put in our heads. Come with me—give it a chance." He believed it fiercely with all his soul.

"This is stupid," Vincent announced, the trails of sweat on his face and chest catching what little light seeped into the sweat lodge.

"That's the sort of open-minded, can-do spirit we were hoping for." Andrew didn't bother opening his eyes. Ron couldn't help being a little resentful at how comfortable Lily's brother seemed in the sweltering heat. Both he and Vincent were drenched, but Andrew and Gerry looked as if they were relaxing in their living rooms.

"It is easier to believe you are broken than to try and heal yourself." Gerry carefully nudged a coal in a new alignment with the others. "You would rather be condemned than risk failure."

"Great. You do horoscopes, too?" Vincent didn't seem cowed by Gerry's offered insight.

Ron had seen men like Vincent before at the VA hospital after he'd returned from Afghanistan. There was Kenneth, whose entire skin was pocked and scarred from shrapnel from an IED. The doctors couldn't remove all the fragments, and Kenneth swore he could feel them digging their way through his body. Al had lost both his legs and half of an arm after his convoy was attacked. He'd spit and swear at the nurses and doctors who came to help him with his prosthetics. Both men were like wounded animals, unable or unwilling to stop themselves from attacking anyone who came close. They used their injuries as weapons against those who would help them. Kenneth left the hospital and ended up self-medicating himself into a coma with drugs and booze. Ron lost track of Al, but he'd heard that the man had discovered only one working hand was necessary to put a gun to his temple.

Complaints were still pouring out of Vincent's mouth. "—no idea what you're talking about."

"I do," Ron interrupted. "Quit your whining."

Vincent's mouth hung open, and his sweat-soaked, greasy curls were plastered to his forehead.

"You heard me. I've seen guys like you before. Always joking and looking for the easy way out. Too scared of failure to even try." Ron fixed

Vincent with his best drill-sergeant stare. "You want to let him win?"

"He already won," Vincent snarled.

"Bullshit. He ran away. That's not winning." His old strength and confidence flowed easily through his body, flushing away the fear he'd lived under for too long. He might not know where he was going, but there would be no more retreat or surrender. Time to fight back.

"He'll be back." Vincent's protest sounded less like a threat and more like an abandoned child hoping for reunion with his parents.

Andrew gave a thoughtful nod. "Is that what you want?"

Vincent didn't answer, but the anguish on his face communicated his thoughts.

"He betrayed you. He betrayed all of us." Ron kept very still, recognizing that Vincent might be on the verge of slicing through the lodge walls and running away.

"Then why do I still want to go with him?" The words burst out of Vincent.

"Because he twisted your mind to make you. I can see the scars in your thoughts and memories." Andrew spoke calmly and with more compassion than Ron could remember hearing before.

Vincent buried his hands in his hair, clenching his fingers as if he could rip out the damage. "I can't even make myself talk about him. Not even in my head."

"Can you?" Gerry asked Ron, his entire body tensing like a predator spotting a fresh trail.

Ron shook his head slowly. His mind skittered away from the memories of his captors. It was like trying to force himself to put his hand on a glowing stove burner. Common sense and protective instincts held him back.

"Interesting." Gerry settled back, his dark eyes hooded once more. "Both of you have been restless since your captivity. Your body fights the trap in your mind. This is where we will begin."

"Where?" Vincent demanded.

"We may have found the remaining instructions he left in your minds," Andrew answered. "Instructions that would prevent you from betraying him. Now that we know they are there, we can work on them."

"How?" Ron doubted Andrew would just be able to go into his

mind and undo what his captors had done.

"Like ice grinding through stone. Great pressure applied over time." Gerry cast a handful of dried plants on the coals. Immediately, the sweat lodge filled with aromatic smoke. "Breathe, and listen to the rhythm of your bodies."

Andrew began to thump on a drum, his voice raised in long, shivering wails. The sound wrapped around Ron's body like a blanket made of nails. It pricked him even as it enfolded him. Uncomfortable and unsettling, it penetrated deep into his consciousness.

"Find the trail in your mind that does not belong. Follow it to the poison left in you," Gerry told them. "See his face. Speak his name."

Sweat coated Ron's body, a visible slippery layer. He felt as if he might melt and dissolve entirely under the throbbing drums. He didn't have the slightest idea how to find a trail in his own mind. He tried to concentrate on his captor, to pull even a single detail out of his memory. Anything to help him crack the wall of silence.

His captor's hair had been dark. Ron was fairly certain of it. He remembered seeing it gleam under fluorescent lights as if it were oiled. Ron had been in a bed, tilted at an angle, with restraints on his arms and legs. He sucked in a shallow breath of steam, the heat and moisture scalding his lungs. His fingertips dug into his palms and then snapped outward as if searching for an intruder in the smoky dimness. Ron's eyes flew open as he panted, unable to draw in enough oxygen to do more than react. Andrew, Gerry, and Vincent—their faces swam in front of his eyes as the light began to dim further.

He could hear Vincent shouting over Andrew's chanting, his words swelling and fading like ocean waves. Vincent held something shiny in his hand, and Ron struggled to focus on it. His heart pounded hard enough to send sheets of sweat flying from his vibrating skin. The shine resolved into a knife, a long dagger with beading on the hilt.

Obviously, Ron hadn't quite managed to subdue all of his anxiety. Seeing a mentally unstable and unpredictable man holding a knife less than two yards away sent his instincts shrilling into full-blown alarm mode. *I have to get out.* Where was the exit? His head whipped back and forth too quickly for him to make out the details. Nausea boiled in his throat.

Andrew grabbed him, his mouth moving, but Ron couldn't make out the words. He tried to break the other man's grip, but his reactions were weak and disoriented. He couldn't resist when strong hands hauled him out of the sweat lodge and into the icy kiss of snow and wind outside.

Ron sucked in great lungfuls of frigid air while Andrew's sure grip kept him from falling over. He kept waiting for the memories of Afghanistan to come in and overwhelm the present, but his mind and senses stayed firmly in the Arctic. Eventually, he began to hear Andrew's words. "Easy. Easy now. Breathe in and out."

He would never have guessed such genuine comfort could have come out of such a sardonic mouth, but gratitude left him weak and shaking. His wet skin began to shiver and ripple, each hair standing at attention in a vain attempt gain heat.

"Let's get you back inside." Andrew held open the flap for Ron to enter. The heat swirled around him like a blanket settling on his shoulders. It held him close the way a father holds his child.

Vincent lay curled up on the leather matting, his knees tucked tightly to his chin and his arms wrapped around his legs as if his body might fly apart if he let go even for an instant. Gerry knelt beside him, holding the knife. No blood darkened its gleam.

"Your mind grew panicked, and your body began to shake as if in a fever. You needed to go outside to cool, but we cannot ignore that it began in the mind." Gerry tilted his head, letting his long hair fall to one side like a sable curtain threaded with patches of grey.

"I couldn't hear. I couldn't make myself move. Everything was spinning," Ron said. At a distance, the experience sounded smaller than it had felt in the moment. Those few seconds had been horrific and devastating.

"Classic panic-attack symptoms," Andrew said, settling back into his place.

The diagnosis took Ron by surprise. He'd expected something more metaphysical or metaphorical. Then he chided himself for being swept up in Hollywood Indian stereotypes. Lily had told him that her brother was trained as an Emergency Medical Technician.

Gerry nodded in agreement. "But you did not become lost in your mind. Only in your body. An improvement."

Andrew held out his hand to Gerry, who reversed the knife and placed the hilt in his grandson's hand. Examining the blade closely, Andrew spoke to Vincent. "You felt the need to arm yourself against us. We have told you many times that we cannot force healing on you."

"I know about the other orders. If you can't fix me, you'll kill me." Vincent ran his hand through his matted curls. "I'm too dangerous to leave alive."

"Who told you this?" Gerry asked.

"I know my family. We're all ruthless bastards. They sent me up here to die." Tears darkened Vincent's lashes, and his fingers tightened in his hair.

"Surrender yourselves to the trance. Only then can you access the deepest part of your spirits," Gerry said. "You must push yourselves past any point of comfort."

Vincent glared at them from his protected posture. "Pass."

"Would you be a slave or a free man?" Andrew asked Ron.

Ron couldn't lie and claim he wasn't afraid. There were a lot of dark and shameful memories inside his skull. He'd turned to bottles and pills to avoid them. He hoped he had the strength to face them, but he couldn't be sure. What Gerry had said made sense in a way he'd never articulated before. He'd experienced it during basic training when he'd pushed his body further than he'd ever believed it could go. He'd transformed, creating a better, stronger, more capable version of himself. He had believed he could stand toe to toe with the evils of the world and refuse to let them pass. He would face anything to get that feeling back.

Gerry passed his verdict. "They are not quite ready. We will continue another day."

Disappointment flared. "I'm ready."

Gerry shook his head. "No, Blue Eyes. You are desperate, which is not the same thing at all. You cannot flee fear by using fear. There is strength in you, but this will take time. Take the time to search your dreams and your thoughts."

"How will I know when I'm ready?" Ron demanded, irritated at the old man's dismissal.

Andrew replied, "You won't have to think about the answer."

"What happens then? He gets the secret ring and access to the

Batcave?" Vincent's sarcasm flung out like blades seeking blood.

The firelight painted Gerry's face in red and gold. "His enemies will be the ones to learn the lessons of fear."

Part Three
ANGIOGENESIS

CHAPTER TWELVE

"You can't keep hiding who and what you are," Lou said as he and Lily picked their way through the snow to Evonne and Bob's. After several hours of combing the forest with Bill, Lou had found the remains of the rogue bear. Doc had begun the necropsy to determine if it had attacked Steve and Dr. Damali. Bill asked Lily and her brother to let the rest of the community know the animal had been caught and make sure everyone was all right. Lily had jumped at the chance to be useful instead of sitting and waiting and chewing her nails to the quick. As Lou continued his lecture, she wished she'd come alone. "Your heritage is nothing to be ashamed of."

"I'm not ashamed of it." Lily's words spilled out too quickly to be anything but defensive. She missed her strong and, most importantly, *silent* brother. "I spend time in the fur."

"You're hiding from your mate." Lou briefly knelt to examine thin scratches at the base of a tree.

"I'm not—what?" Lily sputtered. She wasn't hiding. She'd been ready to tell Ron the truth when Lou had interrupted to drag them on the investigation of the rogue bear. They might or might not be mates, but she wasn't willing to have a lie of omission between them any longer.

"I am not sure whether or not I approve, but we don't always mate with other skinwalkers." Lou shrugged, rising back to his full height. "The Colony is evidence of that."

I very much do not want to have this conversation. Would it be too much trouble

181

to send another crisis to interrupt? Just a little one. Lily pulled her toque off to briefly run her fingers through her sweat-lank hair. She needed to explain everything to Ron, but his potential reaction terrified her. She'd grown up knowing about skinwalkers and other *lalassu.* By his own admission, Ron had never heard of people with supernatural abilities until recently. Would he be able to accept her if she was as much animal as human?

"If the bond is fertile, we can hope that your cubs will be females," Lou continued.

"Okay, we are officially stopping talking about my still entirely hypothetical children finding breeding mates. Ron and I are too different." A part of her mind wailed in protest, demanding to declare her last words a lie.

Lou raised one eyebrow in the sardonic *I don't believe you, but I'm too polite to say anything* gesture she'd hated since childhood. "You should have faith. As your mate, he will accept both sides of you."

"If he's my mate. If." The thoughts and emotions whirling through her mind felt as if they were growing, pushing against the confines of her skull in a desperate attempt to break free. "This isn't how I planned for things to go."

"Life and plans don't work together." Lou pulled down a pine branch to look at scuff marks.

"I like having plans, thank you very much. I don't want some big biological imperative to force me into something. A mating bond should be based on more than pheromones." Her parents had been mated. Grandfather hadn't, although he had loved his wives. Her mother might have physically lived past her father's death, but the fun-loving, singing, playful mother that Andrew and Lou described had left, replaced by someone cold and practical.

"This isn't something you can control or deny, Lily. It is what it is, and no amount of wishing will make it into anything else." Lou took her irritable insistences in stride, leaving her with the childish impulse to jump up and down and demand he agree with her.

Instead, she focused on what she needed to do: tell Ron who and what she was. If he left, she would cope with it. Her mind barely acknowledged the possibility of acceptance. Even if he was *lalassu,* how could he accept her? Revealing everything to a random lost hiker would have been easy—if he then ran shrieking in terror, no real loss. But if the twinkle in Ron's blue eyes turned to icy fear and disgust, his withdrawal would leave scars.

She stepped through the final curtain of trees between her and Evonne and Bob's cabin, feeling relieved. Her best friend would help her find answers, although she suspected Evonne's advice, like Lou's, would require a leap of faith. Mating with an outsider may have worked for her and Bob, yet Lily wasn't so sure for herself.

The door slammed open as they approached, startling her. Bob didn't give her a chance to gather her calm. He charged forward, rifle in hand, his entire body puffed up and quivering with righteous indignation. "He's done it again!"

Alarm leapt higher, fueled by the adrenaline already pumping through her system. Had the rogue been here? Was Evonne hurt? She started to push past Bob to check on her friend, and he grabbed her arm.

"Dr. Damali is dead. How many more will you let him kill?" Bob shouted inches from her face.

"The rogue? When did it happen?" *What if there's more than one?* Panic made it hard to understand the words. Her animal self pushed at her mental barriers, trying to come to the fore to trade her weak human body for a more powerful and robust one. Lily clung hard to her coherent thoughts, resisting the shift.

"If he was here, I'd kill him myself!" Bob lifted the rifle in illustration.

But he's already dead. "It's too dangerous—" Lily began, but Bob cut her off.

"Damn straight! I told you that in Kluane. Where is he?"

Pieces began to fall into place, assembling an entirely new picture from the one she'd initially assumed they were talking about. They hadn't known about the rogue bear in Kluane. Which meant Bob was accusing Ron. A subsonic growl vibrated across her body as her attention focused solely on Bob as the potential threat. With effort, she forced words out of her mouth. "Ron did not kill Dr. Damali."

"I heard the so-called 'official' story about a bear attack. As if any of the Colony animals would let a stray into this territory," Bob sneered.

"The Colony is settled for the winter's hibernation. A rogue bear penetrated our territory and attacked Steve and Dr. Damali. We found its body." Lou's voice was smooth and quiet. If Bob hadn't been half-crazed with fear and speculation, he would have recognized it as a sign of danger. Lou never stayed still and calm except when waiting in ambush.

"It's too convenient, this claim of some random animal coming through. I know he did it! Like he killed Nada. And probably his squad in Afghanistan, too." Bob waved the gun wildly, mentally beyond anything resembling rationality. Lily's vision began to blur, and the weight of muscle began to build on her arms and across her back as the animal within prepared to strike at the threat.

"Bob!" A sharp reprimand came from the cabin.

It was the only thing that could have possibly broken the tension before something terrible happened. Lily's vision cleared, and she blinked at the sight of her best friend standing in the doorway, a long fringed shawl looped loosely over her arms and pinned at her chest.

"They're protecting a murderer!" Bob howled, pointing the rifle at Lou and Lily.

Evonne stepped out into the snow with her bare feet, ignoring the cold to reach her husband. "Lou and Lily would never lie to us about something like that."

"You said it yourself! She's sleeping with him!" Bob snarled, his beady eyes snapping back to Lily.

"I'm not." Lily managed the two words calmly enough, but her face blazed hot enough to start the spring melt.

"Did anyone even see this so-called rogue bear attack?" Bob demanded.

"Vincent did." Unease threaded through her preternatural alertness. Between his drinking, sullenness, and isolation, Vincent wasn't the most reliable of witnesses.

"Doc will be able to tell us for certain soon, but I studied the scene of the attack myself. A bear killed Dr. Damali and wounded Steve," Lou said. "Not a human."

For a single precarious moment, Lily thought they had convinced Bob. He turned to his wife, a stricken look on his face, and his mouth opened for what Lily thought would be an apology.

"You're all in this together," he whispered.

"Bob—" Evonne reached for him, but he staggered back.

"None of you can see it." His round face tightened in grief and determination. "But I'll show you."

He staggered away from the cabin, blindly breaking a trail. Evonne started to go after him, but Lou stopped her. "You need to get inside before your feet freeze."

He picked her up and carried her into the cabin. Her feet were already white and pale. Lily put a wool blanket on top of the stove to warm it. It was one of Georgette's, the weave and threads blending into indistinguishable smoothness, and Lily hoped to avoid scorching it.

"I don't know what's come over him." Evonne's dark eyes shone with tears. "Ever since he came home, he's been obsessed with the idea that Ron is some kind of killer."

"He's worried about you." Lily knelt and wrapped the warm blanket over Evonne's feet, gently rubbing them to restore circulation. She put another one on the stove to warm.

"I know. He's talking about leaving Bear Claw." Evonne rubbed her arm over her eyes, avoiding the supersensitive fingertips. "He contacted Ken through the radio relay, and I heard the two of them discussing how Bob could fly his plane to Vancouver without being detected by the authorities. He said he could put me in a crate to smuggle me in so no one would know I was there."

It was on the tip of her tongue to tell her friend that Bob would never do such a thing. However, Lily had seen too much of his overprotectiveness to doubt it. If he thought it would keep Evonne safe, he'd happily drug her and haul her out.

"It's too late to bring Blue Eyes here as a test case. Even if Bob didn't think he was a killer, I don't think it would matter." Evonne suddenly realized Lou still stood in the room. "I mean—"

"Don't worry. I've heard about your little plan." Lou picked the second blanket off the stove, trading it to Lily for the cooled one. "It's a dumb idea but not worth running around, threatening to shoot people over."

"It wasn't a dumb idea," Lily protested. "Evonne doesn't deserve to be locked away because she's different. Besides, the world is going to find out about us eventually, and it would be better if it were on our terms."

"We can talk about it later. For now, I need to track down Bob before he does something stupid." Lou paused. "I'll do my best to bring him home safe, although we both know it's going to be difficult if he's decided I'm the enemy."

"This isn't him. I should go with you. He'll listen to me." Evonne started to get up.

"No." Lou stopped her. "If he sees you, it's going to trigger all of his protective instincts. My best chance is to find him and talk him down, man to man. I can protect myself, but I can't do it if I have to worry about someone else."

Thank the stars. Lily didn't trust Bob not to shoot first and ask questions later. Lou's skills and his innate skinwalker healing would keep him safe from any accidents.

He left the two women alone. Guilt pulled at Lily like snow and ice weighing down a pine's branches. "I'm sorry, Evonne. This is all my fault."

"Let's save a little blame for my idiot husband. He's been so agitated since Bill came to warn us about what happened to Dr. Damali." Evonne looked at the door as if it could tell her the future or explain the past. "He immediately blamed Blue Eyes."

"He's not a killer, and he definitely didn't hurt Nada." Lily could be sure of that much. She'd seen too much of his pain and grief over his losses to believe they weren't genuine.

"Bob kept saying how none of us understood what we were dealing with. He's always been afraid that something would happen to me. I used to tease him about preparing for a mob of villagers with torches and pitchforks. As if there were enough people around here to put together a mob without it having to travel for a couple of days in either direction. It's not so much of a joke anymore." Evonne stared at the window without seeing anything except the pictures in her own mind. "He didn't grow up with the *lalassu* like we did. I think the idea of such secrets existing in the world ended up undermining his confidence and sense of security."

Lily frowned, trying to understand. "He's worried about the secret getting out?"

Evonne shook her head. "No, more like if a secret as big as the *lalassu* was out there, then what else could be hiding in the world?”

“Unlocking his inner control freak. And now we’ve made it worse.” Lily wondered if she would have saved Ron if she’d known what sort of storm she would unleash. It should be an easy decision—protect Ekurru and the Colony. But somehow, she doubted she’d do anything different, which left her feeling unworthy of her position of Guardianship.

Evonne interrupted. “You’re about to rub holes in my feet.”

Lily dropped her hands and stepped back, embarrassed. Evonne’s feet had returned to their normal tan tone, and Lily hadn’t been paying attention but kept chafing them into redness. Her legs twitched, ready to start pacing, but she forced herself to sit down in the other chair.

“Bob was always protective of me once he understood I was Marked. If he could have built me a tower like Rapunzel’s, I think he would have.” Evonne looked at her grey-tinted fingers. “I miss going out and seeing more than a few acres of forest. I liked meeting new people in Kluane or Juneau.”

Lily remembered their trips together when they were teens. Evonne had hated the gloves she’d needed to wear. The pressure against her hands was like a constant strobe light in the eyes, unceasing overstimulation. Yet they’d also laughed constantly. “I miss it, too.”

“I want to be able to go into a restaurant and eat without wondering if a tourist will notice the gloves. I want to be able to touch the jewelry and stonework in the shops and really let myself feel all the details in them. I want to go out without worrying about making myself a target. Before, those things fed my creativity, and now my world is hemmed in by these four walls.” Evonne gestured at the cabin. “Some days, I feel like an animal caught in a trap, and I have to decide if I’m going to gnaw my paw off to get free. It’ll hit me—the realization that I could spend my entire life stuck in this small box, and then I’ll be put into an even smaller one to be shoved into the ground, and that will be it. I’ll vanish as if I never even existed. It’s terrifying.”

“I won’t let that happen,” Lily promised.

“Remember when we used to lie by the fire and talk about what it would be like to be able to just date boys without worrying about our secrets?”

Like it was yesterday. Lily could almost smell the pungent stew and hear their teenage giggles. Nada had brought them a bunch of teen magazines with articles on all the rituals of prom. Evonne loved the idea of picking out the perfect dress, but Lily had always been more enraptured with the idea of being in a crowd and having someone pick her to dance with. She'd fantasized herself to sleep with visions of music playing and couples swaying around her as a boy held her in his arms and they moved to the melody.

Instead, they'd made their way to an adulthood in which Evonne was trapped in her own home and Lily caught up in her responsibilities. "It's not too late. We'll find a way to fix this."

Evonne wasn't lulled into comfort by Lily's vague promises. "Things are moving too quickly. Dr. Damali's death will attract attention, maybe even the international media. She's a prominent public person killed by the very animals she studied. All sorts of people will want to use her death to push their own particular agenda. They'll converge on us, and with every stranger who comes, the odds are greater that one of them will discover the Colony or Ekurru."

"Bill will handle things. He'll keep it quiet." Lily tried to sound confident, but her friend's words shook her. She'd never considered the implications of Damali's death beyond trying to protect Bart from being hunted and killed by Steve.

"The time for dreams of dancing and stolen kisses is over. We need to be prepared." Evonne turned her haunted gaze back to the window. "Something is going to explode."

"I don't know what I would have done without your invaluable assistance, Ms. Golov." Dalhard clasped Edyta's hand between his own. Karan frowned at the dingy Kluane community hall. He disliked having to do business in such an unpromising location, but it was the closest settlement of any size. From here, they could gather everything they needed to collect his employer's intelligent bears.

The only real barrier was Edyta Golov and her insistence on

personally directing their operation. The initial plan only required her aid in pinning down where exactly the Bear Claw settlement was. They would make it work.

"Nice to be appreciated for once." Edyta's eyes flashed. Her irritation would insulate her against his employer's persuasive influence, but with skin-to-skin contact, it would not take long to break through.

"Has there been trouble?" Dalhard asked, sounding like the perfect impression of a concerned friend.

"Those folk up at Bear Claw are up to something. I always thought they were hiding something." Her mouth thinned, and her chin jerked forward, fury tightening every muscle. "Now you tell me they've been talking with your competitors about exclusive rights to the minerals, cutting me right out of the deal. I've bent over backward for them, and they think they can walk right over me."

"We won't let that happen. At Dalhard Industry, we honor our commitments." Dalhard stroked Edyta's hand with his fingers, and Karan could see the effectiveness of his dual appeal to both the woman and the businesswoman. His employer's gentle flirtation opened her mind, and as she relaxed, Dalhard's influence seeped in.

"I knew I could trust you, Mr. Dalhard. You're a real gentleman." She squeezed his hand but didn't let it go. "I was sorry to hear about Dr. Damali. Were you and she close?"

Karan bent his head to hide a smile, pleased the businesswoman seemed to have forgotten his presence. Her dulled awareness meant her resistance was crumbling.

"We met several times over the years as I supported her work. Her enthusiasm and dedication impressed me. I believe it's important to take the long view with this excavation. I don't want to disturb the wildlife more than we need to. Though I do want to take care of the animal that attacked her."

"Dangerous animals are nothing to mess around with. Most of them have sense enough to be scared of people, but every so often, you find one who isn't frightened." Edyta nodded sagely.

"Hopefully, this will convince the people of Bear Claw that I am not the enemy. I'd like to build some goodwill and show them I'm not like the other corporations seeking to exploit them and run." Dalhard winked, and

Edyta giggled. They had her now.

"Senator Paterson arranged for the Predator Control Unit from Juneau to come in and help with the bear. They are the top people in their field." A blatant lie. The men they brought were mercenaries from a subsidiary of Dalhard Industries. They all had experience as hunters and trappers. An engineer had built the pieces of the massive cages they intended to carry with them on the helicopters. The cages could be assembled once they reached Bear Claw.

"I need to ask you a favor, my dear," Dalhard continued. "I need someone to coordinate things from here."

A hint of Edyta's hardness returned. "I should be there—"

"My dear, you can trust me to look after your interests," Dalhard said, cutting her off and tightening his grip. "And there's no one I would trust except you to handle my affairs here. Besides, I would never forgive myself if you ended up getting hurt."

Eyes glazed, Edyta nodded and mumbled, "Of course."

"I knew you'd understand," Dalhard whispered conspiratorially before releasing her.

Edyta's sharpness returned as soon as his hand released hers. "We should wait for Bob to return. He knows the area better than anyone else and can guide your pilots in."

Dalhard paused in the midst of rising to his feet, irritation briefly poking through his oily politician's façade. Karan wondered if his persuasive gifts were faltering or if Edyta's will was so strong it could not be completely suppressed. They needed to complete the extraction quickly and quietly before the Canadian authorities realized what was happening. Dalhard allowed himself a moment to button his coat and adjust his cuffs.

"He could land everyone right by the ranger station." Edyta took advantage of the pause.

"I don't think we can afford the time," Dalhard insisted, clapping his hand firmly on her shoulder, making sure the fingertips passed her collar to touch her bare skin. Karan admired how he made the gesture look entirely natural.

"Weather makes landing tricky." Edyta shook her head. Karan had seen it before when people were resisting his boss's gifts. As if they tried to shake loose the alien influence creeping over their minds.

"Captain Lind is a competent pilot. I have every faith in his ability. As should you." A hint of steel surfaced beneath the smooth patter.

"If that's what you want." Edyta shrugged, nodding her acceptance.

"It is," Dalhard said firmly before releasing her with another charming smile. "Now, would you be so kind as to bring the maps you promised?"

Ron couldn't shake the uneasy feeling that lingered after his sweat-lodge session. *I have to stop letting paranoia get the better of me.* The idea of his captors leaving undetected instructions in his mind made him queasy and uncertain of which feelings and decisions to trust. He spent the sled ride back to the Charging Bulls' cabin worrying about it. Had they left a prompt for him to abandon the Harrises? Being on his own had certainly left him more vulnerable at times. Which of his reactions were truly his and which were planted?

Despite his efforts to stay calm and rational, his tension didn't subside until he saw Lily waiting for him outside of the small cluster of cabins. He didn't truly think something had happened to her in the few hours they'd been apart, but he was grateful to have proof nonetheless.

Some of the relief evaporated as he noticed how tightly pinched her lips were. Without her usual smile, she seemed like a faded print of herself. "What's wrong?"

"I haven't been honest with you. Not completely." When she looked up, he saw tears shining in her eyes. "I never really meant for things to happen like this."

He began to wonder if his paranoia were wrong after all. A chill that had nothing to do with air temperature began to lock down his muscles. "Is this about us?"

"Yes."

His heart stopped until she continued. "And no. It's about me."

"It's not you, it's me?" A brief, hysterical laugh burst out of his lungs. After the emotional stress of the sweat lodge, he didn't think he could handle a politely worded breakup speech.

"What? No. That's not it. Although it might be, after you've heard what I have to say." Lily hugged her arms tightly to herself. "It's about me and my family. And the Colony."

He snapped his mind out of wondering what would happen next and made himself focus on her words. She kept twisting her fingers and shuffling in place, clearly upset and agitated. Whatever she needed to tell him, it was important. "I know you protect the Colony."

Lily shook her head. "Maybe this will be easier if I show you."

"All right." He followed her as she began to walk toward the Colony.

"We weren't chosen at random to protect this place," Lily began as they hiked along the packed-snow trail. "My family has been intertwined with it for a long time. On my father's side, we've lived here since before Columbus arrived in North America. My mother respected his obligations, so she agreed to live here, too. Her family has similar responsibilities down south, near Yellowstone." She abruptly stopped and spun around. "Do you understand?"

The pleading expression on her face made him want to say yes, but honesty compelled a different answer. "Not really."

Her face fell, crumpling into frustration and despair. It left him feeling like a complete jerk, and he reached out for her, except she'd already begun to walk away again. "Of course not. That's just genealogy and geography. I'm not even coming close." Her shoulders slumped, and he heard a ragged breath as she stopped in her tracks.

"Hey," he said softly, catching up to her and pulling her into his arms. He wrapped himself around her, putting himself between her and the world, creating a space with only the two of them. "Whatever this is, we can get through it. You know all my horrible secrets. I can't believe that yours are any worse."

She replied with a little sobbing laugh. "Wanna bet five bucks on it?"

He pulled back so she could see that he was completely serious. "I'm not sure about much in this world, but I'm sure about you."

Lily's hand came up as if to touch him, but she dropped it back down. "You're not going to make this easy on me. Come on. It's only a little farther. Then I can show you everything."

A few minutes more brought them to the Colony's rocky valley. Ron recognized Setsuné as she came out of her cave to greet her company like a distinguished and respectable matriarch. Bart followed her out of the cave, the wound on his neck healing nicely. The little bear was in good spirits, dashing ahead of his guardian like an eager puppy.

Ron saluted him as a fellow wounded soldier. "Hi, little fella. Glad to see you're feeling better."

"Setsuné chewed dried yarrow and laid it on the wound." Lily pointed out a greenish mash on Bart's fur. "It prevents infection and encourages clotting. She keeps a number of plants stored in her cave and uses them to tend to the members of the Colony." She took a deep breath and faced Ron. "She's not like a regular bear."

"I know. Neither is Litonya. Is she here?" Ron asked before he caught himself. He shouldn't try to distract Lily from what she was trying to say. It was obviously difficult enough for her without adding to it.

"She's here. But I have to finish explaining first, and then you can see her." Lily brushed at a large boulder before sitting down on it. "Have you heard of skinwalkers?"

The term struck a chord. Ron frowned as he mentally chased down the memory. "I think I heard it in an *X-Files* episode once. A woman who turned into a wolf."

"They're a popular legend among the Navajo, but most tribes have their own version. They're bogeymen, able to transform into any animal they choose or sometimes take on the shape of another person, usually with a pelt." Lily nervously plucked at her sleeve. "It's all nonsense, of course. But there's a grain of truth in the legends."

"I'm discovering there usually is." He hoped the gentle reminder would ease her nerves, but instead, her posture tightened up as if anticipating a blow.

"What they don't understand is that those they call skinwalkers aren't really humans taking on the forms of animals. Instead, they have a dual nature. On one side, they are human, with human intelligence and reactions but with stronger primal instincts that come from their animal side. When they are in their animal form, they are that animal—more capable of rational thought and planning but still an animal with all the powerful instincts." Lily looked over at Setsuné. "Once they take on the fur, they're not human anymore. In some ways, I don't think they ever really were."

"What about when they're in human shape?" Ron asked.

"Some skinwalkers are more comfortable in human shape, but others are more comfortable in their animal form." Setsuné came closer to Lily as she tried to explain. The bear dipped her head to nudge Lily's hand with her nose, and Lily stroked her fur as if she were an overlarge dog. "Sometimes they don't go back to the skin."

"You mean they can't change back?" Ron asked, looking at the matriarch with sympathy.

"Can't or don't. The two sides don't always coexist easily. It's hard to explain, but at a very fundamental level, a skinwalker isn't human. Even in human form, there is something of the animal in them." Lily took a deep breath.

Ron thought he understood. It sounded as if she was trying to tell him that Setsuné had once been human. Other members of her family must also be at risk. He guessed Lou was the skinwalker. With his leather and fur clothing and surly manners, he seemed more feral than human anyway. "Is there anything you can do to help them?"

"I don't know. There have always been skinwalkers who chose to live almost exclusively in their animal form. It's where they felt comfortable. In the fur, things are simpler. There's no fight between human intellect and animal instinct. Instead, the animal benefits from greater awareness."

"It sounds like it would be tempting." Ron could see a parallel with the chemical oblivion he'd pursued for his own nightmares. Even if won, the constant inner fight exhausted the spirit. Drugs and alcohol made it impossible to fight, delivering him into the false comfort of numbness.

"I don't know if it's temptation or simply succumbing to our true natures. Is a skinwalker an animal who can take human form or a human with an animal side?" Lily seemed to be losing energy as the conversation continued.

She's worried that I'll reject her because of her family if they're not human. "Lily, I don't want to do my whole 'the world is strange' speech again. Because it doesn't matter. I love you, and there's nothing you could tell me that would change how I feel."

The smile he'd been waiting for broke through the facial gloom. He joined her on her boulder, putting his arms around her shoulders before continuing. "I know it might sound crazy. After all, we've only known each other a few days. But I think I loved you ever since the moment I woke up at Doc's and saw you looking down at me like my own personal angel. Maybe I loved you before that, before I even knew you were out there. It feels like it's always been a part of me." He tugged off his mitten so he could run his finger along her cheek and nose, tracing the contours of her face to keep them safe in his memory.

"If it's crazy, I'll have to be committed beside you," she whispered as she cupped her hand around his neck, pulling him closer. "Because I love you, too."

His heart swelled with happiness, overshadowing the lingering uneasiness. No paranoid suspicion dared to penetrate such a brilliant uprising of joy. A distant part of his mind wondered if he'd ever experienced such untainted glee even as a child. It didn't seem possible. He shoved aside intellectual curiosity and took Lily's lips in the kiss he'd been aching to give her.

Her lips were cool against his at first but quickly warmed into fiery heat. Some basic survival instinct warned him he couldn't strip away the bulky barriers of clothing between them no matter how much he wanted to. Instead, he pulled her onto his lap to straddle him, crushing her against him to explore the delicate curves of her body through the puffy parka.

She moaned softly as his tongue plundered her, a frustrating promise and substitute of what he wished he could do that moment. There was the shack he'd spotted behind the firepit. Maybe it would be warm enough.

"Wait." Lily broke free from the kiss, her breath coming in short pants against his face.

Ron immediately froze. "Too fast?"

She smiled. "I still haven't told you the catch."

"What catch?" His intellect was not up to having this conversation right now.

"The catch that could make you regret what you just said." The smile disappeared from her face. "I never expected to feel this way about anyone."

Setsuné interrupted Lily's halting explanation with a loud bellow. The couple twisted and saw her standing on her hind legs, her snout lifted high with the nose pointed back toward Bear Claw.

"Something's wrong." Lily slid off his lap to peer in the same direction as the bear.

Ron's acute hearing picked up a strange intermittent buzzing. He suspected the noise had alarmed Setsuné.

"Can you tell what it is?" Lily asked.

"I'm not sure." The sound tugged at a subconscious memory, one overflowing with anxiety and trepidation. Yet he couldn't quite place it. He closed his eyes to concentrate on the sound, trying to separate it from the constant hiss and hush of the wind and the creaking and plopping of snow. Too regular to be natural. More like a vibration than an audible noise.

His eyes popped open as the memory burst into awareness. "Helicopters."

Chapter Thirteen

"Stay here!" Lily shouted at Setsuné, taking off toward Bear Claw at a run. Ron followed her. To his surprise, she ran as quickly as he did with his enhanced muscles—faster, since she knew where to place her feet to avoid stumble-inducing pockets of crushed snow. He heard an irregular crashing behind them. Looking back, he saw Setsuné charging behind them.

"I don't think she listened," he shouted at Lily.

"It was a long shot," she called back over her shoulder, skidding along a stretch of ice. She managed to gracefully maneuver through the skid and end up still running in the right direction.

The buzz from the helicopters pulsed and rattled even louder. Despite the echoes bouncing off trees and rock, Ron picked out the direction and height of the motors. No question: they were landing at Bear Claw. He and Lily would be too late.

He spotted two helicopters settling below the tree line, long towlines dangling from their bellies. He heard a third set of rotors slowing, suggesting another was already on the ground. They couldn't afford to go charging in blind. For once, he needed to think the situation through instead of reacting.

Reaching out, he grabbed Lily's arm, although the abrupt change in momentum knocked them both to the ground. Setsuné nearly plowed into the two of them, but instead, she managed to half bury herself in a great spray of snow that left all three covered in icy powder.

Lily shook herself off, fury blazing. She started to get to her feet.

"Wait!" Ron grabbed her arm again to make her listen. "We can't rush in. They're already there."

Lily's legs collapsed underneath her. "This can't be happening."

"We need to think," Ron insisted, amazed he could still think tactically instead of emotionally. He refused to waste the opportunity. His brain could collapse into panic at any moment. "Is there any chance this could be legitimate?"

"No." Her firm denial negated any further consideration. "The only time we get helicopters is if we're getting supplies for the ranger station. Which happens in spring and fall and only takes one helicopter."

"Then we have to assume the worst. They're after me or Vincent." Ron held her hands tightly between his. It was time for his turn to fall on the grenade. "If that's the case, I'll go with them."

"No! You can't!" Lily's eyes were wide in protest.

"We can't let them find out about the Marked or the Colony." The weight of the decision settled on him, somehow less terrifying than worrying about it had been. The worst was happening, and protecting Bear Claw was more important than protecting himself. Besides, Ron wasn't completely out of resources. "I might surrender, but I don't intend to go quietly. As soon as we're away from here, I'll find a way to escape."

"I'm not letting them take you," Lily hissed. Her skin seemed darker, but maybe it was the ferocity of her expression.

"I won't go in blind." Ron got to his feet, helping her up. "We need to get close enough to see what's going on. If they're looking for me, I'll surrender, and you stay out of sight. They might already have people as hostages."

"We can figure out another way." Her fingers dug painfully into his arms. Her fierceness warmed him, but he knew that surrendering might be the only way to keep everyone safe.

"Your people need you. You have to stay free to protect them." The steadiness of his nerves surprised him. The promise of action and danger balanced out his otherwise off-kilter reactions. His only regret was not having more time with Lily. There were dangerous currents in Bear Claw, and he hated abandoning her to swim them alone.

"I need you," she whispered. He wasn't sure she'd intended for him to hear it. Her lips pressed together, and she glared deep into his eyes.

"Only as a last resort."

He nodded, knowing they were already there. "Let's go. Think you can convince Setsuné to be quiet?"

Lily turned to the bear and said something in a melodic language. The ursine matriarch huffed once but didn't immediately resume her charge. A plaintive wailing interrupted them.

Bart peeked out from his perch in a tree. Setsuné hummed and clacked at him, which seemed to reassure the little bear.

"She's telling him to stay put. It's a sequence that mother bears use with their cubs when investigating a potentially dangerous situation," Lily said quietly. "We need to move quickly."

Ron nodded. They crept the last half mile to the ranger station, taking more time with that stage than the two or three miles from the Colony. They stayed low, hoping to keep below visual range of whoever waited for them.

Finally, they got close enough to see the station. Men in pale snow-camouflage gear moved with purpose around the small cluster of grey, flat-sided cabins. They carried plastic tubs and boxes of gear, piling them in some arcane dictate of organization. Most of them wore rifles strapped across their backs.

He and Lily needed to be closer. He heard the muffled sounds of a heated argument from the main station. If he timed it right, they could crouch between the supply bins and peer in the windows without any of the soldiers noticing them. The intruders seemed more interested in getting their camp set up than in protecting the perimeter.

He caught Lily's attention, pointing at her and himself before indicating the bins, signaling that they could hide there. She nodded and pointed at Setsuné.

Ron shook his head. There was no way the men wouldn't notice a giant bear. Two humans could crouch in the shadows. Setsuné would be too obvious even if she tried to hide.

Lily nodded. She stroked the bear's muzzle, pointing firmly at the ground. Setsuné started to puff up, but Lily leaned in and pressed her face against the bear's cheek, deep into the fur. A massive paw lifted off the snow, and Ron tensed, preparing to yank Lily away before the animal could hurt her.

Instead, Setsuné balanced her heavy paw and its lethal claws gently on Lily's shoulder, cupping her like a mother hugging her daughter. The sight represented everything worth sacrificing himself to protect.

Setsuné released Lily, nudging her in the chest with her snout. Ron took Lily's hand, watching the soldiers' movement, searching for the inevitable moment when they would all be looking somewhere el—*There.*

Lily followed him easily as he ran lightly to the shadows between the supply bins. They found shelter not a moment too quickly. A soldier glanced toward them, frowning. Ron held his breath, keeping perfectly still. People didn't do well picking out details without motion to help them focus. After a few seconds of staring at the shadows with a puzzled expression, the soldier shrugged and continued carrying his crate to its designated location. Next to the wall, the details of the argument were much easier to make out.

"… expect us to believe that?" an unfamiliar gruff male voice barked.

"Your opinion means very little to me." Doc's irritated tones made Ron wince. Doc was treating this as if it were an academic review. Except no one brought armed soldiers to a remote location for something trivial.

"You always hated her!" Steve shouted. The placid cowboy had vanished, leaving a man barely hanging by a single cracked hinge.

Doc tried to respond reasonably. "Steve, you're grieving and not thinking clearly. I don't know why you called these people in, but—"

The sharp crack of fist on flesh suggested Steve was not in a mood to be reasonable. Ron's shoulders tightened under Lily's restraining hand. Listening to Doc being brutalized without charging in to stop it felt wrong on every level, but experience had taught him the hard way: he wouldn't be the only one at risk if he charged in without knowing the circumstances. He couldn't handle any more deaths on his conscience.

He could hear a scuffle. The gruff male ordered, "Get him out of here."

"He killed her!" Steve shouted again, close to tears. "Him and that murderer!"

Doc's voice cracked with regret and compassion. "Steve, I've confirmed that this bear killed Dr. Damali."

"It's a lie! I remember seeing them both there!" Steve shrieked.

"You saw Ron?" Doc asked, sounding puzzled. *Guess that answers the question of who they're looking for.* Doc wouldn't have used his name casually. The intruders must know he was here, but he couldn't walk in and surrender if they already held Doc. He and Lily needed to figure out a way to get him out first.

"I saw a tall man hurrying away. And then I saw her lying there, dead, with your bloody bear nosing at her," Steve said.

Doc tried to soothe the ranger. "Steve, you were hurt—" Another voice interrupted, ordering Steve's removal. The commander of the troops was inside the cabin. Steve's accusations that Ron had killed Dr. Damali struck a tender soul scar. With a shock, Ron realized he didn't even know the biologist's first name. He'd been so caught up in his own thoughts and Lily's distress that he'd failed to realize how upset Steve would be. A certain sympathy for the man softened his frustration. If something had happened to Lily, Ron doubted he'd be any closer to sanity than Steve.

The front door clacked open, and Steve's ranting became much clearer. The soldiers had finally obeyed the commander and removed him. With the ranger gone, it meant one less complication, which should have relieved Ron. If the commander was honorable, then Ron could go ahead and surrender. But his instincts warned him the real danger still lay ahead.

"I'm sorry about that, Doctor," the commander apologized.

"You still haven't explained what you're doing here." Doc didn't sound impressed. Ron mentally congratulated the biologist on his caution. He wouldn't be caught by a good-cop, bad-cop routine.

"We've received a report of a sighting of Corporal McBride in this area and another about a confirmed human kill by dangerous wildlife. Either would require an investigation." The commander's words confirmed Ron's worst fears. *They're here because of me.*

"McBride is long gone, and the rogue bear is dead," Doc insisted.

"This bear might be dead, but it isn't the only dangerous predator out there." Metal grated against metal, probably a medical tray scraping against the steel surgical table. "This animal has been ripped apart, nearly shredded."

"Scavengers—" Doc began.

The commander interrupted. "The wounds are consistent with a single animal, most likely a bear but significantly larger than any bear ever recorded. Dr. Damali was studying extraordinarily large bears, was she not?"

Ron glanced over at Setsuné, still hiding in the shadows. He remembered the blood on her fur when they'd gone to check on Bart. At the time, he'd assumed it was from the little bear, but now he wondered if the matriarch had gone after the rogue herself.

"Rumors. They've never been documented," Doc said.

"Until now. I would say we have an obligation to investigate this potential threat to our personnel. We do a large number of training sessions here after all." The commander wasn't going to accept any of Doc's arguments.

"A dozen soldiers with guns strikes me as more of an attack force than an investigation," Doc replied scornfully. "We're used to handling our own wildlife issues."

"True. But let's get back to the other potential threat. You have no idea how dangerous McBride is. I don't intend to lose him through complacency." He sounded like a good commanding officer, Ron determined. One who didn't let his pride get in the way of making decisions. Which made him a very dangerous opponent, but he would probably accept a surrender without collateral damage. Except Ron's instincts held him back, insisting he'd missed something.

"Either way, like I told you earlier, he's long gone. He took off yesterday, and I haven't seen him since." Doc's voice grew louder, and Lily squeezed Ron's shoulders. The biologist's lie was kindly meant, but the consequences could be disastrous. This wasn't a poacher or trespasser. The commander wouldn't accept Doc's word for it.

"So, you claim he left before the attack on Dr. Damali? We found clothes matching the description of those McBride wore inside your cabin." The commander sounded like a neighbor chatting over a fence, but the casual and friendly approach didn't fool Ron for a second. He hoped it wasn't fooling Doc.

"Rags. He traded work for new gear. And yes, he's long gone. I don't know who Steve thinks he saw, but it couldn't have been Ron," Doc insisted. "You can take your men and go."

The commander persisted. "There is still the animal that killed this so-called rogue bear which you claim killed Dr. Damali. We intend to capture it."

"We can handle it on our own. Your help is not needed, and your presence will only make things worse." Doc spoke as if he really expected the men to simply pack up and vanish on his word. *I can't let this keep going.* Ron took a deep breath and met Lily's eyes, hoping she could see his regret. She scowled and shook her head, refusing to accept it.

"Dr. Svensson, there are too many holes in your story for us to accept it." A thump suggested the commander had pounded the table for emphasis. *I'm sorry, Lily. It's time.*

"Allow me, Captain. I've read the good doctor's work, and I know he cares about protecting others." The new speaker's voice made Ron's hands shake. He recognized that voice. His captor was here in Bear Claw. All thoughts of surrender vanished.

"We have to get Doc out of there now!" he hissed at Lily.

"Wait, Ron—" Whatever protest she might have made was lost as Ron rose up and slammed his shoulder into the cabin's rear door, trying to break in.

The door didn't budge. It barely shivered in its mountings, having been built to withstand much larger and stronger potential home invaders.

The commander shouted orders, but Ron heard them only as a distant buzzing. He barely noticed Lily's vain attempts to drag him away from the door. Instead, all he knew was the need to break down the barrier standing between him and his captor.

Unfortunately, his enemies were not hampered by hyperfocus. Soldiers came charging around to the back of the cabin, weapons drawn and ready to fire. Ron's higher brain functions finally kicked back online, recognizing the immediate threat. He began to turn, preparing to shove Lily out of the way of the inevitable rain of bullets.

Despite his enhanced speed, he still couldn't move fast enough. His altered senses left him acutely aware of everything. The refracted gleam of sunlight on oiled handgun barrels. The opaque frost building and receding on the soldiers' protective goggles as they breathed. The bits of ice and snow clinging to Lily's parka and toque as she stepped in front of him, her hands upraised.

Ron scrambled to grab her so he could get her out of the line of fire, but his fingers missed, skimming along the plasticized fabric in a fingernail rasp of failure.

The gun muzzles erupted in a blaze of light. For a moment, Ron could have sworn he saw the bullets slowly gliding through the air. For a moment, he thought he still had time to save her.

It was only an illusion. One borne of hope and adrenaline. His desperate grasp left him off balance, and he crashed into the snow as the blast of gunfire slammed into his eardrums, leaving him temporarily deafened.

Lily fell to the ground in front of him, landing heavily on her hands and knees. Her hair came loose, tangling over her face like inky tendrils. She looked back at him, anguish on her face.

Ron reached for her, a child's denial in his heart. If he could only touch her, it would make everything okay. The last few horrible seconds would become a lie or a bad dream.

A forest of legs closed in on them as his hand struggled to close the final inches between them. Lily sagged down as if the weight of her body had become too much to support. Soldiers moved between him and her, knocking aside his hand, denying him the opportunity to make things right. They grabbed his arms and wrenched them behind his back to put handcuffs on him. He screamed and fought, not caring if he tore his arms right out of his body as long as he got the chance to reach her.

Frigid metal burned on his wrist. *No!* He threw himself to the side, breaking loose from the men holding him.

A terrible roar shattered everyone's concentration—low, on the very edge of human hearing, but so loud that it became a physical presence. It swept through the clearing with such ferocity that Ron expected to see trees bend and walls shatter in its wake.

It slammed into the soldiers in front of him, tumbling them in a tangle of limbs and weapons. A furry wall rose up above the heads of those still standing. Higher and higher it climbed, dwarfing them. Then it turned, and Ron's dazzled senses finally made sense of it.

A bear, standing over twelve feet tall, with dark-brown fur except for a golden crescent on one shoulder. Litonya. Her mouth stretched wide, sharp canines glistening in the sun, and her throat vibrated with the roar. The open maw looked wide enough to swallow the soldiers whole.

The soldier trying to cuff him began to fumble with the handcuffs, the metal clanking in evidence of his fear. Ron threw his weight backward, taking advantage of the distraction to get free. Litonya must have followed them like Setsuné. She would be protecting Lily, although Ron couldn't see her anymore through the milling curtain of military men.

The soldier let him go, scrambling backward. Ron rolled onto his feet and began to shove through the men between him and Lily. Litonya was smart, but she could still accidentally crush Lily by stepping on her. Except Lily wasn't there.

Fragments of her red parka were scattered across the snow, ripped apart and left like blood drops at a crime scene. Ron's mind whirled, trying to reset his expectations so he could understand what he was seeing. Litonya's subsonic roar finally ended, and her forelegs crashed down onto the snow, rattling the cabin walls and threatening to knock the aggressors off balance.

We weren't chosen at random to protect the Colony. Is a skinwalker an animal who can take human form or a human with an animal side? Lily's words rattled around the inside of his skull.

"Lily?" Ron whispered, reaching out. She nodded, raising and lowering her head quickly in a gesture that looked alien on a bear even as it conveyed the meaning clearly enough.

A click warned them that the element of pants-wetting surprise was wearing off. Litonya growled and charged at the man who'd raised his rifle. The shot blasted out, breaking the temporary truce.

"Run!" Doc's voice cracked through the din, and Ron whirled, looking for the biologist.

The old man struggled against two soldiers, his long grey hair and beard loose and unkempt from his efforts to break free. Ron didn't need his tactical training to know the old man didn't have a chance, particularly with the cast still around his ankle. Doc shouted again, and one of the soldiers lifted his rifle, ready to club his captive into cooperation.

Ron leapt toward Doc, not caring if these men saw his supernatural abilities if it meant he got to Doc in time. But once again, he was too late. The rifle swung and made contact, thunking into the back of Doc's head with a hollow sound. Doc went sprawling into the snow, red blood swelling up from the wound.

A fuzzy black streak charged out of the forest, snarling. The men swung their rifles to face the new attack. Ron twisted in midair, trying to catch Bart before he charged right into the firing line.

He landed heavily on his side, grabbing the little bear in his arms. His enhanced strength barely held on as two hundred and fifty pounds of muscle coated in slippery fur tried to keep going. Bart might be a small bear, but he weighed more than Ron did. It took everything he had to stop the charge.

But not the bullets.

The sharp crack of rifle fire ripped through the air, and Bart shrieked in agony as the slugs bit deeply into his flesh. He went limp, his weight crushing Ron, pinning him into the churned snow.

Ron couldn't see anything except bristly black fur. He tried to get leverage to move out from underneath, but the angles were too awkward. Men shouted orders and then screamed in panic amid the thunder of gunfire.

Someone lifted Bart's limp body off him. Ron crawled out and saw Litonya holding the little bear's neck ruff in her jaws, easily holding his weight long enough for Ron to escape. Ron got to his feet, ready to fight, and ended up standing there, blinking. He'd been pinned for only a few seconds, and in that time, the firefight had become a massacre.

Gunfire barked off to the side, and he saw two men firing at Setsuné. She ignored the bullets, some of which must have struck despite their terrified aim. Instead, she walked deliberately and silently to them and swatted them with her paw. The gesture looked idle, like someone sweeping aside a pile of papers from a tabletop. It sent them flying through the air, and when they landed, their necks were bent at angles never intended by nature.

The sight sickened Ron, bile rising in his throat. He gagged, and Setsuné's head swung around to focus on him. He winced at the madness in her eyes. He'd seen the human intelligence in Litonya's eyes long before he knew her true identity. Setsuné's gaze held all the pain of a sentient creature avenging the death of a loved one. As he stared at her, he accepted the truth of what Lily had tried to tell him. She was aware and intelligent but not human.

Litonya stepped in front of Ron. He guessed she didn't entirely trust

Setsuné's sanity either.

The adrenaline began to drain out of Ron, pulling his energy with it. He couldn't help looking down at Bart. The wind stirred his dark fur as if trying to rouse a sleeping playmate. His brown eyes stared blankly ahead, ignoring the flecks of snow and ice in the wind. Ron closed them, sliding the delicate lids together with a brush of his fingers. He stroked Bart's head, marveling at the velvety fur under the coarse guard hairs.

The snow crunched as Setsuné approached. Litonya growled.

"Easy. It's okay," Ron assured her, looking up as the ancient bear came closer. "I'm sorry, Setsuné. I tried—I swear I did."

Setsuné still didn't look entirely sane, although the craziness didn't gleam in her eyes anymore. Ron and Litonya backed away as the matriarch knelt beside Bart's body, keening softly as she snuffled at him. Tears threatened to freeze in Ron's eyes as he watched. One more death to add to his conscience. He looked away and saw Doc sprawled in the snow. *Make that two.* He never should have let himself be seduced into staying here. His presence had just cost the people of Bear Claw everything.

Leaving Setsuné to her grief, Ron walked slowly to Doc, unsure what he could possibly do but unable to leave him lying in the snow like an abandoned toy. At least the biologist hadn't seen Bart get shot. It would have hurt him as deeply as Setsuné.

Litonya stayed between him and Setsuné. Ron thought about saying something but stopped. She was the expert, and he trusted her to keep him safe while he dealt with Doc. His sorrow-numbed brain wondered if she could change herself back to human or if she needed to wait for sunset or something else. He might have gotten used to the idea of people with superpowers, but actual shape-shifters still seemed too much like Hollywood special effects to feel completely real.

He knelt beside Doc and rolled him over, intending to lift him up. Sometime in the chaos of the last few minutes, he'd lost his mittens. He should worry about frostbite, except he found it hard to shift mental tracks. At least until his chilled bare fingertips caught the steady thumping of a pulse.

It can't be. It's a trick of the cold. Ron huffed on his hands to warm them. Then, taking a deep breath to steady his nerves, he checked Doc's neck again. He closed his eyes, trying not to get his hopes up, but a pulse definitely beat under his fingers. Ron noticed that blood still seeped from the purpling gash on the back of Doc's head. More proof. *He's not dead. He's unconscious.*

As if to confirm Ron's diagnosis, Doc stirred and moaned, his hand coming up to touch the sticky blood on his head. "Hang on," Ron told him. "We have to get you out of the snow."

He picked Doc up and got to his feet, his mind newly awakened by the necessity of caring for someone else. Doc would need dry and warm clothes. *The ranger station.*

"Get away from him, you bastard!" A sudden shout stopped Ron in his tracks.

Slowly, he turned, easily holding Doc's weight. Steve stood on the far side of one of the cabins. He'd obviously taken shelter there during the fight, but the ranger wasn't what held Ron's attention now. That honor went to the wide-barreled shotgun trembling in Steve's hands.

"Steve, he needs help." Ron kept his voice calm. He guessed Steve had become unhinged by everything he'd witnessed. Ron knew from experience how unsettling it could be to have the fundamentals of a worldview ripped out from under his feet. He himself had fled in terror to try and drown himself in a bottle as a reaction to that kind of disturbance. From the look of Steve's pale face and trembling hands, the ranger wasn't handling it nearly as well as Ron had.

"Leave him alone!" Steve shouted. The barrel of the shotgun shook, and Ron tensed, ready to leap away if the ranger began to blast at random.

"Steve—" Ron tried again.

"Shut up! This is all your fault!" Steve rasped. "You should be the one who's dead."

Litonya moved surprisingly quickly for an animal that weighed over two thousand pounds. Ron didn't hear her or see her change position, but suddenly, she stood between him and the shotgun.

"Lily, don't!" Ron shouted. Steve was ready to fire—every soldier's instinct confirmed that. Ron couldn't put Doc down safely, at least not quickly enough to protect Lily. If he jumped over her with Doc in his arms, then Doc would take the brunt of the shotgun blast.

"That's not Lily," Steve snarled, his lip curled in revulsion as he looked at Litonya.

"Steve, listen to me. I know you're scared." Words spilled out of Ron in a desperate attempt to defuse the situation. "You have to put the shotgun down. Doc's hurt and needs help. We need your help. You're supposed to help people."

"I have to protect him from you." Steve lifted the gun. Litonya reared back on her hind legs, blocking Ron's view.

He ran to the side, hoping to get around her quickly enough to make a difference. He dreaded hearing the deafening blast of Steve pulling the trigger.

Instead, he heard a hollow thump. Skidding to a stop beside Litonya, he saw Bill standing over Steve, the butt of his rifle firmly in hand. The older ranger surveyed the scene with cool practicality. "Get Doc inside, and then come help me with Steve."

Ron obeyed, relief leaving him weak. Too many shocks had hit him for him to be functioning with anything near competence. He was reacting on gut instinct and emotion. He needed to wake himself up, but he couldn't summon the strength to do anything differently. He'd felt the same way when he'd staggered away from that truck stop.

"This is a surprise," a familiar voice interrupted him.

With everything else that had happened in the last few minutes, he'd forgotten why he'd broken cover in the first place. Adrenaline spiked through his body, nailing him to the floor in frozen fear.

"I rarely underestimate my opponents," his captor continued, staring at Ron through a video interface. A large flat-screen monitor was perched on the rangers' map table, topped with a webcam. "Perhaps you'd like to tell me why exactly my men failed?"

Ron's vocal cords locked as he simultaneously tried to obey the instructions and keep Bear Claw's secrets. He was appalled to discover the man still held power over him and that his body leapt to obey his captor's whims.

"I didn't expect it would be easy to capture you. I spent too much time and money making you into a superhuman. But I didn't expect you to destroy them all." His captor nodded in approval. "Well done. This demonstration should increase your value on the market even more."

Bile surged up, but it couldn't get past Ron's throat and left him choking and shaking. The dead men around him meant less than nothing to the man onscreen. They somehow ended up being an economic benefit to him.

"I arranged this little surprise on the advice of Commander Lind, who did not underestimate you. The prototype works exactly as Northstar promised, giving me an opportunity to give you the proper instructions." Lips parted in a cruel smile, and his captor delivered the final blow. "Come back to me."

No. No. NO! Ron's denial might have been silent, but it screamed inside his head with every bit of strength he could summon up.

"You don't have a choice, you know. Come—" The picture abruptly winked out.

Ron blinked, still locked into place. The command echoed and tugged at his awareness, alternately bullying and seducing him to obey.

Bill straightened from outside the window, holding a wood-handled axe in his hands. "Looked like you were having some trouble, so I cut the power line to the generator."

Ron opened his mouth, wanting to tell the ranger not to trust him anymore. Bill should knock him out, like Steve. Nothing emerged except a hoarse whimper.

"It's all right, son. We're going to get you to someplace safe."

Nowhere is safe. Sweat beaded and ran across Ron's skin, the only evidence of his internal struggle.

"Ron, it's going to be okay." Lily stepped through the door, draped in a blanket. Her bare legs peeped from under the ragged edge. She didn't seem to be injured, but Ron's mind was busy struggling to fight the lingering command.

"Hhimm." Ron managed to force a single blurred syllable through his frozen lips.

Understanding dawned in Lily's eyes. She said something in rapid staccato syllables to Bill, who hefted the axe.

"Got it, Lily." The ranger disappeared from the window.

"You need to give Doc to me," Lily said quietly.

Ron understood. Doc couldn't afford any more injuries. He still hadn't completely regained consciousness. Lily slipped her arms under Doc.

His hands resisted letting the biologist go. He suspected the need to care for Doc was a big part of why he hadn't instantly obeyed his captor. Ron closed his eyes and surrendered Doc's weight to Lily. As soon as his hands were free, he clutched at the rough-hewn edge of the map table to anchor himself.

"It's all right, Ron. Just another minute," Lily reassured him, her voice dim and distant as he battled the demons in his head. He kept his eyes closed, not wanting to tense up and fight Bill when the ranger came in to knock him out.

"Just a minute." Lily sounded closer now. A sharp pressure jabbed his arm, and his eyes snapped open despite his intentions.

Lily had plunged a syringe into his arm through his parka. He looked at her in shock as chemical blackness swiftly began to swallow his awareness.

"I'm sorry, Blue Eyes."

Chapter Fourteen

Lily caught Ron as he slumped forward. The ketamine she'd injected from Doc's supplies was intended to fill the tranquilizer darts for bears. She lowered him to the rough wood floor and checked his pulse and breathing. To her relief, both were strong and regular. She glanced to where Bill tended Doc, who was beginning to come around.

"Is he still breathing?" Bill asked.

"Yes." Lily got up to get a cloth to wash Ron's face. Dots of sticky blood were drying on his hands and face. He'd hate it if they were still there when he woke up.

"Damn stupid thing to do, injecting him like that. You have no idea what kind of dosage is safe for him," Bill said.

"Because inflicting a head wound to incapacitate someone is so much more precise," Lily snapped back. She clutched her wet cloth in her hand. "Did you even check to see if Steve is still breathing?"

Bill wasn't inclined to take her criticism constructively. "Don't take that tone of voice with me, young lady. Without your grandmother—"

"Don't fight." Doc's weak voice cut across the argument. "We don't have the time."

Lily knelt beside Ron and began cleaning the blood from his exposed skin. His face was still creased, and his lips pinched together as if he was in pain. As much as her heart ached to see his anguish, she hoped it meant she hadn't overdosed him with the drugs. The thought of him dying sent a ripping tornado of knife-winged butterflies swirling in her gut.

He'd been ready to sacrifice himself to keep her and the rest of Bear Claw safe and without a second thought about what would have happened to him if he'd been captured. The close call left her shaking with fury and melting on the inside. He'd decided too quickly, not giving her time to come up with something else, but he'd done it to save them. He understood how vulnerable they were and would rather turn himself over to his worst nightmare than risk them.

She kept her fingers pressed against the pulse in his neck, drawing comfort from the steady beat. A flicker of his eyelid had her peering down with swallowed breath. He needed to wake up so she could tell him how sorry she was, and then the guilt storm could stop tearing her into pieces. Did he hate her for being a skinwalker? For lying to him? Would he see her as an animal now? The questions kept pounding at her nerves, leaving them loose and quivering.

Setsuné's display of savagery would make anyone think twice about trusting a skinwalker. Ron's face had been white and his hands shaking when he'd realized what her great-grandmother had done. And yet the idea of him hating her somehow didn't matter to her as much as it had before. As long as he was alive and unharmed, she'd thank the spirits and swallow her broken heart.

A small flare of hope inside refused to be extinguished. Maybe he would understand, and maybe he would still love her as much as she loved him. Heavy, thumping footsteps interrupted her thoughts.

"I brought him inside. He'll be okay." Bill coughed. "Lily, we can't stay here."

"Of course not. They'll be back with more soldiers." Common sense told her as much. This hadn't been a courtesy call or an inquiry. Somehow, Ron's enemy had known what to expect. She'd seen the massive cages lying in pieces and the heavy tow cables attached to the helicopters. If they hadn't stopped them, those men would be hunting the Colony. "We need to destroy the cages."

"They're reinforced steel." Bill shook his head. "We're not going to be able to destroy them without welding torches and a lot of time."

"Break the hinges," Doc suggested, holding a cloth to his face to staunch the blood.

"Let's go, then." Lily got to her feet.

Bill coughed, his face flushed. "Maybe you should… ah, put some clothes on?"

Lily tugged her draped blanket closer. In fiction, skinwalkers always seemed to have extra clothes handy or could generate them out of nothing. Dramatically bursting into animal form served as punctuation for effect. She'd never done anything like that before. Transforming had always been a conscious decision, requiring mental effort.

When she saw those men holding Ron down and putting cuffs on him, it had certainly sparked a strong emotional reaction. Fury, fear, and a fierce urge to protect had overwhelmed any semblance of conscious thought. She hadn't been on the verge of a transformation, though. Not until she'd seen the naked terror on Ron's face as he'd struggled to reach her. Then everything had shifted to the fur before she'd even been aware of it. Uneasiness pricked at her, and she wondered if this was the first step in losing herself.

"Where can we go?" Doc asked weakly. Propped up on the bench, he leaned against the wall. Obviously, he wouldn't be up to any kind of strenuous trek even if his ankle hadn't been already injured.

"We have to go to Ekurru and warn Evonne and everyone there." Lily made the decision quickly. "I'll get clothes there."

"You'll freeze—" Bill began, but Lily cut him off, shaking her head.

"I'll go in the fur and carry Ron. We'll need blankets or something to keep him warm enough."

"What about Steve? We can't leave him here." Bill didn't look at his partner, who lay slumped unceremoniously in the corner. Lily hesitated, a certain level of guilt creeping into her confidence as she realized she'd forgotten about him entirely. Bill was right. Steve needed someone checking on him regularly until he woke up and recovered from the blow to his head. But she couldn't forget seeing the twin barrels of his shotgun pointed at her like monstrous maws. Nor could she ignore how he'd clearly been working with the soldiers, threatening Doc to get him to betray secrets.

"I stay." It was a woman's voice, but rough and uneven as if the speaker hadn't used it for a very long time.

All of them turned to look at the doorway. An elderly woman stood there, calmly shrugging into a ripped and bloodstained parka. Her pale-grey hair spilled down her shoulders in a long, matted tangle, and her tan skin was deeply folded and pitted with wrinkles.

"Setsuné," Lily breathed. She'd never seen her great-grandmother in human form before. She held out a blanket. "You don't have to do this."

Setsuné cuffed her great-granddaughter affectionately. She pointed a gnarled finger at the bodies strewn in the snow. "My fault."

Bill cleared his throat before beating a hasty retreat. "I'll deal with the hinges."

Setsuné clutched at the blanket over her heart, her dark eyes bright with tears. "Hurt."

Lily didn't have to ask what she meant. Big Bart's little body still lay in the snow, visible through the open door. "I know. It hurts me, too."

"Kind girl. Smart." Setsuné cupped Lily's cheek. "I watch. Wake, I go. Other comes, I go."

A repeated metallic dinging announced that Bill was attacking the cages with his axe. Setsuné winced at the noise, her shoulders rounding up to her ears.

"Don't risk yourself. We've lost enough today." Lily wrapped her arms around her great-grandmother. Setsuné hesitated, and Lily guessed she needed to remember how to use her spindly and oddly jointed human limbs. Her great-grandmother's arms folded around her, holding her close, to allow the love and pride to seep between them.

"Litonya." Setsuné pulled back, holding Lily at arm's length. "Must make choice. Two here and in here." She tapped Lily's heart and head. "Live in both, very difficult. Much hurt. Better to choose."

Her great-grandmother was obviously struggling hard in her efforts to communicate, which surprised Lily as much as the message. Grandfather always encouraged them to find a balance between the fur and the skin. He'd warned them against getting caught up in one form. Yet Setsuné felt choosing one was important enough to make a tremendous effort at speaking verbally.

Were they expressing different opinions, or did Setsuné understand something Grandfather didn't? The tug of trying to live two different lives kept Lily off balance, and sometimes she felt as though she wasn't living either fully. Walking away from her bear form was more like an amputation than a lifestyle choice. Even when she worried about disappearing inside the fur, she didn't want to give it up entirely.

She watched her great-grandmother brush aside debris on a bench with the back of her hand, the fingers rigidly cupped together as if she still had a paw rather than a hand. All Lily's life, she'd been told that Setsuné had lost herself in the fur. But if her great-grandmother hadn't been trapped by her animal side but had, instead, chosen it, then Lily didn't need to be afraid of losing herself. Both sides of her nature felt right to her. Or was she reading too much into a few words from a woman who hadn't spoken or possibly even thought in human language for over six decades?

Introspection could wait. She needed to get Ron and Doc out of there. Mindful of the door's narrow dimensions, she stepped outside and willed the transformation. Settling evenly onto all four paws, she snuffled the air, searching for any hint of more intruders.

Litonya pointed her nose toward the cabin and waited. Bill brought Ron out and laid him on her broad back. The weight triggered an automatic discomfort from her animal side, but her human one overrode it immediately. Bill covered Ron with a blanket and tied it down over him, looping the coils around her belly to hold her unconscious passenger in place. Between her body heat, Ron's clothes, and the blanket, he should stay warm enough for them to get him safely to Evonne's.

Bill came back out, helping Doc to limp along. The four of them set out, moving slowly. Litonya found the rubbing and binding of the ropes uncomfortable and unnatural, but she continued with her plodding walk. She monitored the steady pounding of Ron's heartbeat and drew comfort from each fur-ruffling breath. Bill held his rifle in one hand while the other supported Doc. He kept scanning the trees and what could be seen of the horizon. Doc was pale with pain, his lips bloodlessly clenched against his teeth as he alternately limped and hopped.

It seemed to take forever for them to reach Evonne's, moving slowly through a dark forest that seemed to have switched allegiance to their enemies. The ever-shifting wall of tree trunks no longer offered a concealing curtain of protection. Instead, each one was a hole in their vision, a potential ambush. Constant vigilance rapidly beat them down toward exhaustion. Litonya felt it instinctively, the shift from predator to prey. As an omnivore, she understood both sides of the exchange.

No further ambushes sprang out at them from the deepening Arctic twilight. They reached the Running Elk cottage without incident. Bill banged roughly on the door.

"Bob?" Evonne cried out as the door flew open. Her face fell as she realized it wasn't her husband but tightened in concern as she took in their condition. "What happened?"

"Soldiers. They came for us. They know about us." Bill explained it succinctly if dismally.

A shadow separated itself from the interior of the cabin, resolving into Vincent. "Where are they now?"

"Dead." Bill's hand tightened on his rifle, suspicious. "What are you doing here?"

"He came when he heard the helicopters. He wanted to make sure I was safe," Evonne answered, her shoulders straightening at the implied insult. No one impugned a guest in Evonne's house.

Vincent stepped forward to support Doc's weight. Litonya took a deep breath, expecting to catch the harsh bite of alcohol. Its absence shocked her. Vincent appeared to actually be sober. Bill let go of Doc after a long glare, and the two men staggered forward to a seat by the warm stove.

Bill turned to untie Ron from Litonya's back. The ropes fell away, but the places where they had rubbed still burned. Bill made a clucking noise. "You should have said something."

Litonya let out a sharp huff and glared at him.

"Point taken." After lifting Ron, Bill brought him into the cabin as Evonne hurried out with a shirt and pants draped over her arm. Litonya hefted herself up onto her hind legs and let herself shrink back into her skin. As soon as Lily's hands were functional, she grabbed the clothes, grateful the two of them were near enough in size to make it work. The velvety-soft texture of the closely woven wool slid over her skin, and Lily allowed herself a girlish moment of enjoying the sensation.

"I don't know where Bob went." Evonne bit her lip. "I thought he'd come back, especially when we heard the helicopters. I'm afraid he's gotten hurt."

"He wasn't at the ranger station, so I'm sure he's fine," Lily said.

"Vincent checked on Georgie at the retreat. She's okay, and Bob wasn't there." Evonne used the back of her wrist to shove her hair out of her face. "She's worried Bob might come back and take me away."

"We won't let him." Lily hugged Evonne, feeling her friend tremble. The weight of her guilt crushed her. So much trouble crashing down on her friends and family because of her decision to rescue a lost hiker in the woods.

Bill tapped his fingers on the table. "I don't think any of us are going to be able to stay here. The man on the television is going to send more people. We can't be here when he arrives."

"How can we get everyone out?" Lily demanded, aghast. "Even if we move all the people, there's still the Colony! Where will they go?"

"Sesame Street?" Vincent snarked. Everyone ignored him.

"There's the plane." Doc raised his head limply. "The river is still running."

The door thumped, and all of them jumped as Andrew opened it. Lily could have screamed at him for ratcheting up the tension in an already unbearable situation. Luckily, Bill took him aside to explain what had happened at the ranger station. That way, Lily didn't have to deal with his sardonic commentary.

Lily sat down beside Ron, trying to think. Bill had put him on Evonne and Bob's bed, and he lay on the brilliant orange-and-red quilt as if he slept. She smoothed his fine sandy-brown hair, letting her fingers skim over the network of fine creases at the corners of his eyes. Most of the scars left by his life were internal, hardened places in his soul and heart. He'd cursed himself for failing, but he still kept trying. Maybe her thinking stemmed from a life defined by scarcity, but the battering he'd suffered only made him shine brighter in her mind. He'd proven his worth. If only he could see it.

Andrew walked into the room without knocking. "How are you doing?"

His lack of sarcasm told her how worried he was. Her answer wouldn't help the situation. They might not be physically hurt, but the threat hanging over their heads wasn't something she would define as okay. Their sanctuary was broken. The protective stone walls they'd relied on had been abruptly revealed to be cheap cardboard stage sets. "Still here."

"Grandfather is going to the retreat with Lou. They're planning to evacuate the Colony."

Evacuation. The five-syllable word wrapped around her throat, blocking the air. She barely managed a squeak. "Where?"

"Apparently, Lou found some potential sites a few years ago. He's been keeping an eye on them in case we needed them." Andrew sat down on the bed next to her, his elbows balanced on his parted knees. "He needs to work on his communication skills."

Lily chuckled at the old joke, letting it puncture some of the tension between them. "We aren't going to be able to stay here. This entire place will have to look deserted when they come back."

"Some of us are going to have to be bait to draw the hunters away," Andrew said. "Those men wanted Blue Eyes and Vincent. I assume you will come with us as well."

"You're coming?" Lily ran her hand over her tangled hair. "Of course you are. If you can break the mental hold, then they can be potential weapons." She doubted Vincent would be able to destroy the link. He'd spent too long running from it. Even asking him to change felt uneasily like being complicit with mental torture. Yet her discomfort paled in comparison with the wave of emotional protest against using Ron as a weapon against their attackers.

She barely kept her objections behind her teeth. Only one thing stopped her from speaking out: if her brother suspected how much her loyalties had shifted, he would leave her behind. "That's four—five with Doc, who has to fly *Angel*. That leaves room for one more."

"Me," Evonne said from the doorway.

Lily and Andrew both started in surprise. Neither had heard her come close.

"Evonne, are you sure?" Lily asked.

"I'm sure. I'll write a note to Bob." Dry tear tracks dulled her dusky cheeks. "It can be the first link on the trail. When he finds it, he'll go straight to the ranger station and find Steve."

Lily rubbed at her forehead as if the movement could knock her thoughts loose. Those cages hadn't been put together in a few days. Someone had been hunting them before Ron's arrival, but how? *Of course. Dr. Damali's research.* Based on legends of large, intelligent bears. The deeply unpleasant conclusion slugged her in the gut. Dr. Damali's project had never been about documenting unusual wildlife for mining. She'd been working for their attackers, led by the same man who'd held Ron and Vincent. Their enemies were even closer than they'd realized. "We need help from the greater *lalassu* community if we're going to get through this. All of us are in danger."

"I'm reconsidering our hiring policies for subcontractors." Dalhard poked at one of the frozen bodies with the toe of his elegant designer boots.

"They have been somewhat ineffective of late," Karan agreed, scanning the area. The soldiers must have been taken completely by surprise, given the paucity of bullets fired. Superficially, their injuries appeared to be a common animal mauling, but no animal struck as precisely as that. Broken spines and claw marks that unerringly hit major arteries, causing instant bleed outs—these injuries were the work of something intelligent.

"This should have been simple." Dalhard seethed while Karan knelt to examine the cages. The hinges were flattened or broken open, making it impossible to pin the sections together. A masterful bit of sabotage.

"Get the other team up here now," Dalhard ordered.

"Sir, that may not be wise." Karan rose to his feet. His employer had gone very still except for twitching muscles in his jaw. "They have gone into hiding after destroying the cages to ensure we could not come after them. We cannot expect ordinary soldiers to go up against *lalassu* and walk away unscathed." Karan watched Dalhard's jaw flex more rapidly, a sign of an impending explosion. If Karan's employer believed he would remain silent and risk becoming the scapegoat for this ill-advised failure, then Dalhard was even further from reality than Karan had guessed.

"We don't have anything in the stable that is suitable. That was the point of recruiting soldiers for experimentation." Dalhard studied the five claw marks slicing across a cabin wall. He stretched his fingers wide but could not match the width of the slashes. "McBride is the only one to show a useful level of enhancement. We need him to study. We never should have left him and the other one."

This was not a point Karan wished to debate with his employer. He had seen McBride's expression after the old woman was shot. The man had been on the verge of breaking free of his conditioning. If they had taken him, he would have inevitably rebelled or destroyed his mind, either of which would have ended his potential usefulness. Time had been of the essence; even a few seconds of delay could have undone them.

"We should return in the spring," Karan suggested. "Harvest the cubs. They will likely prove more tractable and trainable if taken young."

Dalhard grunted, the closest he was likely to come to an admission. Karan picked his way across the snow toward the ranger station. His employer's tendency to rewrite history to salve his own ego was appalling. How could Dalhard expect to deal with failure if he never acknowledged it?

Karan bent to enter the shabby little structure. Compared to this, his rustic hotel room was a paragon of sturdy construction. The two men inside went stiff as soon as he entered. *Good.* Their fear would be useful.

The ranger still held a compress to his head above a sulky expression. Karan had dealt with his type many times. Physically powerful and athletic, the ranger was used to getting his way, likely only suffering the sting of failure on rare occasions. His sense of self was rooted in his success, leaving him incredibly vulnerable and open to suggestion in the wake of failure. His bruised eyes, twitching fingers, and clenched teeth were all promising signs of obsession.

The other man was harder to read. Short, with rounded features and the stout body of a professional strongman, his stance declared a pugnacious and determined spirit. He had shown up shortly after their arrival, demanding information about his wife. Karan saw the signs of deception—fidgeting, avoiding eye contact, and short, evasive answers to questions. This man hid key information—likely that his wife was one of the *lalassu.*

"Mr. Villeneuve, Ranger Harker, we are preparing to depart." He needed to cement their loyalty. "We need your help, Mr. Villeneuve. Ms. Golov tells us you are an accomplished pilot. Do you know how to fly a helicopter?"

The pilot nodded slowly, eyes never leaving Karan. "I've flown them before."

"Excellent." Karan widened his mouth in a smile he hoped would reassure. "Are you both ready to proceed?"

The pilot did not hesitate to climb into the cockpit while the ranger lingered, buckling his harness with unnecessary slowness. Karan drew his headset on as the noisy rotors pulled them into the sky. Bear Claw dropped away beneath them.

"Are you all right, Ranger Harker?" Dalhard asked, the concern in his voice evident despite the static popping over the communication frequencies and the dull roar of the rotor blades.

"I've never seen anything like that." Steve shook his head, his fingers gripping his bag even tighter. Karan's knuckles ached in sympathy. "One minute—"

"Steve," the pilot warned. *Interesting.* Karan deducted that the ranger had only recently learned of the *lalassu*, and the pilot was trying to keep him from saying too much.

Dalhard nodded, showing the predatory patience that Karan wished his employer would use in other circumstances. "We'll have time to talk when we land."

Steve nodded, accepting Dalhard's proposal.

"We'll have our doctors check you out. It's the least we can do under the circumstances." Dalhard made the offer in an appearance of generosity. Only Karan could appreciate the practicality of the gesture. It would keep the ranger under their control and give them a chance to run a genetic-compatibility profile. With his obsession, it should not be hard to convince the man to undergo the process for the prospect of vengeance.

Karan made a few discreet notes on his tablet as they flew back to Kluane. Would it be best to send the ranger south or to bring the necessary personnel here? The dilemma preoccupied him, distracting him from underlying irritation.

The pilot proved surprisingly competent, managing the short flight easily and landing safely with a light touch on the controls. Perhaps they would offer him a position with the company. After they landed, the pilot slipped away, and Karan let him. Kluane was not particularly large, and he had people strategically positioned. The pilot's movements would be tracked and reported.

Karan still winced when they returned to their accommodations. Dalhard had bought out the single hotel in Kluane, but it was little more than a hunting lodge that catered to ruggedly independent outdoorsmen. Karan had arranged for adequate wireless communication relays and shipped up appropriate food, but nothing could change the deliberately rustic nature of the place with its wood-paneled walls, roughhewn furniture, and brilliantly checkered curtains. He supposed he should be grateful the owners had decided to opt for indoor plumbing rather than outhouses.

Mood rapidly souring, Karan flipped open his laptop to attend to the necessary inconvenience of running a multinational company. Instead, he received a pleasant surprise. His little fish had taken the first piece of bait. **Caligo>> Are you serious about a truce?**

Karan smiled. His former partner was so easy to read, despite his attempt at tough-guy attitude and suspicion. **Pujari>> I would not have offered otherwise.**

The response came so quickly that Caligo must have prepared it in advance.

Caligo>> What exactly are you offering?

Pujari>> Identify the people you wish left alone, and we will do so. An offer will always be open to them to join us, but we will not risk further upset by attempting recruitment. Karan had planned his opening offer carefully, proposing enough to seem serious while still allowing his former partner to dismiss him as greedy.

Caligo>> How do I know this isn't a trap to identify them and collect them yourselves?

Pujari>> We are still nursing our wounds from our last entanglement, old friend. It is not an experience we are eager to repeat. This is simple business—nothing more, nothing less.

Caligo>> You were always good with the numbers.

Karan frowned. Was the comment intended as a slur? So many of their disagreements boiled down to idealism versus practicality. He had constantly insisted that Caligo was not thinking of the numbers. Or was it finally an acknowledgement of his particular talents? **Pujari>> Do you** agree then?

Caligo>> I want to trust you, my old friend, but our history makes it difficult. If we could meet face-to-face, it would be easier to strike a bargain.

The hook had been swallowed, but the fish was not yet secure. It could still slip away from him. **Pujari>> Or for you to set your own trap? Our history cuts both ways.**

Caligo>> A fair point. I will bring your proposal to the Priestess. A small step of trust.

Pujari>> It is all I ever asked.

Ron didn't know anymore if he was dreaming or awake. He watched Brian and Adam step through walls, leaving behind crosses that grew into solemn forests standing in silent judgment. He ran between the tree trunks, which unfurled like flower petals to reveal men standing at attention, their blank eyes staring ahead in solemn sentry duty. Big Bart poked at the men in their tree coffins, leaving great black smudges on them from his nose. Ron tried to shout at him, to warn him of the danger, but the little bear never saw the men reaching for him with blackened fingers. They clutched at his fur, and he screamed for help. Ron fell, and when he looked up, he saw black claws ripping away the fur, and then it wasn't Bart but Lily lying there. Cadaverous hands dragged her into a waiting trunk.

He tried to run, except his legs were too heavy and the air was too thick. He could only watch as the bark folded around Lily. Just as it closed, she opened her eyes. Her loving, sparkling dark eyes were blank and white. Dead, without any hint of life or laughter. He shouted and pounded at the trunk to release her, his cries swallowed up by the silent forest. His hands turned blue with cold and then shimmered into ice. His next blow shattered his fingers into crystalline pieces. His entire body began to vanish like loose snow in the wind, a glint of swirling refracted light and then nothing.

"Ron?" He could hear Lily calling, but he had no body to answer her with. Or did he? He felt dreadfully tired and heavy but still somehow scattered.

Lily's face hovered nearby, but it quickly began to change, her skin getting darker and rougher. Long canines yawned from Litonya's long snout. She huffed at him, and he wanted to tell her that he was sorry he hadn't understood who she truly was.

"He's still out of it." Lily sounded so sad. She reached out to him, and her hands became claws that penetrated deep into his arms, injecting him with numbing drugs. He tried to protest, but his throat had swollen into an impenetrable barrier. Panic started to set in. He remembered Lily injecting him with a drug. Was this an overdose? If he was dead and this was the afterlife, it was as horrible as he'd always feared: fully aware and trapped inside a decaying body.

"He'll wake up soon," Doc said. Was Doc okay, or was he stuck in this place, too? Ron wondered if any of it was real or if these were just the final spasms of a dying brain. It all felt like too much to worry about. He curled up at the base of a tree as the bark wrapped around him, holding him close. He grabbed at it, ready for oblivion. To his surprise, the bark felt like a knit blanket.

No matter how he tugged, he couldn't get it to cover him completely. Someone held his head, hands wrapped around each side like the two sides of a vise. He jerked away, and one hand slipped, allowing a horrible roaring sound to invade deep into his brain.

"Careful," Lily said as the hands returned and the sound dropped to a bearable background level. Ron reached up and touched a smooth curve of plastic cupping his head. He blinked and saw Lily again, her face a pale smudge against a darker background.

His lips and tongue were still numb and stiff. He frowned, rubbing at his mouth. Lily had done this to him—left him helpless, weak, and trapped in his dreams. He reminded himself that she'd done it to protect him, but panic had him firmly in its steel claws.

Doc reached out to pat his arm, and Ron twitched, trying to escape what his brain interpreted as an attack.

"The effects will wear off soon, boy." Bright-yellow ear protectors blazed on either side of Doc's head like little suns.

"You're quite lucky, you know." Andrew's sardonic voice drifted to him. Ron strained but couldn't see him—only regular bands of darkness, overlapping in a crisscross pattern. *Cargo netting,* his dazed brain identified. The buzzing was an engine. He was on some kind of cargo plane or maybe a helicopter.

"Do you want some water?" Lily asked cautiously.

He realized he heard her directly through the headphones wrapped around his head. A headset. Now he could see the microphone hovering in front of her lips.

Anger slowly started to boil, creeping forward to cover his hurt. They had drugged him and dragged him somewhere. After all their talk of trusting one another. He managed to get his body and brain together enough to ask a single word. "Where?"

"We're on our way south," Andrew answered grimly. "When we land, we'll figure out our next step."

"We're flying?" Ron asked, words coming together easier the second time.

"Welcome to the *Angel.* I use her every spring and fall to bring up my gear and supplies for the year." Doc patted the narrow fuselage fondly.

Ron blinked, trying to resolve his blurred vision into something coherent. He noticed two other people sitting across the narrow fuselage: Vincent and a young native woman wrapped in a thick blanket. She curled up against the netting with her eyes squeezed tightly shut and her mouth wincing in pain. Vincent's head lolled on his shoulders, and his wrists and ankles were wrapped in duct tape.

"He didn't come quietly," Lily answered Ron's unspoken questions. "This is my best friend, Evonne. She's one of the Marked."

"The others?" Ron was slowly returning to life. Whatever preflight cocktail they'd given him, there didn't seem to be too many physical side effects. Too bad his emotional reactions weren't settling as quickly. Everything flashed through his mind too quickly to process, scraping nasty raw wounds with every pass.

"Lou took Grandfather and the others deeper into the woods. Bill is watching over the Colony. Hopefully, those people will follow our trail and overlook them." Lily hugged herself tightly across her body, rubbing her arms. Ron's first instinct was to hold her and tell her everything would be all right, but two things stopped him: his emotions were bouncing so rapidly he didn't trust himself not to snap at her, and he couldn't reconcile the petite young woman in front of him with the massive bear who had sent him running through the forest when they'd first met.

It didn't seem physically possible. Litonya was ten times Lily's weight at a minimum. How could so much mass compress or expand without flying apart? When he'd lifted her, she hadn't been extraordinarily heavy.

"I know you have questions." Lily hesitated.

And when I'm not recovering from a drug overdose, I'll ask them. He tried to dismiss his anger with reason. He'd been begging them to knock him out rather than risk hurting them or returning him to his captors. She'd done it in a much gentler fashion, and yet, he couldn't stop himself from reacting as if she had attacked him. His faith in her was shattered by the lies she'd told, leaving him to wonder if she'd been manipulating him from the beginning. He'd thought he'd found sanctuary, and it had ended up being just as false as the previous one.

He closed his eyes to pretend to sleep, aware he wasn't being entirely fair but unable to stop his internal seething. A small, mean voice in his head told him to walk away from all of them. They'd hurt him, so he didn't owe them anything.

Doc hadn't owed him anything but still gave him a place to stay and nursed him back to health. Andrew hadn't owed him anything but tried to help him with his post-traumatic-stress flashbacks. He could rage against them like Vincent, or he could swallow his pride and try to get back to being the sort of man he'd believed he was before Afghanistan. Then he could try and figure out what to do about Lily and his feelings.

CHAPTER FIFTEEN

"I look over, and suddenly it's not Lily anymore—it's a giant bear. And it starts attacking us." Steve's red-rimmed eyes and arm-waving gestures made him look more like an End-Is-Nigh street preacher than a confident cowboy. "I saw that murderer go after Doc, and I threatened to shoot him. I couldn't let him kill Doc the way he killed Rachel."

The ranger's boot heels bounced against the industrial carpet in muffled staccato. After the fiasco at Bear Claw, there were a number of empty rooms in their rustic hunting lodge, and Karan had simply installed their new acquisitions in one of them. The pilot had left early that morning to meet with Ms. Golov, giving them the perfect opportunity to recruit the ranger.

"We were all greatly grieved to hear of Dr. Damali's death," Dalhard interjected smoothly without interrupting Steve's flow of complaints.

"I thought I had him. I was ready to pull the trigger, and then someone took me out from behind." Steve reached up to touch the bandage covering the gash on the back on his head. "I didn't wake up until just before you got there."

"Who else was there?" Karan asked. It had taken them several hours to reach the isolated clutch of cabins after the video feed was severed. Enough time to allow their prey to escape and leave their homes abandoned. But someone had cared for the unconscious ranger. The shattered door to his cabin left the interior freezing, and an unconscious man would have quickly perished without the fire in the stove. A fire that had been tended well enough to still be burning brightly when they arrived.

Steve shook his head. "I thought I saw someone moving around when I first woke up, but I must have dreamed it. There wasn't anyone there."

Karan kept his face perfectly still despite an urge to let his lip curl in disgust at the ranger's obtuseness. The man could not see past the superficial basics of the situation. He had not seen anyone, and therefore, no one must have been there despite the evidence of someone having tended the fire and the ranger. It made the ranger a useful tool, but Karan could not help looking at him with contempt. The man was a follower, prey for anyone who cared to use him, and he did not even seem to realize it.

"Where would they have gone?" Dalhard pushed.

Steve shook his head. "I don't know. Lily and her family did some trading here in Kluane and down in Juneau and Whitehorse. Her brother is at the University of Alaska. Doc has friends at the universities of California and Alaska. He's got a little water plane he uses to go back and forth."

"That gives us some promising leads to pursue." All the potentially useful information had been squeezed out of the ranger. Karan sent a message to check local radar towers. If they had escaped by air, they might have left a radar trail.

"It doesn't seem fair," Dalhard said suddenly.

"What?" Steve raised his head in surprise.

"The story shouldn't end here. A drifter and murderer shouldn't get the drop on a fine young man such as yourself, an officer of the law, and live to get away with it." Dalhard tapped his fingers on the tabletop.

Karan watched the ranger's expression shift into sullen bewilderment. Reminding him of his failure tied yet another string to this puppet.

"We could help you. Make sure the next confrontation is more…" Dalhard paused for dramatic effect. "Even."

Greed kindled in Steve's weary eyes. "How?"

Dalhard put his hand on Steve's arm. "Let me tell you."

From there, the deal was sealed. The puppet would dance to

Dalhard's tune. Karan began to plan forward, mentally shuffling personnel and resources to put people in place for a transformation.

He retreated, leaving Dalhard to finish. As he walked down the long, chilly hall with its flickering and humming fluorescent lights, he made notes on his tablet, sending instructions to various personnel. Out of long practice, his steps were silent, which allowed him to hear the whispered conversation from the lodge's office.

"Things are out of control."

Karan recognized the pilot's voice and held perfectly still to listen.

"No, Ken," Bob whispered. His voice held the notes of a man trying to convince himself. "You don't understand. Evonne would never leave me like this unless someone coerced her. She knows what's out there."

Karan could not catch any hint of the other half of the conversation. Too bad the pilot had not chosen a cell phone for his conspiratorial communication. Still, the landline in the office would make it easy to trace the call.

Bob continued. "I don't trust them."

Perceptive. If the ranger looked beyond the surface, he would not trust them either. Most people were too lazy to look past what they wanted to see, and Karan had no problem with taking advantage of that fact. The pilot might be one of the rare individuals who saw through the verbal smoke and mirrors.

"Once I find her, we have to get out. I'll need your help."

If the pilot thought he could run, he was less clever than Karan hoped. Allowing him to think he had escaped might prove helpful, though. After careful research, Karan suspected Bear Claw might be yet another of the *lalassu* refuges. Such sanctuaries began during the early years of medieval persecution, when to be different invited violent torture and death. The early ones had been monasteries and nunneries. No one in those days grew suspicious if people shut themselves away in the name of the Christian god. Today, they needed greater physical isolation to evade the increasingly connected world. The challenge must drive Caligo mad.

The best way to harvest the *lalassu* of Bear Claw would be to leave them to their isolation. The exodus had not been a well-planned transition but a reaction to a hasty invasion. Pretend to look elsewhere, and they would inevitably crawl back, congratulating themselves on having escaped notice. Then they could be collected in force by an adequately prepared team.

"Thanks, man. I knew I could count on you."

Karan faded back into a blind spot by the door. As he expected, the pilot emerged without checking carefully. Preoccupation always left people with gaps in their vision and unseen vulnerabilities he could exploit.

A pattern of mysterious and abrupt disappearances was being repeated worldwide. Karan had noticed it soon after taking the Harris brothers, and he began to track it then. His old partner had sent out some kind of alert but had not realized how visible the movement would be. Karan had already identified several substantial *lalassu* communities in Perdition, Galveston, and Olympia, as well as some in Europe and the Mediterranean.

The days of hiding in the dark were over.

Doc brought their tiny plane down safely on the water, coasting to a stop on one of the hundreds of finger lakes carved between the mountains by glaciers. The icy waters reflected the starry scape above with perfect clarity, creating an illusion they were landing among the stars. No cabin windows or fires outlined the shore. Ron could only figure out where the edges of the lake were by looking to see where the starlight suddenly vanished. He took a deep breath and coughed on the whiff of sulfur in the air. He tried another breath, but the scent faded quickly.

"Are we swimming to shore?" he asked. "Or do we paddle?"

"Lily?" Doc swiveled to look at her. "Is it too heavy?"

She shook her head, taking off her headphones. "I'll make it work. Get the ropes ready."

They were practically stacked on top of each other in the narrow plane. The *Angel* wasn't designed to carry so many people. Doc grabbed a coil of bright-yellow nylon rope and began tying a large loop. Lily lifted the hem of her shirt and then hesitated, looking at the others.

"We'll keep our eyes closed if you want," Evonne said quietly. "Vincent's out, and he's the only one you'd care about peeking."

"I care. I don't want to go blind." Andrew ostentatiously stared out the window.

Ron didn't close his eyes, but he did look away as Lily hastily hauled her shirt over her head and shucked out of her pants. He'd spent plenty of time fantasizing about the first time he'd get to see her naked, and this wasn't anywhere near the scenario he'd hoped for. She dove into the water, causing the stars to disappear and shift in an expanding black hole of ripples.

When a bear's head broke the surface, he was more prepared. Wrapping his mind around the concept of Lily and Litonya as the same person was easier now that the effects of the ketamine were wearing off. *So much for not being surprised anymore.*

His anger was easier to shove aside, as well, though he still twitched every time someone made a sudden movement. No matter how well intentioned the drugging, he'd been caught off guard, which kept his adrenaline pumping strongly. He'd held back from Lily during the flight, at first because of resentment but now because he wanted space to come to grips with his own reactions.

When he thought about Lily, it was easy. He loved her and wanted to spend his life with her. He also had no trouble thinking of Litonya as a friend. He'd stopped thinking of her as just a bear, but he wasn't attracted to the bruin. But now he had to accept they were the same, that Lily was fundamentally and physically different than he'd first believed. Was he ready to date outside his species?

"Okay, Lily, here you go." Doc tossed the loop he'd made over Litonya's head, and she began to swim to the shore. The floor jerked under Ron's feet as she tugged the plane toward the ice-rimed trees.

He wondered if Lily even thought like a human while she was in her bear form. The way she'd described skinwalkers suggested that the person he thought of as Lily was completely subsumed beneath the animal. Or had he misunderstood? His head ached with too many competing thoughts doing battle.

"She wanted to tell you, but she was scared." Evonne's statement rang loudly in the relative silence of lapping waves.

Ron reluctantly turned away from watching Litonya swim through the stars. "It's a big secret to trust someone with."

"It's more than that. And it's my fault." Doc pulled his glasses off his face to pinch his nose with his fingers before confessing. "I pointed my gun at her."

Ron's fingers curled into fists, and his anger abruptly reignited, swelling his shoulders and arms. The idea of anyone pointing a weapon at Lily brought an instinctive flare of protective fury.

"I'd been following her mother for a few months, studying her and her cubs. Gerry helped me to settle into the cabin, and Lou and Andrew helped a lot for surly teenagers." Doc tossed out the teasing insult, but it fell flat. He hurried to continue. "I didn't know anything about *lalassu* or skinwalkers. I was there strictly for the bears. I called her mother Datsá because of her unusually dark fur. It means raven. She trusted me, letting me get incredibly close. She was my favorite." Doc smiled as he remembered.

"None of this is explaining the gun," Ron growled, knowing he was being irrational and unable to stop himself.

"Ah, yes. I suppose not." Doc's smile vanished, leaving Ron feeling like a jerk. "Datsá was killed by another bear. I heard the growls and went running toward them. When I got to her, she was fighting with a male who'd gone after her cubs. It's not unusual for males to do that, especially in spring when they're hungry. The cubs were curled up in a tree, wailing and crying for their mother. I had my rifle, and I was ready to say to hell with my scientific objectivity and shoot the bastard attacking her when he managed to get a grip on her throat." Doc swallowed hard, and when he spoke again, Ron could see the tears gleaming on his cheeks. "I shot, but it was too late. They were both dead. The cubs ran to me, cuddling against my legs and crying for their mother. I didn't know what else to do. If I left them there, they'd be dead in days. So I brought them home."

Doc's obvious grief finally softened Ron's anger. He reminded himself that whatever happened, it had been a long time ago, and Doc regretted it.

"It took me a while to get them to follow me. I sacrificed bits of my lunch to lure them along. I thought I'd put them in the shed, but I went into the cabin to get some blankets first. As soon as I opened the door, they pushed past me and dashed inside like they were escaping Hell's own demons. I ran in to try and chase them out and found myself staring at a pair of five-year-olds, a little boy and a little girl—Lily and her twin brother, Mark. It scared me half to death, and before I could even begin to guess what to think, I lifted the rifle and pointed it at them." Doc wiped at his tears, too choked up to continue right away.

Ron rolled his shoulders, trying to release the angry tension tightening them down. He could imagine it all too easily. Terrified children who had just seen their mother killed. An isolated biologist suddenly confronted by the scientifically inexplicable. He'd reacted out of fear the way humans had reacted for generations: if it is new and frightening, try and destroy it.

"They started to cry, bawling their little hearts out. I've never felt like a worse person, and I couldn't believe what I'd seen. Gerry and his family arrived soon after. They'd found Datsá and tracked the cubs back to me. I was freaking out, and they were crying. Gerry took me aside and explained everything to me." Doc put his glasses back on, and Ron could see the tears still glittering in his eyes.

"She's never forgotten it." Evonne's quiet voice held so much reproof that it threatened to flatten Doc under the weight.

The biologist didn't say anything for a long moment, swallowing several times before he could make an audible response. "I imagine neither of them have. I'm lucky that Lily hasn't held it against me, but I know I hurt her more badly than I can guess. There's nothing I can do to take it back."

The plane bumped to a stop against something solid. Ron looked out the open door to see Litonya standing on a steep and narrow ice-lined beach, shaking gleaming water out of her dark fur. He started to leverage himself up to get out of the plane, but Doc's hand clamped down on his arm.

"Try to do better than I did," the biologist ordered.

Ron nodded, cracking through the thin, dark ice to splash ashore. His boots kept his feet dry, but the cold still seeped through. He took the rope off Litonya and found a tree to tie it to. Then he used the second tie at the back to further secure the small plane.

Another set of splashes announced Andrew's arrival. "We need shelter, a fire, and somewhere we can hide the plane before sunrise. They'll be after us."

"I'll keep an eye on Evonne and Vincent," Doc offered.

Ron's feet ached from the cold. If he didn't get moving soon, they'd start to freeze. "I'll search down the shore that way. You take this side, and we'll meet back here in half an hour?"

Litonya growled, swinging her head back and forth in a clear negative.

"You have a better plan?" Andrew asked, folding his arms over his chest.

She pointed her snout into the forest. Ron squinted but couldn't make out anything in the deep shadows. Doc passed out a flashlight from the plane. Litonya didn't wait and started into the trees. Ron shone the light ahead of her. It looked like some kind of trail, an old, overgrown one.

"Do you know this area?" Ron asked Andrew.

"Not in any detail. We're a couple hours' hike out of Juneau," the shaman replied grimly. "Doc spotted the open water. From the smell, it's fed by a volcanic spring."

Ron nodded, approving the decision. First rule of hiding: don't be where your enemies can expect you to be. By delaying their entry to Juneau, there was less of a chance of being detected. People couldn't be vigilant forever—they slipped up and got complacent. Of course, there was the risk the delay could give their enemies time to set up something elaborate. He tightened his grip on his flashlight. He'd deal with that when the time came.

Litonya clacked her jaws together, the sound echoing through the silent woods like a gunshot. She'd stopped a few paces ahead of them. Ron steadied the flashlight and saw the sagging roof drooping over a splintering porch among the trees. The faded front door leaned partially open and appeared to have fallen off at least one hinge. *An abandoned cabin.* It didn't matter if it was infested as long as at least some of it was intact. He hurried forward in his excitement.

"Thank you." Ron petted Litonya on her thick ruff as he passed. For a moment, it felt like one of their long nights standing guard in front of Doc's cabin.

Luck was with them. Two windows were knocked out, and the room was full of debris from the forest, but the overall structure was surprisingly intact. Ron shoved a piece of a shelf over one broken window while Andrew swept a place clear under the other. Since the chimney was stuffed with birds' nests, pine needles, and other highly flammable trash, they wouldn't bother with the fireplace. With luck, the smoke would go out the broken window instead of building up in the cabin.

It didn't take long to get everyone settled. Ron carried an unconscious Vincent from the plane, and then he and Litonya found a small open area near the beach. He guessed whoever owned the cabin had used it as a place to store a boat. They managed to drag the plane onto the shore and wedge it between the trees where it wouldn't be easily seen from the air. By the time they returned, the cabin had been swept out and a fire burned on top of an irregular platform of lakeside rocks. Ron braced the broken front door into a semblance of being shut.

"You people all suck," Vincent grumbled, holding his head in his hands.

"You'd rather be back there, reattaching puppet strings to your arms?" Ron shot back.

Vincent didn't reply, curling up in a corner to sulk.

"We have to dig out whatever that son of a bitch left in your skulls." Andrew held up his hands, palms out, when Ron glared at him. "Metaphorically, not literally."

"How can we do that?" Lily asked, shivering in her shirt and jeans. Evonne picked up a blanket, pinning it between her palms to carry it. She draped it over Lily with a surprising level of ease.

Ron wished he'd thought of it. A stupid sense of pride held him back from putting his arms around her. Doc's words kept pounding at him, demanding better of him. A distant, sarcastic part of his mind pointed out he'd lost the bet. He thought he'd seen how weird the world could get, and it turned out that he'd barely dipped his toe into a vast ocean of incomprehensible new possibilities. He welcomed the chance to turn away from his confusing emotional morass and concentrate on what Andrew was saying.

"… part of our tradition. With my help, you both should be able to sever the deep ties this man left in you. I can't explain it clearly to someone who doesn't have the shamanic gifts, but if you trust me, I'm telling you that I can do this."

"Then why didn't you?" Vincent's accusation hung in the air amid the grey wisps of smoke from their fire.

"You didn't trust me. I thought we had time to build up your trust, make a gentle transition. Evidently, I was wrong." Andrew shrugged, leaning back against the grimy walls. "Without your willing and eager participation, the ritual is useless. I could drum until my arms fell off, and you'd still be trapped."

"You can really do this without Gerry?" Ron asked quietly.

His face limned in shadow, Andrew's voice rang clear and calm in the silence. "I can see what needs to be done. Much like I know how to read a trail or set a trap. It's no longer something I need to think about. I can process what is necessary on an unconscious level."

It all sounded rather vague and new-age-ish for Ron to put his faith in. Except he couldn't deny that the waking nightmares had vanished after the sweat lodge. The danger was greater than it had ever been, and his mind and senses were clear. He wasn't fighting flashbacks and panic attacks.

"We should get some sleep." Doc curled up on the floor near Evonne.

Lily looked over at Ron. *Time to man up.* He straightened up and held out his hand to her. The best way to get past his uncertainty was to understand what was happening. "You promised me answers."

"I did." She nodded and got to her feet, holding the blanket tight to her.

Evonne made a soft sound, equal parts concern and questioning. Lily smiled gently at her best friend and nodded. The sadness of it wrenched Ron's heart into jagged pieces. He wasn't any better than Doc with his gun pointing. Evonne glared at him, promising a world of pain if he didn't improve.

They stepped away from the fire. Ron would have liked to go outside, but Lily would quickly freeze. Instead, he settled for a few purloined cushions from the plane in the darkest corner of the cabin.

"Guess it's time to talk," she said. "I suppose I won the bet."

He balanced his arms on his knees, feeling awkward and

conspicuous, like a teenage boy on a first date. "I thought I understood this new world, and now it's bigger than I imagined. Doc told me what happened with your mom. I'm sorry."

"I heard him. I don't blame him for freaking out." Lily rested her chin on her blanket-wrapped hands.

"Still. It's not okay. And what I did isn't okay either." It wasn't the best start, but he needed to begin on familiar territory to have any chance of progressing. "Tell me about your mom."

"I don't remember much about her. Grandfather told me that she loved music and was a beautiful dancer. She could find honeycomb anywhere and never be stung as she collected it, regardless of her form. She kept her distance, but sometimes I heard her humming to us when she thought we were asleep." Lily's face was half in shadow and half lit by golden firelight. Her ruddy skin glowed in the light, but the shadows made an impenetrable black mask flickering along her features. "The only thing I remember from that day is being afraid. I thought Doc was going to shoot me, and I kept crying because he was supposed to be my friend."

Her memories sparked ones of his own mother pretending to bake cookies. They would take them out of the box and put them on a cookie sheet and then pull them out of the oven to enjoy. He'd always enjoyed "tricking" his father with their home-baked treats. He cleared his throat and took the plunge. "So, you've been a skinwalker since you were born?"

"That's right. Until my mother died, I had no idea that other people were restricted to only one body. I thought everyone could do it. I used to switch back and forth constantly. Now I spend most of my time as a human." She sounded as if she regretted the choice.

"Why?"

Lily took a deep breath. "I told you how we're not just humans who can shape-shift—we have an animal side and a human side. Most skinwalkers are pulled toward one or the other. For some, it's the human, and for others, it's the animal. You met my great-grandmother, Setsuné. She always was more comfortable as a bear. She'd spend entire years without shifting to the skin even once."

Ron slowly connected the family dots. "But your grandfather spends more time as a human."

"The only one of his siblings to cross over. He's told me about how isolated it left him. He tried to stay as a bear to please his mother, but he couldn't suppress his natural inclinations." Lily reached out as if to take his hand before stopping in midair and pulling back. "I know this is hard."

"Yeah. What you do should be impossible. Enhanced strength, enhanced senses—those are a different version of what I already knew. But shape-shifting is something that defies physics." Ron scrubbed his hands on his jeans as if he could wipe away his discomfort.

"Only as you understand them. A bumblebee is technically too heavy and unaerodynamic to fly, but it still does." Lily rubbed at her forehead.

"Actually, I don't think they still believe that." Ron stopped himself. "Sorry. I'm interrupting."

"You make my point for me. I don't think anyone's done actual studies on shape-shifting." Her smile briefly flickered into existence. "Doc tried once before he realized it would reveal too much."

"What does it feel like?"

"I have to decide to shift, like deciding to put on a particular outfit. Once I do, it feels like stretching. My body gets longer and bigger, and I begin to feel heavier, like gravity is pulling me down harder. My bones change shape, getting longer and denser, and the flesh flows over them. It happens quickly, so I don't get a lot of time to analyze it."

"Do you… lose yourself?" Ron asked.

Lily shook her head. "No, I'm still me. The bear side thinks differently, notices different things, but it's still me under the fur. I used to be afraid that I would get lost, like Setsuné. Except maybe she wasn't as lost as I thought."

"So, you could choose to stay human?" The words fell past his lips before he could snatch them back.

Tears caught in her thick lashes and shone in the light. "I don't think so. I might lean toward skin, but I can't pretend I don't have an animal side. I can't stay in my human shape forever." She sniffed and looked up with a brave and trembling smile. "I know it bothers you. I saw your expression when you realized I was Litonya. You weren't ready to fall in love outside your species."

"I wasn't ready to fall in love at all." He cupped her cheek, unable to resist touching her. "I've spent the last years hating myself. I wanted to be a hero. It was all I ever wanted to be, and when I lost it, I felt worthless."

Understanding dawned in her eyes, and he smiled, relieved—until the expression morphed into hurt, and she pulled away from his hand.

He started speaking quickly. The words spilled out of his mouth as if they could bridge the gap growing between them. "I've spent months on the run, only to find soldiers on the doorstep of the one place I had begun to feel might be a home. I've watched people I care about get hurt and be killed in front of me without being able to save them, and I include Big Bart on the list. I've put an entire people in jeopardy. Yet I wouldn't want to have missed any of those experiences, because without them, I wouldn't have met you."

Ron took Lily's hand in his, stroking his thumb over her warm skin. "Ever since my friends died in Afghanistan, I've felt horribly selfish for being glad to be alive when they're dead. My country called me a hero, but I knew I was a fraud, because I was lucky, not brave. I still don't know if I would ever have the courage to throw myself on a grenade to save anyone else because I've been too late every single time I've had the opportunity. I ask myself if I'm subconsciously hesitating because I'm too selfish to give myself up. And now I feel even less worthy because I'm hurting myself and everyone around me, and yet, the idea of not having you in my life hurts worse than all the pain our connection has caused."

Lily smiled, although with a tinge of sadness. "Guess that makes us awful together, because I feel the same. So, what do we do now?"

"Wish I knew."

Vapor sat in his darkened apartment, staring at the log of conversations with his old partner, Pujari. *Karan,* he reminded himself. *He's Karan now.* The bank of monitors over his desk flickered with constant updates. The changing lights set up a constantly shifting pattern of brightness and color on his walls and ceiling like the reflections from a meditation pond. After millennia of watching over the *lalassu* community, his intuitive sense for impending danger was highly developed. He'd sensed the fall of the Roman Empire and the rise of the witch hunts decades before they'd actually happened.

Now his intuition warned of an even larger storm. Something unprecedented. And his intuition pointed squarely at his old partner, Pujari. *Karan.*

He buried his face in his massive hand, the metal from his pierced eyebrows and lips biting into his palm. He'd been wrong in London all those years ago. He'd seen too many statistically significant targets hit during the long months of the Blitz, and he'd been certain Pujari was aiding the Nazis in their bombings. They'd argued so much over the *lalassu's* role that it splintered their relationship. Pujari wanted to come out of hiding and rule the humans. Vapor had never liked hiding, but taking on such a major change without the Goddess's blessing struck him as too risky.

He'd watched Pujari support the Third Reich's view that not all men were created equal and the superior were born to rule. Neither of them had known how far Hitler would take his rhetoric, or at least, Vapor hadn't, and he hoped his bond-brother had not. He'd been so sure Pujari was involved beyond making speeches at parties and encouraging members of Parliament to surrender that he'd done something unthinkable: he'd walked away from a friendship that had survived centuries, and he'd betrayed his bond-brother.

He and Pujari were both gifted with unaging youth, but they could still be killed. Only natural, gentle death was denied them. To save the world, Vapor had arranged for a bomber to destroy Pujari's home in Germany. He'd seen images of the devastation. At the time, he assumed his friend was dead. Instead, Pujari had been horribly injured and would have spent many long and painful years healing. He wouldn't be able to continue helping the Nazis.

And yet the Blitz continued to destroy an improbably high number of targets. Vapor had never felt such guilt in all his existence. He'd sacrificed part of his soul and the one person who meant more to him than any other, and he'd done it for nothing. Even at a distance of over half a century, it ripped him apart.

Now he had the second chance he'd always prayed for. Pujari was alive. Vapor would be able to make things right with his bond-brother, to show the compassion and understanding he should have always given him. Pujari was reaching out, offering a truce. Vapor wanted to believe him.

Except he still faced the same dilemma. He'd received word from Gwen and Dani Harris. As the Goddess of the Night's Chosen Priestess, Dani was a direct conduit to the divine for all *lalassu,* and her sister, Gwen, was the most powerful medium ever to have existed with access to the knowledge of all the dead from all ages. Both warned of great danger about to fall on the *lalassu* and possibly the entire human race as well.

He couldn't tell the Harrises about Pujari and his connection to Dalhard. Dani was already furious about the government's fumbling with the investigations. She'd threatened to hunt Dalhard down personally, and only Michael had been able to talk her down. He definitely would not be telling her that her brothers' captor had returned to the United States.

Vapor needed to know the truth of what was happening. He couldn't falsely accuse his bond-brother again. But he also couldn't let him destroy the world.

He rubbed his hand over his shaved pate. Give him a digital environment, and he could find the truth in heartbeats. If it wasn't here, then Pujari must be hiding his information on non-networked computers. He needed someone with experience investigating in person instead of online—someone not connected with the *lalassu* but who was aware of them. Then, when he had his facts in hand, Vapor could confront his bond-brother.

Chapter Sixteen

Lily woke early, still curled in the far corner of the cabin beside Ron. She opened her eyes to see Andrew creeping toward the door in his pea-green thick wool coat, fur-lined leather mittens, and hat. He paused, noticing that she was awake, and put his finger to his lips.

Does he think I'm stupid? Everyone was exhausted, and she wasn't about to disturb them. But she also wasn't going to let her brother get away without an explanation. She used the abbreviated hand signals Grandfather taught them for hunting to ask, *Where?*

He held his hand up and wiggled his fingers in the air, cupping his other hand over them like a shelter. It wasn't an approved sign, but Lily understood. He was going to look for a place for a sweat lodge.

She tapped her wrist and pointed at the sky. *How long?*

He signaled back that he'd return by dawn, which Lily guessed was still several hours away. She nodded her acceptance.

Andrew rolled his eyes but didn't make any other protest. He slipped out of the cabin and disappeared into the grey-lit predawn. She checked the others by the fire. Vincent's chin rested on his chest as he slept, braced in the corner, his fists and knees pulled tight to his body. His knuckles were white and clearly visible even in the dim light. It was horribly unfair they couldn't soothe his pain before putting him through the torturous mental challenge of breaking psychic commands.

Evonne lay on her back with a tarp from *Angel* between her and the filthy floor. She'd pulled her arms inside her parka to keep warm. Lily had seen it hundreds of times over the years. Her friend would have her hands flat on her belly. Evonne called it keeping a fingertip on her internal functions. The fluttering of her pulse and the rhythmic beat of her organs formed a complex interweaving rhythm she could feel through the hypersensitive grey hairs on her fingertips. It soothed her, bringing good dreams.

Doc sprawled, snoring lightly with his glasses askew. *Have to remember to ask Andrew about the cast when he comes back.* Birch bark was strong, but it didn't hold up very well under hard usage. If it had begun to break, Doc might have permanent damage to his ankle. She hoped that he would come through all right. She hoped they all would.

Lily settled back against Ron, enjoying the warmth and strength of his broad chest under her cheek. His arm tightened around her, but his breathing stayed steady and even, suggesting he hadn't been disturbed by her conversation with Andrew. She held her fingers tight in a fist so she could resist the temptation to trace his features. She settled for using her eyes instead so she wouldn't wake him. So strong and handsome, even in sleep, he exuded a confidence-inducing aura, reassuring those around him that they'd never have to worry and that he would stand between them and any harm.

It was who he really was, even when he battered himself over his failures. She dared to brush back the crisp hairs falling against his forehead, marveling at how far he'd come in his internal battle. Most people would have slid into a chasm of oblivion, weighed down by trauma dreams and the bottle. She glanced over at Vincent. The two men had both suffered so much, and while Vincent found himself buried beneath what had happened to him, Ron found the strength to keep fighting. He wasn't better than Vincent, and he hadn't suffered less. Maybe it was luck or maybe Ron's own inherent refusal to accept that the bad guys could ever win.

A true hero. She smiled sadly. Last night, a horrible explanation had occurred to her, and even now it nipped at her contentment, washing everything in a sense of disillusion. Ron prided himself on being a hero, on saving others. She'd seen his desperation to reach her when the soldiers separated them. It had matched her own, triggering her transformation. Forget options and consequences—all that mattered was protecting him. She'd always been a protector, standing guard over the Colony and Ekurru. It was a large part of who she was, but she'd never felt such an intense and uncompromising instinct toward another person, not even Evonne.

Ron was also a protector, and he'd begun to pull back after seeing her in the fur. What if his withdrawal wasn't because she was a skinwalker? What if it was because she didn't need his protection? The suspicion ate at her. She wanted to believe he loved her and that, given a little bit of time, he would come to accept both sides of her. She wanted to believe he'd withdrawn because of the shock.

He was her mate. She knew it deep in her bones. It wasn't only because she loved him or because of his compassionate and generous spirit. They were connected, a true match of heart, mind, and soul. If he rejected her, she wouldn't get another chance. When he returned to his home, he would carve out a piece of her and walk away with it. If he knew how it would affect her, he would feel obligated to stay.

She wouldn't tell him. Couldn't tell him. Perhaps it was the mating bond or maybe her own instincts, but she refused to build a cage around him, even one made of affection and love. If he stayed with her, the choice must be his. Even if it left her soul maimed and limping, she would survive if he chose not to stay. Her mother had survived being left alone, after all. She shoved aside the creeping urge to hold tight and beg him to stay. She wouldn't put her own ego and pride above building the relationship the right way.

Movement by the fire caught her attention. Evonne sat up and threaded her arms through the parka sleeves again. "I don't suppose anyone packed breakfast."

"This wasn't our best-planned excursion." Lily got up to kneel beside her friend. "How are you doing?"

Evonne pushed the escaping wisps of her hair out of her face with her forearm. "Would it be stupid to say I feel happy? Given the circumstances?" She spread her grey-tipped fingers on the tarp. "Everything feels so rough and ragged. I can feel the floorboards bend and tremble whenever someone shifts their weight and the vibrations in the walls from the breeze. It's not overwhelming me. In fact, it feels great to experience something different than the cabin."

"You always were the optimistic one." Lily smiled.

Evonne didn't smile back. "The only thing I don't feel good about is Bob. I don't understand what happened. We went from knowing each other better than anyone else to being two strangers sharing the same house. I don't even know when it all changed."

Lily wrapped her arms around her best friend, careful not to touch the sensitive grey skin. Evonne leaned against her, trembling.

"Was I too stupid to see it from the start? Did I only imagine that he loved me?" Evonne's body shook from holding back tears. "How can you love someone and still want to cut them off from everything and put them in a box?"

The right words escaped Lily. When Evonne had met Bob, both women thought the way he'd pursued her was so romantic. When Evonne revealed that she was *lalassu*, Bob hadn't hesitated. He'd joined their community and become an enthusiastic protector.

"He's not bad or vindictive, but somehow, we've ended up on opposite sides of everything. He cares about me more than anyone else in my life and would literally walk the world to fetch a blade of grass if it would make me smile." Evonne held up her hand with her fingers stretched wide. "I'm afraid we're broken past any hope of repairing, but I don't want to go back to being trapped, even if leaving him costs me everything."

Lily remembered Ron's words about how he would accept all the pain they'd experienced and caused because otherwise they wouldn't have met. She agreed and still felt that way, but her friend's marriage was too steep a price. How much more pain could they accept without hating each other? Her mind flashed to the bodies of the men sent to Bear Claw. She doubted they were evil, but as Evonne so eloquently put it, they'd ended up on the wrong side. They probably had families and responsibilities and took the job to make a little money.

"I know nothing is ever going to be the same again," Evonne whispered, her eyes still dry. The dullness haunting them was harder to watch than tears would have been. "There's no way to go back to where we were before."

"We'll find a way," Lily promised recklessly. "Maybe not exactly like before, but we'll find someplace good again. It'll be better. We won't be trapped again. And Bob will come to his senses, and you'll forgive each other and live happily ever after."

Evonne laughed weakly, not out of any kind of genuine amusement but in a weary effort to humor Lily. Which hurt even more.

"You'll see. Darkest before the dawn and all that," Lily insisted.

Her best friend pulled back, anger pinching the corners of her mouth. "Lily, I know you want to believe that. You're in love and want to believe in a beautiful and shiny universe. Except we don't know anything about the people chasing us or what they want beyond putting us in cages. We're running blindly, which means we're probably being stampeded toward a cliff."

"Then we won't run blind." Ron's quiet declaration took them both by surprise. The two women twisted to look at him.

"How long have you been awake?" Lily asked.

"Since you got up." Ron rose smoothly to his feet and came closer. "Evonne, I know my words won't make it any better, but I will do everything in my power to get you your life back. As soon as Andrew gets back, I want to get started on the ritual to break my ties to the man who held me captive."

"Make that two of us," Vincent added, saluting them with an imaginary glass.

Lily frowned at him. She'd been sure that he was passed out.

Vincent shrugged, indifferent to her embarrassment and irritation. "Yeah, I listened. It's not like this place has TV. Besides, I was hoping my extensive experience with late-night TV would be accurate, and the two of you were only a few minutes away from a pillow fight."

"Eww." Evonne stood up and glared at him.

He grinned at her, a hint of the old carefree joker slipping past the sardonic mask. "Can't blame a guy for hoping."

"Are you sure about this, Vincent?" Ron asked, sobering the mood.

His knuckles whitened. "I'm sick of being a puppet. It's time to cut the strings."

"Ken? It's Bob." He stared at the clunky office phone as if the antique held all the answers.

"Bob, you wouldn't believe the chatter going on down here. A training mission left for Bear Claw, and now it's vanished from the records." Ken sounded worried, but Bob heard the thrill of the hunt in his old friend's voice. Ken always had a gift for figuring out when silences meant people were covering something up. It had made his reporting career.

Bob swallowed, refusing to look behind him. He needed to be very careful. "They're all dead."

Silence on the other end of the line. "It can't be possible."

"It's more than possible. It's what happened. Watch, and I bet they'll release a cover story of some kind of crash that killed everyone deployed on the training mission." Bob rubbed his hand over his pate, his fingers slipping across the sweat-slick skin. "I was there. I saw the bodies."

"Jesus, Bob." The reverent profanity hung between them. "Are you okay?"

"Evonne's missing." He could barely force enough breath between his lips to make the two words audible.

"You don't think—"

"McBride has her. I don't know if he's hurt her, but I need your help." Bob felt suspicious eyes boring into him. It took all his determination to keep focused on what he needed to do. *It's the only way to save her.*

"What do you need? I can be there in a few hours," Ken said immediately. He'd had always been like that. He wouldn't care if the paper ended up firing him. He'd walk away without a second glance to be where his friend needed him, just as Bob would do if the situation were reversed.

"I need you down there, pal." Despite his attempts to stay casual, his fingers tightened in the phone cord as he used the code phrase they'd agreed to long ago. Now Ken would know that things were even more dangerous than Bob implied. It told him Bob needed him to hold a refuge and escape route ready.

"Got it. Tell me." Ken's terse sentences showed he understood.

"I need to drive McBride out from cover, but I don't want Evonne dragged into it." He needed to be precise. There was too much room for disaster in a misunderstanding. "I need you to break the story. Tell everyone how dangerous he is."

Ken tried to caution him. "Are you sure? If he has Evonne, we don't want him getting desperate."

"I'm sure. It has to be this way."

"All right. Evonne's a smart girl, even if she did marry you. I'm sure she can take care of herself."

The feeble banter still made Bob smile despite the fear clogging his gut. "She doesn't understand what he is. She thinks he's helping her."

"We'll find her."

Bob hung up the phone delicately and slumped down into his chair.

"Well done, Mr. Villeneuve," Dalhard's assistant said. The man reminded him of a scavenger hovering nearby, waiting to see if an injured elk was quite dead before taking a bite.

"He's on his way." Bob had promised himself he wasn't going to ask again, but he couldn't stop himself. "Any word on the plane?"

"We know they didn't land in one of the major harbors. We have people watching and a network of cameras equipped with facial recognition. Eventually, he will show his face. At most, we will be only a few hours behind him."

Karan's smooth promises meant nothing to Bob, not since Steve had disappeared in the middle of the night without explanation. Trapped between predators, there was no safe route to fly. Ken's promise was the only hope Bob had for himself and Evonne to escape.

Evonne was unhappy with her isolation. He knew it and wasn't unsympathetic. Last year, he'd begun searching for somewhere they could move to and still be safe. A small village in British Columbia seemed like the best choice, and he'd asked Ken to help him find something suitable. They could find a rural property, and Evonne could have a proper garden and spend time outdoors all year round. No one would have to know she was *lalassu*.

There was the challenge of how to get Evonne into the city. She had no papers or identification. As far as the government knew, she didn't exist. They hadn't even been able to get legally married. He and Ken came up with the solution of smuggling her inside the plane, pretending she was cargo. Lots of illegal immigrants did it, hiding inside shipments. He could keep her safe if he could only get her away from Lily before the skinwalker and her killer boyfriend got his wife killed.

The last thing Joe Cabrera expected after a sixteen-hour shift was a knock at his apartment door. Actually, knocking would be an overly polite description of the rapid-fire pounding threatening to warp his door off its hinges. He'd been about to collapse on his leather-and-chrome couch to mindlessly zone out on the survival shows recorded on his DVR and try to catch some sleep before he needed to go back. Now his hands trembled a little as adrenaline zapped away his weariness.

He eased his gun out of its holster and adjusted the chain holding his badge in plain sight on his chest. He'd collected his share of enemies after ten years on Perdition's police force, and that had been before his little side trip down Freak Alley.

"I know you're in there," a deep and raspy male voice shouted through the door. "I need you to open the door."

"Who are you?" Joe shouted back, easing the safety off his pistol. After what he'd seen, he wasn't about to take any chances. *It might be a thief. Or someone with a grudge.* It said a lot about the last few months that a thug gunning for him was the optimistic option.

"Michael sent me, and I'd rather not shout my name for everyone to hear."

Joe leaned in to take a brief look through the peephole to see a tall, heavily built man with a shaved head and piercings in his lip, eyebrow, and ears. Grey-blue abstract designs swirled over his skull. "That's too bad because I don't let strangers into my apartment." *Not unless they're pretty and female.*

"I need your help. Please."

Joe heard the note of desperation he'd grown all too used to over the years—the one people got in their voices when they thought the door was closing on their last chance. Whether it was a traumatized coed learning that the police couldn't arrest her psycho ex-boyfriend until he'd actually done something to hurt her, or a multiple offender discovering that this time his charm wasn't going to keep him out of jail, their voices held the same mixture of panic, disbelief, and rising terror. His common sense told him that he should call for backup. His compassion made him open the door.

"How do you know Michael?" Joe asked, holding the gun steady on his visitor. He was compassionate, not stupid.

"I've been helping Dani's family for a long time. I coordinate between the different groups of *lalassu*," the bald man said quietly.

Michael had mentioned someone. A hacker who arranged for forged papers and could make inconvenient records vanish. "Vapor."

"That's me. Can I come in?"

Joe lowered his weapon and stepped aside. Vapor stepped inside, moving lightly for such a large man—he could have done work as a burglar. Joe closed the door but stayed beside it, keeping his gun in hand. He still didn't trust his visitor. Preparing for a quick exit seemed like the smart choice.

"I need your help," Vapor repeated. He glanced around the apartment, and Joe doubted any detail escaped his notice. Joe loved to renovate, and he'd spent a lot of time making his condo comfortable, replacing the crap carpet with wide hardwood and building his own custom shelves and cabinets. Next year, he intended to rip out the kitchen and redo it. Having this stranger in his space, judging his home, only pissed him off.

Vapor settled himself on Joe's couch, keeping his hands flat on the cushions and well away from his body. Joe recognized the posture. It was one they taught police for situations in which they needed to defuse tension. Keeping the hands wide meant there was plenty of warning if someone decided to go for a weapon. "What is it you want?"

"You remember what happened last summer?"

"Hard to forget. I'm still getting tinfoil hats in my locker for having dared to say something about it." Joe hadn't meant to say anything, but somehow, it all came spilling out. Ancient gods and people with strange powers living in secret societies. A company collecting those people as if they were their own personal action figures. He'd tried to convince the FBI investigators to take precautions going after Dalhard, but they'd only laughed at him.

"I think there was more to it than we thought. I need your help to find out." Vapor's hand lifted off the couch as if he wanted to rub his head, but he put it back down before it made Joe twitchy.

The last time he'd helped these people, Joe had ended up trapped in a building wired with explosives and left for dead. "Thought you were an all-powerful hacking god."

Vapor's breath exploded out of his chest in a coughing fit. He curled up and pounded on his chest.

Joe left his post to get the man a drink of water before he died on the pristine black-leather sofa. It meant holstering his weapon, but he was already getting the impression that the man's visit wasn't a trap.

"Thank you," Vapor croaked as he accepted the glass. Once his breathing steadied, he continued. "Give me electronics, and I can do what you need. But there are ways to get around my skills, and our target knows them. It's a long story—"

"I got time." Joe shrugged.

The metal stud flashed as Vapor raised a disapproving brow. "I used to have a partner. Someone who helped me with my work for the *lalassu*. I thought he was dead until a few days ago when he contacted me. He told me his boss was involved in recruiting Eric and Vincent, Dani's brothers."

"Dalhard." This could be the lead he'd been looking for: someone who would testify about Dalhard and his illegal activities.

"I think he's back in the States. There's a chance we can find out what's really happening. My partner says he targeted the High Priestess line by mistake and wanted to make sure it didn't happen again. He asked me to trust him."

Joe didn't need Michael's psychic powers for his next statement. "You don't."

"No. I don't. It's been a long time since I saw him, and we had some fairly strong divisions of opinion before that. Taking Eric and Vincent might have been a mistake, but he still intended to take, hold, and experiment on *lalassu*." Vapor's eyes were hard, reflecting everything back like dark glasses.

"I can't get caught up in another quasi-illegal investigation," Joe warned. His shoulders still tightened with fury every time he remembered the fact that he couldn't testify about what Dalhard had done to him. "If I go after him again, I want everything aboveboard and legal so I can nail the bastard."

"That's not something you have to worry about," Vapor promised.

"Do Dani and Michael know he's back?" He'd seen what Dani could do as High Priestess and wouldn't have minded having her as a backup.

"I can't tell them. Not until I know what's going on. Dani is many things, but forgiving isn't one of them. She'd call for war. I need solid ground before committing to full-on hostile intentions. That's why I need you." Cracking his knuckles, Vapor didn't look like a man who would hesitate before an act of violence. "I need to know if he's really trying to work things out or if this is more bullshit. I can't search online—he's a ghost. He's been avoiding me for deca… a really long time. I need someone good at finding stuff out in the real world." He sounded more concerned about his old partner than with taking down Dalhard. Joe could respect that even if he didn't agree with it. Protecting the partner would be a lot easier once Dalhard was in jail.

"So, why pick me? Isn't there some hotshot detective out there with superpowers you could call on?" Joe slumped into a chair. When exactly had his life taken a turn into the Twilight Zone? But he couldn't walk away from someone who needed his help. He'd never been able to, no matter what it cost him.

"I can't use one of the *lalassu*. But I still needed someone who already knew about us. I've arranged for you to have a five-day paid absence. Tickets are waiting for us at the airport." Vapor got to his feet.

"Hold on! Five days? Plane tickets?" Joe jumped up, furious. "I haven't even said I'd go."

"No. But you will. I've read everything there is to find on you, Detective Cabrera. So I knew before I came that you would come with me." Vapor's posture and voice held no hint of apology.

"Where the hell are we even going?"

"Alaska."

"Take deep breaths to calm yourself," Andrew instructed.

Ron sucked air in through his mouth, his ribs pulling apart to accommodate the extra volume in his lungs. He tried to concentrate on the physical sensations to get the whirling thoughts in his mind to settle. His captor knew where he was. And his hooks would reel Ron in like a trout in a stream and prevent him from identifying the man even in his private thoughts. Could hooks like that even be carved out? Ron swallowed and refused to ride further on that train of thought, but another immediately took its place.

He'd hurt Lily with his withdrawal, which stung him into action like the flick of a whip. The gap hadn't closed completely after their talk yesterday, as much as he wanted it to be gone. He'd tried to say the right things, but he felt a lot shakier than he'd let on. Realizing his captor could still control him left him doubting all his reactions. Which were real and which were created? The uncertainty kept his nerves sparking and jumping.

At the moment, his mind and soul were too scattered and at the mercy of a madman. Hopefully, he could keep up the confidence act until he could match it for real. He would not be another Doc in her life, someone she trusted who'd turned on her.

"Your head is spinning fast enough to qualify for Exorcist Frequent Flier miles," Andrew interrupted. "Concentrate on breathing."

Ron nodded, his chest expanding as he filled it with oxygen.

"Kind of hard to concentrate when we're on the run for our lives. Again." Vincent's snark wasn't helpful, but it did sum up the situation.

"Do you want to be free of this man?" Andrew asked as if it didn't matter either way to him.

"Yes," Ron answered immediately.

"Do you want it enough to face the most frightening, darkest parts of yourself?" Andrew sprinkled water on the coals to create a fresh wave of steam. "He buried his command in the deepest part of you, in a place where you cannot lie to yourself. When you go there, you will not be able to hide from what you truly want. If being left alone is more important than being free, this will not work."

It made a weird kind of sense to Ron. He'd seen it at the VA when he was recovering. Some people fought past grievous injuries, refusing to surrender for even a single moment. Others went through all the motions before plateauing. They surrendered because the pain of therapy wasn't worth the promise of possible recovery. The idea of digging deep into the dark places of his soul sent panic signals flying even as it made him more determined. "How can we know if we're ready?"

"You'll only know when you try, but I think the restlessness you've both been experiencing is a sign your mind is already fighting." Andrew shrugged and began to drum. It wasn't a proper instrument—there hadn't been time or space to bring one. Instead, Andrew had found a section of hollow log in the forest and was beating on it with a large stick. The resonance was different, but he could coax a surprising variety of tones from it. "Let yourselves go into your heads."

Ron ignored Vincent's snort of derision and closed his eyes. This time, he wasn't going to let himself get sucked into a panic attack. He could remember a woman visiting the homeless shelter he was living in. She'd offered a chance to get clean and make a difference, and he'd signed up for the program.

The pounding beats and Andrew's tonal chanting buoyed Ron as he pushed his way through the memories. *What had she said the job would be?* Bodyguard. That had appealed to him. He'd been tired of constantly searching for his next fix, of having to choose between awful possibilities. He wanted to feel proud of himself again. They'd driven him and the other recruits to a house somewhere in the New York suburbs. Then they'd injected him with something that knocked him out.

Just like Lily. He refused to get sidetracked. When he'd woken up, he'd been in the facility where he'd met his captor.

Dark hair gleaming in the light. It flashed off his teeth, too, when the man spoke. What had he said?

What if you'd been stronger, faster? Able to leap across the compound and take them out in the blink of an eye?

He'd been big, a powerfully built man. Ron's breathing started to speed up as if the air might betray him if it spent too long in his lungs.

Don't you owe it to your friends to try? The words sank claws into him, holding him down.

He needed to see the man's face. Hear his name. Ron could barely hear the drumming any longer over the pounding of his own heart.

There had been a fight. Ron remembered a struggling body in his grasp. Why had there been a fight? The details were foggy, refusing to crystallize. He gritted his teeth, trying to remember what happened next.

Pain.

Horrible, mind-searing pain. So intense it left him unable to even beg those around him to kill him. Lily spoke of feeling her bones lengthen, and now he glimpsed what she meant. The grinding of pulped fragments rubbed against each other as they rebuilt themselves, stretching his muscles until they snapped. Her transformation might be painless and natural, but his had been imposed against all of nature's ironclad laws. He'd been broken, ripped apart at a cellular level as they shoved him back together to suit themselves. Agony was too mild a word to describe it.

His body couldn't tell if the assault was a memory or fresh pain, but he was too deep in his own mind to avoid it. Ron tried to scream for help, except his body stayed locked around him like a rigid prison. He couldn't get it to do anything. *Don't panic!* He held onto emotional control with mental fingernails, but he wouldn't be able to escape the knife-edged whirl of a panic attack for long.

Part Four
EPITHELIALIZATION

Chapter Seventeen

Lily couldn't shake the restless certainty that something was wrong. Healing ceremonies sometimes took days, and it had only been a little over an hour, but she couldn't stop pacing. She reminded herself that her presence would not be welcome. Aside from the sweat lodge being one of the places that still held a gender divide, her grandfather had warned her that if she was there, Ron might not have the strength to do what he needed. He might be tempted to rely on her as a crutch rather than stand on his own.

"Go and check on him," Evonne ordered abruptly. She held two thick sticks in the crook of her elbow, ready to put them on the fire.

Lily stopped, only then becoming aware of how quickly she was moving back and forth across the cabin. The vibrations must be driving Evonne nuts. She blushed and dropped onto one of the logs they'd dragged in to serve as seats. Doc lay by the fire, drowsing as best he could. His ankle had begun to swell and ache, but they didn't have anything to give him for the pain.

"Sorry." She noticed her knee bouncing in place and consciously halted it.

"I wasn't kidding. Go." Evonne used her toe to nudge the new logs into place. "You're not going to be able to settle until you do."

"He's my mate." The words blurted out like a cork popping out of a bottle. Lily hugged her arms tight to her body, hoping to relieve the pressure building inside.

"Oh." Evonne settled back on her seat. "Are you sure?"

Lily nodded, her fingers tightening on her biceps.

"That explains the obsession and sense of impending doom. You're worried he won't accept you."

Lily wished her friend's pointed observations were less accurate. "I need to keep perspective. He's going to be leaving when this is over."

Evonne nodded slowly, biting her lip. "He might stay."

"He wants to go home. I can't trap him." Lily's nails scraped against her scalp as if she could dig her way free. "I don't know what to do."

Evonne's mouth narrowed. "You need to try. Go."

They hadn't stayed friends for twenty years in an isolated community without learning the fine art of timely retreat. Lily wrapped one of the blankets firmly around her shoulders, stuffed her feet into Doc's boots, and stepped out into the snow.

The hint of sulfur in the air from the lake gave at least one reason why the cabin had been abandoned. She'd be willing to bet that there wasn't much to eat in it either, which would explain the lack of wildlife in the area. The trees were very quiet, not like the woods near Bear Claw. There, she knew almost every animal, from the mated pair of foxes who liked to den under the ranger station to the eagles who made their summer homes in the tall trees near the river. She understood those woods, their daily and seasonal rhythms. These ones left her feeling dangerously out of place and exposed.

Her feet pulled her toward the muffled thuds of Andrew's makeshift drum. After a moment of trying to convince herself that she should really do a circuit and scout the area, she gave in to temptation and allowed herself to follow the tracks to the sweat lodge.

There hadn't been much time for finesse when building it. They'd used bunches of pine branches for the walls instead of smooth leather hides. The branches providing the frame were either dry and dead or leaking pitch. It held none of the serenity and dignity of their lodge at home, but Lily hoped the urgency of their purpose would compensate for the crudity of their efforts.

Spirituality wasn't a natural trail for her to follow. She didn't know much about the patron goddess of the *lalassu*, the Lady of the Starry Skies. Crouching in the silent, snow-filled forest, Lily wondered if a prayer from a relative agnostic such as herself would even have an effect. *If I were a goddess, it would probably annoy me. It'd be like a neighbor who only spoke to me when he wanted to borrow something.* Still, she couldn't help picking up the smoldering bundle of cedar from the flat rock outside the lodge and wafting the smoke toward herself.

Hopefully you're not like me, Lady. The cedar smoke was sweet and comforting. The scent always lingered around her grandfather. Lily closed her eyes and tilted her face toward the clear sky. *Please, we need to get our feet on the ground again. I hope Evonne and Bob can find their way back together after all of this. He really does love her even if he's confused right now. And I know she loves him.* A painful swelling caught at her throat, making her grateful that she wasn't speaking aloud. *Please help Doc to heal. He's an old man and needs all the help he can get. It's my fault we're stuck out here. He shouldn't be punished for that. And please help Ron to find what he needs.* She clamped her mental mouth shut as her traitorous emotions begged her to ask the Lady to make Ron want to stay. If he decided to stay, she would accept that, and if he didn't, she would take that, too.

Kind girl. For a moment, she thought she'd actually heard the words drifting in the wind—a female voice, one she didn't recognize. But the words were so faint and distorted that she dismissed it, shaking her head to clear her senses. There wasn't a trace of anyone else out there, particularly not a strange woman. Perhaps it was a trick of sound bouncing off the mountains, trees, and snow, or so she told herself. The idea of the alternative, a divine response, terrified and humbled her.

The drumming from inside the lodge abruptly stopped. Dread swelled in Lily's chest, and before she could even consider innocent explanations, she crawled through the low entrance.

Shadows coated her vision as she blinked against the dim light, but when her eyes adjusted, she saw Andrew struggling to hold on to Ron as he sprawled and twitched dangerously close to the pile of gleaming coals. Lily immediately wrapped herself around him. "Ron, it's safe."

At the sound of her voice, he stopped flailing, and Lily breathed a short-lived exhalation of relief. His skin was clammy and cool with sweat despite the humid air inside the lodge, and his eyes were open but not focusing. She looked at Andrew, hoping for guidance.

"He hit something, one of the psychic hooks, and his mind froze in that moment." Andrew's mouth twisted with the effort of putting what he sensed into inadequate human words.

Ron's pulse pounded against her hands hard enough that she didn't need to be anywhere near a pulse point to feel the galloping rhythm. Whatever moment of time trapped him, it wasn't a good one. "How do we bring him back?"

"He's responding to you." Andrew knelt beside Vincent, his fingers on the other man's throat. "Keep talking."

Lily nodded, but when she opened her mouth, her mind went blank. What should she talk about? The weather?

Sorry I forgot to tell you that my fur coat is a necessary lifestyle accessory.

Hey, I know things have been rough between us, but let's ignore that and go for a make-out session?

How do you feel about having cubs?

"Lily! Start talking!" Andrew shouted.

"Ron, I… I wish I didn't have to do this. I wish we really were a lost hiker and a girl from some weird Northern community. I wish we could be finding out about each other instead of on the run from people who want to hurt us." Lily let the words pour out of her. "And at the same time, I don't wish for any of it. Because then you wouldn't be you, and I wouldn't be me, and I don't know if we would have fallen in love if we were different people. We belong together. I can't imagine loving anyone except you, and I'm sorry for all the horrible things that have happened to you, but they made you who you are, and I love who you are."

"Oh gods, spare me," Vincent moaned as he came awake. Andrew dragged him out of the sweat lodge, only pausing to issue final instructions for Lily to keep talking.

"You can do this, you know. I know you blame yourself for letting Nada, Bart, and your friends die, but you weren't the one who pulled the trigger. It was the man who hurt you, who is still hurting you, and when I think about what he's done, I want to rip him into tiny pieces and use him to bait my fishing nets. You're strong, Blue Eyes, stronger than you ever thought you were. And now we need you to come out of this so that you can protect us." She squeezed his hands.

That got a response. Ron's eyes twitched to one side, and his fingers flexed.

Lily abandoned the comforting approach. If he needed a drill sergeant, then she would give him one. "We're in danger, and you'll never forgive yourself if you aren't there to save us."

His breathing and pulse slowed, and his feet curled onto the floor.

"You need to wake up and get moving," Lily barked through her tears, not needing to feign a roughened voice.

His head turned.

"On your feet, soldier!"

Ron rolled out of her arms and into a kneeling position. Lily held her breath as he dashed out of the lodge. She wouldn't have guessed anyone could dash on hands and knees if he hadn't accomplished it so effortlessly.

Her relief at his return was tempered by dread. The steamy air coiled in her lungs as she drew in rapid, shallow breaths. Ron hadn't responded to her passionate outpouring of love. He'd come alive as a protector and soldier. A lost and lonely part of her mind could only howl, *Whyyyy?*

It doesn't matter. Whatever works to bring him out of the trap. Her confidence still lay broken on the dirt floor. She tried telling herself she was overanalyzing, being ridiculous. But she couldn't rip the seeds of doubt out of her mind. She wanted to hide inside the lodge, but she forced herself to crawl outside with the others. Once there, she didn't want to look at Ron, yet she still couldn't help stealing glances his way.

He stood tall and proud, ignoring the cold despite the goose bumps pebbling his skin. He scanned the horizon, or as much of it as was visible through the trees. Like a good soldier. Lily swore her heart was physically sliding out of place down through her body to land with a thud in one of her boots.

"I smell smoke," he said. Not a word about what she'd just said.

"The lodge is leaking. I'll put out the coals." Andrew ducked down to go back inside.

Inside, Lily's mind and heart screamed, demanding answers. Outside, silence locked her in as firmly as any deadbolt. She might not be the most romantically experienced person, but she refused to be the needy, demanding girl. Lies born of obligation would give no comfort. Her lips and chin firmed as she straightened. She wasn't going to pretend to be weak or that she wasn't proud of both sides of her heritage.

She turned to focus on Vincent, curled up in the snow and rubbing at his head as if enough pressure could erase whatever he'd seen. His confused and vacant expression told her he had been forcibly ejected from a trance rather than being brought out naturally. "Are you all right?"

"Oh, I'm outstanding," he muttered. "Can't wait to try it again."

If he had the strength for sarcasm, he was on the road to recovery. She pulled his blanket tighter around his shoulders.

He jerked the blanket away from her. "You know there's no way we can win."

Lily hesitated, unsure how to answer him. This didn't sound like one of his usual depressed and drunken rants.

"No joke. No punch line. We can't win. Not against him." Vincent stared at the ground, his arms braced against the snowy dirt.

"That's something he put in your head. Not the truth." She was back on solid ground.

"This isn't his influence. It's a fact." Vincent lifted his head, his shaggy curls limp against his skull. "He has money, power, and the ability to convince people to do what he wants by touching them. He is every conspiracy theorist's nightmare come to life. We can't hide from someone like that."

"Then what should we do?"

Ron interrupted. "I still smell smoke. It's not the lodge." From his expression, Lily would have guessed that he was upset at her for paying attention to Vincent. Except he couldn't be jealous, not when he'd ignored her as soon as he came out.

She caught the acrid scent of smoke in the air, and it wasn't sweet cedar smudge. "The cabin!"

Ron raced the short distance between the sweat lodge and the cabin, his heart pounding. The trees ahead gleamed with crimson-and-saffron light, but he couldn't pretend it was from the sunset. Not when the sun was sinking off to his left.

Lily's footsteps crackled right behind him, and he fought the urge to look back. He'd hurt her somehow, coming out of the sweat lodge. His memory was blurry. He remembered hearing her voice, but the words were lost. When she finally came out, she'd barely looked at him, going to Vincent instead.

His jealousy vanished as he arrived at the cabin. Thick smoke poured out of the holes in the roof. He whipped his head back and forth, looking for Doc and Evonne. He turned away from the cabin, hoping they'd gone to the lake to fetch water to fight the flames. But the snow on the thin track was unbroken.

There must be something they could use to carry the lake water to the fire. Could they scoop snow onto the flames?

He started to ask when he realized Lily's crunching footsteps hadn't slowed. She'd kept running. Which meant… she'd gone into the cabin.

Ron's chest imploded as all the air vanished. The front door had been knocked aside, and he could see the flames licking the walls inside. "Lily!"

Someone came stumbling out of the smoke—a woman with long, dark hair, muffling her face. Ron grabbed her and immediately realized he held Evonne, not Lily.

He wanted to fling her aside and go after Lily, but he couldn't leave her. Evonne was coughing so badly she couldn't speak. He carried her away from the cabin to where Andrew emerged from the trees. His usual impassiveness vanished, leaving him gaping in open-mouthed shock.

"Take care of her," Ron ordered, handing Evonne to Andrew.

"I was… trying to get Doc out," Evonne hacked out the words. "She pushed me out… and went after him."

"The roof!" Andrew shouted.

It all seemed to happen in slow motion, like a nightmare. The flames sprouted in the roof, and Ron heard the neglected timber supports creaking and cracking in the heat. He started to run, but the air held him in gooey suffocation like thick treacle. His strength was useless. His speed wasn't enough. He roared, the vibration rumbling and resonating in his chest, except he couldn't hear it over the crashing of the porch roof as it came down, sealing the door behind flaming debris.

Failure. Just like before. The word pounded him, threatening to send him to his knees and drown him in memories.

No. He refused to surrender. His mind clicked through possibilities with eerie calm. Doc had been toward the back of the cabin. The flames were at the front and side, near their makeshift fire. If Lily pulled him back, away from the smoke and fire, she would be trapped at the back of the cabin with no exit. The windows were all on the fire's side.

Ron ignored the others shouting at him. It didn't matter what they said. He would not acknowledge any other possibility. He scrambled to the back, slipping in the icy snow. He ran his hand along the wall, searching for chinks between the thick planks, something to give him a handhold. The boards burned with the heat of the fire behind the wood, and despite his single-minded focus, he knew time was running out.

"This one. It's got several large cracks running through it," Evonne said.

She stood beside him, her grey hands spread wide over the wall. Her fingers and thumbs looked distorted as her fingertips expanded to half again their proper width. She lifted one away and nodded at him. "This one."

He didn't waste any time, backing up a few steps before launching himself at the place she'd marked. He ran with his full strength, his feet anchored firmly in the ground to give himself the maximum impact. He slammed into the wall without any hesitation or thought of sparing himself.

His shoulder and arm screamed in agony, trying to warn him of bruises and possible breaks, but he shoved aside the pain. The boards gave—only a fraction. But it was a start.

Again.

And again.

On the fourth ram, the plank splintered, and he ripped it away with his bare hands. Then he grabbed the one beside it and wrenched it aside, ignoring the jabbing pains and warning cracks in his fingers and palms.

The gap was barely wide enough to get through, but he didn't hesitate. He saw Doc lying on the ground immediately in front of him. Grabbing the man's ankles, Ron unceremoniously hauled him through the gap, shouting Lily's name as loudly as he could.

Once Doc was clear, Ron took a deep breath and plunged again into the smoky inferno. His eyes burned, filling with tears in a desperate attempt to avoid being scorched. The heat tightened around his skin, gripping him tightly in a toxic shell. He dropped to the ground to crawl, blinded. He fumbled for any sign of Lily.

His blind patting found a leg. Immediately he grabbed it and dragged her toward him. He turned, unable to see the opening he'd made through his blurry vision. His skin pulled taut, stretching painfully like the start of a sunburn.

A vibration rolled through the floor. Then another. It was someone beating on the wall—probably Andrew. Pulling Lily over his back, Ron crawled on his elbows toward the side where the trembling was strongest. He caught a whisper of fresh air against his cheek. He must be close.

There. The rough boards dropped away under his questing fingers, revealing the ragged edge. Lily's weight on his back lightened as hands grabbed her and lifted her out. Ron twisted himself sideways to follow her out.

He dragged clean air into his scorched lungs despite their protests. Then he lifted himself up to see Lily. Andrew frantically checked her pulse and nose. The panic Ron had been shoving into a mental box threatened to break free. Had it all been for nothing?

"She's alive. Doc, too," Evonne rasped. "But she swallowed a lot of smoke."

The pain of his injuries started to demand Ron's attention, but he pushed himself to crawl closer to Lily. He needed to know for himself.

His fingers stood out like tight pink sausages against her cheek as her breath fluttered against them. Her eyes stayed closed, the lashes thick enough against her cheeks to cast shadows. His strength began to fade, and he let his weight settle onto the ground beside her, still stroking her skin. He whispered, "Come on, Lily. You can do this."

Joe would have bet any amount of money that the advertising copy for their hotel promised an "authentic Alaskan experience" or "built with traditional Native methods," but all the fancy wording wouldn't change the fact that their hotel room leaked like a sieve, letting icy fingers of freezing air snatch at him during all hours of the night and day. He knew this because his companion insisted they needed to stay hidden in the room, barely leaving long enough to grab something cheap and greasy from the diner next door.

"If I was a suspicious kind of guy, I'd be a little concerned about how you've whisked me away from my home and work and then virtually imprisoned me in this hotel room." He stared up the ceiling.

The rapid-fire tapping of Vapor's typing slowed for a moment before resuming its frenetic tempo. "It's for your protection."

"So you say, except you've also admitted that your old friend isn't here. Not that you've given me his name or any other identifying information." Joe rolled up into a sitting position. They'd been there for over a day, and so far, the only thing he'd learned was that he really didn't like salt fish. "You told me that you needed my help as an investigator. I can't investigate from in here. Do you want me to find out what your friend is up to or not?"

"Of course I do. It's why you're here." Vapor frowned, seeming confused by the question even though he remained focused on his computer. "But I have no intention of rushing into anything."

"We only have another three and a half days. If Dalhard isn't here, we should go where he is."

"If we do that, he'll detect us in a second. He'll be here soon, and then we'll get to work. You know better than anyone how dangerous Dalhard can be." Vapor didn't look up from his screen, green-and-blue lights painting his face so he looked like one of the guys from *Braveheart*.

Joe's temper began to simmer. Damn right, Dalhard was dangerous. Vapor wasn't taking the situation seriously. "I know that no police force has ever been able to find someone to testify against him. I'd do it, except no court would ever accept anything I said after I admitted to sneaking illegally onto his property." The memory provoked hate and humiliation in equal measure, and Joe took a deep breath to get back onto rational territory. "He's been under suspicion before from different groups. The Medical Research Council investigated him for improperly explaining the risks of medical experimentation, the Port Authority suspected him of not declaring cargo to avoid taxes, the Security and Exchange Commission looked at him for insider trading, and that's only the stuff in the US. There's also stuff in Europe, Asia, and India. All related to paperwork, and not a damn one of them ever came to anything."

"Language." Vapor raised his studded eyebrow without looking up.

"Language? That's the only part you heard?" Joe burst onto his feet, his fury reaching critical levels. Bad guys should not be able to circumvent justice. "It's bizarre. The best possible interpretation of the data is that he's skating close to the edge. The worst makes him into a monster mix of

Al Capone and Hitler. Someone starts to investigate, and suddenly every single witness interviewed insists the paperwork is wrong. Of course, Dalhard's people explained everything—it's all mistakes and oversights. And when we do have someone to tie to something bigger, they either disappear, recant, or turn out to be unreliable witnesses. They can never link Dalhard to anything questionable, let alone illegal. It's not possible for him to have bribed and threatened everyone!"

"He didn't. From what you and Michael have told me, he is an empath—one with a very limited range, restricted by touch. Within that range, he can override a person's emotional reactions to create artificial loyalty, distort memory, or implant commands. He is probably descended from one of the Siren lines." Vapor delivered the information with the exact same dispassion and precision he'd used to discuss meal options the previous day. "Their persuasive powers are legendary."

"I thought the Sirens were like mermaids or something." Joe was admittedly drawing his information from Saturday morning cartoons, but he was still on remedial *Weird Shit for Dummies.*

"A group of females gained a reputation for luring sailors to their deaths through song. Through history, male and female Sirens often dabbled quite successfully in politics and trade. Now most of them have gone to Hollywood."

Okay, there was no way Joe could let that tidbit slide without exploring it. "So like Tom—"

"I'm not personally acquainted with the heritage of every celebrity," Vapor interrupted. "And we have other things to focus on. You haven't reached the necessary conclusion from what you've learned."

Feeling like a stupid kindergartener never brought out the best in Joe's personality. "Maybe it's because my partner hasn't seen fit to fill in the actual information."

"You have all the necessary details to understand what is at stake. Dalhard has been investigated, and yet, every time, the agencies involved fail to find corroborating witnesses, only suggestions of improper paperwork. Once a witness reaches a certain level of involvement, they invariably change their story. He has persuasive empathic powers that can only affect those he touches."

Spelled out in detail, it was hard not to see the shape in the dots. But Joe had not risen through the ranks of police because he accepted easy or plausible explanations at face value. "You're saying that he corrupts the witnesses?"

"More than corruption. I spent several months working with Vincent after his return. He literally could not say Dalhard's name or even hear it when I used it first. He could only refer to what happened to him in vague terms. His brother, Eric, is still recovering physically, and many of his memories from captivity are blurred to uselessness. If Dalhard could invade their minds despite their strength and ability to fight back, what chance would an ordinary human have, particularly if Dalhard is clever enough to select his victims from the ranks of the dispossessed in the first place?"

I really don't like where this is heading. "So, what are you saying?"

"Conventional justice will never be able to apprehend him. I understand why you and Michael needed to try. Both of you have a strong attachment to legal authority and due process." Vapor's tone suggested he could have substituted *stupid* for *strong*. "If I had understood the depth of what we were dealing with, I never would have allowed the farce to continue."

"Our investigation wasn't a farce!" The accusation stung like a slap in the face.

"It couldn't be otherwise when the subject of your investigation can manipulate the tools you rely on."

Joe would have given a great deal to crack Vapor's impassive façade. He forced himself to pause and count to ten before he lost his temper. *Time to look at the flip side.* As much as Joe didn't want to believe it, Vapor had a point. The justice system assumed that people would actively seek to right the wrongs against them. It already had problems when intimidation or corruption discouraged victims from coming forward. Throw in someone who could mess directly with a victim's head, and the chance of conviction dropped to almost nothing.

"This is why we've kept our own systems in place for millennia. The gifts of the *lalassu* place them in a position that tempts them to act outside the law. Giving in to the temptation only puts all of us in danger. Eventually, the sheer number and determination of the rest of humanity would bring us all down no matter what powers we brought to bear."

Listening carefully, Joe realized Vapor's impassiveness came less from not caring and more as a result of exhaustion, as if Vapor had been personally losing this fight for far longer than anyone might guess.

"So, what would your people do about Dalhard?" Joe asked.

"Find him and execute him." Not even for this statement could Vapor lift his eyes from his screen. Joe mentally floundered, trying not to instinctively draw his gun and arrest his companion for uttering threats. Every time he made some progress in understanding the *lalassu*, he got hit with something showing him just how alien the culture really was. "You can't kill him."

"We don't have the authority or resources to imprison him. Rehabilitation is out of the question. Who could we ever trust with determining his recovery? He would circumvent any safeguards we put in place. We don't have any telepaths strong enough to wipe his personality—which would still effectively kill him while leaving his body alive to make restitution. He is a mad dog running through the streets. We don't have the luxury of alternatives." Vapor laid each sentence down into an impenetrable wall, leaving Joe without escape.

Joe sank back down onto the bed, his fingers pressed hard into his temples as if he could squeeze out a different plan.

Vapor finally stopped typing and looked at him. "We don't come to these decisions lightly. He is not going to stop until someone stops him."

Joe nodded. He'd studied serial killers in the Academy and even gone to visit some at Riker's. This wasn't any different. But he couldn't bring himself to say that it was okay to kill someone even in an effort to defend and protect others. In the heat of the moment, the rules were different. But Vapor was proposing cold-blooded, premeditated murder, and nothing could change that. Just as nothing could change the threat Dalhard posed.

He took a deep breath and put it aside. "Let's concentrate on finding him for now. Worry about what we're going to do later."

Vapor nodded and resumed his typing. The light from the screen flashed red, and Joe couldn't help thinking it was an omen. Dalhard might be evil, but Joe couldn't shake the feeling he'd made a deal with a devil to take the man down.

Chapter Eighteen

Something's not right. The thought skated through Lily's mind, breaking the serenity of unconsciousness. She tried to put it aside. It couldn't be too bad—she felt warm, safe, and protected in a way she couldn't remember ever feeling before. She wanted to snuggle into the feeling the way she was snuggling into the strong arms carrying her.

Wait. What? The fogginess of sleep blew away as her mind unrelentingly ascended the levels of consciousness. She was being carried. From the gentle sway, she knew he was walking, his arms cradling her securely against his chest. Her breath caught and scraped painfully against her lungs, which stung and burned like wind-chapped skin. She tried to cough, but the spasm sparked instant agony.

"Easy now," Ron soothed. His voice rumbled into her, vibrating through the contact between them. "We need some water here."

Her eyes were gummed shut despite all her efforts to open them. Ron shifted her in his arms, raising her head up to his shoulder so that she was half sitting. The roughness of a bark cup scraped against her lips. The water was earthy but deliciously cool against the tight scorched folds of her throat.

"It's going to be okay," Ron said as someone wiped at her eyes with a damp cloth, being careful to dry them quickly to avoid freezing. She managed to pry her eyelids apart, although she guessed her eyes would be bright red and inflamed, based on how sore they felt.

"What...?" Her voice croaked like a raven.

"Do you remember the fire?" Evonne hovered blurrily in front of her.

The fire. That explained why she felt so horrible. She remembered realizing Evonne and Doc were still inside the cabin and dashing inside. The heat and smoke had dropped her in her tracks. She'd found Evonne trying to drag Doc out the door and shoved her friend out into the clear air. Her last lucid memory was the horror of realizing the porch roof had collapsed across the door. She'd known there were windows, but she'd been too dizzy and disoriented to find them. "Doc?"

"He's safe. He woke up a few hours ago. Andrew's been carrying him," Evonne said.

Ron turned so Lily could see without having to move. Her vision began to clear, and she made out Doc waving at her, sitting astride a pale-blond blur. Another few blinks, and she recognized Andrew's bear form, one of the rare "ghost" grizzlies considered sacred by the Dene. His light coloring was the mark of a skinwalker shaman. Her sore eyes focused past the two of them to see Vincent slouching along, his gaze fixed firmly on his boots, defeated and broken but still moving. It was more than she would have believed after his "we can't win" speech but less than she would have hoped for.

She breathed a very cautious sigh of relief, careful not to jar her burned lungs. She'd been sure both she and Doc were dead when she'd collapsed.

"We need to keep moving." Ron began walking down the path again. Lily heard Evonne's light footsteps squeaking in the snow behind her and Andrew's steady crunching. Vincent's were inaudible, like a ghost's.

"Where?" Single syllables seemed safest for her roughened voice.

"If Andrew is right, we're about an hour outside of Juneau," Ron answered. "We walked through the night. We'll get a doctor to check you out."

Grumbling behind her gave Andrew's opinion of that plan. He would have explained that she would heal quickly once she felt strong enough to shift. *No doctors.* The words couldn't emerge through her raw throat. The brief period of alertness exhausted her, and she began to sink into the darkness again.

A surge of sadness followed her down. Carrying the damsel in distress away from disaster, Ron owned the role of hero. He sounded confident, at peace with himself. This was the role he was meant to play and the one that would inevitably take him away from Bear Claw.

"Define 'disappeared.'" Dalhard rubbed his eyes with his fingers.

"There is no trace of them with their usual associates. They have not made contact or sought sanctuary. We cannot find the plane that is registered to Doctor Svensson." Karan kept the resentment out of his voice. His boss had no right to make him report like a bungling minion.

"What about the brother? The one at the university?" Dalhard demanded.

"His absence appears to be legitimate. Our agent confirmed he is with his class in the field." *Not an idiot.*

"They have to have gone somewhere," Dalhard growled.

"Most certainly." Karan inclined his head regally, agreeing with his employer but not submitting to his ridiculous expectations.

"What do you intend to do about it?"

Karan had answered that question in detail two days before and then dutifully gone over it again. He was not as undisciplined as Dalhard. Irritation would not make him shed the proper decorum. "They cannot hide indefinitely. They need food, shelter, supplies. Even if they barter, the persons they barter with will have to replace what is taken. McBride's face is spread across every media outlet. Eventually, they will make a mistake that I can track. Until then, we need to be patient."

His boss hated that word, and Karan used it quite deliberately. If Dalhard had been willing to be patient, they would not be in this mess. Dalhard ignored the subtle jibe. "What of the ranger?"

"Adapting nicely." Surprisingly well would have been a more accurate description. He had gone far past the threshold of their other test subjects. There must be some variable he shared with McBride, something overlooked in their screenings.

Both had been highly motivated, he mused. McBride wanted to be a hero, and Harker wanted to avenge his lover's death. Most test subjects signed up for bonuses or other cash incentives. Such determination could make a difference, Karan supposed. He would arrange a full genetic workup once they were back in civilized society. Sooner or later, a test would reveal the connection. Everything came down to practical and tangible reality, even so-called altruism.

"I need to go to Juneau. Senator Paterson is wavering and needs reinforcement." Dalhard fixed his piercing eyes on Karan. "You will stay here and continue to monitor the situation."

Karan's mind began to click through the implications and calculations immediately. Dalhard was consolidating his power base. Ordinarily, he would want Karan with him. Ordering his aide to remain suggested that Karan's boss doubted his loyalty. *Very well. If that is how it must be.*

"Find them." Dalhard waved his hand dismissively.

Karan inclined his head and withdrew, the perfect image of an obsequious servant. For the last ten years, his goals and Dalhard's had meshed. Now, a significant separation appeared to have formed between them—as it had with Caligo so many decades ago.

He had known his fill of being ignored and taking orders from those who could not see the larger picture. His family had been abysmally poor, barely able to afford a single meal each day. They cleaned the home of a wealthier family, and Karan and his sisters often stole scraps from the trash to fill their growling bellies. If caught, it meant lashes with a whip or stick as well as immediate dismissal. He had been clever, able to determine when their masters were paying attention. He had always been able to predict how others would react and, if permitted, use those reactions to his advantage.

His professionally symmetrical teeth ground against each other. He had warned his father when their master's son took an interest in Priya, his eldest sister. Yet his father clung to willful blindness, insisting that a high caste meant honorable behavior. Karan tried to get his sister to flee, but she would not leave their family. When she disappeared, he knew who to blame.

It is all in the past now. They were all long dead. No one else in his family had inherited the gift of longevity, which was a strange quirk of genetics. His mother had often berated him for his cold view, but as he watched the years pass without touching him, he came to understand: his was the perspective of eternity, the objective view of the gods who could seed the world with plagues and disasters to spark new growth. *Too bad*

Caligo could not share in my vision.

His old partner had been strangely silent over the last few days, ignoring the digital overtures Karan left for him. Caligo probably assumed that Karan would believe he was considering the proposal, but his silence only held one possible interpretation: his ex-partner was preparing to challenge him. Little did he recognize that Karan had already won. He had only needed time to make his preparations, and the farce of negotiation had provided that.

You always thought you were so clever, Caligo. Karan permitted himself the luxury of smirking at the blank computer screen. *You never understood how to plan ahead. You never understood the essential truth of people and how easy they are to manipulate. Or how easy you are to manipulate. You taught me the harshest lesson of all: never trust anyone, not even those who call you brother.*

"Let's hope Mark is home," Andrew muttered. Lily couldn't argue with him. Their group looked like a disreputable bunch as they walked swiftly down the row of narrow, bland townhouses that served as the University of Alaska's student housing. She noticed Ron's clenched hands and guessed his nerves would be acting up. He was out in public in broad daylight—he wasn't safe. She also felt the urge to hide until the reassuring cover of twilight, but Doc was getting worse. He needed shelter, food, and medicine fast. They'd left him, Vincent, and Evonne hiding nearby.

Andrew spotted their brother's assigned home, distinguishable from the others only by the number bolted above the door and a torn poster from an action movie taped over the front window. A plastic clown fish hung from a thin string looped over the porch light. Lily braced herself on the wall while Ron scanned the street and Andrew banged on the front door. After some disgruntled shouting and thumping from inside, it opened, revealing a skinny, blond young man with heavy glasses resting askew on his face. He blinked in surprise. "Andrew, man, we didn't know you were coming."

"We need to come inside, Jason." Andrew didn't wait for a reply, shouldering the young man aside. Lily turned to signal Evonne, using it as an opportunity to avoid Ron. She'd refused to be carried through the streets of Juneau. It felt close enough to what she wanted that it hurt to know it couldn't be.

It was too early in the school year for the summer industrial cleaning to have completely worn off, but a heavy overlay of old pizza and unwashed laundry did its best to challenge the harsh buzz of disinfectant and carpet soap. Books and papers littered the main room, piled anywhere with a flat surface, including the low, mass-produced sofa and the mismatched wooden chairs.

"Mark's out in the field." Jason waved his hands helplessly, tugging at his worn greyed T-shirt. He'd been Mark's roommate for the last two years. Driven by his own academic pursuits and relatively oblivious to everything outside of them, he made a perfect choice for someone who needed to keep a secret. From the way he looked at them, his book-oriented mind had clued in and realized something wasn't quite right.

"Jason, something… unpleasant happened back home. We need to talk to Mark, but we also need to keep this quiet. Please don't tell anyone else we're here." Lily ushered Evonne, Vincent, and Doc inside. Doc was coughing badly, and Evonne needed to support most of his weight. She kept her fingertip on his neck to monitor his pulse and temperature.

"Okay. Yeah. No problem. Todd and Matt are off doing on-site training this week, so you can crash in their rooms," Jason offered quickly, eager to help.

Vincent disappeared into Mark's bedroom at the back of the house without saying a word to anyone. Evonne and Lily helped Doc up the stairs and into one of the two bedrooms. They picked the room on the left, the one plastered with maps and pictures of various national parks over the dull grey walls. She guessed it was Todd's room from the family pictures tacked to the wall. Lily spotted an electric kettle and immediately filled it up and plugged it in. Searching the drawers, she found a collection of teabags and instant soup mixes as well as generic ceramic mugs liberated from the cafeteria.

Evonne helped Doc strip off his filthy, worn clothes and borrowed a set of university-logo sweats from the closet. Then they tucked him into the bed beneath as many blankets as they could find. His eyes immediately rolled shut. Lily stopped, a mug of steaming tea ready.

"I think he's just exhausted," Evonne said in answer to Lily's unspoken fear. "I could use a hot drink, though."

Lily handed over the tea and poured another for herself, savoring the warmth seeping through the mug into her swollen fingers. They pulled up the two chairs as close to the baseboard heater as they could and stuck their sock-clad feet on top of it. After a night and part of a day marching through the forest, they needed the heat to prevent damage.

"Are we still following a plan?" Evonne asked, balancing her mug with her palm through the handle and her fingers outstretched to avoid contact.

"I think Andrew is making it all up as he goes," Lily muttered.

"All right. Start talking." Evonne nudged her with a sock-clad foot.

"There's nothing to talk about," Lily insisted.

"*Au contraire.* You've barely looked at Ron since the cabin. The man pulled you out of a burning building with his bare hands, and you act like he forgot your birthday."

"Okay, fine. I don't want to talk about it." The bitterness clung to her words despite her best intentions, and yet she wouldn't change it. She'd earned the right to some anger to balance her humiliation.

"Don't make me push you. I'm too tired."

"He's a hero." Lily leaned back, closing her eyes.

"So are you! You came in to save Doc and me." Evonne's chair scraped against the floor as she scooted closer.

"I did what I had to, but it's more than that with him." Lily tried to find the words for what she instinctively understood. "He won't be happy being pinned down in Bear Claw."

"Neither am I. Still not seeing the point." The mug clinked as Evonne set it down on the windowsill.

"He's my mate. If I tell him what that means, he'll stay, and he'll be miserable. I told him I wouldn't put strings on him." Lily opened her eyes. No sense in hiding from the truth. Nothing would change it.

"He likes you. He'll want to stay." Evonne rubbed the back of her forearm along Lily's side, offering comfort.

"Right. What guy doesn't dream about hooking up with a girl who's not even human?"

"All that *Avatar* and *Star Trek* fan fiction can't be wrong."

Evonne's reply sparked a smile and took some of the immediate boil off Lily's simmering hurt. "And how would you know about that?"

"Bob's told me a lot about this whole Internet thing. You're not the only one interested in the outside world. Lily, you didn't see him when he realized you were trapped in there. He wasn't going to let anything stop him from getting to you. He ripped open the wall like it was birch bark."

Lily hated to burst her friend's romantic delusions, but suspicion pried the words from her lips. "He's a protector, a rescuer. He'd have done the same for Doc or for you. I wanted to believe there was something special between us." She told Evonne about her impassioned plea in the sweat lodge and how Ron only responded when she'd ordered him like a soldier.

"What about the first night in the cabin? He said he was glad he met you and that he wouldn't change any of it." Evonne refused to be easily derailed.

"It doesn't mean he wants to spend his life with me or even a weekend." Lily slumped. Her energy had escaped along with her hope. "I'm not saying he hates me or is preparing to burn me at the stake because I can turn into a bear. I won't always be the one needing to be rescued. Someday, he's going to leave to find someone else to protect."

Her friend did something she almost never did: she pulled Lily close and wrapped her arms around her.

"I can't look at him without already feeling that emptiness, the promise of pain." Hot tears rose, tightening her throat and spilling down her cheeks.

"You can't let your fears hold you back," Evonne said. "Maybe he'll hurt you, and maybe he won't. If he does, I, as your best friend, solemnly swear to hunt him down and stick icicles in his shoes."

Lily laughed weakly through her tears. "Don't. I can't make someone feel something for me that they don't. It's not his fault if I love him and he doesn't feel the same way about me. It just hurts." She buried her face in Evonne's shoulder, letting the pain flow out in silent sobs.

"I know." She could hear the tears in Evonne's voice, too. The two of them held each other, sharing in the primordial heartbreak of uncertain love.

Ron winced at the prices the student store asked for a few simple groceries, but Andrew paid it without hesitation. He'd thought Lily's brother was exaggerating when he said their pooled cash might not be enough, and now it was nearly gone. They picked up the bags and left, keeping their heads lowered and their pace steady to avoid drawing attention.

Andrew hadn't needed any coaching, a fact that began to nibble at Ron's suspicions. When had the shaman practiced the art of inconspicuousness? There wouldn't have been a need in Bear Claw, but somehow, Andrew knew what to do and had clearly practiced enough for it to become automatic.

"Perhaps you could hold off on the paranoia until we're out of public," Andrew said quietly.

Ron stiffened. "How—"

"It's not telepathy. You're not exactly an enigma." Andrew conspicuously glanced down at Ron's clenched fingers. "I wouldn't try to bluff at poker if I were you."

"We're not going to be able to stay here for long." The muscles in Ron's back and shoulders were aching from the accumulating tension.

"Tired of the scenic North already? I thought you'd promised Lily you were going to stay." Andrew kept his voice casual and jocular, though Ron picked up on the layer of steel underneath. *Hurt her, and I'll hurt you*, it promised.

"That was before we got chased out by armed soldiers. The game has changed." *Leaving me scrambling to learn the new rules, as always.*

"If you've been playing a game, I understand why you've been having trouble." Andrew opened the door to Mark's unit. After a quick check to make sure Vincent still sulked in the back, they brought some fresh bread up to where Doc and the girls were staying. Doc was sleeping uneasily, packed in towels that the girls had warmed on the heater. Evonne rummaged through the closet, running her grey fingers along a pair of hiking boots.

"Are we going to have to send Mark's roommates a check for stolen goods?"

"Survival situation." Evonne shrugged, putting the boots down. "The leather is almost worn through on those ones anyway."

Lily wasn't looking at him, Ron realized. She turned away from them, rubbing her arm as she stared out the window. The narrow confines of the room meant he couldn't get to her without shoving Evonne out of his way. Lily's friend glared at him as if aware of his thoughts.

"We got some food." He held up the bag, unsure why he needed to make a peace offering.

"Lily, let's go and see if we can scavenge some gear out of the lost and found." Evonne nudged Lily with her sock-clad toe.

"Sure." Lily squeezed past Ron, barely acknowledging his existence as anything other than an odd piece of furniture. He let her go, a flurry of emotions struggling for supremacy. Hurt: her rejection stung, biting deep into his heart. Confusion: why was she upset with him? Or was it even about him? There was plenty to be upset about. Maybe he was taking things too personally. Lily wasn't a game player. He'd always been able to count on her honesty, except about being a skinwalker. And in hindsight, he understood why she'd been reluctant to tell him that.

"I'll go out and find a computer where I can make contact with the others. We need to warn the other *lalassu* what's happening here," Andrew said. "How are you doing, Doc?"

"Better than Ron. You've stepped in it now, boy." Doc struggled to prop himself up with the thin pillow.

Ron somehow doubted Doc meant his boots. "Stepped in what? Do you know why Lily is avoiding me?"

Doc coughed as Ron helped to steady the biologist's shoulders and head against the wall. "Lily's got it in her head that you're going to leave her at some point."

"But why—oh." Ron sank down on the bed. He'd known from the beginning that, despite her promises, Lily wasn't a no-strings kind of girl. She was pulling away to protect herself. When she'd pretended to sleep until they reached Juneau, Ron had let her keep her illusions, trying to give her time and space to cope with the trauma. He'd still been floating on the relief-high of knowing that she was safe and in his arms. He'd needed the physical contact to reassure himself that she was really safe.

"I eavesdropped. Girls really do talk about everything." Doc fiddled with his glasses. "She says he's her mate."

"Oh, damn." Andrew set the bread down on the desk with a dull thud.

"What does that mean?" Ron asked, desperate to understand. The idea of losing Lily had his hands and legs shaking. His adrenaline demanded that he go fix the problem immediately. Only, he wasn't sure what needed to be fixed.

"Because of our animal side, we have a profoundly strong mating urge. We bond strongly, but because of our human side, the bond is unbreakable for life. If you reject her, she won't be able to bond with anyone else." Andrew's words were short and clipped. The shaman turned to Doc. "I suspected she had bonded with him, even though she kept refusing to admit it."

"She's admitting it now." Doc tugged at his beard.

There must be a mistake. "Lily knows I love her. Why would she think I'd leave her now?" Ron demanded. Lily not knowing how he felt seemed far more ridiculous and improbable to Ron than humans turning into bears.

"She's convinced herself and Evonne that you need to be a hero more than her partner," Doc repeated.

Ron stared at his hands, scrubbing at his thighs, unable to quite process what he'd heard.

"As comfortable and relaxing as it is to discuss my sister's romantic entanglements, there are other issues we need to deal with," Andrew interjected. "We need to try the sweat-lodge ritual again. You were close to breaking through the barriers."

"If he's her mate—" Doc began.

"They'll have time to sort it out after we escape with our lives," Andrew said.

"No." The word slipped out before Ron came close to making a decision to speak.

"The ritual might have been difficult, but it doesn't negate the progress we've made." Andrew's hand squeezed Ron's shoulder reassuringly.

"No. I have to fix things with Lily." It was surprisingly simple. If Lily was hurting, he needed to make it right. Ron didn't care if his captor and the entire US Army were waiting for him outside the door. Or rather, he did still care, but it didn't bring anything near the panic at realizing that Lily might be leaving him at that very moment. He'd nearly lost her once in the last twenty-four hours. Twice wasn't going to happen. "I have to make her understand how important she is to me."

Doc coughed, an unpleasant rattling that sounded as if he were trying to hurl the accumulated smoke out of his lungs. He needed a doctor, and Ron would make sure he got one. But first things first. "You know Lily. Both of you."

"If it's a mating bond, she won't have any choice." Andrew folded his arms over his chest, his fingers rapidly tapping on his bicep. "She's never been interested in a relationship before now. Steve tried, but she ignored him. One of the other rangers a few years ago wrote her some poetry, but she ignored him, too."

"She and Evonne read a lot of romance novels. Edyta sends them up." Doc paused to drink some water. "She's asked me a lot of questions about high school, about prom. I didn't go to mine, and she's always been disappointed about that."

"Prom?" Ron looked between the two men, lost.

"It was the dancing. She wanted to go dancing," Andrew explained. "We'd have to promise her dancing to get her to meet with the other skinwalkers. Not that it ever mattered. She wasn't interested in them."

"She's always been focused on her responsibilities with Ekurru and the Colony," Doc mused. "She's never come into heat before."

"We do not go into heat, and this is not a conversation I want to have." Andrew glared at Ron. "Contemplating setting up a date for my sister is enough of a trip on the ick side for me. The last thing we need to do is attract attention."

Ron was not enjoying the gist of the conversation. His emotions flicked with distressing rapidity between a grim elation that Lily hadn't fallen for the superficial charms of rangers looking for someone to enliven their postings, clawing jealousy that her family had been actively searching for a mate for her, and determination to make things work between them. All of it was punctuated by alarms of panic at the thought of discovery. "You're right. Lily would even agree. We should concentrate on the crisis at hand. But if we wait, we'll be too far apart. I don't care about being spotted—I care about making this right." *And we might not survive long enough to make it work.* If he could just take a drink, then he could cope with the overwhelming emotions. College campuses had bars. He could find one easily and numb the despair creeping up.

Except if he did that, he wouldn't be worthy of Lily anymore. He would never be able to go home, whichever home he chose. He needed to draw a line for "never again" and make it stick. He couldn't afford to fall back into old patterns.

"I think I may have an idea," Doc said.

It was a good thing Evonne came with her. Blind and preoccupied, Lily could have been searching through term papers instead of lost-and-found bins. She told herself that she was worried about the Colony, and she was. All communication had been cut off, leaving good or bad news trapped inside the Bear Claw borders. It didn't help. She recognized a lie even when it was woven out of truths. Things were playing out exactly as she'd always feared. She'd fallen in love with a man, and he'd taken over everything she relied on to get herself through hard times. She wanted to curl up and cry and write bad heartbroken poetry with tundra imagery.

"I'm telling you, a few cold things in his shoes would make us both feel better. I'm sure I can find some frozen scat near the dump that we can use." Evonne's supportive vindictiveness only left Lily exhausted. This wasn't like when Steve had tried to corner her in the ranger station and they'd arranged for Evonne to make some delicate alterations to his long underwear, removing the insulation around his crotch.

A tiny smile crept through at the memory, proof her sense of humor hadn't entirely deserted her. "Thanks for the offer. But I think we just need to talk."

"That sounds mature and less fun, but if it's what you want, it's what we'll do." Evonne gave her a one-armed hug as they arrived back at Mark's house.

"Hello, ladies. Your afternoon has been productive, I see." Andrew met them at the door. "Lily, I need you to go to On the Rocks. Right now."

Not now. On the Rocks was a mining bar and the hub for under-the-table deals. They'd met with a number of black market contacts there over the years. "I was hoping to talk with Ron first."

"He's out. I have a contact who can help us get out, but he's insisting on meeting you instead." Andrew might be an inch shorter than his sister, but somehow, he still managed to look down his nose like a disapproving parent.

She could fight. She could argue. It would waste time and energy, and she'd probably still end up doing what Andrew asked. Or she could accept the mission gracefully and get it over with. Then she could talk to Ron. "Who's the contact?"

"I don't know his name. It's a friend of a friend. He'll be in a plaid shirt—"

"Him and every other guy in the bar," Lily interrupted irritably.

"And carrying a toy fish."

"Okay, that might be unique." Evonne stepped between Lily and her brother. "Are you sure about this?"

"It'll be fine. Andrew's right—we need to concentrate on survival now," Lily replied.

Andrew punctuated his impatience with a long-suffering sigh. "He should be waiting by the time you get there."

Lily ran a self-conscious hand over the length of her hair. Bits were slipping out of the braid, and her clothes looked exactly as one would expect after a few hours crushed in a plane, escaping a fire, and trekking through the wilderness. She and Evonne had cleaned up as best they could when they'd arrived, but there was only so much they could do.

On the other hand, On the Rocks mainly catered to off-duty miners instead of the cruise-ship crowd. It was close enough to campus that a fair number of students probably went there too for slumming thrills and cheap electronics and other goods. She might not stick out as much as she thought.

She threaded her way down the darkened streets, picking through the filthy mix of slush and mud. The usual mix of snowmobiles and motorcycles squatted at various angles to the bar, although not as many as someone might expect based on the level of noise inside. Lily remembered the controversy when the mine had announced a free shuttle service to the bar. On the one hand, fewer drunks would be attempting to drive or walk back to the housing barracks. On the other hand, in a community that already struggled with alcoholism, it could be seen as enabling bad habits.

She pushed open the heavy door, releasing a burst of country music and laughter into the night. Inside, red-and-blue lights flashed from various neon beer advertisements. The jukebox blared the usual mix of country music and rock. Most of the crowd consisted of men from the surrounding tribes, out for a relaxing night of drinking, not flirting. And nearly every single one of them wore a plaid flannel shirt, the unofficial off-duty uniform of the North.

Everything inside showed an innovative approach to recycling. Empty chemical drums had been turned into tables, and the chairs were irregular stumps of wood. Only the bar—a long, polished slab of slate from the local quarry—showed a hint of sophistication. She remembered the first time she'd come here to visit Andrew. She'd been barely thirteen, and the busyness and press of people in Juneau had been overwhelming to a girl who'd known fewer than twenty people her entire life. Andrew had brought her to the bar, and although it had been crowded, the rough-hewn walls with decorations of antlers and pictures of the forest reminded her of home.

It wouldn't remind Ron of home. He was used to more put-together places such as tourist bars with custom-made tables and stuff on the walls designed by someone with a degree in interior design. He would be used to the type of girls who went to those kinds of places, too, she suddenly realized. Girls who knew how to do their makeup and had pretty hair like the ones she'd seen on the computer—delicate girls with practice flirting. Not a grubby little Northern girl with rough skin who knew four different ways to gut an elk. Lily slumped into a seat.

"Buy you a drink?" The invitation pierced the numbing cloud of self-pity, reminding Lily of her job. She shook her head, preparing to give a polite refusal.

Only to freeze in shock.

Ron stood beside her in a buttoned plaid shirt, carrying a small plastic toy in the shape of a clown fish. Lily's dazed brain recognized it as the same one from Mark's house. "What…. did you already meet the contact?"

"I'm the contact." Ron smiled, making her insides melt and reminding her why she hadn't kept her head in the first place. "We didn't think you'd meet with me otherwise."

She resisted the urge to comb through her hair. "You shouldn't be here. We should go—"

"Doc told me what you said to Evonne. How you think I need to be a hero more than I need to be with you." Ron shook his head when the bartender approached. His knuckles were white around the little fish, and Lily realized how difficult it must be for him—a recovering alcoholic in a bar. *The definition of temptation.*

"I know it's important to you. How you hated feeling like you'd failed as a hero. We shouldn't talk about it here." Lily started to stand. He might have told Litonya instead of Lily, but that didn't mean she didn't remember it all.

"No. We need to be here so I can show you how important you are to me." He took her hand in his and began to play with her fingers. She settled back onto her stool as he continued. "You're right. It is important to me. All my life, I was the hero. I saved puppies and rescued cats from trees. I was the kid the adults depended on to watch the others and keep them safe. Joining the army was a way to be even more of a hero. And then I failed, and they still called me a hero, but I couldn't believe it anymore." Ron leaned forward on the battered lid of the drum table. "You're wrong about the rest, though. When I realized you were trapped in that fire, I didn't care about being a hero or protecting myself or anything except the fact that I might never get to see you again."

Lily didn't know what to say. It hurt too much to let herself believe and hope.

Ron gripped her hand and brought it to his lips before fixing those brilliant-blue eyes on her. "I've never been more frightened or more clear in my life. The idea of losing you is so terrible that I will do everything I can to make sure it never happens. You are more important than anything else in my life. I don't care about clearing my name or finding my captor except that it would make you safer. I want to be with you any way you'll let me." He smiled. "Even if it means curling up in one of the dog sheds."

"That doesn't strike me as comfortable." Lily took refuge in the distance of a joke. But humor didn't dissolve the tension. Instead, it only brought it into focus, making her acutely aware that this was a turning point in her life. Balancing on the edge of a knife, she knew that whichever way she let herself fall, nothing would be the same as before she'd found Ron McBride in the woods. She could keep trying to protect herself, or she could take the leap of faith. Maybe heartbreak was at the bottom of the cliff, but she'd never know until she jumped.

He wrapped his big hands around hers again. "Don't try and

convince yourself this isn't real. It's more real than everything else, and I'll do whatever I have to so I can prove it to you."

Time to let go. Lily took a deep breath. "The smart thing would be to wait until we've gotten through this. But I guess I'm not that smart."

"I'm not willing to wait either." His thumbs skimmed along the back of her hand. "I've spent too much of my life waiting for a right time that never seemed to come. I always thought that if I were faster and smarter, my life would come together. Now I'm better than I ever could have been, and my life is complete chaos. I'm fighting for what I want, and what I want is you."

How could any girl stand firm in the face of a declaration like that? Lily bit her lip. "What do we do next?"

"Dance with me." Ron got to his feet, still holding her hand in both of his.

So many times, she'd fantasized about the moment someone asked her to dance, and she'd come up with dozens of witty acceptance speeches. None of them floated up from the depths of her memory.

"I know it's something you've always wanted to do. Dance with me. Here. Now."

She looked around at the noisy bar full of miners in various stages of drunkenness. It wasn't exactly how she'd hoped this dream would come true.

"Please." Ron's fingers tightened around hers, and his confidence started to look a little ragged around the edges. "For one song, give me a chance."

Chapter Nineteen

Lily allowed Ron to tug her off her perch and lead her to the tiny clear area in front of the jukebox. He slipped a coin into the slot, and a slower song obediently began. She was acutely conscious of the puzzled and irritated looks from the other patrons, but Ron ignored them, cupping his hand across the small of her back and wrapping his other hand around hers. Lily felt awkward, unsure where to put her free hand or how to move.

"Relax." Ron began rocking gently on the balls of his feet. His hand on her back guided her to match his movements.

"This isn't really a dancing kind of place." Lily's fingers tightened on Ron's sleeve as she intercepted a glare from a burly man with close-cropped hair, and his mouth twisted downward. This wasn't how her dream was supposed to play out.

"Nothing about us conforms to the rules." Ron turned the two of them in place, swaying lightly.

"Ron, you don't have to do this." She tried to pull back, but Ron held her close.

"I do. I need to restore your faith in me. I'm sorry I hurt you." His thumb caressed the back of her hand.

His words pulled her attention away from the men around them and back to Ron. She looked up into his brilliant-blue eyes and tender smile, and the rest of the world fell away. Her fears quieted, giving her the mental and emotional space to remember how good it felt to just be Lily and Blue Eyes. No complications, no duties. She laid her head on his shoulder, giving herself up to the sway of the music. "I'm sorry, too."

"I realized something when I thought I'd lost you. You can't protect someone you love by staying away from them. You can only do it side by side, and I don't intend to ever leave your side again."

His words reminded her of the dangers they still faced. "You can't know that. Neither of us knows what will happen, but we can fight together."

He leaned down to whisper in her ear, barely audible over the music. "See, the thing is that I do know. Because I have the best guardian ever— a magnificent grizzly able to take down men with a single swipe of her beautiful paw. She's also a beautiful and magnificent woman, one I love more than anything else in the whole world."

He meant every word of it. Lily's heart swelled with radiant joy.

"I should have guessed about Litonya. Being around her felt like being around you. For a long time, I've been on my guard, afraid that if I let myself slip, people will get hurt. With you and Litonya, I was at peace because I knew I could trust you."

"I wanted you to feel safe," Lily whispered, enjoying the warmth of his arms around her, the smoothness of his shoulder against her cheek. Maybe the setting wasn't how she'd imagined it, but this part felt exactly right.

"And I do. I know that as long as we're together, we can deal with anything. You were afraid I wouldn't want you because you're strong, but it's because you're strong that I love you. I don't need someone else to protect. I need someone to stand with me."

Tears threatened to blur the moment she was desperately trying to preserve. The puzzle pieces were fitting together into a new picture. He was a soldier at heart, true. So was she when it came down to it. She stood between the Colony and Ekurru and any danger that might approach. Their relationship wasn't based on him being the hero and her being a victim. They could be guardians together. She smiled. "Evonne will be upset."

Ron frowned in puzzlement. "Won't she be happy for you?"

"She will. Eventually. But right now, she's searching for something cold and unpleasant to slip into your bed tonight. I believe she also planned to put icicles in your shoes." Laughter bubbled up through the collapsing tension.

Ron grinned, pulling her even closer against him. Lily tucked her head into the nook between his neck and shoulder, savoring the warmth of his firm muscles. He pulled their outstretched hands close in to their bodies, intertwining their arms. "Doc and Andrew will explain it to her. First, you and I deserve a little privacy, though. It'll give her a night to cool off."

Lily stole a kiss, a featherlight brush of her lips against the rough stubble coating his throat. "That sounds like a very good idea."

She heard hoots and whistles as Ron bent his head to capture her lips with his, but she didn't care. He tasted sweet and a little smoky as he sought to claim her mouth with soft, explorative lip bites. She squeezed closer to him, letting herself enjoy and map every inch of his tall, lean body. She could feel the long length of his hard-on behind his worn-out jeans, and the realization set a slow burn simmering deep in her own belly.

"Let's go," he whispered hoarsely against her lips.

They slipped outside, Ron barely remembering to grab his coat. As the frigid air slapped them, he guided them back to the student housing. Lily hung back. "I'm not big on audiences."

"You forget they're all in on the plan." He held up the keys, and Lily recognized the mittens they'd sent with Mark when he left. "We've got one of the rooms to ourselves."

The heat burning in Lily's belly didn't allow much mental space for questioning. Her sense of responsibility pricked at her conscience, and she shushed it, reminding herself that they couldn't do anything else at the moment. Tonight could be about her and Ron, no complications and no regrets.

Fortunately, the house was dark and quiet when they arrived. She wasn't in the mood to listen to Andrew's sarcasm or explain things to Evonne or even humor Doc's long-winded lectures. The silence let her continue to cling to her illusions. Tomorrow, it would all hit home: being on the run from their enemies, not knowing what happened with her family, the urge to return to Bear Claw.

"You're pulling away," Ron said quietly as he opened the door. "Second thoughts?"

Lily shook her head. "I have responsibilities. So do you. But tonight isn't about them. It's about us, and I don't want to bring them into it. I do need to tell you something about the mating bond, though."

"Andrew explained a little bit." He didn't rush her, waiting for her to tell her what she needed to in her own time.

"It's not romantic like finding a soul mate. It's a biological imperative that doesn't pay much attention to what the human mind thinks. Or at least, that's what I always believed. I fought against it. I didn't want to be forced into a permanent bond with someone who was only geographically convenient. I wanted a chance to fall in love, to feel the thrill I'd read about in novels." Lily remembered how her heart would ache at the idea of a dark, romantic hero who'd come to sweep her away. "Instead, I bonded with you, and as much as I tried to pretend it wasn't true, I couldn't stay away or lie to myself."

Fear widened his eyes and tightened his mouth. "Andrew said that if I leave you, the bond will hurt you. Maybe we shouldn't consummate it until after."

"It's too late for that." Lily loved the fact that he was willing to hold back if it was best for her. "I've already bonded with you. Tonight is about making a memory that we can hold on to no matter what happens in the next few days. Life is pain. That's why we need joy to hold on to. You are my mate, Ron McBride, and you always will be."

"I can't imagine ever being without you. I don't want to imagine it." He kicked the door shut and pulled her tightly into his arms as if daring the universe to separate them. "But if tonight is about making a memory, I want it to be the best one possible."

He began nibbling on her neck, tiny biting kisses along the length of her jaw and down her throat. Lily tilted her head back, shivering under his ticklish touch.

"Is that a shower back there?" he asked between kisses.

"Mm-hmm," Lily answered coherently.

He pulled back, a devilish grin spreading his cheeks wide. "Then I have a fantastic idea."

It took a few moments for the water to begin to flow through the pipes, but Ron occupied the time by gently removing their worn clothing. Anticipation and self-consciousness warred in Lily as he tugged her snug sweater up over her head. Although she wasn't entirely inexperienced, this was new territory for her.

Ron had already stripped off his shirts, leaving his chest bare except for a dusky sprinkling of hair. He laid aside her sweater and cupped her face in his hands. "I won't do anything you're not okay with. This is too important to mess up by being impatient."

Lily nodded. She didn't want to make the mistake of getting caught in her head. For once, instead of thinking and planning, she would let herself feel and explore. To answer him, she slid off her leggings and put them with the other clothes. Her action left her clad only in a tight tank and panties.

Ron's indrawn breath sounded gratifyingly appreciative. Steam began to fill the tiny bathroom as he quickly shucked off his jeans. His swollen member stood temptingly erect, jutting toward her like the needle in a compass. His big fingers grabbed the hem of her tank and paused. "Okay?"

"Oh yeah." She was ready—slick, swollen, and aching. He pulled the tank over her head and then knelt before her. Hooking his thumbs into her panties, he slid them down her legs, letting his fingertips score fiery lines along her skin. Lily's knees started to shake, and she leaned back against the narrow sink.

Ron began to kiss the top of one thigh, the raspy roughness of his stubble contrasting with the tenderness of his lips. His hands reached back to cup and shape her buttocks, helping to support her. Lily closed her eyes and tilted her head back as he nibbled his way closer to the join between her legs. Hot droplets hit them through the open shower curtain.

"Come on." Ron stood up, still grinning as he pulled her into the narrow shower stall. "No need to waste the hot water."

They nearly filled the tiny space, but Ron turned her so they were pressed front to front, letting her back enjoy the full force of the spray. His clever fingers undid the ragged remnants of her braid, finger combing through the worst of the tangles. Water quickly soaked through the strands, and they clung to her body like inky tentacles. To her surprise, he reached for a bottle of shampoo.

"I'm going to learn every inch of you," he promised, working the lather into her hair and then letting his soapy hands explore. He cupped her breasts, teasing the nipples with his thumbs until they tightened despite the heat. The steady flicking sent a new wave of heat to dissolve Lily's strength. His hand skimmed down her side, hooking her leg and drawing it up around his waist so he could caress and knead her thigh.

She nearly swooned as his erection rubbed against the swollen folds between her legs. She felt ready to explode, vibrating with the urge for completion. But he didn't push into her. Instead, he pressed her against the wall for a penetrating kiss, postponing the other penetration she longed for.

His tongue plundered and plunged, claiming her mouth as its own. *Mine,* it said with each swipe and lave. *Mine.* His fingers tightened on her body, and he ground against her. *Mine!* She grew dizzy with surrender, all too willing to participate in her ravishment.

She buried her fingers in his spiky wet hair, returning passion for passion. She met his thrust with one of her own, deepening the kiss between them.

Need for oxygen eventually broke their clinch, leaving them panting and clinging to one another. Ron cradled her in his strong arms, his forehead pressed against hers. The hot water sputtered, drumming against their bare skin, while steam swirled around them. Ron whispered, "Ready for round two?"

Her legs were recovering their basic skills, letting her stand on her own. He bent his knees, lowering himself into a kneeling position. His mouth grazed her thighs. His lips felt cool compared to the steam. "Put your leg on my shoulder," he said.

Lily complied and then immediately braced her arms against the side of the stall as his kiss found her sweet depths. A last coherent thought surfaced: Evonne had been right. The description in books didn't do this justice. Then she lost herself to the coaxing of his nibbling lips and tongue.

His hands gripped her hips, holding her in place as her bones swiftly liquefied while her muscles wound tighter and tighter in exquisite tension. Dizzy and floating, she felt herself crying out but couldn't hear over the roar of her heartbeat. He kept up his relentless pace, building her higher and higher with every expert touch. Until she slammed into the pinnacle.

Everything spun and vibrated, tossing her like trees in a storm. Ecstasy bloomed, cascading through her like the Northern Lights, a shimmering blanket of brilliant pleasure. As she came panting back to herself, she realized the water had gone cold at some point, raising chill bumps along her skin. Yet she couldn't quite summon up the energy to move.

Ron supported her as he stood, turned off the water, and guided her wobbly steps out of the stall. Wrapping a thick towel around her, he lifted her easily, carrying her to the waiting bed. He settled her on the sheets as if she were something precious and sacred. His eyes crinkled as he smiled at her. "You are so beautiful."

"You too." She smiled. With his wide blue eyes, sensual mouth, and ready smile, he was the image of masculine beauty. Add to that a body refined over years of training, with firm, rounded muscles defining his arms and broad shoulders and a wide, powerful chest and back nipping down into a trim waist and the legs of a long-distance runner, and a girl would have to be three days dead not to drool. Lily reached up to him. "Guess it's time for round three."

"Yes, ma'am." He saluted her before crawling over her into the bed. He fastened his mouth over her breast, rolling the nipple with his tongue. Lily closed her eyes, her hands tight on his shoulders, eager to draw him up and get to the finale. Her body ached and clenched with wanting to feel him inside. Her blood thrummed in a low fever, burning restlessly in her veins.

"Still good?" he asked, releasing her. Her eyes popped open as she bucked, trying to reach him again. A teasing smile haunted his swollen lips.

"Definitely," she panted, reaching for him.

"Are you sure?" He hissed the last word as she wrapped her hand around his jutting shaft.

"It will be when you get back over here." Her lips stretched in a seductress's smile. "Don't make me wait."

He grinned back at her. "Definitely not, ma'am."

Their lips joined in a kiss, which only strung Lily's tension tighter. He probed her slick folds with a finger, and she squirmed against him, ready to be filled. He took the hint and positioned himself between her open thighs.

Finally, she felt what she had been waiting for: the delicious stretch as he entered her. He groaned as he rocked back and forth, sliding deeper with each thrust. She held on to him tightly, her awareness vanishing in bright electrical fireworks that exploded along her nerves. Suddenly, the second peak clamped onto her, sending her high into the stratosphere. She was made solely of pleasure, a thrumming drum skin of delight, pounding out her orgasm in deep, resonating bursts.

Slowly she returned to herself, becoming aware of her sweat-slick skin clinging to Ron's, the harsh rasp of his panting breath against her ear, and the trembling of her limbs as she floated down on waves of aftershocks.

She wanted to stay in the moment and not ruin it by remembering all the things they needed to do and all the forces aligned against them. Her brain never stayed silent while she was awake. She refused to let it interrupt. This fragile interlude belonged to her and Ron. No one and nothing else had any business encroaching on it.

She barely had enough energy to turn her head and press a kiss to his cool, damp shoulder. He lifted himself up enough to hover over her, braced on his elbows on either side of her head. Reaching up, she cupped his face with her hands, letting her fingers trace the line of his brow.

"I don't have the words," he murmured.

"That makes two of us," she whispered.

"You're everything I could never dare to dream for." The tenderness in his eyes brought tears to hers. He turned his head to snatch a kiss against her palm. "You're my Lily, and I never want to even imagine a life without you."

"And you said you didn't have words," she teased.

A wicked gleam flared to life in his eyes. "I've always been more of a man of action. Ready for round four?"

"Ms. Golov." Karan took a selfish pleasure in startling the businesswoman. He had watched her walk into Ptarmigan's conference room, her eyes skimming over where he waited in the shadows. She tried to regain the upper hand, scowling and folding her bony arms over her chest. These cold climates simply withered people away. Karan could not wait to return to more civilized temperatures.

"What do you want?" She scowled, clearly used to dominating those she dealt with. He allowed himself a small smile. She might be top shark in her little community, but he was a great white. Her posturing meant nothing to him. He glanced around the room where the businesswoman met her clients and suppliers. She likely believed its bland, fabric-covered prefabricated wall segments and sturdy metal table appeared intimidating. They would have been imported at great expense, yet to him, they made the room look cheap and industrial.

"Mr. Dalhard is growing impatient with the lack of progress." He glided forward, delicately positioning himself behind the head chair—a padded black-leather thing—as a subtle reminder of his position relative to hers.

"If he wants instant results, he should hire a magician." Edyta's growl held a promising note of defensiveness. "Why is he so all-fired eager to get his hands on the folk from Bear Claw anyway? There are plenty of reservations and other communities out here that could give you access to the mineral beds."

Karan noted her growing suspicion. Dalhard's influence was wearing off, letting her question his decisions. Which would not be a problem if Dalhard were still in Kluane. Left on his own, Karan would have to respond to her doubts the old-fashioned, direct way. "He is worried about them. They fled for their lives from a vicious attack." Edyta frowned. "They took their dogs and stuff with them. That's not fleeing—it's running from someone. Why would they be so scared of your boss?"

"I am afraid they may have been influenced by Corporal McBride." He needed to be careful, sprinkling judicious truths in the right position and proportions. The woman had already proved to be unusually sharp at spotting outright lies.

"The fellow from the news? The one who Bob's always going on about?" Edyta settled herself in a chair with a snort. "I've known Bob for ten years, and I can tell you right now that the man is not acting rationally."

"He is terribly worried about his wife and family." Karan let his phrasing insinuate that the woman should be as well. "I believe there is more to his fears than he has shared."

"Bob's always been crazy protective about Evonne. I've invited him to bring her up for any number of things, and he always has some excuse. I think he's worried she's run off with the soldier man, no matter how much he whines about Lily." Edyta's shrug suggested she wouldn't have blamed Evonne in such a case.

"You do not believe McBride is a murderer?" He widened his eyes, attempting to appear innocently confused.

"He wouldn't be the first fellow with a past to find his way up here. Way I see it, there's lots of talk about might and maybe with damn little proof being offered. Could be the government trying to keep things fair, but the real key is this: I can't see the Charging Bulls tolerating a killer in their midst. Lily's a smart girl with a good head on her shoulders. She wouldn't get mixed up in that sort of thing."

Irritation threatened to overwhelm Karan's carefully composed expression. He should have been able to use her concern to trigger an emotional response, but she remained coolly logical. Emotions were far easier to manipulate and maintain than logic. He needed to find the correct trigger.

"If your boss really wants to bring easier communications to the North to sweeten his mining deals, Slate River would be a much better place to start than Bear Claw." Edyta pulled out a map and pointed out the small mining town. "From there, he could build out to the east and north. Forget going into the mountains—it's difficult territory to get around in. It'll eat up your profit. Better to get your kinks worked out in the tundra."

She continued outlining a business plan that would consume a fair amount of their available revenue for the forthcoming decade, and Karan realized his mistake. They had initially approached her as business people but had allowed their true focus to detract from their apparent cover. If they were only interested in the mineral rights and mining, or even only in developing their communication prototype, then they would have abandoned Bear Claw at the first sign of resistance.

Clumsy, he scolded himself. He had been too caught up in Dalhard's rapidly evolving plans and dreams to exercise the usual caution and thoroughness.

"The network could be made profitable within five years. People are damn starved for entertainment up here, especially in the winter," Edyta finished.

"A well thought-out and thorough presentation." Karan inclined his head and watched the woman preen. Her pride in business acumen defined her. That was the key. "I will certainly present it to Mr. Dalhard, although I doubt I can do it the justice you could."

"I can go over it with both of you. I know all these places—the climate, the territory, and the people. With my help, you'll get what you need." She folded up the map to put it back in her bag.

"We have not been completely honest with you about our needs." Karan bent his head, keeping his gaze fixed on the woman, peering through his lashes.

A flash of triumph rippled across her features. "I knew you weren't showing me all the pieces. Thought I wouldn't figure it out?"

"Not at all. Forgive me, Ms. Golov, but deception does not come naturally to me." He fidgeted with a pen, trying to appear sheepish and nervous. This sort of acting had never been easy for him. He could conceal his emotions well enough, but manufacturing a false reaction was difficult. "The truth is that we are not only representing our own interests. Other parties asked us for help."

"What other parties?" She leaned back, and Karan forced himself to stay steady. If she believed him, she would be leaning forward, eager to hear the secret. Leaning back meant she suspected a trap.

"I hope you can understand that I have not been at liberty to speak of this and that I am breaking many laws in doing so. I rely on your discretion." Karan watched as her back slowly came forward. "Because of our interest in this territory, we were contacted by the RCMP and Homeland Security. They were afraid McBride might be in this area and asked us to find out quietly, one way or another."

"That's how you got so many soldiers so quickly." Edyta nodded, accepting his interpretation of events. Karan breathed easier.

"He is far more dangerous than publicized. Your friend Bob is right to be afraid. The corporal took out the entire team we sent after him and did it quickly enough that they could not call for help." He looked away, trying to convey a sense of guilt and vulnerability. "That was our fault. We underestimated him, and good men paid for our mistake with their lives. I do not want to make the same mistake again."

"What do you want me to do?" she asked. The surge of triumph intoxicating Karan must have been similar to what an ambush predator felt when his prey stumbled into a snare. The fly was caught in the spider's web. Now he could wrap it tight and drain it dry.

The pieces were coming together. Vapor could feel the electronic skeins intertwining into a net—one being wrapped around the escapees from Bear Claw by an unknown hand.

The Charging Bulls finally contacted him, saying they were leaving Bear Claw to escape—an extraordinarily useless and outdated piece of communication. He suspected they would make contact with Mark, but he wouldn't return from his training trip until the morning—just in time to see the shit storm of articles and media broadcasts calling for any information on the escaped murderer Corporal Ronald McBride.

Damn you, Pujari. He'd tried to shunt aside the broadcasts and kill the links to the articles, but for every one he managed to quash, another five popped up. A relentless stream of data was driving Pujari's prey into a trap.

He'd sent Joe out to see if he could track down the Charging Bulls and McBride. The detective possessed good instincts along with an unfortunately idealistic sense of morality. Joe relentlessly insisted on coming up with plans to take Dalhard down legally. They could insist on complete isolation. They could pretend he had some highly contagious disease.

He refused to track down Dalhard until Vapor agreed to do things his way. He wouldn't deliver someone into a death sentence. Vapor could admire the man's determination even as it frustrated him.

Luckily, he didn't need Joe anymore to track down Dalhard. The man currently sat in the most expensive hotel in Juneau along with a senator, ensuring the charges against him would vanish. Worryingly, there was no sign of Vapor's old partner. Karan must be managing the data stream—whoever was behind the broadcasts was unbelievably good, matching the skills Vapor had acquired over decades of practice.

For the moment, he had a different angle to pursue. A man named Bob Villeneuve was posting very vocal diatribes on a large number of sites, exhorting people not only to share information about McBride, but to physically attack him on sight. Villeneuve's current address was listed as Bear Claw, Yukon Territory. Vapor doubted it was a coincidence.

He found Villeneuve ranting on a conspiracy-theory site. It was child's play to yank him into a private chat room.

V>> We need to talk, Bob.

Bob>> Who are you?

Vapor activated the web camera in Villeneuve's computer to see the little man sweating and twitching. He suppressed his irritation. Frightened people had a tendency to focus on what they thought others wanted to hear rather than the truth.

V>> My name is Vapor. I'm a guardian to the *lalassu*. Now stop looking behind you and concentrate. We don't have much time.

Bob>> You can see me?

V>> Your computer has a webcam. We can talk about that, or we can talk about how to save your wife.

Bob>> Do you know where she is? He looked so hopeful, like a puppy begging for treats.

V>> No. But I know you don't want the people you're with to get hold of her. The man couldn't be so stupid as to believe whatever promises Dalhard had spewed, unless he was under the man's psychic influence.

Bob>> You can't know that.

V>> They're here for profit. Their own. Whatever they've told you, they don't care about your wife or about you. If you're not careful, you'll both end up as corpses.

Bob>> Why should I trust you?

Did he have any other options? **V>> Trust is overrated. I'm offering you help, but I need your help to do it.**

Bob>> What do I have to do?

It would be nice if Vapor could convince him to lay off his attacks on McBride, but any suggestion of it would only cause Bob to log off immediately. Instead, he focused on another immediate concern. **V>> I need to find Karan Samil. Do you know where he is?**

The man onscreen glanced to one side, nodding. **Bob>> I can find out.**

The little bastard wanted to play games. With his wife at risk, he still sought to cater to both sides.

Bob>> How do I contact you?

Vapor gave him a disposable cell number. **V> Call, or open your computer and leave a comment or message anywhere. I'll get it.**

Bob logged off. Vapor shook his head again. Bob didn't even realize he'd already told Vapor where his old partner was. Bob's computer was logged into a network in Kluane, which meant Pujari was there, too.

Chapter Twenty

A sputter resembling a stubborn engine turning over woke Lily up from a sated sleep. She smiled and stretched, glancing over at Ron, still snoring beside her. He'd earned his rest. *Go back to sleep, or wake him up for round ten?* It was good to finally have pleasant decisions to make.

Impulsively, she decided to rummage in the common area and see about making them something to eat. It was still predawn, and the house and neighborhood were quiet. She could keep the focus on her and Ron for a little while longer. She slid carefully out of the covers, preventing the cold drafts from getting underneath the warm blankets. It took her a few minutes to find all her clothes and pull them on—enough time for the chill to wake her up as thoroughly as a cup of coffee.

Humming, she picked her way to the common room at the front of the house. Turning the corner, she froze as she saw the image on the television screen: a giant picture of Ron in his military uniform. Jason stood in the corner of the room, his blond curls limp and dark with sweat as he clutched a baseball bat. His fingers were white where they gripped the wood.

"I recognized him," he whispered. "They said he killed people."

"Jason, they lied. I can explain everything." Lily kept her voice calm and her hands up in a nonthreatening position.

"I'm not stupid." Jason thrust his chin out defiantly. "You and your family, you're always keeping secrets from me. Think I don't notice when you hustle me out of the way or stop talking when I get near. I saw it all and thought, it's okay. It's not my business even though it leaves me on

303

the outside." Tears threatened to spill down his cheeks, fogging his glasses.

"I'm sorry. I'm sure Mark never meant to hurt you. I know I didn't." Lily stepped forward slowly, wondering if she could get close enough to grab the bat. Jason's accusations struck too close to home. They had dismissed him, but now he had her full attention.

"This isn't about your stupid family drama," Jason shouted. "He's dangerous!" He lifted the bat higher as if expecting Ron to pop out of the shadows at any moment.

"I swear he isn't." Lily decided to stick with a version of the truth. "There are some very bad but powerful people looking for him. They're telling lies so no one will help him."

"You expect me to believe you?"

"It's the truth." Lily heard pounding feet on the stairs and in the hall. Jason's eyes flicked over her shoulder and bulged wide like a frog's.

"Jason, man, what the hell?" Mark's normally cheerful voice was rough and cracking. His short black hair stood up at all angles in thick tufts like an anime character. Lily noticed the dark circles under his eyes and guessed he had arrived home late last night. His sweatpants and T-shirt were creased and stained as if he'd collapsed into bed without bothering to change.

Lily sensed Ron's presence behind her, although he didn't say a word. He would be evaluating the situation, ready to haul her out of the way in a second if things went wrong but trusting her to deal with it until then. Like a true partner. She kept her attention on Jason. "You need to put the bat down, Jason."

"The news says to call the police if you see him." The tip of the bat lowered, more as if Jason was losing strength than deciding to put it down. His skinny arms trembled, jiggling the weapon.

"Tell me you didn't," Mark pleaded.

"Mark, go upstairs and check on Doc," Lily said. For once, her twin actually listened to her.

"I can't get dragged down in this. I don't know if you're running drugs or whatever, but I worked hard for my scholarship. I can't lose it over something like this." Jason sank down into the corner, a lost little boy in flannel pajamas, clutching the bat like a teddy bear.

Lily started to reassure him, but someone pounded on the front door. Her heart sank.

"They're after me. I can draw them away," Ron whispered.

"Maybe it's a neighbor, complaining about the fighting." She wanted to believe it.

The person outside shouted. "We know he's in there. Open up."

"They said to call." Jason peered out through his fogged glasses.

"I'll find you!" Ron promised, slamming a hasty kiss onto her mouth before bolting for the back door.

Lily didn't hesitate—she ran after him. Mark and Andrew could get Doc and Evonne out. She refused to leave Ron's side. She followed him out into the back alley, the frozen gravel biting into her bare feet—and skidded to a stop when she saw a powerfully built Hispanic man standing in the alley, arms folded. He shook his head. "I guessed you'd try and rabbit."

"Joe?" Ron whispered, and Lily saw the shock of recognition on his face. "What are you doing here?"

"You tracked us from the bar?" Ron struggled to grasp what Joe had told him. He'd gotten so used to ignoring the warnings in his head that he hadn't cared about being in public. And yet, he couldn't bring himself to regret it. A goofy smile stretched his cheeks at the memories.

A growl from their guests banished his good vibes too quickly. Ron focused on the silent, burly man with a tattooed shaved head, introduced as Vapor. Bikers and gang members didn't intimidate Ron, but something about the man had Ron's primal protective instincts working overtime. A glance at Andrew told him the shaman felt the same way. Despite a nonchalant pose and crossed arms, Andrew's fingers kept twitching against his sweater.

"Jason's out, and Doc is sleeping," Evonne announced as she came downstairs, her face pale and her eyes dark with exhaustion.

Andrew nodded. He'd been the one to inject a little chemical sleep assistance into the weeping roommate. Ron didn't ask if they'd done the same for Doc. The biologist had been coughing all night.

Evonne went to Lily, and the two women exchanged quick words in their native tongue. Hopefully, Lily was convincing Evonne to give Ron another chance. He didn't want to come between her and her best friend. Or find something cold, wet, and possibly biohazardous in his shoes.

Last night had been incredible, washing away the clutter in his mind and heart. Her grandfather was utterly wrong. His love for her fueled him, gave him strength and hope. She gave him a mental refuge, one that drugs and booze could never hope to match. Realization slugged him, knocking aside his train of thought: he'd slept through the night without a single nightmare. Lily was who and what he needed, and he would do whatever he must to make things right so they could go on together. She'd made him into a hero again by giving him something to protect.

Andrew and Mark pulled Vincent out of the back bedroom. Grumbling loudly, he'd taken one look at Vapor and immediately shut up, which was a first in Ron's experience and left him wary. Ron shifted slightly to keep Vapor, Vincent, and Joe in his line of sight. He remembered Joe from the disastrous rescue attempt. His mind still skittered away from the details, but he knew which side the cop was on.

"We wouldn't have needed to track you if you told us where you were going." Vapor delivered the scolding like a teacher chiding a student for failing to study.

"How did you know where to find us?" Ron asked, offended by the armchair quarterbacking of their escape.

"Hiding with your girlfriend's brother isn't exactly difficult to figure out." Sitting on a squat chair like a king on a throne, Vapor resembled an ancient mountain as it was lashed by a thunderstorm, unmovable and untouched. "You're lucky—" The next word refused to register in Ron's ears. "… didn't figure it out. Especially since he's here in town."

The buzz could only mean one thing: his captor. Panic seized Ron's throat in clawed hands. The memory of his body being taken over with a single phrase locked his muscles tight. Lily immediately came to stand beside him, wrapping her arm around his back and resting her cheek on his shoulder. Her touch released the suffocating tension long enough for him to draw a long, ragged breath.

"We need to get Ron and Vincent out of here." Lily's voice came very close to being an order as she glared at Vapor and Joe.

"Can you magic up some tickets or something, like you did with me?" Joe asked.

Vapor shook his head. "We have a bigger problem than—" The word buzzed and skittered. "My old partner is with him. He has many of the same skills I do and an uncanny ability to spot artificial patterns against the background of everyday transactions. We need a way out that he won't anticipate. I don't know whose side he's on, but I doubt it's ours."

Again, Ron heard only a distortion when Andrew spoke. "—'s probably pulling your friend's strings. We've been trying to break the protections he put in Vincent and Ron's minds, but so far, it's proving difficult."

"So, you still wouldn't be able to testify about what he did to you?" Joe scraped his hand over the close-shaved stubble on his head. "Damn."

"What's the rush?" Vincent grumbled.

"If we can't find a way to neutralize him legally, then Vapor wants to execute him." Joe glared at the bald man.

"From what you've said, that makes sense." Evonne shrugged.

Ron stared at her in shock before turning to Lily for support. "We can't just kill him!"

"Didn't you say he was unraveling the charges you managed to bring?" Lily asked. "And he's done it before, too." Joe reluctantly nodded, and Lily continued. "Vincent was right. We can't keep running and hope he doesn't find us."

It wasn't the whole-hearted endorsement of a non-murder plan that Ron hoped for, but her observations were valid reasons why the traditional justice system wouldn't work.

"Look, you can't go after"—buzzing—"like you would any other *lalassu*," Joe argued. "He's a public figure. You can't make him disappear and assume no one will come looking. He's on different boards and schmoozes with high society. Lots of money and power aimed right at you."

Vapor tilted his head, considering the policeman's words. "You make a good point. Yet we can find no one to stand against him."

"I'll do it." Ron straightened, moving away from the wall.

"And the Boy Scout volunteers. There's a shock," Vincent muttered, ignoring the dirty look Lily shot in his direction.

"You can't even hear his name as we speak it." Vapor's stare evaluated and weighed, a weary guardsman examining and putting aside a faulty weapon.

"Put me in another sweat lodge. I'll break through this time." Ron refused to let his captor win, and more importantly, he refused to put the people of Bear Claw in any more risk because of him.

"As pleased as I am to hear your renewed enthusiasm, psychic healing is not an on-demand service." Andrew drummed his fingertips against each other. "It may take many more lodges to break through your barriers. Adding extra pressure to yourself will not help."

"Lily can help." He reached out to slide his fingers through hers. "If she's willing."

She smiled, squeezing his hand.

Andrew began. "Grandfather told you—"

"Grandfather was wrong," Ron interrupted. "Lily isn't a crutch. I'm not dependent on her, and I won't trap her. I trust her to watch my back, which will let me do what I need to do."

"As touching as this is, we still have an escape to plan," Vapor reminded them. "We need to get you all out as soon as possible."

"I might be able to help with that." Mark half raised his hand, sticking the other sheepishly in the front pocket of his jeans. "Edyta's left a bunch of messages on my cell. At first, she wanted me to call her if I saw you or heard from you. But the last one said not to, that it wasn't safe."

"Did she say why?" Joe asked.

"She said she didn't trust her new partners. That they weren't what they'd said. She said she was coming to Juneau and offered to get me out before they realized who I was, but she wouldn't be able to do it until late." Mark pulled his phone out, offering it to Lily. "She's been calling every hour."

"Please. It's a trap." Vincent jumped to his feet. "You can't win! Not against him. He sees everything, and he can snap his fingers to bring us running. We're only kidding ourselves."

"Sirens aren't invincible. Their powers fade without frequently renewed contact." Vapor fixed his steely gaze on Vincent. For once, the younger man didn't back down. Instead, he stared back, twitching like an animal in a snare.

"Do you trust this woman?" Joe asked.

"She's been a friend to our family since I was a child. She doesn't know about the *lalassu* or any of the rest, but she's always done right by us," Lily said confidently, accepting the slim silvery cell phone from her brother.

"So, her baseline personality could be reasserting itself." Andrew paused. "I don't see any better options on the table."

Ron didn't like this. Like Vincent, he knew how insidious his captor's influence could be. If neither of them had managed to break their mental bonds, how could this woman have done it?

"Count me out of this shit. You're all crazy." Vincent bolted for the back door.

Ron caught him before the other man could go more than a few steps. He held on tight, locking his elbows under Vincent's armpits and his hands behind the man's head. Vincent might be stronger, but now he had no leverage to use his strength. He flailed and shouted at Ron to let him go.

"Listen to me. We can do this. We can break free." Ron believed it with all his heart.

"You have no idea what you're talking about!" Vincent struggled, trying to throw his head back and catch Ron in the face. "You've been enhanced for a few months. You're not really one of us! You're a fucking copy!"

The accusation sank its fangs deep into Ron, poisoning him with a fear that had haunted him since his original escape. Caught between worlds, he risked being rejected by both of them. He wasn't a real *lalassu*. He hadn't been born with his gifts. They'd been imposed on him, stolen from Vincent and his brother, Eric. *No, not going there.* Lily loved him and accepted him, and he wasn't going to let this bitter bastard steal his contentment.

Vincent sagged, and Ron held on tight in case it was a trick, using his own weight to drive the man down onto his knees. Vincent pleaded. "He's too strong. I can't fight him."

"You can. I know you can." Ron looked at Lily. "We both can."

Vapor knelt down in front of the two of them, his flinty eyes reminding Ron of the merciless drill sergeants who'd pushed him throughout basic training. "You come from a strong line, Vincent. As long as I've known you, you've never done what someone else wanted.

Are you really going to start toeing someone else's line now?"

Bitter laughter spilled out of Vincent's mouth. "You think that bullshit psychology is really going to work? I told you what you needed to do before you sent me out here."

The corners of Vapor's mouth tightened. "Not an option."

"It's the only option." Vincent laughed, the sound colder than the ice outside. "Shame you don't have the guts."

Andrew stepped forward, Mark shadowing behind. "We'll take him upstairs to rest."

Ron let go, and Vincent didn't resist being led away. He stumbled limply between the two skinwalkers like a broken toy. Ron turned to Vapor. "What did he ask you to do?"

For a moment, Vapor was silent, and Ron didn't think the other man would answer. When he finally spoke, the blandness of his words belied their content. "He asked me to kill him before he could hurt anyone else."

When the phone finally rang in Lily's hand, she'd worked herself into such a state of tension that she actually jumped. She didn't recognize the number on the display and took a deep breath. If this was one of Mark's girlfriends, she might kill him. Ron's hand on her shoulder steadied her, although he took care to be completely silent.

"Hello?" she said cautiously, closing Todd's bedroom door so the others wouldn't be overheard.

"Lily? Thank God you're okay." Edyta sounded genuinely relieved. "Listen, I don't have a lot of time. I snuck out to use the phone so they wouldn't hear me."

"Who's there?" Lily asked, wondering if Edyta would be able to say Dalhard's name. If she was under his influence, they couldn't trust her.

"Mr. Dalhard's assistant, Mr. Samil. I don't think Mr. Dalhard knows what that man is up to." The affection in Edyta's voice when she said his name didn't reassure Lily. "He says the government asked them to investigate, but I don't believe him. I pretended to because he frankly frightens me."

"Did he threaten you?" Lily asked, meeting Ron's worried gaze with her own.

"No threats, but there's something about him. Like he'd happily put us all in coffins. I'm telling you, Lily, I've been in business a long time, and I've got good instincts about people. He's dangerous." A long silence followed.

Lily's imagination went wild. Had Dalhard's people found her? "Edyta?"

"Sorry. I don't have much time. Mr. Samil asked me to fly him to Juneau this afternoon. I don't want you anywhere near that man. Meet me at the Ptarmigan hangar at nine o'clock, and I'll fly you out anywhere you want to go. Then I can come back in the morning before he realizes I'm gone. I know the air traffic controller on duty, and he'll make sure there's nothing about me leaving."

"Are you sure? It's a big risk," Lily asked.

"Not as big as dealing with that man anymore. I know if I explain things to Mr. Dalhard, he'll be as shocked and appalled as I am."

Lily foresaw the potential disaster. "Edyta, do us a favor, please. Don't talk to Mr. Dalhard until we're gone."

"I'm not a fool, girl. I know better. I can take ten people but not a whole lot of luggage. Decide who's coming, but I don't want to leave any hostages behind. Steve has vanished completely, and no one will tell me what's happened to him."

Lily closed her eyes. Had he died from his injuries? She might not have liked or respected the ranger very much, but he didn't deserve to die from having known them. "What about Bob?"

"I assume Evonne is with you?" Edyta asked.

"She is."

"He's broken up about her leaving. He blames you, but I think Mr. Samil has been working him up. He's spouting crazy talk like a conspiracy nutjob." Edyta snorted in scorn. "She's better away from him until he calms down."

"Thank you, Edyta." Relief that their family friend hadn't been completely overwhelmed by Dalhard's Siren influence left Lily feeling giddy.

"I'll see you tonight." The line clicked off.

"You think we can trust her?" Ron asked, holding her close.

"She used his name, and although she still thinks he's a great guy, she's agreed to get us out." Lily shook her head slowly, unsure. "She'll know where she took us. What if she tells him after?"

"We'll have her take us to a major travel hub. Vancouver or maybe Seattle. From there, we can be on a plane or a boat within hours and vanish." Ron spoke with the confidence of a man who already held multiple vanishings under his belt.

"She said his assistant gave her the creeps." The assistant must be Vapor's old friend. She'd never met Vapor before this, although she'd heard of the mysterious hacker in whispers for most of her life. He inspired a feeling of unsettled creepiness. She wondered if it was the same sensation that *lalassu* gave the ungifted. Like being in the presence of a powerful predator, she had a distinct sense of being shuffled down the rungs of the food chain.

She savored the warmth and strength of Ron's arms around her. All her life, she'd stood strong and alone, the one facing the dangers rather than the one protected from them. Now she had a shelter and someone to fight beside her. She couldn't be happier, and that feeling segued immediately into guilt about her best friend. "I should go and talk to Evonne. Let her know about Bob."

Ron nodded. "I'll be here if you need me afterward."

Lily stepped across the darkened corridor to the other bedroom where Evonne and Vincent sat with Doc.

Evonne immediately stood up, but Vincent continued feeding Doc a bowl of chicken soup. His tenderness and care seemed uncharacteristic, as did the lack of complaining.

"I talked to Edyta." She quickly shared the information she'd been given. "He still loves you, Evonne. I think you can make it work."

Evonne's long black hair fell in her face, hiding her reaction as she turned away. "It's gone too far. We're too different now."

"It's not too late," Lily insisted, her friend's pain shredding her own joy.

Evonne glared back over her shoulder. "Of course you believe that. You're in love, and it's all new and shiny. You want it to be forever. But it doesn't matter how much you love each other now. It'll all fade."

Lily stepped back as if physically slugged by the words.

Her friend's face softened out of its angry twist. "I'm sorry."

The apology felt meaningless, but Lily refused to lash out with more angry words and drive a bigger wedge between them.

"You and Ron are different than Bob and I. We're done, but that doesn't mean you will be." Evonne returned to staring out the narrow window.

Lily retreated, stumbling back through the hall. Ron held out his arms and pulled her close. He'd heard what Evonne had said. He didn't say anything, allowing his love for her to flow through his arms, wiping away the sting of her friend's prediction.

"Good luck, man." Mark offered his hand to Ron. He and Evonne were taking Doc to the hospital. Andrew had shared his worrying fear that the old man was developing pneumonia. Without proper care, Doc might not see his beloved bears again. With a few clicks, Vapor's skills ensured that no one would connect Doc with Bear Claw or question his "daughter" about his injuries.

"Thanks. I'm sorry we didn't get much chance to know one another." Ron liked Mark. Under different circumstances, he could see the two of them being friends. Unlike Lou's surliness and Andrew's mystic reserve, Mark was down-to-earth and friendly.

"It'll happen. You're mates, which means you are stuck with us, my friend. We're like a black hole of familial ties: we'll suck you in, and you will never escape." Mark grinned. "We're like maple syrup. Once it's on the plate, you can never get rid of it. We seep into everything with sticky fingers." He waggled his fingers in the air.

Lily interrupted, tugging her brother aside for a hug. "Enough metaphors. I'll find a way to get in touch with you."

"Be safe. Both of you." The flash of concern vanished quickly into a cheerful smile and wave as Mark climbed into the car where Evonne and Doc were waiting. Ron noticed Evonne pointedly looking out the car window. "Should I check my shoes for icicles?"

"I hope we get enough time for both of us to move past this." Low and rough, Lily's voice shattered with heartbreak. "I hate the idea of leaving things like this."

Ron put his arm around her and held her tightly as they watched the car drive away. Then they didn't have any more excuses. A traditional sweat lodge wouldn't be possible in this urban environment, but Mark suggested a rather ingenious solution while they waited for Edyta to arrive.

After hanging a hasty Out of Service sign in the athletic center and making a quick test of Ron's lock-picking skills, they had the gym's sauna and steam room to themselves. Andrew kept wincing away from the machine-smoothed wood paneling and benches. Ron guessed the shaman wasn't happy with trying to transform commercial athletic equipment into a spiritual retreat, but since he didn't make an objection, Ron assumed the setting was workable. Steam vented through grates in the wall rather than from heated stones, and a steel-and-glass door instead of a leather flap separated them from the outside, but the surroundings weren't the most important element. Their intent was what mattered. Vapor and Joe stood guard in the outer corridor to discourage random visitors.

Despite a few choice phrases muttered under his breath, Andrew efficiently smudged the entire room with cedar smoke to purify it, making it into a sacred space. His chanting, drumming, and dancing filled the room with a physical presence, weighty and powerful. Vincent looked as if he might be sick at any moment, but Ron was determined. He'd be damned if he let himself live as a puppet.

"Try to get comfortable," Andrew said.

Ron settled onto the floor, breathing deeply. The steam slithered into his lungs, warm and wet. Lily sat behind him, her hands on his shoulders and her breath matching his. He tried to concentrate on himself and his own blocks, but he couldn't help comparing himself with Vincent, shivering and shaking by himself on the farthest bench. Ron had Lily with him, and he felt as though he could leap tall buildings in a single bound. Vincent looked like a miserable child waiting for a blow to fall.

"Concentrate," Andrew snapped. "Breathe in… and out…"

The routine was familiar, and Ron settled into the peculiar combination of alertness and blindness that he'd felt in the other sweat-lodge sessions. He concentrated, trying to pull up details of the first meeting from the blurry mass of memories.

White. The room was white. So white it glowed with antiseptic purity under the harsh blaze of surgical lights. He'd been uncomfortable, still edgy from withdrawal yet thinking more clearly than he had in years. Two men were beside him to his left. Doctors buzzed around the equipment at the edges of the room, studying readouts and ignoring the three of them. Ron remembered how the roughness of his clothing chafed against his skin, scraping him raw. He hadn't liked the waiting. He'd spent too much of his life waiting—for orders, for drugs, for help. The empty time had left his nerves scraped thin and ready to snap.

What happened next? Ron pushed himself to remember, trusting Lily to anchor him to the present. The wall had gaped open, revealing the shining steel walls of an elevator. Two men got out. One was slim and precise, with tan skin and dark hair cut neatly against his skull. From India, Ron guessed. A bodyguard of sorts, the man had stayed behind the other man, constantly making notes on his tablet. Ron forced himself to concentrate on the other one, and a chill swept his body despite the steam. This was the forbidden territory.

"Sir, may I speak freely?" Ron had asked even though he didn't have to seek permission outside the military. The man intimidated him. He was large and physically strong in a way that couldn't come solely from working out at a gym. His eyes were cold, like those of a man considering a purchase. Right then, Ron decided he didn't need to be a part of whatever the man offered. He asked to withdraw from the trial. "The money is good but not worth risking my life for, sir."

"Money never is," the man agreed, and relief swept through Ron. Maybe he'd misjudged these people, but he still preferred to take his sobriety on the road. Maybe he could find another way to deal with the nightmares and flashbacks.

"Thank you for all your help. I'll find a way to pay you back." He'd held out his hand to seal the deal. The other man took it, and then everything fuzzed and softened in his memory.

Lily's hands held him upright as his body sagged, trying to collapse into blank sleep. Ron fought to stay awake, to stay focused. His mind clung to the steady rhythm of Andrew's drumming and the atonal chanting. He would not be defeated by his own body and on someone else's instructions. *I'm coming for you, you bastard.* He snarled mentally.

His captor had played on Ron's guilt at having survived when Adam and Brian were dead. "Come on, Corporal. Don't you owe it to your friends to try?"

"Devil!" One of the other men screamed and attacked their captors. The man grabbed a plastic-tipped syringe off one of the trays. "Have to kill you! Demon!" Ron hadn't had time to think—he'd reacted purely from instinct and training, trapping the attacker's arms in a lock.

Looking back, he had more sympathy for the attacker's accusations, but he refused to allow his captor to assume the awful power of a supernatural demon. His adversary was a man with a man's weaknesses. Those weaknesses could be exploited, and his efforts could be overcome. Ron became dimly aware of his body shaking badly. Lily's arms wrapped around him, and he could hear the muted tones of her voice—not the words, just the rise and fall of blurred speech.

Lily. So strong and yet so vulnerable. Warmth crept outward from his heart, banishing the chill. Ron might not have been worthy of surviving, but Lily made him feel as if he might one day be. She'd never seen him as just an experiment. She believed he had a hero's heart and saw him as more than he could have ever hoped to be. She'd given him the strength to believe in himself again—she and Doc and Andrew and Bill and all the others he'd met in Bear Claw. He wasn't relying on them as crutches. Instead, their faith in him formed a life raft, giving him the strength to pull himself back to shore.

In comparison, his captor was nothing, a bully hiding behind superpowers, and a coward who preyed on fear. He didn't have any true power, only illusions that built an apparently impenetrable house of cards.

The doctors had led him away after he'd subdued the attacker. "Mr. Dalhard wants the protocols started immediately."

Mr. Dalhard.

Like wire stretched too tightly, his mental bonds burst suddenly with a flurry of pings. Ron opened his eyes, dizzy from the steam. Lily's arms gripped him tightly, and her body pressed against his back. He croaked, "Dalhard. His name is Dalhard. And he doesn't own me anymore."

Vincent shrieked wordlessly from across the room, still curled in a ball.

Andrew stopped drumming and knelt in front of Ron, his eyes boring into a place above Ron's head. "You've done it."

Ron put his hand over Lily's, holding it against his bare chest. "I couldn't have done it without you. Especially you, Lily. I trusted you to keep me safe."

"I'll always have your back," she whispered. "Even if not quite as literally as right now."

He laughed, giddy with sudden freedom. "I did it. I finally did it."

Vincent collapsed onto the bench, his eyes rolling in his head as he twitched in seizure. Ron leapt up and steadied his fellow captive before he could vault headfirst to the floor. "Come on, Vincent. You can do it just like I did. Cast the bastard out of your head."

Vincent moaned, his fingers digging bloody furrows into his rigid arms.

"I have to bring him out." Andrew knelt at Vincent's side.

"No, we can help him break free," Ron said.

Andrew's gaze seized his, and Ron's elation drained away. Lily's brother held the agony and compassion of ages, as if he'd lived dozens of lifetimes instead of a mere three decades. "You can't be a hero for him. He's not ready to save himself."

Ron tried again, his voice small. "We can't leave him like this."

"We can't force him." Andrew put his hand over Vincent's face and began a different chant. Lily came to lend her silent presence, and tears began to prick at Ron's eyes. It wasn't fair. Once again, he found himself cast into the role of lone survivor.

No, he corrected himself, his shoulders squaring. He'd worked hard for his freedom, and it was no shame to him or Vincent if Vincent wasn't ready. He wasn't responsible for the other man and shouldn't be measured by what he did or failed to do. Ron had a job that needed doing and people to keep safe. He wouldn't let Dalhard get his hands on them.

CHAPTER TWENTY-ONE

The sun had long since disappeared when Ron and Lily made their cautious approach to the Ptarmigan Industries hangar. They waited behind a set of wooden platforms, watching as a few crewmen finished up some task before heading home. Lily fidgeted with her small backpack of borrowed clothing, rolling her shoulders, uncomfortably aware of her animal side. The bear lurked barely beneath the surface, its instincts roused by the tension and potential danger. Glancing back, she spotted Vincent and Andrew, loitering a few steps behind.

Something had broken in Vincent after the sweat lodge. They'd caught him twisting a bedsheet into a rope, and later, he'd tried smashing a mirror into razor-sharp shards. After that, Andrew refused to leave him alone even for a moment. Lily wouldn't have expected anything else, but she saw the doubt trembling at the edges of her brother's confidence. He wasn't sure anyone could help Vincent anymore. Joe and Vapor would stay in Juneau to continue investigating. Vapor would ensure that Mark, Evonne, and Doc all got out.

At least Ron broke free. Even a brief thought of him washed away her sadness and fear. For once, Lily allowed herself to revel in her own joy without feeling guilty at another's misfortune. Edyta would help them get away from Juneau, and from there, the family could decide what to do. Grizzlies migrated up and down the West Coast each year. Perhaps they could move the Colony down to Yellowstone or somewhere else along the Rocky Mountain range. It would be nice to have sunlight every day and more than a few weeks of summer. And they'd be closer to Ron's family. *This might all actually work out.*

The two men in their dusty coveralls finally walked away, joking and laughing with each other. Ron signaled Lily and the others to move quickly before anyone else came along. The four of them made it into the hangar without attracting any attention. Edyta waited by a pile of plastic cargo containers, her thin arms folded over her chest. "You're early."

"Didn't want to miss the flight." Lily smiled at her old friend, but Edyta didn't return it. *Not a good sign.*

"There's a heap of trouble and lies floating around. I don't know who to trust—Dalhard's assistant with his smooth lines or the man accused of multiple murders." The older woman fixed Ron with a shrewd stare.

"Forget them, Edyta. You've known us a long time. Trust us." Lily stepped between them, meeting the older woman's steely glare with unmovable certainty.

"There's a lot of dead people up in Bear Claw who might think it's time to reconsider." Edyta hadn't become a successful businesswoman by accepting other people's opinions.

"We didn't ask to be invaded. We've only ever sought to go our own way." Andrew stepped forward.

Edyta snorted. "I know it. Caused me no end of trouble. Who doesn't want progress and convenience?"

"We don't. We're happy with our lives." From the squaring of Andrew's jaw and the stubborn set of Edyta's, Lily knew neither would give in easily.

"Edyta, you told me to give my heart a chance and not to spend all my energy on responsibilities and duty," Lily reminded her. "We can't tell you everything that happened. There are secrets that aren't ours to betray. But I can tell you we didn't do anything to provoke the attack. We only defended ourselves. Please, trust your heart on this."

Edyta slowly nodded. "Using my own words against me, girl. Always knew you'd make a heck of a saleswoman. You're right. There's no proof and no time to dig some up, so we have to go with what we know about each other. And I know that you're good people who wouldn't want anyone else to get hurt."

Lily exhaled sharply, relieved that Edyta hadn't changed her mind about helping them. She squeezed Ron's fingers to let him know it would be all right.

"With that said, there's someone I need you talk to before we leave." Edyta walked a few steps over to the conference room and opened the door. Bob stepped out into the hangar, clutching his hat in his thick fingers. The sweat shone through his thinning hair.

"Please, where is Evonne?" he begged.

Lily shrugged, trying to disperse the extra weight in her shoulders. Her animal side saw Bob as a threat to her family and her mate. But the human part of her heart softened and tore, unwilling to tell the man that her best friend considered their marriage to be over. *Evonne is upset. She can't really mean that she's going to throw everything away.* Love was supposed to last, no matter what bitter words were spilled. "She's safe, Bob."

"What have you done with her?" Bob demanded.

Ron moved closer, his comforting presence overshadowing her like the ancient trees. Lily kept her voice calm. "I haven't done anything to her. She made her own choice."

"She wouldn't have left the safety of our home! She knows how dangerous it is out here for someone like her." Bob pounded the plastic cargo boxes with his fist.

A dry little chuckle escaped Andrew. "We've been operating at the edge of this world for thousands of years. We know a little something about how to function in it."

Bob flushed red at Andrew's mockery. "I'm only doing what you did."

"I somehow doubt that," Andrew replied in a bored tone.

Bob leapt at the shaman, fist whirling. Lily reached out, aware that she was too far away to stop the attack. Ron was only a step behind her.

Andrew slid aside at the last second, evading Bob's belligerent charge. The stout pilot went tumbling forward, sprawling on the concrete.

"Enough," Edyta snapped. "This isn't the time or place for a brawl. You said you wanted to talk to them, Bob, and I agreed to help you. Don't make me regret it."

"I know you care about Evonne." Lily knelt beside Bob. "I do, too. She's been my only friend for a long time."

Bob glared up at Ron, who was standing less than a foot away, ready to unleash violence at the slightest threat to Lily's safety.

"Look at me, not him," Lily said.

Bob's eyes darted back to her. "We were happy until he came."

"No. You weren't." Lily rested her hand on Bob's trembling fingers. "Evonne felt trapped and unhappy for a long time. And you were always worried and afraid. That's not being happy."

"I only wanted to keep her safe." He whispered the words like a mantra before gesturing to the private room. "Ekurru was supposed to be safe. That's why she needed to stay."

"Ekurru was never meant to be a prison. Only a sanctuary," Andrew said.

Bob's head snapped up, and anger twisted his features. "When people are out to hurt you, there's no difference."

Lily's bear was fighting to come out, demanding that she assume her stronger side before the powder keg of tension could explode. From the way Andrew's hands were trembling, she knew he faced a similar struggle. She needed to defuse the situation before it erupted.

"Easy," Lily soothed Bob, forcing his attention back to her. "You and I, we can talk. We'll get this sorted out."

She held her breath. She owed Evonne so much. If there was even a chance that Evonne could know happiness in her marriage again, then Lily intended to return the favor. Twenty-four hours ago, she'd been certain that the relationship between her and Ron was an illusion, destined to shatter. Now she was ready to take a leap of faith.

"It's going to take some time to get *Tallulah* ready to fly out." Edyta nodded at the bulky cargo plane filling the hangar. "You two can talk in the conference room."

"She's not going anywhere with him," Ron interrupted, his fists clenched tight.

Lily stood up and put her palm flat on his chest. "Ron, you have to trust me. Don't try and put me in a cage to keep me safe."

He covered her hand with his own. His heart thundered against her fingertips, even through his clothing. "He tried to hurt you before."

"I can take care of myself. And I think he'll be calmer if he's away from everyone else." Lily glanced back. Bob had curled up, his elbows propped on his knees and his fists pressed tightly to his temples.

"They've both been working with our enemies." Ron's thumbs rubbed her shoulders, his big fingers wrapped around her upper arm.

"I know," she whispered. "I'll be careful."

Ron let her go, his fingers lingering reluctantly before releasing. She turned back to Bob. "Do you want to get Evonne back?"

Bob unclenched his fists and rose slowly to his feet. "What do you want from me?"

"This isn't a ransom. It's a question. Do you want to be with Evonne, not as her jailor but as her husband?" Lily hoped Bob understood. If he didn't, there wasn't any chance at all.

"It's all I ever wanted. I can't imagine my life without her."

Bob's reply was everything she could have wished for. "Then let's talk privately while Edyta and the others get the plane ready."

"Fine," Bob said grumpily. He started walking toward the conference room.

Lily reached back to give Ron's hand a final squeeze before following Bob. She caught up just as he reached the dull metal door. "This won't be easy."

Bob opened the door, gesturing for her to precede him. As she stepped inside, he said. "I know. But once you're gone, I know I can make Evonne see sense."

His words sparked alarm, and she whirled. Bob pushed her into the conference room and pulled the door closed. "You don't know what you're playing with. You're a kid testing out matches in the woods, and the forest is already burning. Once the flames are high enough, Evonne will have no choice but to come to me so I can keep her safe."

"That's crazy," Lily panted, holding back the fur with all her strength.

"Actually, it's love. Quite touching, really," a smooth male voice interrupted. "Would you like a handkerchief?"

Adrenaline shot through her, and she scrambled back from the new threat, thudding into the wall. She recognized the man sitting at the conference table in his immaculate suit. Slicked-back hair, confident, and with powerful features. Dalhard.

It'll be fine, Ron reminded himself. He'd been on edge all day. Vincent had been needling him after the sweat lodge, snarking and jabbing. The man insinuated Ron had broken free because he wasn't a real *lalassu*. Ron barely managed to keep his temper in check, his fury aggravated by his nerves constantly jangling. His nerves didn't care about an escape plan— they just kept agitating his primordial brain and signaling that he needed to be running. Anywhere.

The conference room door thudded shut, and he discovered his internal panic could actually go higher. Lily was out of sight with a man who kept uttering threats against both of them. Ron decided he'd had enough of fighting his internal caveman. Lily and Bob could both live with him looking at them through the door.

He started to walk across the concrete hangar floor when he heard a thud from the conference room. Immediately, his brain locked into combat mode. All senses went on high alert.

Then he heard the scream. Memory, self-doubt, and confusion all got shoved aside. Ron covered the distance to the conference room in three long strides, grabbing at the door handle. It rattled in place, locked. Ron immediately seized the knob, using all his strength to wrench the metal, popping the cheap latch. He burst into the room with Andrew only a step behind.

It can't be. Horror-locked, his mind refused to comprehend what he saw: Dalhard standing quietly, hands folded behind his back and a smirk on his face. Another man held Lily, one whose eyes and cheeks poked prominently from behind tightened skin. It took Ron a second to recognize Steve. It looked as if extra muscle and bone had been shoved into him like an overstuffed backpack. *He's not dead. Dalhard experimented on him.* The ranger had been transformed into the same kind of out-of-place monstrosity as himself.

"Corporal McBride, a pleasure to see you again." Dalhard greeted him as if they were old friends meeting by chance on the street. Belatedly, Ron noticed Edyta quietly locking the door behind her, cutting off their escape. Vincent was the only one still free.

"Steve, I know what you're going through. You don't want to hurt her. Let her go. It's me you want. I'll go with you." Ron's attention stayed on Lily. Her lips were pressed together in pain, and he could see bruises forming where Steve gripped her.

"Maybe I should just snap her neck, and then you can spend a few hours staring at her corpse," Steve growled, looking like the very picture of insanity with his bloodshot eyes and pale skin. "Then you'll know what I'm going through."

Red drenched Ron's vision, and only the knowledge that Steve wasn't bluffing held him back. "Let her go. It's me you want. I'll go with you if you let her go." Ron didn't have to think about the offer. Nothing mattered except keeping Lily safe. She shook her head slightly, her eyes begging him not to give up.

"It's not always about you. Steven won't be harming the young woman." Dalhard raised an eyebrow at the ranger, who reluctantly loosened his grip. "Her family has some fascinating and useful talents. Ms. Golov and Mr. Villeneuve revealed quite a store of knowledge once I realized the right questions to ask." He patted Edyta on the shoulder.

"How could you betray us like that?" Lily jerked in Steve's grasp, nearly breaking free in her effort to get to Bob.

"You should have told me where my wife is." Bob glared, his lips raw and cracked from him chewing on them. "You stole her from me."

"I wasn't aware she was a possession." Andrew managed to pull off a perfect impression of aristocratic impassiveness.

"All of you are overreacting," Edyta frowned with impatience. "Mr. Dalhard's proposals could help us all a great deal. That's why I brought you all here."

"We trusted you!" Lily spat at her former friend. Ron couldn't be angry with Edyta, though. He'd experienced Dalhard's insidious mental restructuring firsthand. It could make a person betray almost anything they held sacred.

"No, you didn't. I put in weeks trying to make this deal happen, and you never intended to follow through. Too busy hiding your little secrets to care about the money and time I was flushing down the river." Edyta stood straight, drawing her petite frame up rigidly to stare down her nose. "Mr. Dalhard understands, and his work in the North will make me rich. I told you that you needed to meet with him in person to understand."

"He's using you!" Ron shouted, hoping to cut through the conditioning but all too aware he and Lily sounded like crazy people in comparison to Dalhard's suave coolness.

Edyta's eyes hardened. "Everyone uses each other. Bear Claw is sitting on a fortune in natural resources. I'm not waiting anymore."

"It's what they do. Pretend they're better than all of us when they're nothing but freaks." Steve's lip curled, and his fingers clenched around Lily's arms again. Her mouth tightened, but she didn't cry out.

The word *freaks* sent a jolt through Ron. Steve submitted to medical experimentation, and he dared to call Lily and her family freaks? It left Ron's teeth grinding and his fists eager to deal out some justice.

"Do you really think you can coerce us into cooperation?" Andrew demanded. "Even with your persuasive gifts, do you believe we don't have defenses?"

Dalhard laughed. "Defenses always have weak points."

"You have what you wanted. I'm going to get my wife." Bob's interruption sounded more pleading and desperate this time. He unlocked the door.

"Of course," Dalhard said. "Do tell Vincent to come in and be a good boy. He'll tell me where they've gone."

The door opened, revealing Vincent slumped against the doorway. "I told you there was no point in fighting."

"Quite right. You've caused me a great deal of inconvenience with your misguided attempts to break free." Dalhard shrugged, adjusting the sleeves of his suit.

Ron's hand itched to smack the self-satisfied smirk off Dalhard's face. "No soldiers this time?"

"It's been somewhat difficult to find qualified personnel in the wake of the previous attempt. Besides, you're going to come along quietly, aren't you? I've invested a great deal to acquire all of you, but I won't hesitate to destroy you if you give me too much trouble."

Steve released one of Lily's arms to press his forearm against her throat again, obviously eager.

Ron looked at Lily, ready to fight. He couldn't bear to see anything happen to her. "If you let them be, I'll go with you."

"No," Lily whispered fiercely. "I won't let you do this!"

That was his girl—willing to fight to the end. But Ron wasn't willing to gamble with her life. He turned away from Dalhard even though his training screamed at him not to shift focus away from the enemy. Except this wasn't about the enemy. This was his last chance to tell her how he felt before Dalhard wiped away everything that made him Ronald McBride. "Lily, I love you."

"Don't do this," she pleaded. "We can fight him." Steve's arm tightened around her throat, and her words choked off.

"Stop!" Ron shouted, raising his hand.

Dalhard nodded, and Steve reluctantly let go. Dalhard smirked at his audience. "This is not a negotiation. Do you need a reminder of who is in charge here?"

"You're on thinner ice than you know. Take what's being offered, and don't be greedy," Andrew said.

The glare Lily shot at her brother could have ignited a forest fire. Ron caught Andrew's gaze, and the shaman slowly nodded. They understood each other. Andrew would make sure Lily got out.

Dalhard's jovial façade vanished. "You don't understand. I never intended to walk away with only part of the collection. Vincent, bring him to me."

Vincent grabbed Andrew and began to drag him toward Dalhard. Ron could see the tears in Vincent's eyes and knew a terrible battle raged inside the man's mind. Lily took advantage of Steve's distraction and tried to break free, knocking aside the arm against her throat. Ron lunged, hoping to grab her out of Steve's reach. Instead, Vincent and Andrew ended up crashing into him and knocking him down.

Lily shrieked, and Ron looked up to see Steve holding her, his arm wrapped back around her throat and the other pinning her arms down.

"Stand down, Corporal." Dalhard smirked. "Or he'll snap her neck."

Ron glared at his enemy, longing to attack. He imagined the satisfying crunch of the ranger's bones under his fists. The man deserved no less for threatening Lily.

"Ron," Lily squeaked hoarsely. "It's okay."

She closed her eyes, and panic surged in Ron as he thought she was passing out from lack of air. Steve began to shift in place, as if trying to recover his grip. Lily opened her eyes, and they were rounder, with the beautiful chocolate-brown irises filling the entire eye. She opened her lips, exposing razor-sharp fangs in a mouth that stretched wider than a human's should.

No. Whatever Edyta and Bob had told Dalhard, Ron doubted it was the truth about skinwalkers. If Lily shifted, there would be no hiding it. He tried to lunge at Dalhard, but it was too late. His captor stood with his jaw open and hands raised.

Lily surged forward out of Steve's grasp, landing heavily on four furred legs and growling. Shredded, her clothes fell away onto the floor. Litonya roared at the men, her claws digging into the industrial carpet.

Edyta raised a shaking hand, her skin doubly pale against her russet hair. "It's not…"

Renewed avarice lit up Dalhard's eyes. "It's more than I'd hoped for. Steve, contain it."

Steve knelt, coming up with a tranquilizer handgun. Ron tackled the other man, grabbing at Steve's arms. The ranger broke free of Ron's grasp easily, and Ron lost his next opportunity to attack from shock. Steve swung at him, the blow smashing into Ron's chest to knock the wind out of him.

Unfamiliar helplessness sapped Ron's strength. For the first time since his transformation, he was fighting someone whose strength equaled his. He'd allowed himself to get sloppy in his fighting techniques, using his enhanced strength to dominate his opponents.

Steve raised his arm to punch Ron again and then flew to one side. Litonya stood on all fours where the ranger had been, one massive paw still raised from swatting him. Ron saw a glint of concern in her eyes as if she worried that he would resent her interference in his fight.

"Thanks." He ruffled her thick fur as he got to his feet.

Steve picked himself off the floor nearby, his shadowed eyes promising murder.

"Steve, I know what they've done to you, but this isn't you." Ron tried to reach the other man, hoping a spark of the original personality still burned.

"It's me now." Steve laughed, the bitter sound tainting the air with foul anticipation. "Now I can have whatever I want."

Ron dodged a clumsy kick. "You can't. You have to break free of him."

"Why would I want to do that? He made me strong, so much stronger than I ever was before." Steve's eyes narrowed as he rocked back and forth. "You're nothing but a whining coward, afraid of the power he gave you."

"Rachel wouldn't have wanted you to be like this." Ron watched the ranger's hands. He had a habit of twitching them before he attacked.

Steve went still, his hands tightening into fists. "I could have saved her if I was like this."

"I thought the same thing—that if I was stronger, I would never lose anyone ever again. But it's not true. No one can promise that." The words settled into place like a soothing bandage over the open wound in his soul. "Sometimes there isn't anything you can do to stop bad things from happening."

Litonya stepped forward, her head and shoulders beside him and nearly to the top of his chest. Ron reached out to the ranger. "You can stop this, Steve. You might not have been able to save Rachel, but you can save Lily. They'll put her in a cage and dissect her. Please, you have to break free and let us go."

For one glorious moment, Ron thought he'd convinced the other man. The fury faded, leaving Steve looking sick and lost. Then it snapped back into place. "She's not even human."

"Neither are we," Ron said.

Steve's hands shook before he roared and charged at Ron. "I'm not like them! I'm not a freak!"

"We're not freaks." Ron caught Steve's arm, twisting it painfully behind his back. No matter how strong the ranger was, his joints remained vulnerable. Locking his elbow and wrist meant Steve remained pinned. "Lily is strong, compassionate, wise, and the best person I've ever known, on four feet or two. Her family dedicated their lives to protecting and helping others for generations. I'm proud to be one of the *lalassu*."

Litonya's eyes softened, and she clacked her jaws in approval. Ron searched the room, suddenly realizing they were the only ones left in it. The door to the hangar hung open.

His grip loosened in surprise, and Steve wriggled free. The ranger landed a solid blow to Ron's temple, knocking him back and sending painful points of light sparking across his vision. He fell into the heavy steel table. Cracking agony rippled through his ribs, and Ron numbly wondered if they were broken. He staggered, shaking his head to try and clear his eyes.

Someone grabbed him from behind, fingers digging for his throat. Ron grabbed his attacker's arm and pulled, bending swiftly at the waist. Steve went flying over his head, slamming him into the prefabricated wall.

The impact knocked the paneling loose, revealing the concrete before it overbalanced to fall on top of Steve. Ron raised his fist but hesitated. He needed to take the ranger out of the fight but didn't want to kill him. They were both Dalhard's victims, and the real villain was escaping.

Lily loudly clacked her jaws together, drawing his attention. She pawed at something shiny on the ground: the tranquilizer pistol.

Ron bent down and picked it up, lifting it just as Steve rose to his feet. He fired and saw the green tufted dart appear in the center of Steve's chest.

The ranger grabbed at it, yanking it out. "You can't stop us."

"I can, and we will." Ron flattened his hand to fake a strike at Steve's face before slamming his fist into the man's stomach.

Steve folded over, coughing. He still tried to head butt Ron from his bent-over position. Litonya shouldered the man, knocking him down again.

Ron clicked the second dart into place and fired again. It struck Steve in the shoulder, and this time he collapsed, his eyes rolling back into his head.

It was time to hunt bigger prey. Fury filled Ron's vision. He wasn't letting that bastard get away again.

Chapter Twenty-Two

Lily would have led the chase into the hangar if the door had been built to let grizzlies through. Luckily, the prefabricated wall sections were also not designed with grizzlies in mind. Rearing up on her hind legs, she shoved the wall with both stout forelegs, sending the entire frame down. Her claws bit into the mass of stretched fabric, and her weight crushed the cheap plastic supports, slowing her down as she clambered awkwardly into the hangar.

Edyta crouched by the plane, eyes wide with terror. Her body blocked the airplane stairs, her fingers wrapped so tightly around the metal handrail that Lily would not have been surprised to see dents. Dalhard stood over the businesswoman and Vincent, demanding that Vincent get her out of the way. Vincent's arms were wrapped around Edyta, but Lily could see his heart wasn't in the attempt. Or maybe he really was weak after months of steady drinking and hiding in his cabin.

Andrew stood to one side, offering sarcastic commentary but not making any other movement to help or escape. Lily's hackles rose as she spotted Bob behind her brother, holding a gun on him. The barrel kept wavering as Bob's hands shook, his face locked in a rigor of agony and determination. She didn't doubt he would shoot Andrew in a heartbeat.

"Dalhard!" Ron roared.

The skirmish at the plane froze at the sound, all of them turning to look at Ron and Lily. She curled her lip back from her teeth, displaying her fangs. Her back legs tensed, ready to hurtle her forward. Anyone who thought her size would hamper her speed was about to learn a painful truth about the futility of outrunning a bear.

"Let them go, and step back from the plane." Ron's words snapped in the silence with military precision and authority.

"I'm beginning to see you as a bad investment." Dalhard shook his head as if contemplating a less-than-perfect appetizer. "Vincent, get her on the plane, then deal with this idiot."

Vincent collapsed onto the ground, his face buried in his hands. Edyta shook and gasped as if about to have a heart attack, her bony hand clutching her chest.

"You are worthless," Dalhard sneered. "I should have killed you as soon as I harvested you. You're nothing but a pathetic fool, a waste of space and air."

Vincent flinched as if physically struck.

"Care to pick on someone your own size?" Ron stalked forward. Lily circled to one side, keeping an eye on Bob and her brother.

"You forget, Corporal. I own you."

"Not anymore." Ron reached out to grab Dalhard, and Lily clacked her jaws together as loudly as she could. *Don't touch him!*

Ron didn't look back, but he stopped short of grasping his opponent. Maybe he'd remembered Dalhard's Siren powers on his own, or maybe he'd understood her warning. Lily didn't care as long as it worked. She started to stalk to the side, blocking their prey's escape.

Dalhard laughed at them both, clearly not intimidated in the least. "Do you know how often I've heard that? How many people were certain they'd broken free of my influence? Do you know how many of them became monsters at my final instructions? You can never remove all of my hooks, and all I need is one to make you live out your worst nightmares!"

An unanimal-like panic began to swell inside Lily's brain. Andrew had been so sure they'd eradicated all of Dalhard's influence. She trusted her brother's shamanic gifts, but this wasn't something they'd ever dealt with before. What if he missed one? What could Dalhard force Ron to do? Her imagination painted vivid, horrifying pictures of the possibilities.

"I will make you kill everyone here." Spittle flew from Dalhard's lips. "Then I'll send you back to the gutter, your brain crawling with nightmares every waking and sleeping moment—"

Lily rose onto her hind legs and roared. The sound penetrated the hangar, leaving ears ringing and legs wobbly. She slammed back down onto the ground, the impact rocking the pavement. Her human and animal side united in a single evaluation: dangerous. She ceased to see the man before her as a unique individual with a name and history. Instead, she saw a competing predator, one who needed to be killed to protect herself and her family. And bears never allowed anything to threaten their families.

She charged, fangs and claws stretched wide. Dalhard scrambled backward, abandoning his pose of arrogant superiority. The overhead lights picked up the fresh layer of sweat gleaming on his skin as she drew close enough to catch the stink of fear.

Snapping at him, she caught the fine cloth of his suit. It tore easily, her sharp teeth shredding it as he scrambled up onto a stack of crates, which was too tall and precariously balanced for her to follow him. She roared again as he yanked a phone out of his pocket and began shouting into it, demanding someone come and help him.

Movement. Behind, her instincts warned. A deep breath rolled Ron's distinctive scent over her tongue. He was moving slowly and carefully, probably to avoid triggering an instinctive chase response. Lily huffed, a low vocalization to let him know she wasn't about to attack randomly.

A popping crack burst through the air as something hit her from behind. It stung and burned, driving into her body and shocking her mind out of its balanced union. Her human half recognized the sensation. A bullet. *Someone shot me with a small-caliber bullet.* The indignity and pain sent her animal side into a blind fury, and Lily struggled to keep her attention on Dalhard. He was the true threat.

"Destroy the bear, Vincent!" Dalhard ordered, hunched low on the wobbling crates.

She couldn't make out the details since Vincent crouched outside the blurry range of her vision, but he didn't move any closer to her. She heard a metallic clatter behind her.

"I'm worthless. Not suicidal." Vincent's bitter sarcasm reassured her.

"Andrew took the gun from Bob," Ron whispered as he knelt beside her. "Are you okay?"

Blood trickled and matted her fur around the wound. Her right back leg hurt badly enough that she didn't think she'd be able to stand on it for long. It would slow her down in a fight, but she wouldn't retreat. She swung her head back around to focus on Dalhard, and a growl curled out from between her exposed teeth.

"Looks like you're out of toy soldiers." Ron stood up to face his captor, his hand still stroking her neck ruff.

"Kill the bear!" Dalhard ordered, his demented gaze seizing on Ron.

"No." Ron didn't hesitate in his denial. No symptoms of inner or outer conflict showed on his face or stance. Lily rumbled with satisfaction and pride in her mate.

The stunned look on Dalhard's face was priceless. He shouted again. "Obey me! Kill the bear!"

"Not gonna happen." Ron shrugged. "Guess your hooks weren't as deep as you thought."

"One touch, and I'll—"

"To touch me, you'd have to come down," Ron interrupted. "Do that, and I'm pretty sure she'll rip you to tiny pieces before you have a chance to do any damage."

Dalhard tried again. "I could take over her mind."

"Then I'll take you down. You won't have the time to take both of us. I remember from before. It takes you almost a minute to forcibly take over someone's mind. You won't survive long enough." Ron's delight in besting his opponent faded from his face. "You've done enough damage. It's over."

Dalhard's gaze flicked frantically over the hangar. Lily couldn't catch details, but she guessed the blurry tan figure on top of the pale one was Andrew sitting on Bob to restrain him. Edyta and Vincent were an unmoving mass of shadow near the blurry hulk of the plane. No movement, no struggle. A rumbling echo built in her chest. They'd won.

The outer hangar door slid open, and the sense of victory vanished into new wariness. Lily cursed her ursine vision, which didn't allow for much detail beyond thirty or forty feet. She studied Ron and took comfort. He didn't seem worried about the newcomer.

"Looks like you're not in a position to make demands, Mr. Dalhard." The familiar voice set her concerns to rest. Joe came close enough for her to verify his identity. "Seems to me that it's time to deal."

"You want to try sending me to prison again?" Dalhard glared at Joe, arms spread to keep his balance as the crates shifted beneath him. "I'll destroy your career."

"It's true, prison hasn't been a great threat for you before. Not with your assistant pulling strings." Joe shrugged. Despite his nonchalance, he kept shooting nervous glances her way. Ron kept scratching and rubbing her fur to remind her of his presence. Or perhaps he was trying to reassure the policeman about her.

"The thing is, your guardian angel abandoned you. So it might be time to start talking about a deal." Joe stayed a careful distance from Lily and Ron.

Dalhard raised a skeptical eyebrow.

"It's true. He's not running to your rescue this time. He's not even answering his phone for you." Joe slid his gun out of its holster. "We can do this the easy way or the hard way. I've spent the last few days arguing that we shouldn't kill you, but I'm starting to see the appeal of letting the bear eat you. Less paperwork for me."

Lily clacked her jaws together, recognizing a prompt when she heard one. Ron's fingers tightened around her fur.

"Karan would never betray me!" Dalhard straightened.

Joe shook his head. "It's a done deal, dude. He already handed over a bunch of really interesting papers. Evidence of tax evasion, money laundering, illegal trade. Juneau PD faxed it to the feds with a downright embarrassing plethora of high fives."

Enough banter. Lily's leg and hip hurt more with every passing moment. She bounced up on her back legs, despite the screaming pain, using her front legs to knock down the unsteady stack of crates.

They came crashing to the ground, plastic cases warping and cracking while the wooden ones shattered. Dalhard fell hard among them, and Joe instantly appeared at his side, wrenching the man's hands back to slap handcuffs on him. Alarm stabbed through Lily until she got closer and realized Joe wore thick leather gloves, eliminating the risk of skin-to-skin contact.

"You can't hold me!" Dalhard shrieked and writhed.

"I'm pretty sure we can." Joe hauled him unceremoniously to his feet. "Stop thrashing. The bear-eating plan is still open for discussion."

"I'm not for it. He probably tastes terrible." Ron stroked her fur. "Lily shouldn't have to suffer."

"I'm sure there are less picky bears out there." Joe winked at Ron, but Lily noticed he was stepping back, increasing the distance between them as he steered Dalhard toward the ruined conference room. "Too bad he's cooperating."

"How did you even know to come here?" Ron asked.

"Vincent called me. Told me something was going down. The rest of Juneau PD should be here shortly," Joe replied. "I wanted to make sure I could wrap up any unmentionable loose ends beforehand. They've been warned that Mr. Dalhard here is an expert poisoner. They're never to touch him without precautions." Joe paused to look at Lily. "I don't want to have to dodge a call to Predator Control."

She nodded stiffly. Bear necks weren't really made for that kind of motion. She padded back to the conference room, grasping the straps of her backpack in her teeth. She wasn't quite sure where Mark had gotten clothing to fit her and Evonne so quickly and didn't want to ask. Some things a sister should never know about her brother. Once she was out of sight, she braced herself to wrestle with her animal side, prepared for it to resist the switch back to human.

Instead, she found herself shrinking into her other side easily. Muscles compacted, sliding together, her fur retracted into her skin, and she balanced easily on two feet as her center of mass shifted. As she quickly dressed in the chill air, Lily tried to puzzle out the reason for her painless shift. Why would her bear side have been so agitated before and now be so calm? The easy answer was that she'd sensed Edyta's duplicity on a subconscious level, which had gotten her hackles up, and with the crisis over, the fur had settled. However, she'd experienced similar warnings before, and it had always taken a long time for her animal side to calm down after a fight.

The only thing that was really different was the mated bond between her and Ron. She'd never believed the stories about the power of love before. Watching Evonne and Bob's marriage crumble had further undermined her confidence in love's durability. She'd pictured it like brittle birch bark, snapping under the slightest stress. But after watching Ron fight so hard to save her life, she knew love wasn't so simple. It was more like a fishing net—pliable and encompassing and needing to be kept constantly in repair. The work didn't frighten her, but she still worried about Ron's happiness. He'd been through so much, and it wasn't really fair to ask him to stick to a decision made under such stress.

She looked out the broken wall to where Ron stood, talking with Joe.

They'd taken Dalhard down together, and now they could concentrate on their future. She wanted to wake up beside him every morning and talk to him about the Colony. She wanted to tease Doc and hear Ron laugh. She wanted to watch his beautiful blue eyes turn smoldering with heat and know she inspired it. She wanted to reach out in the middle of the night and hold his hand. She wanted it all.

At peace with herself, Lily walked out slowly to Vincent, still curled against the airplane stairs. "Thank you."

"For not being stupid enough to attack a grizzly who could bite off my head? Glad I could surpass that particular low bar of expectation." He shrugged, not meeting her eyes.

Lily gently tilted his chin so he had to face her. "You defied him. You called Joe."

"When I realized he was here, I knew it was only a matter of time before he started pulling my strings. I knew I needed to call for help before he realized his own personal action figure was available." Vincent pulled his chin out of her fingers, staring blankly at the hangar again.

Lily thought she'd lost him to his despair, but he finally spoke again. "When they rescued me the first time and I realized what he'd done, I tried to kill myself so he couldn't use me." He chafed his arms. "I never took things seriously. Find me a party and a pretty girl, and that's all I ever wanted out of life. I thought that was why the Beast could turn me so quickly. I thought I deserved what he did to me because I never wanted anything bigger, not like Dani and Eric did. They fought and resisted him and ended up scarred and broken. I didn't fight."

"You fought now," Lily reminded him.

"Yeah, but that's not what's important. I might not have wanted some grand goal, but that doesn't mean I deserved what happened. I didn't ask for it." Vincent slowly got to his feet. "I didn't deserve it."

"No. You didn't." Lily hugged him, all too aware of his vulnerable frailty.

"Think your brother will still be able to help me?" he asked, stepping back.

"I'm sure he will." Together they walked to where Andrew still stood over Bob. Her best friend's husband slumped on the ground with tears soaking his cheeks. "Please, where is Evonne?"

Lily knelt beside him. "She's safe, Bob. I wouldn't risk her."

"You took her away from me. I protected her." He rubbed his face on his shoulder to wipe it, his hands still pinned behind his back.

"You were willing to sell us all out for her." Andrew's dry voice cut through the whimpers. "Women tend to have difficulty with that."

"Irrational creatures that they are," Vincent added. "It's why their menfolk have to lock 'em away in towers to keep them safe. Happens all the time."

Bob's grief flashed over to anger at their mockery. "It's no different from what you were doing! Making your grand plans like lords of the manor. Look where it got you all!"

"Am I arresting the loudmouth?" Joe called over.

"No," Lily said quietly. "Let him go. Take him to his wife. If she'll see him."

Andrew opened his mouth to object, but she shook her head, stopping him. "He loves her. He might have been stupid about how he showed it, but it wasn't the love that faded—it was the common sense. If he can understand that, maybe they can work it out." It didn't matter how old the net was, it could still be mended if people cared enough to try.

"Controlling someone isn't love." Vincent glared.

Lily kept her attention on Bob. "No. It's a separate issue. Evonne won't be controlled anymore, but maybe you can show her you can change."

Police sirens began to creep up. Joe took charge. "Time for anyone who doesn't want to be officially questioned to vanish. Ron, are you ready for this?"

"Ready for what?" Lily froze in place, her mind whirling and her gut clenching.

"Now that Dalhard is in custody, I'm going to stay behind and testify about how he and his people killed Nada," Ron explained gently, each reasonable word driving a spike into Lily's heart. "Murder and kidnapping make this more than a white-collar case and make it more certain he'll spend time behind bars. Preferably in isolation."

"I see." Lily couldn't quite figure out what to do with her hands, feet, or tongue. Her body felt awkward and swollen with all the things she wanted to say. She hadn't expected this, and now her dreams were frozen around her, waiting for the single tap that would shatter them all.

"What's wrong?" Ron asked, his hands tight on her elbows.

Lily took a deep breath. "You're going."

"Don't worry. I'll be careful," Ron said. "And I'll come back to you."

Lily exhaled, looking into those beautiful crystalline blue eyes. Warmth crept slowly through her veins, banishing the chill of doubt. "I know."

"We have to go. Now." Andrew dragged her and Vincent away before she could say another word.

"Come to watch the finale?" His old partner's voice had not changed. It was still husky and rough enough to polish rock. Karan always felt it made Caligo sound common and coarse, though he admitted it cut through a crowd effectively when issuing commands. He preferred the precision of high-class turns of speech for himself.

"I learned my lesson about leaving loose ends," Karan replied without turning. Below, red-and-blue lights lit up the night as Juneau police escorted André Dalhard into custody. "I assume you have arranged for him to be put into isolation rather than with the general population?"

"It's in his file. But people are people. Someone will screw up." Caligo stepped into Karan's view. The man had made visible changes in the last sixty years, adding piercings to his eyebrow, lip, and ears. A shaved scalp revealed the ancient tattoos covering his head as well. *Most unattractive.*

"He will not find things as easy as he once did." It might be unprofessional to take satisfaction in the well-executed downfall of an obstacle, yet Karan could not help allowing a faint smirk to curl the corners of his lips. His former employer had underestimated him and chosen to ignore his advice. The man deserved what he had coming to him.

"He knows you betrayed him. He'll be out for revenge," Caligo warned.

"He will have difficulty getting it. I have been a ghost for decades. There are no records of me anywhere. I am the one who ran his illegal dealings. I doubt he even knows half of the contacts he works with, contacts who will be quite happy to continue to work for me." Karan turned to face his old partner. "You did not come to see me out of a sudden, if belated, concern for my welfare."

"I never wanted to fight with you, Pujari." Caligo ran a hand over his face, tugging down his mouth. He looked sad and briefly old, as if feeling every year he had walked the earth.

"I am Karan now. Karan Samil." Pujari had failed and been rightfully executed for his sloppiness. Karan did not make such mistakes.

"I go by Vapor now. Guess we've changed more than either of us might like to think." Vapor paused before continuing. "We don't have to be on opposite sides of this."

"You came to your senses and now understand that our gods-given talents give us the responsibility to bring order to the chaos of modern life?" Karan doubted it but had no interest in prolonging false hope.

"Can't you see how setting ourselves up as kings will only get all *lalassu* persecuted and killed? The humans outnumber us exponentially. They won't tolerate being second-class citizens."

"They already are. Give them their television and their fast food and nightly titillation, and they will not care who is in power. They have traded freedom for security before and celebrated the bargain. We could offer them true freedom and safety." Karan's irritation grew. Why did his partner always insist on living in some idealistic-dream version of reality?

"We'd be hunted down as weapons and tyrants." Vapor's shoulders slumped. "I didn't come here to fight with you."

"Why did you come? To persuade me of the wickedness of my ways? You have already made your opinion quite clear. The barrage of bombs aimed at my home made a rather direct point."

Vapor winced, and Karan's fist tightened in satisfaction.

But the reminder didn't stop his old partner from continuing. "I'm sorry. I'm sorry for what I've done, and I'm sorry for what I'm going to have to do."

Karan sniffed. "Take those who want to hide and continue to hide. I will take those who are tired of being locked behind walls of fear."

"Secrecy is our best defense. As long as no one knows we exist, no one comes looking for us." Vapor firmed his stance and face, his determination clear.

"How secret do you think we truly are? The police detective knows and already bends under the teasing of his colleagues for his knowledge. The biologist and ranger know and have been drawn into battles. Across the globe, the *lalassu* interact with humans and leave traces of themselves behind. The only way to truly keep our secret would be mass genocide." He did not mention which side of the human-*lalassu* equation he would choose to destroy. Let Vapor struggle with the consequences of his chosen path.

There was no point in prolonging the conversation. It wasted time and resources when Karan already had plenty of work to do. He turned on his heel and walked away, confident that Vapor would not have broken his precious code of secrecy and arranged for an arrest.

"Please, Pujari. I don't want us to be enemies," Vapor called out.

Karan despised him for his weakness. And despised himself for the tiny piece of his soul that longed to go back to the old days when he had a brother whom he trusted more than any blood relative. He stepped over the edge of the roof onto first rungs of the ladder to the ground. Only then did he trust himself to reply. "We were always enemies. We simply never admitted it to ourselves."

Part Five
MATURATION

Chapter Twenty-Three

All for nothing. Bob slowly brought his plane to a halt on the tiny rural runway. He'd been flying for two and a half hours and with none of the usual euphoria of riding the wind. Instead, all he felt was sick with grief and battered by numbness.

He'd gone right from the Ptarmigan hangar to the hospital to see Evonne once the damn Bull siblings decided to actually share that information with him. She was with Doc, who was receiving IV antibiotics to combat the infection in his lungs. Bob was relieved to see her unharmed until he noticed her bare hand resting on the biologist's arm.

"What the hell are you doing?" He'd rushed in and pulled her away.

Why didn't I tell her how worried I'd been about her? How glad I was to see her safe?

His gentle Evonne had shocked him with the strength of her glare. "I'm monitoring him. I can sense his heart rate, oxygen flow, and temperature better than the machines—"

He'd tried to shush her, terrified someone might be listening from the corridor.

"There's no one nearby. I can feel the vibrations if anyone approaches. So we might as well speak frankly." As she sat back down on her chair like a queen on her throne, Bob could feel the distance between them growing.

"You made a deal with Dalhard." Evonne's kind eyes narrowed in accusation.

"It seemed like the best way to keep you safe. I already had everything set up with Ken. You always talked about seeing more of the world. He found us a quiet little village in British Columbia. It would keep us away from Bear Claw when Dalhard's people came back." The words poured out of him as he tried to explain.

Each syllable only hardened her expression. "You never thought to talk to me about these plans?"

"You don't understand what the world is like, Evonne. I know you want to believe people will welcome you with open arms, but they'll see you as a monster." He wished he could unsay it. He'd gladly make any sacrifice if he could erase that moment from both of their minds.

"Do you see a monster?" Five words that had sliced into his soul with righteous guilt.

"Of course not! But you're different, and I don't want you to be hurt." He wasn't the bad guy here. He hadn't put everyone in Bear Claw at risk with crazy schemes. It was too late to go back there. People would be coming to investigate, and he fully expected more collection teams to slip in, too.

"We needed to stick together," she said. "You put us all at risk."

"I don't care about the others. I only care about you." He thought it would reassure her.

Somehow his answer only made things worse. "You can't care about someone and keep them in a cage."

He'd lost his temper after that. He'd yelled at her, calling her ungrateful and a traitor to their marriage. He'd never shouted at her before, but his frustration overcame his intention to persuade. In the past, Evonne had always tried to calm him. She'd always been so calm and soft-spoken. In the hospital, to his surprise, she met his anger with a fury of her own. She accused him of seeing her as a shameful secret, something to be hidden away. She'd questioned his love for her, claiming that if he truly cared about her, he'd treat her as an equal.

This was all Lily's fault. She'd built up a fantasy and convinced Evonne it was real. He needed to make Evonne see the truth. If she had only listened to him, none of this would have happened. They could have been well away before everything hit the fan. Before he could make Evonne understand, she'd told him to leave and not bother coming back. "I'm going to see the world, as you put it. And I don't mean finding a new hiding spot."

He couldn't believe she'd said it. More, he couldn't believe she meant it—standing there with tears in her eyes, telling him that they couldn't be together anymore. He was willing to forgive her for her foolishness, but she looked at him as though he was personally responsible for everything that had happened when all he'd ever tried to do was protect her. He'd walked away, not seeing any other choice.

Lily had poisoned Evonne's mind all too well. *Damn her.* That had left him no option but to show the two of them he was right. Terror dug away at his sense of purpose. What if Evonne was hurt before he could make her see? A new vengeful idea took shape in his mind. If he could focus attention on gifts entirely different than Evonne's, then it would be easier to keep her safe. And what could be more different than a shape-shifter?

After the hospital, he'd made his way back to the Ptarmigan hangar. As he'd expected, with people already in custody, the police hadn't bothered to do much in the way of a search within the hangar. There wasn't even a strip of police tape across the entrance. Using his key, he entered and made his way to the ruined conference room.

His little camera had fallen from the table and lay among scattered magazines, still intact with the memory full. He'd initially hidden it here to collect hard evidence to use against Dalhard, blackmail material to keep the man away from Evonne. But now he saw a different opportunity. He grabbed his overnight bag out of his locker, gambling that the night's events had disrupted the usual procedures at the airfield. He'd been right. No one had even tried to contact him when he taxied down the runway and took off into the black night.

Dawn peeked over the mountains as he arrived at his destination. He'd radioed Ken and asked him to meet the plane. They'd used this airfield before when one of them needed to get in and out of the country quietly. Flying low under radar levels, he'd avoided any official notice, and no one ever visited this particular set of overgrown runways. For a pilot used to navigating the irregular terrain of Alaska and the Yukon, the landing was easy.

As promised, Ken waited for him in a truck at the end of the runway. Bob shut down the engines, his movements slow and methodical with dread. Ken looked around as Bob locked up the plane. "Where's Evonne?"

"Not coming. She left me."

The sympathy on his old friend's face nearly cracked through Bob's resolve, but he pulled himself together.

"I'm sorry, man," Ken offered as they wheeled the plane into one of the abandoned buildings. They'd come back later to retrieve it. "You can stay with me as long as you want. No problem."

Bob nodded, accepting the offer. He pulled the camera out of his pocket. "This should help even things up."

"What's on it?" Ken examined the little device.

"Something that will make your career."

Back in the familiar hush of the trees and snow, Lily curled up in Setsuné's cave. It had only been a few weeks since she'd first found Ron half-frozen in the woods, but it felt like several lifetimes ago. Each day that passed without word from him dragged like an eternity. An empty, aching hole gnawed at her, keeping her awake at night and preoccupying her mind during the day. She'd achieved a precarious equilibrium, concentrating on what she needed to do and trying not to think too much about Ron. He'd promised to come back. She believed him, but her newfound faith was too fragile to hold up to any rough handling or doubts.

Grandfather and Lou didn't understand. They kept poking at her, pushing her. Their well-meant anger chafed and unsettled her hard-won balance. So she began coming to the Colony. Lou had followed her once, but a few snaps of Setsuné's fangs convinced him to give Lily the space she needed.

She unfolded Evonne's letter to read again by the light of an oil lamp. She and Vincent had settled into an apartment in Perdition. Andrew had taken up lodgings with a *lalassu* healer nearby. Evonne had gotten a job with a local tailor, one who made fantastical costumes for theatrical performances. She sounded excited and happy, which brought a sad smile to Lily's lips as she leaned against Setsuné's rough fur. There was no word about Ron.

Setsuné rumbled and purred, offering what comfort she could. Lily patted her, although the movement awakened a sharp pain in her right hip. She winced, staring at the flickering shadows on the ceiling. The bullet wound wasn't healing as it should have. Thus far, she'd managed to keep it a secret from her family—one more wall solidifying between her and them.

"I miss him," she whispered to Setsuné.

Her great-grandmother rumbled agreement. Lily closed her eyes, trying to picture Ron happy and safe with his family. Warmth soothed her exhausted muscles as she imagined his mother hugging him. He'd have a big smile on his face, and his father would be off to one side, proud. The details were blurry since she had no idea what they looked like or where they lived. But it was the feelings that were important. Imagining Ron happy was the only way she found peace.

Setsuné made a short growling noise, breaking the mental vision. Lily blinked, sitting up. Evonne's letter lay in her lap, and she picked it up. "Maybe I should try writing to him again."

Snorts from Setsuné. Lily smiled, agreeing. Every effort to put her feelings on paper came out horribly mawkish or juvenile. *Hi, how are you? Feel like coming back to the land of Eternal Snow?* She'd burned every sheet in the stove rather than risk anyone else finding them.

She tried to distract herself with the letter again. Evonne was delighted with their small apartment off the main drag, although she complained about the texture of the cheap plastic cups and plates that Vincent had bought. She loved watching the throngs of people but hadn't yet built up the courage to mingle freely without concealing gloves.

Both Evonne and Andrew were proud of the small steps Vincent had achieved. Refusing Dalhard and calling Joe might not seem huge compared to breaking free as Ron had, but it was still a direct step of defiance. Lily paused to let the familiar sharp ache recede back to manageable levels before letting her thoughts continue. Vincent had recognized his inability to act directly against Dalhard, so he'd done what he could in advance and then tried to slow the Beast as much as possible. Evonne said he was talking about visiting Steve, who had been sent to a hospital facility after his arrest. Vincent thought he might be able to help Steve understand what had happened to him. He'd certainly do a better job than the doctors, who wouldn't believe Steve's accounts.

The ability of people to rationalize away what they had seen continued to surprise Lily. Mark had written to say that Jason didn't seem to remember much of the events that had happened in Juneau. Even so, Jason had requested a new roommate for the next semester. He claimed he needed more privacy to study, but Lily suspected his two-year friendship with Mark had fallen through.

Mark also mentioned that Edyta believed everything she'd seen had been a hallucination brought on by a heart attack. Her heart had suffered an arrhythmia but nothing worse, at least physically. Knowing the depth of her greed and stubbornness, Andrew had insisted on a long talk with her before he left Juneau. After he left, Edyta had agreed to begin plans to sell her freight business and retire on the proceeds. Lily wasn't entirely happy about her brother's tactics. Using his shamanic gifts seemed too close to Dalhard's type of persuasion.

Mark would be coming home to Bear Claw tomorrow, bringing Doc back from the Juneau hospital. The biologist had recovered completely from his ordeal and was eager to get back to his bears. She'd kept detailed notes for him, though she doubted he'd be satisfied with them. *He never is.* She smiled.

She heard footsteps crunching in the snow. Lou was probably coming to check on her. He worried she would collapse into a fatal depression the way their mother had. Lily had reached an accommodation with him: he didn't try to talk to her or come into the cave, and she ignored him as he walked by. She rubbed Setsuné's fur. "You've got my back if he changes his mind, right?"

Rather than growling her solidarity with her great-granddaughter, Setsuné raised her head. Lily immediately rose to her feet. The crunching rhythm didn't sound like Lou's footsteps. She picked up her walking stick. It wasn't much of a weapon, but with Setsuné beside her, it would be enough. The squeak of snow gave way to a steady thud. Whoever it was had reached the clear stone path down to the Colony.

Lily leapt out onto the path, ready to confront the intruder. And froze.

Ron stood on the switchback trail, dressed in a new brilliant-blue parka with matching black-knit hat and mittens. Her brain stuttered, performing all kinds of system checks to see if she had somehow lost her mind in the last few hours.

"Hey." He smiled at her, and she didn't care anymore if it was a dream or hallucination. She threw herself into his arms.

"Guess you missed me. I know I missed you," he whispered tenderly, his arms holding her tight as if he never intended to let her go again. She breathed in his scent, letting it permeate and relax her entire body.

They might have stood there long enough to turn into abstract icicle art if Setsuné hadn't interrupted, snuffling them with her nose and pushing her enormous head between them.

"Hi, Setsuné." Ron grinned, still holding Lily tightly. "Thanks for taking care of her for me."

Her great-grandmother yowled, stretching her jaws wide to flash her fangs in an unsubtle warning.

"Trust me, I'm not going anywhere." He tilted Lily's face up toward his, studying her. "I even left Doc and Mark back at the cabin so I could see you right away. Did you think I wasn't coming back?"

"I knew you would. But I'm glad not to be waiting anymore."

"Me too. Wherever you are, that's my home now. And I never want to leave again. No more running." He captured her lips with his, claiming them. She savored the sweet coolness of his mouth on hers, teasing and exploring. It warmed her right to her core.

"I'm hoping you'll still help me fulfill a promise I made," he murmured against her lips, punctuating the words with hungry little kisses.

"And what would that be?" she asked, returning the favor.

In answer, he stepped back from her and pulled a little plastic box out of his pocket. She recognized it, having rescued it from Doc's cabin and brought it back to her own to keep safe: the box of Nada's ashes.

As true night replaced Arctic twilight, they gathered around a large bonfire outside Evonne and Bob's cabin. Grandfather drummed and chanted as Ron opened the box.

Georgette, as Nada's niece, claimed the first handful of ash. She spread her grey-tinted fingers wide, and Ron poured a small amount of fine grey ash onto her palm. She looked similar enough to her sister to be her twin, although they were actually almost five years apart. Georgette glared at Lily, unhappy with Evonne's decision to leave.

Tilting her hand, Georgette let the fine-grained ash catch the updraft from the flames. It flew upward in pearly wisps among the bright orange-and-yellow sparks floating to the sky. She whispered, "She was the first one to believe in my art and bring my blankets and clothing down south to sell."

"She taught me to make the softest leather I've ever seen." Lou took the box next, hurling his handful to the stars as if launching it. The ash hung briefly above the bonfire like a pale, shimmering cloud.

Mark sprinkled his handful of ash over the flames as if decorating a cake. "She told me never to worry about what other people thought."

Lily took her share of the powdery ash and softly blew it over her fingers as if blowing a kiss, wishing Nada's soul peace and joy. "Without her, I never would have found my other half."

Ron intertwined his fingers with hers as he cast ash into the flames. "She saved my life at the cost of her own. It's a debt I will always honor and can never repay."

They took turns sharing memories, watching the ash glint as it soared above the flames, until the box emptied.

Doc stepped up with a large tin. Lou had cremated Big Bart's body and saved the ashes for Doc so the biologist would have a chance to say good-bye.

Ron held out his hand, and Doc nodded. He dug a handful of ash out of the tin. "He saved my life. Not because of any plan or calculation, but because he was a friend, and he loved without reservation." The ash curled upward in a thin grey-white spiral.

Bill took a handful. "He was trouble, but he had great spirit."

Doc hefted more upward. "He deserved more. He was a fighter and friend."

A dark shadow separated from the forest, resolving into Setsuné as she approached the fire. Doc and Bill both froze briefly, no doubt remembering her bloody rampage at the ranger station. Then Doc held out the tin, from one grieving parent to another.

Setsuné grasped the tin in her teeth before jerking her head. The remaining ash spilled out across the snow and along her fur. She rumbled sadly, rising up on her hind legs with her muzzle pointed at the sky. She stayed poised, her grief all the more potent in its silence.

When she'd settled back onto all fours, she plodded to Doc, pushing her nose against his chest. He nodded, daring to smooth the thick fur around her ears and forehead. He whispered, "We'll both miss him."

Lily slipped her arm around Ron as they stared at the steady light of the stars blazing above them. He squeezed her back. No matter what loss lay in front of them, they could draw strength from each other and their friends and family. She didn't need to choose between fur and skin. He loved her in both forms. They were together, and nothing could take that from them. Mates, lovers, and partners.

Vapor cursed in his native tongue, one that hadn't been spoken in millennia, aside from the linguistic mangling of archeologists.

He'd already removed dozens of copies of the video from various sites, but it kept popping up faster than he could remove it. For every copy he deleted, another ten went live. Someone was actively fighting him—someone with skills to match his own. The national media had picked up the video. Some of them called it a hoax, but a few were taking it seriously. More would as it became clear that it had no special effects or clever editing.

It was too late to bury the video. All they could do now was try and weather the storm.

Thank you for reading.
If you enjoyed this book and have a moment,
please leave a review.
It's one of the best ways you can thank an author.

If you're not ready for the fun to end,
check out my website www.jclewis.ca
for a chapter by chapter author commentary.
I share inspirations for my characters and scenes,
some of the more interesting bits from my research,
and all sorts of other tidbits.

Look for the mirror and step on through…

You can also sign up for my newsletter to find out about new
releases, contests and my appearances.
Sign up at www.jclewis.ca.

The story continues in book three: *Inquisition*

"Hey, Detective Cabrera. Good catch today."

The newbie's words caught the attention of the other Perdition police officers bustling around the bull pen. The rustle of paperwork and murmur of conversations dropped, leaving an eager silence.

"Thanks…" Joe Cabrera let his voice trail off, unsure of the kid's name. He knew he should walk away rather than risk tainting this kid's career with his presence. The guy was so new he was practically quivering in his crisply pressed uniform and glistening shoes.

"Rob Salazar." The rookie held out his hand. "If you have a minute, I'd like to talk about the case. How did you track down the firm that makes the weighted dice?" He'd probably read a book on how to introduce himself and create a presence at work. Joe's own eager rookie days were too distant to dig up from his memory. After the last few months, he was too tired and cynical to even try.

"I just followed the leads." *Dammit, it was a good catch.* But he didn't dare brag about the work he'd done to track down the trio of scammers who'd been counting out cards and swapping out dice at the local casinos. He'd managed to catch them before the organized-crime family who ran the place caught up to them. "Nothing special."

"How did you know that one guy would go back to his ex-girlfriend's to hide out?"

The other cops in the precinct were starting to snicker. Joe shook the boy's hand as quickly as he could. *Time to bail.* "Another time, Salazar."

Joe turned and found himself blocked by a tall man whose girth ensured there would be no convenient retreat. Detective Dave Hampton carried a grudge stretching back to when Joe made detective first. Staring at the flecks of crumbs and lint dotting the man's once-expensive wool trench coat, Joe reminded himself not to react and give Hampton the satisfaction of knowing his blows had struck home.

"Don't waste your time, Salazar." Hampton gave a broad grin, clearly eager to delve into old ground with a fresh audience. "Not unless you want a front-page story for the tabloids."

"I don't understand." Salazar glanced between the two of them, eyes round and uncertain.

"Tell him what they call you." Hampton smirked, his grin displaying yet more crumbs caught in his sandy-blond beard. Joe despised the man's slovenliness, especially since it carried over to his police work. Hampton never bothered finding the right suspect if he could beat a convenient one into a confession.

"I wouldn't dream of depriving you of the pleasure." Joe gritted his teeth in a pleasant, professional smile. *Don't react. Don't give him the satisfaction.*

"Creepy Cabrera." Hampton should be in charge of crowd control. He didn't need a megaphone to project his voice. "Guy's a regular X-file."

Salazar shook his head, confused. Joe tried not to roll his eyes. The kid probably didn't even remember *The X-Files*.

"Once they figured out you were loony tunes, they took away the Dalhard Industries investigation and gave it to a real detective." Hampton puffed himself up, tucking his thumbs into the nonexistent gap between his paunch and his belt.

Joe pushed past the bully, not trusting his temper to remain under control much longer. Obedient chuckles echoed down the hall as Hampton proceeded to loudly explain the facts to Salazar. "Creepy Cabrera used to be a hotshot, but no one trusts him since he started spouting off about the little-green-men brigade."

It was psychics, not aliens, you moron. Try to keep your prejudices straight at least. Joe's jaw tightened, and he ground his teeth hard enough to squeak.

The elevator doors slid shut, and Joe let himself slump. If only he'd kept his mouth shut this winter. The ancient machinery whirred in the walls as the elevator ascended slowly, giving Joe plenty of time to brood about what went wrong.

He was open-minded, willing to believe that the universe still held plenty of surprises. Tía Agata was always babbling about positive and negative energy, blessings and curses. He didn't put much stock in such things himself, but he didn't dismiss them either. But what had happened went far beyond a mere surprise.

Seven months earlier, he'd discovered that there were people walking around with the sort of superpowers that belonged in comic books and movies. The discovery hadn't just yanked the rug out from under him—it had shattered the bedrock of his beliefs about the nature of the universe. He'd been doing all right with it, managing to pick up the pieces and fit them back into some semblance of order, until his so-called friends dragged him out to Alaska to hunt down André Dalhard, a man who could control people by touching them. Dalhard had used his skills for murder, kidnapping, extortion, fraud, and any number of other crimes. None of which Joe could prove.

Why did they even bother? He knew the reason. They'd needed his help to track the man down, but then they'd expected him to turn his back while they took care of the problem. Instead, Joe had insisted that even a man like Dalhard deserved due process, and he'd brought him back and put him on trial.

That was when the trouble started. Other officers could mock the tin-foil-hat crowd, but Joe knew that at least some of those dangers were real. He'd begged for enhanced security precautions to keep Dalhard in jail. But he hadn't been able to come up with a rational explanation for why staff should avoid all skin-to-skin contact with the prisoner. Joe had gotten frustrated one day, and it all came spilling out. Two minutes of babbling had ruined ten years of his career and reputation.

His sergeant insisted on Joe seeing a psychologist. He'd gone, and he'd made all the right noises, claiming stress, bad medication, and whatever he thought might make a difference. Of course he understood that psychics weren't real, and he'd been tired and had made a little slip while joking. No big deal.

His verbal footwork had kept his badge safe but hit his pride hard. Cops were worse than frat boys for holding on to an embarrassing joke. At least frats only lasted through college, though. He'd be Creepy Cabrera until the day he retired. Especially with Hampton stirring the pot at every opportunity.

Even worse was the knowledge that his brothers in blue were walking out there, ignorant of the dangers that Joe now knew existed. Keeping it to himself made him feel like a traitor, but how could he convince them of the truth if they hadn't seen it for themselves? Joe's eyes had been forced open, and slipping back into the shadows of ignorance wasn't an option any longer.

The elevator doors dinged as they began to close, and Joe realized he'd been standing there, staring into space like a shell-shocked trooper from World War I. Grabbing the door to keep it open, he gratefully realized no one seemed to have noticed. *I need to go home and start working on the end table for Mamá and try to forget that I'm the only one who knows we're balancing on the verge of some kind of superpowered apocalypse.*

"Detective Cabrera!" his sergeant, Fran Modnik, called out before he could escape, her blond ponytail swinging like a hangman's noose as she stalked across the lobby.

Shitshitshit. "Sergeant," he replied politely.

"We need your help on something." Modnik passed him, her sensible flats squeaking softly against the linoleum. She didn't bother looking back to see if he would follow her as she made her way to the tech department without a single wasted step. A great believer in efficiency, Modnik didn't use makeup or wear fashionable clothes or indulge in idle chitchat. Dark slacks and a department T-shirt were her uniform unless she was forced into something else by political necessity. Some cops didn't like working for her, finding her cold and unforgiving. But Cabrera was impressed by her Sherlock-worthy detective skills and hoped the department would continue to recognize her incredible potential.

I was almost home free. He kept a discreet distance behind the sergeant. As they opened the door, the temperature rose—too many machines and too little air conditioning. The sheer number of storage units, tables, and monitors made Joe twitchy. They blocked his lines of sight and could potentially hide a half dozen intruders.

"You've heard about the series of break-ins at data-storage facilities across the state?" Modnik logged into the main terminal, powering up the large central screen.

"It was in the morning briefing," Joe said cautiously. The higher levels were frustrated and spreading a wide net, asking local cops to keep an eye out for anything that might be connected.

Modnik nodded. "Lockbox here in Perdition got hit yesterday. The thief is a pro—set the cameras on a loop, disabled the alarms. The only thing she tripped was a routine maintenance alert, which noticed the missing file."

"She?" Joe's interest perked its ears. His sergeant didn't drop details like that by accident.

"Thanks to the alert, we knew the file was removed at 2:13 a.m. The security cameras at Lockbox were affected but not the street cameras." Modnik delivered the news with grim satisfaction. She always told her officers to be patient, because criminals were invariably sloppy. They made mistakes, and then the cops could reel them in.

"A big oversight for a pro to make." Joe frowned. After the last few months, what others called "easy" smelled more like a trap to him.

"She didn't know about the red-light camera at the intersection of Roosevelt and Third. Tourist blew through the light at 2:16, and look what we found." Modnik pointed at the high-resolution traffic photo. The prominent feature was a grey sedan midway through the intersection, but Joe focused on the area behind the car.

The steel doors to Lockbox had the company name and logo clearly stenciled on them. A woman wearing a long, cream-colored designer coat over a grey business suit held them open. The photo resolution was sharp enough that Joe could see a flash of coral pink on her painted nails and the heavy stitching on her slim leather briefcase.

"Any chance she's an employee working late?" Joe asked.

Modnik shook her head, a smirk curving her pale lips. "Nope. Checked the employee records, and there's no match. And no record of anyone in the building either. That's our thief."

"It's a nice clear shot of her face." Joe leaned in. She'd be easy to identify. She looked more like a model or actress than a criminal. Her makeup and dark hair were even done up like one of those fifties pin-up girls, emphasizing big eyes, pouting lips, and sharp cheekbones. "Were we able to track her movements?"

"The bank on Roosevelt has twenty-four-hour coverage of the street. Same with the drugstore on New Orleans Ave." Modnik began typing again.

"Then we've got her." Joe started to warm up to his sergeant's enthusiasm. The two streets were a block apart and close enough to Third to have partial coverage of the area in front of Lockbox, although they were at the wrong angle to see the actual building.

"You'd think so." She split the screen into two views, one from the bank and one from the drugstore. As the timestamp crawled from 2:10 to 2:25, the streets remained deserted except for the grey sedan roaring through the light and a homeless couple, both bundled so heavily against the cold that their features were impossible to pick up. The man was definitely African American, with a worn knit cap pulled low over his forehead. The woman was dark skinned as well, possibly Latina, with filthy bleached-blond hair. They meandered over to the dumpster in the alley across from the drugstore and picked through it. Modnik paused the playback. "They go through the dumpster for another half hour and then wander off. No sign of our Jane Doe."

"How?" Joe's mind began to click through possibilities. "She'd have to pass at least one of the cameras. Could the feeds have been tampered with?"

"No. The sedan confirms the recording isn't from a previous night. I'm still having tech go through it to make sure, but it looks clean. Our mystery lady simply vanished into thin air." Modnik clicked off the screen and faced her detective. "That's where you come in."

"Me?" Joe tried to keep his voice nonchalant while his heart sank deep below his belt. *Another weird case for Creepy Cabrera.*

"Too many cops get focused on what they expect to see. You keep an open mind and follow the evidence. I don't need someone screaming ghosts or conspiracies. I need someone to find out what happened. The truth, no matter how strange."

His reluctance seeped through his professional mask. "I'm not sure I'm the best choice."

"Because they call you Creepy Cabrera?" Modnik hit the nail with a blunt-force sledgehammer. "I don't care about a bunch of status-happy idiots poking at you because they haven't heard a good joke in a while. You're a good detective, Cabrera. You find the connections—you find the bad guys."

"And what about the other stuff? This isn't going to help my reputation, Sergeant." Joe decided to be equally blunt.

"Trust me. You want this case." Modnik paused, glancing around the room to make sure they were alone. "The data firms that have been hit all have a client in common: Dalhard Industries."

Joe's head snapped up. He wanted to ask if the sergeant was sure, but she'd take it as an insult. *Careful.* Dalhard's lawyers had already slapped Joe with a police-harassment suit.

"I see I've piqued your interest," Modnik said dryly.

"Hampton is the lead officer for the Dalhard investigation." Joe forced his shoulders down, trying to appear relaxed.

"Officially, that's not going to change." She held up one finger to forestall any reply from Joe. "I've known you long enough to trust your gut instincts. This is too big a coincidence to leave unchecked, and I'm offering you a chance to prove what you've been saying. Find this thief, and you might find your evidence against Dalhard." She offered him the slim file.

"Find a thief who disappears without a trace. Easy. And what should I do after lunch?" Joe accepted the file.

Modnik smiled briefly, and the weary sergeant morphed into an attractive woman. "Could be worse. The department is also asking for someone to look into that shapeshifting viral video."

No need to ask for details. Joe suppressed a wince. He'd caught the live version of the event during his trip to Alaska. "It's fake. Probably a publicity stunt for some movie."

"It's caught the attention of some very prominent people. All sorts of experts are insisting the footage hasn't been tampered with. Now I'm having to field ridiculous calls asking what I plan to do if we catch a suspect with unusual abilities." She rolled her eyes. "If they find out about our mystery thief, I could end up having to handle a crackpot task force. So don't thank me yet."

"So you need me to keep this quiet." Could their target be one of the *lalassu*? Was invisibility one of the possible powers? Joe made a mental note to get in touch with his best friend, Michael, to ask. After years of bringing Joe useful tips, Michael had found the secret society of people with an astonishing variety of supernatural gifts, and he'd dragged Joe down the rabbit hole after him.

Modnik nodded. "Whatever you find, you bring to me. And one more thing—stay away from Otisville."

That was the prison where Dalhard currently lived. "Understood."

"I mean it, Cabrera. This is your one chance, and you have no margin for bullshit. You don't talk to Dalhard again until you have enough to hang him with." Modnik delivered her final orders and stalked into the hall, ready to take out her irritation on the next hapless victim who crossed her.

Enough to hang him with. Only a figure of speech, but the words echoed what the other *lalassu* had suggested for Dalhard back in Alaska: a summary execution. Joe had stopped them, but lately, he wondered if his ethics had trapped him into making a fatal mistake.

To be continued…

FOREIGN LANGUAGE AND NAMES:

I am not an expert in native cultures, though I've done my best to be fair and respectful. Any mistakes made are my own. Although the Dene are indigenous to Kluane, I've chosen to create my own amalgam of different cultures for the Charging Bull family. This is a work of fiction and while I strive for accuracy, it should not be seen as an authoritative depiction.

I used words from both the Dene and Miwok language for names. The Miwok language is used by four tribes indigenous to Northern California. The Charging Bull family migrated from there (along with many other grizzly bears) to Alaska. Dene is the language and name for the tribes who inhabit the northern boreal and Arctic region. The Guardians use names from that language to name the bears of the Colony.

Miwok:

Litonya: (Lily) Darting Hummingbird
Lokni: (Mark) Rain falls through the roof (lovable idiot)
Notaku: (Lou) Growling Bear
Uzumati: (Grandfather/Gerry) Grizzly Bear
Yenene: (Andrew) Medicine Man

Dene:

Exleli – drummer
Jtsólé – rose hips
Setsuné – Grandmother

THANK YOUS

First of all, thank you to my husband and sons for continuing to support me as I pursue my dreams. I couldn't do it without you. From helping me to find time to write to holding my hand when I need it, you've been my strength. And for the rest of my extended family, thank you for shouting to the rooftops and cornering people in the grocery stores to tell them about my books. Keep up the good work.

Thank you to my best friends, Sarah, Erin and Christina. You read my very rough original drafts and listened to me go through endless permutations for this story. You told me I needed to keep going and not give up. You believed in me first and I will never forget it. Thank you to Judy, who has been my woman-on-the-street and great with promotional tips.

Thank you to the ladies of ORWA who continue to be the best group of mentors and friends that an aspiring writer could ask for. Thank you, Teresa and Susan, for continuing to guide me along the path of self-publishing, and thank you to Katie for your great suggestions and advice on my manuscript. Thank you to Lucy for your humor and support, it means a lot.

Thank you to the fantastic people at Red Adept for your editing work. Lynn, you keep us all running on schedule and your patience with my questions is always appreciated. Jessica, thanks for your suggestions to improve my story. Sarah, thanks for all the detail work you did on my line edits. Your explanations and sense of humor made the process go much faster. And thank you to Susie for the final polish.

Thank you to Streetlight Graphics for another awesome cover and to Samianne for her amazing interstitials.

Thank you to Maghon, Lauren, Nada, Beth, Elle and Jessica for your great reviews and help. Your encouragement keeps me going.

And thank you for reading this book. If you enjoyed it, please consider sharing it with friends and family or posting a short review. It makes a world of difference and is very much appreciated.

© Ryan Parent Photography

About the Author

Jennifer Carole Lewis is a full-time mom, a full-time administrator and a full-time writer, which means she is very much interested in speaking to anyone who comes up with any form of functional time-travel devices or practical cloning methods. Meanwhile, she spends her most of her time alternating between organizing and typing.

She is a devoted comic book geek and Marvel movie enthusiast. She spends far too much of her precious free time watching TV, especially police procedural dramas. Her enthusiasm outstrips her talent in karaoke, cross-stitch and jigsaw puzzles. She is a voracious reader of a wide variety of fiction and non-fiction and always enjoys seeking out new suggestions.

For more information about *Metamorphosis* or the first book in the series, *Revelations*, (including behind-the-scenes commentary), more books on the *lalassu* and updates, you can go to www.jclewis.ca or find Jennifer on Facebook or Goodreads. You can also follow her on Twitter at @jclewisupdate or email her at jclewis@pastthemirror.com.